AESTHETICS
FROM CLASSICAL GREECE
TO THE PRESENT

ACKNOWLEDGMENTS

Grateful acknowledgment is hereby made for permission to reprint in this volume selections from:

THE ENNEADS, by Plotinus, third edition. Translated by Stephen McKenna. Pantheon Books, a Division of Random House, Inc., New York, and Faber and Faber Ltd., London. All rights reserved.

SOURCE READINGS IN MUSIC HISTORY, edited by Oliver Strunk. W. W. Norton & Company, Inc., New York, and Faber and Faber Ltd., London, 1950.

AUGUSTINE: Earlier Writings. Translated by John H. S. Burleigh. Published, 1953, The Westminster Press, Philadelphia, and Student Christian Movement Press, Ltd., London. Used by permission.

THE SUMMA THEOLOGICA OF SAINT THOMAS AQUINAS. Translated by the Dominican Fathers, second edition, 1927. Benziger Brothers, Inc., New York, and Burns & Oates Ltd., London, publishers and copyright holders. By permission.

LAOCOON, by Gotthold Ephraim Lessing. Translated by Ellen Frothingham, 1910. Farrar, Straus & Giroux, Inc., New York.

CRITIQUE OF JUDGMENT, by Immanuel Kant. Translated by J. H. Bernard, second edition, 1914. Macmillan & Company, Ltd., London.

LETTERS ON THE AESTHETIC EDUCATION OF MAN, by Friedrich Schiller, 1954. Translated by Reginald Snell. Routledge & Kegan Paul Ltd., London.

GERMAN ROMANTICISM, by Oskar Walzel. Translated by A. E. Lussky. Copyright 1932 by G.P. Putnam's Sons, New York.

THE WORLD AS WILL AND IDEA, by Arthur Schopenhauer, sixth edition, 1907. Routledge and Kegan Paul Ltd., London.

WHAT IS ART? by Leo Tolstoy. Translated by Aylmer Maude, 1924 edition. Oxford University Press, Inc., New York.

EXPERIENCE AND NATURE, by John Dewey, revised edition, 1929. The Open Court Publishing Co., LaSalle, Illinois.

TO
MY FATHER
AND TO THE MEMORY OF
MY MOTHER

Contents

Preface

For the purposes of this history of aesthetics, it is probably not necessary to be extremely scrupulous in marking the boundaries of the subject. A certain measure of generosity in conceiving its scope seems appropriate to so variously mapped a field. But a few preliminary distinctions may be helpful. We can distinguish at least three levels, so to speak, on which questions may be asked that have a bearing on works of art. First, one can ask particular questions about particular works: "Is this melody in the Phrygian mode?" "Where is the peripety in *Oedipus Rex?*" To answer such questions is clearly the task of the critic, not the aesthetician. They do not invite theoretical reflection, but demand factual information and interpretive skill. Yet even on this level some theoretical interest and activity may be presupposed, in the formation of such concepts as *Phrygian mode* and *peripety*: comparison and classification have begun. On the second level, one can ask such questions as: "What is a musical mode?" "What are the fundamental, or general, characteristics of tragedy?" To answer these questions is the task of the literary or musical theorist, or systematic critic. Such questions call for an inquiry into the nature of music or literature, or some important features of these arts—for theory and explanation, analysis and induction. Some of these questions are broad, basic, and far-reaching in their import; they are consequently of interest to the aesthetician, and are often considered part of his business. On the third level, one can ask questions about criticism itself, about the terms it uses, its methods of investigation and argument, its underlying assumptions. These questions obviously belong to philosophical aesthetics. When Socrates asks in the *Greater Hippias* what "beauty" (*to kalon*) means, or when Aristotle asks in his *Poetics* what defenses may reasonably be given for a tragedy that has been disparaged as implausible, the philosophical concern is central and evident.

So let us agree to draw our line somewhere near the middle of the second level, but with no claim to finality or exactness, and no suggestion, I hope, of arbitrariness. And let us not rule out, when they are reasonably general and fundamental, questions about certain aesthetic aspects of nature. Many questions that we shall encounter we shall shy away from, on the ground that they are somewhat narrow, and probably belong to the history of literary criticism or music criticism or some other area, rather than to aesthetics; but if some of them could also be considered aesthetic questions, and would be so considered by some philosophers, the exception is hereby noted.

As to terminology, I have no quarrel with those who wish to preserve a distinction between "aesthetics" and "philosophy of art." But I find the shorter term very convenient, and so I use it to include matters that some would place under the second. I claim sufficient warrant in prevailing competent usage—e.g., the *Journal of Aesthetics and Art Criticism* and the *British Journal of Aesthetics*.

There are now in English three histories of aesthetics—Bosanquet's pioneering work, the second part of Croce's *Aesthetic* in the Ainslie translation, and the comprehensive volume by Gilbert and Kuhn. Each of these is interesting in its own way, and together they cover a good deal of ground. But none of them is very new. Thus none could take advantage of recent work on many important philosophers and periods. And none brings to a consideration of the past the best concepts and principles that have been developed by present-day philosophy.

There are several histories of literary criticism and critical theory, of which a few—notably the valuable works of Wellek and of Wimsatt and Brooks—deal with many philosophical problems (not that the border here is very clearly marked!). The sole or primary concern of these histories, however, is with literature and its special problems.

I am sufficiently aware of the inadequacy of my own scholarly equipment not to undertake a study on the order of my distinguished predecessors'—much less one with a larger range. Recently Thomas Munro, in a paper read to the American Society for Aesthetics, spoke of the need for internationalism in aesthetics, and voiced the hope that the day will not be far off when we shall have a genuine world history of our subject. That is far beyond my competence. But though this book is small in scale, may its proportions be just—and may the ideas I have judged most valuable to recall and discuss be found equally so by the reader.

Fifty years ago, Clive Bell opened the first chapter of his little book on *Art* by saying, "It is improbable that more nonsense has been written about aesthetics than about anything else: the literature of the subject is not large enough for that." Like others, I have sometimes felt that to be prodded into more rigorous, more thorough, and more careful work in aesthetics, we should remind ourselves of the alternating neglect and over-indulgence that have sometimes been the lot of our subject in the past. But after writing this short history, I confess that Clive Bell's irony no longer seems to me historically fair, even in his day. And the half century since his words were published has brought solid achievement and even greater promise.

A number of extremely helpful (but wholly guiltless) scholars have commented on my manuscript. The whole book was read by Professor George Dickie, of the University of Illinois at Chicago Circle; Professor Alexander Sesonske, of the University of California, Santa Barbara; Professor John Hospers, of Brooklyn College; and Professor Elizabeth Lane Beardsley, of Temple University. And various chapters were read and helpfully criticized by Professor Helen North, of Swarthmore College; Professor P. Linwood Urban, of Swarthmore College; Professor Sidney Axinn,

16 *Preface*

of Temple University; Professor Samuel Hynes, of Swarthmore College; Professor Stefan Morawski, of the University of Warsaw; and Professor George L. Kline, of Bryn Mawr College. It is a pleasure to thank James E. Thorpe, then at Swarthmore College, whose scrupulous checking of references and quotations saved me (and the reader) from a number of mistakes. And I am also grateful to Mrs. Natalie Pearlman, for unusual helpfulness in the typing.

M.C.B.

General Bibliography

♦

Bernard Bosanquet, *A History of Aesthetic* (London, 1892; New York, 1957).

Benedetto Croce, *Aesthetic as Science of Expression and General Linguistic*, Part II (trans. Douglas Ainslie, 2d ed. London, 1922).

Katharine Gilbert and Helmut Kuhn, *A History of Aesthetics* (New York, 1939; Bloomington, 1954).

Karl Aschenbrenner and Arnold Isenberg, eds., *Aesthetic Theories: Studies in the Philosophy of Art* (Englewood Cliffs, N.J., 1965).

Albert Hofstadter and Richard Kuhns, eds., *Philosophies of Art and Beauty: Selected Readings in Aesthetics from Plato to Heidegger* (New York, 1964).

Alexander Sesonske, ed., *What is Art?: Aesthetic Theory from Plato to Tolstoy* (New York, 1965).

William K. Wimsatt, Jr., and Cleanth Brooks, *Literary Criticism: A Short History* (New York, 1957).

J. W. H. Atkins, *Literary Criticism in Antiquity*, 2 vols. (Cambridge, 1934); *English Literary Criticism: The Medieval Phase* (New York and Cambridge, 1943) ; *English Literary Criticism: 17th and 18th Centuries* (New York, 1951).

General Bibliography

René Wellek, *A History of Modern Criticism*, Vols. I and II (Yale U., 1955).

Allan H. Gilbert, ed., *Literary Criticism, Plato to Dryden* (New York, 1940).

G. W. Allen and H. H. Clark, eds., *Literary Criticism from Pope to Croce* (New York, 1941).

Barrett H. Clark, ed., *European Theories of the Drama* (Cincinnati, 1918).

Oliver Strunk, ed., *Source Readings in Music History* (New York, 1950).

Elizabeth Gilmore Holt, ed., *Literary Sources of Art History* (Princeton U., 1947).

Lionello Venturi, *History of Art Criticism*, trans. Charles Marriott (New York, 1936).

(Special bibliographies are given at the end of each chapter. The order in which works are cited is approximately the order in which the aestheticians are discussed in the body of the text, except that where several works concern a particular aesthetician those judged likely to be most helpful to the reader are placed first.)

AESTHETICS
FROM CLASSICAL GREECE
TO THE PRESENT

ONE

First Thoughts

Though we cannot say when men first began to reflect philosophically on the arts, we can get some glimpses of the stages that must have preceded the appearance of aesthetics in the full sense. For one thing, works of art, or the activities that produce them, would have to be distinguished, however vaguely, from other things. The generic concept of art might come later, but stories, or songs, or dances, for example, would have to be recognized as belonging to special classes, in virtue of their peculiar properties or a noteworthy sort of value. And this means that, at least on occasion, art objects would have to be spoken of—described and judged—in certain ways. Then the philosophically reflective mind, turning about for interesting objects of concern, could find a range of phenomena to be puzzled about in a fundamental way—and could begin to frame propositions (both about the works themselves and about other propositions about them) that, on account of their generality and penetration, might claim to be truly philosophical.

Before aesthetics could emerge in a particular culture, it would not, of course, be necessary that certain objects be set aside by that culture as specialized aesthetic objects—as connected with that interest alone. But at least something like an aesthetic interest, appropriately directed to some objects and not to others, would have to exist. And the philosophy of art would no doubt involve quite early an attempt to puzzle out and clarify the nature of this interest: asking what makes some objects and not others valuable in this peculiar way.

We may doubt whether the ancient Egyptians achieved this consciousness of the aesthetic as such, at least to that degree of explicitness which would make philosophical reflection possible. This is, indeed, strongly doubted by one leading authority, E. Baldwin Smith, who finds it "difficult to imagine" that the Egyptians "had an aesthetic attitude towards art"—"all the evidence indicates that the Egyptians had very little interest in the aesthetic appeal of their artistic creations."[1] We, who can be so moved by the abstract hieratic qualities of their sculpture and wall reliefs, may find it difficult to imagine that they did not respond to them as we do, but Professor Smith has offered some interesting arguments. Though the Egyptians appreciated fine craftsmanship and flowers, their sculpture and painting were seldom located for the benefit of a spectator, and most of it was hidden away in the darkness of tombs. They elevated the profession of the architect to a high level, but in tens of thousands of inscriptions in which these masters are praised, by themselves or others, it is never the beauty of their works, but only strength and everlastingness or richness and lavishness of metal that are cited. Their massive columns, covered with delicate bas-reliefs, suggest an indifference to the aesthetic difficulty of combining these features, but reveal an overriding interest in mass and size as guarantees of durability—in making permanent records of royal possessions and divine connections.[2]

"When they do employ the word *nefer*," says Smith, "or other words such as *'n* as an adjective, and it is translated 'good,' 'fine' or 'beautiful,' we have to be sure in what sense the Egyptians meant a thing was beautiful. . . . Usually when applied to architecture, it has the significance of 'fine' as applied to the quality

[1] E. Baldwin Smith, *Egyptian Architecture as Cultural Expression* (New York: D. Appleton-Century-Crofts, 1938), p. 252.

[2] Ibid., pp. 239, 249, 252. When Neb-hepet-Rē Mentuhotep decided to enlarge his funerary temple, the new wall covered up most of the reliefs on the earlier shrines, "but, to the minds of the Egyptians, the existence of the reliefs was the first consideration; whether they were visible or invisible was less important" (I. E. S. Edwards, *The Pyramids of Egypt*, Baltimore, Md.: Penguin Books, rev. ed., 1961, p. 216). As early as the IId or IIId Dynasty, "the principle of substitution by means of a representation had been recognized," and "scenes depicting [the deceased] hunting, fowling, or inspecting

of material and the thoroughness of the execution."³ "Usually" is properly cautious, but the general bent of the civilization seems evident enough. The Egyptians do not seem to have distinguished their response to art as such from their religious and political attitudes, or, consequently, to have become aware of art as presenting special problems. Apparently they were not a very philosophical people, in any case. Philosophy did not pull away from religious domination, and so we find very little that can be called philosophy of religion—even as late as the inscription called the "Memphite Theology," ca. 700 B.C.—and nothing that can be called philosophy of art.

The Greeks, on the other hand, achieved this distinction, though not as clearly as it was made in modern times. We cannot say exactly when they became able to think of art as raising philosophical problems, but we can guess at some of the first steps. Bosanquet, in his *History of Aesthetic*, quotes a passage from Homer as "one of the earliest aesthetic judgments that Western literature contains." On the shield of Achilles, made by Hephaestus, says the Homeric speaker, "the earth looked dark behind the plough, and like to ground that had been ploughed, *although it was made of gold; that was a marvellous piece of work!*"⁴ Modern aestheticians could provoke an interesting discussion as to whether this is really an aesthetic judgment: whether we should take it as simple admiration of representational accuracy, an imitative tour de force—or whether it is a genuinely aesthetic response to the plastic embodiment and intensification of the richness of the dark loam, setting off the

---

his estates were therefore believed to provide him with the means to continue these pursuits after his death. Likewise, scenes of harvesting, slaughtering of animals, brewing, and baking were thought to guarantee a constant supply of the commodities thus produced" (p. 50; cf. p. 52).

Irmgard Woldering (*The Art of Egypt*, New York: Crown, 1963) also notes the Egyptians' apparent unconcern with aesthetic value ("In the Egyptian language, characteristically enough, there is no word for 'art' or 'artist,'" pp. 72–73), but says that this attitude began to change during the Middle Kingdom (see p. 110).

3 Ibid 252–53. Professor Smith also quotes a letter from W. C. Hayes of the Metropolitan: "In general the stem *nfr* refers almost always to the virtues of an object or person, rather than to its aesthetic appeal."

4 *Iliad* XVIII, 548; Bernard Bosanquet, *History of Aesthetic*, p. 12. Cf. Odysseus' description of the golden clasp, *Odyssey* XIX, 227–31.

golden ploughs, with all that might mean to an Achaean warrior long distant from his native soil. But the Homeric exclamation—"that was a marvellous piece of work!"—certainly is a remark that can give rise to aesthetic questions, as soon as the first authentic and unmistakable thrusts of philosophical speculation begin to be felt in the Western world.

For one thing, it raises profound questions about appearance and reality, about the relation between the image and that which it represents. For a picture is somehow like those other images —dreams and illusory perceptions—that present philosophical problems about the legitimacy of our claim to sensory knowledge. We cannot trace exactly the extent to which puzzles about pictorial representation were connected, by the fifth-century thinkers, with puzzles about knowledge, but reflection about the nature of imitation seems to have been part of a larger growth in awareness of the problems presented by the distinction between appearance and reality. The term *"mimesis,"* and its cognates, which were to have such an important history, appeared in the fifth century, and were applied to musical imitation of other sounds, imitation of people's voices and actions in drama, and (in Herodotus) to the Egyptian wooden statues of the dead. *"Eikon"* (likeness) was also not used before the fifth century, though the existence of an earlier synonym has been inferred from the fact that sixth-century inscriptions on sculpture bore the genitive form ("of Ajax"), suggesting an ellipsis. There is a fragment of an early satyr play by Aeschylus, in which the chorus approaches a temple of Poseidon, carrying pictures of themselves, and exclaiming in wonder at the sheer verisimilitude. In the famous fragment of Democritus (born about 460 B.C.), "One ought to be good, or pretend to be," the word is *"mimeisthai."* Democritus was the first philosopher to work out a full theory of the relativity and subjectivity of secondary qualities as contrasted with the properties of the atoms—though before him Parmenides (about 500 B.C.) had titled the two halves of his great poem "On Truth" and "On Seeming" (or Opinion).

A second development in Greek culture helped prepare the way for the full-fledged aesthetic inquiry first undertaken by Plato. Homer and Hesiod were held in the greatest respect and awe for a long time after their deaths. The functions of poet and seer, or prophet, were already distinguished in Homer, but there was a standing temptation to unite them again. For both the poet and the seer, like the oracle, spoke in heightened language, in words that moved and dazzled, with an inexplicable magic power. And the works of the two ancient bards were accepted wholeheartedly on more than one level, at first no doubt not clearly distinguished. They were history, or what came as close to history as the pre-Periclean Greeks wanted and needed. On a second level, they provided images of moral and religious virtues, of courage and piety, and in this respect they were regarded as fit vehicles for instruction in conduct. With the rise of natural philosophy in the seventh and sixth centuries, a third method of interpretation developed—one that lasted long after Plato. It was claimed that the ancient poets had expressed profound hidden truths through symbol and allegory. The most notorious of these allegorizers was Metrodorus of Lampsacus, who proposed physical meanings for the characters in the *Iliad*—Agamemnon representing aither, Achilles the sun, Helen the earth, Demeter the liver, etc. What was behind all this is not wholly clear—but, for one thing, the natural philosophers may have wanted to borrow the acknowledged authority of the bards in support of their naturalistic speculations about the physical world.

The effect of all these developments was to stamp Homer and Hesiod as wise men and teachers, and to link poetic greatness with epistemic value. The counterdevelopment, which was to bear so much fruit later, in a clearer conception of what literature is and does, began with scathing remarks by Xenophanes and Heraclitus, a few of which survive and have been cited as the first Western examples of literary criticism. "Homer and Hesiod," says Xenophanes, "attributed to the gods all things which are disreputable and worthy of blame when done by men; and they told of them many lawless deeds, stealing, adultery, and deception of each other." This was one important line of thought, which gained adherents—Homer's account of the battle of the gods in Book XX of the *Iliad* was especially objected to. Heraclitus' criticism is based on his own metaphysics, and suggests that the deeper truths are not to be found in mere poets:

"Teacher of most men is Hesiod: they are sure that he knows very many things, who continually failed to recognize day and night: for they are one."[5]

Some early thinking must have been done also about a third problem that was to flower in the fourth century: the nature and source of the artist's creative power. Interest in the origin of the world and of the world-order appeared in Homer and Hesiod, and it grew with the reformations in Greek religion, for example Orphism; and while it was too early, no doubt, for any very elaborate analogy between the artist as creator and the divine creator (world-genesis was thought of on the analogy of procreation), the notion that painting and poetry involve something supernatural goes back a long way. Greek theology taught that poetry and music had been invented by the gods for their own delectation, then taught to men by such chosen spirits as Orpheus, Linus, and Musaeus. Democritus, in the fifth century, may have been speaking somewhat metaphorically when he said (if he did) : "Having a divine nature, Homer carpentered a world of varied stories." But the oldest poets themselves were not unaware of the problem posed by their own productions. When Hesiod and Homer invoked the aid of the Muses, they were not just making a formal bow. Indeed, each of them took pains to explain (Homer in the *Odyssey*, Book VIII; Hesiod in his *Theogony*, 22 ff) that, when the poet speaks, in some sense a god is speaking through him—though it is interesting that Hesiod's Muses tell him that "We know how to speak many false things as though they were true; but we know, when we will, to utter true things" (26 ff; trans. White) . Parmenides opened his poem with the confession that his philosophy had been revealed to him by a goddess. And Pindar apparently gave a good deal of thought to his theory that the poet's own art and skill can be immediately responsible for his work, though his talent and inspiration are ultimately a gift of the gods.

Though intensive study of the arts was not to be undertaken until the general humanistic movement of the fifth century,

[5] The Xenophanes translation is from Milton C. Nahm, ed., *Selections from Early Greek Philosophy* (New York: Appleton-Century-Crofts, 2d ed., 1944), p. 109; the Heraclitus translation from G. S. Kirk, *Heraclitus: The Cosmic Fragments* (Cambridge U., 1954), p. 155.

which we observe in Socrates and the Sophists, an important contribution to that study was made by the earlier developments in natural philosophy. Interest in the observable order of nature —the cyclical processes of growth and seasonal change, the regularity of behavior in physical things—and an urge to discover greater underlying order that will explain what we observe, were the first stirrings of what we recognize as natural science. And it is fortunate that Pythagoras and his followers came quite early (Pythagoras established his Order about 532 B.C.) to conceive of the design in nature, its underlying intelligibility, in mathematical terms. By means of an important empirical discovery, some bold physical and astronomical speculations, and an interest in applied psychology and ethics, the Pythagoreans came closer than anyone before Plato and Socrates to sketching an aesthetic theory about one of the arts, namely music.

The empirical discovery, there does not seem any reason to doubt, was made by Pythagoras himself: it was the discovery of the relation between the lengths of stretched strings and the pitch of their vibration, or, in other words, between the ratios of lengths and the corresponding intervals—thus, 1:2, the octave; 2:3, the fifth; 3:4, the fourth. The idea that qualitative differences might depend on, might be ultimately controlled by, mathematical ratio was a profound revelation to the Pythagoreans, and the interval of the octave (the Greek name for which was *"harmonia"*) appeared to be particularly fundamental: for it involved the opposition of Odd and Even, Unity and Duality, but "harmonized" them completely. The Pythagoreans extended this thinking into a general theory that the elements of the material world either are, or are imitations of, numbers. And they worked out an elaborate astronomical scheme in which the heavenly bodies emit constant tones, corresponding to their distances from the earth, though this music of the spheres is not heard, or not ordinarily heard, by men—perhaps because they lack the refined sensitivity to respond, or perhaps because it falls below the threshold of awareness by its very constancy, as the waves are no longer noticed by those who live on the shore. From these general views about the importance of mathematics in music as well as in nature, the Pythagoreans turned with a very strong ethical interest to the problem of strengthening, and when necessary restoring, the "harmony" of the individual soul, and according to Aristoxenus they used music in this therapeutic fashion, to purge and purify the soul, as medicine is applied to the body.

It will become apparent shortly that some of these ideas had in them the seeds of important developments; the influence of the Pythagoreans upon the thinking of Plato was undoubtedly very considerable. But the maturing of Plato's aesthetics required, as a point of departure, more than the rather vague and tenuous early reflections that we have been reviewing. In the latter part of the sixth century, and increasingly in the fifth century, the more self-consciously theoretical masters of various crafts and arts began to think about the principles on which they worked, and to write them down. Thus, for example, Damon of Athens (fifth century) apparently wrote a kind of Pythagorean treatise on music, in which he said that certain melodies and rhythms are capable of imitating certain types of character (*ethos*) and modes of life. And there was another treatise on music by Laius of Hermione (born about 548). Sophocles wrote his famous book *On the Chorus*, of which only a few remarks survive. Aristophanes put a good deal of literary criticism into his plays—for instance (in the *Frogs* and elsewhere) his condemnation of Euripides' objectionable plots and characters, the music accompanying his odes, and his unfortunate influence upon the citizenry. Polyclitus wrote on proportions in sculpture, Parrhasius on painting, Agatharchus on scene painting, Anaxagoras on perspective. And if we may trust Diogenes Laertius' copy of a catalogue made by Thrasylus, Democritus, interested as usual in everything under the sun, wrote books *On Rhythm and Harmony, On Poetry, On Beauty of Verses, Of Painting, Of Song*, and a book with the long title: *Concerning Homer, or On Correct Epic Diction, and On Glosses*. These works were probably on the level of critical theory—theory of literature, of music, of fine arts—rather than aesthetics. But the most fruitful work in philosophical aesthetics would have to await the completion of some of this research, safely to bridge the gap between philosophic generality and particular works of art.

Bibliography

E. Zeller, *A History of Greek Philosophy from the Earliest Period to the Time of Socrates* (London, 1881), I, 306–533.

Theodore Gomperz, *Greek Thinkers* (New York, 1901), Vol. I, Bk. I, chs. 3–5, Bk. III, ch. 4.

John Burnet, *Early Greek Philosophy* (4th ed., London, 1930), chs. 2, 7.

J. W. H. Atkins, *Literary Criticism in Antiquity* (Cambridge, 1934), chs. 1, 2.

Gerald F. Else, " 'Imitation' in the Fifth Century," *Class Philol* LIII (1958): 73–90.

T. B. L. Webster, "Greek Theories of Art and Literature Down to 400 B.C.," *Class Quart* XXXIII (1939) : 166–79.

Alice Sperduti, "The Divine Nature of Poetry in Antiquity," *Trans and Proc of the American Philol Assoc* LXXXI (1950): 209–40.

Kathleen Freeman, "Pindar—The Function and Technique of Poetry," *Greece and Rome* VIII (1938–39): 144–59.

Richard L. Crocker, "Pythagorean Mathematics and Music," *Jour Aesth and Art Crit* XXII (Winter 1963; Spring 1964) : 189–98, 325–35.

E. H. Gombrich, *Art and Illusion* (New York, 1960), ch. 4.

T W O

Plato

From the numerous passages in Plato's dialogues where aesthetic matters are broached we can guess that some of these matters were familiar topics of intellectual conversation among his contemporaries. Educated Athenians, not only the rhetoricians and rhapsodes, must often have engaged in lively disputes over the truthfulness and authority of Homer, over the sources of beauty in the sculpture of Phidias, perhaps over that thesis on which Socrates is found still discoursing to his two befuddled companions at the end of the *Symposium*—that "the same man could have the knowledge required for writing comedy and tragedy" (223d; trans. Lamb). But some of the aesthetic questions that Plato raised he may well have been the first to formulate, and he certainly was the first to formulate so clearly and penetratingly.

In any case, Plato asked an extraordinary number of the right —the necessary and the illuminating—questions about beauty and the arts. Some of them he asked in language, and with presuppositions, deriving from his own metaphysical theories. Others owe little or nothing to his metaphysics, and must be faced by any aesthetician, whatever his metaphysical persuasion— but it must also be conceded that Plato's metaphysics, whatever its ultimate truth or falsity, led him to open up important lines of inquiry that he might otherwise have missed.

Plato did more than ask good questions; he set forth some noteworthy answers, and he backed them up with some persuasive lines of argument. These trains of thought, the reasoning out of logical consequences that ensue from the adoption of certain initial positions, were an extremely valuable contribution to all later work. The commentators disagree about whether, or to what extent, they may be said to compose a system—a coherent philosophy of art. We must inquire into this below, but without insisting upon the unity of Plato's thought to the point where we ignore important suggestions that he may not have succeeded in reconciling with his other views.

I do not propose to attempt a distinction between Plato's theories and those that may be attributed to Socrates independently of Plato. Some of the Platonic doctrines set forth in the dialogues can with some confidence be said to have been taught by Socrates, but the situation is much less clear with the aesthetic theories, and scholars differ greatly. What we have to understand here is a body of ideas that were developed, perhaps in some part by Socrates, but certainly in large part by Plato himself. The principal dialogues in which these are set forth mostly fall into two groups: (1) the *Ion, Symposium,* and *Republic,* presumably written by Plato in his early period, between the death of Socrates and the founding of the Academy, roughly 399–387 B.C., and (2) the *Sophist* and *Laws,* written during the last fifteen years of his life (428/7–348/7), with the *Phaedrus* somewhere in between, but closer to the latter group. But there are important passages in other dialogues, as we shall see. Though authoritative opinion seems to be divided on the genuineness of the *Greater Hippias,* it, too, may safely be drawn on, for, if not actually Plato's, it is nevertheless very Platonic.

ART AND IMITATION

Plato likes to let his key terms shift senses according to the movement of his dialectic, and while the shifts are usually quite traceable, this practice makes it extremely difficult to be sure about the consistency and coherence of his thought. If Socrates says, at one stage of a dialogue, that all the members of a set have a certain property, and, later, or in a different dialogue, that only some of them do, shall we say that Plato has contradicted himself, or has changed his mind, or has chosen to present a perfectly consistent pair of theses in a verbally puzzling way? This problem arises with regard to some of his most important terms. Another serious hazard in understanding Plato's aesthetics is provided by the English words that now offer themselves most readily as translations of them.

The first and most fundamental of these terms is the one that is usually, and understandably, translated as "art" (*technē*), but is closer to "craft." *Technē* is skill in doing something that takes an uncommon and specialized ability; it involves knowing how to achieve a certain end. In the *Sophist*, where Plato presents, by way of example, an elaborate definition by dichotomy of the craft of fishing, he divides crafts in general into "acquisitive" (such as money-making) and "productive," or creative, which bring into existence what has not existed before. The productive crafts include a wide range of skills—for example, carpentry, flute-playing, "painting, weaving, embroidery, architecture, the making of furniture" (*Republic* 401a; trans. Cornford). Plato suggests several ways in which all these crafts might be sub-divided—including, for example, a division into human and divine (*Sophist* 265b). He does not make the distinction most expected by a modern student of aesthetics—between "fine arts" and utilitarian crafts. Yet the momentous consequence of his thinking was the first theory to cover all of the former.

His own terms are not always decisive guides. "Music" (*mousikē*), for example, can mean music, or fine arts in general, or even something like general culture. Socrates notes in the *Symposium* (205c; trans. Lamb) that "of anything whatever that passes from not being into being the whole cause is composing or poetry;" though only "the business of music and meter" is usually called poetry. But he does not explicitly make a special category of the visual arts (painting, sculpture, architecture), various forms of literature, and certain mixed musical arts—dance, song, and the "choral art" that combines both dance and song. It is, of course, to these that we would now usually confine the term "art."

Plato seems implicitly to acknowledge a distinction between the arts in this narrower sense and the other crafts. They are, for one thing, the only crafts which the young guardians of the Republic are to have any traffic with; they have prestige. And this difference is echoed in a telling Platonic usage. The highest, noblest, and most all-encompassing craft, Plato says in the *Laws* and the *Republic*, is statecraft, the political or royal "art" (*Republic* 342c; cf. *Euthydemus* 291c): and when Plato wants to say most vividly and forcefully what task it is that faces the legislator who proposes to construct a social order worthy of man, and to set its institutions up in a way that will make them flourish and endure, he always seems to compare statecraft with one of the arts—composing a tragedy (*Laws* 817b), coloring sculpture (*Republic* 420c), painting (*Laws* 769 and *Republic* 484c). Moreover, it is the arts that present the hard philosophic problems. Not much, if anything, needs to be said by way of justification for making shoes and building shelters—though the architects of the Republic may at times be tempted into providing too many luxuries for their citizens. But drama, and music, and the adornments of buildings—these are extremely puzzling in many ways to Plato, for it is by no means plain why they should exist at all.

Certain things can be said about all the productive crafts. By means of them, something new emerges; to make it, material media must be manipulated in some way, assembled or transformed; there must be a relevant skill, or set of skills; and there must be a kind of knowledge—the musician, for example, is one who has "the art of recognizing the sounds that can or cannot be blended" (*Sophist* 253b; trans. Cornford). But intelligent productive work also has a goal and follows a plan, which guides the craftsman throughout. Therefore, in one very broad sense, all production is "imitation."

Here we come to the second key term in Plato's aesthetics— one that inevitably gives the interpreter much trouble, and one that Plato himself, despite occasional energetic attempts at clarification, leaves in a far from satisfactory state. As we shall see, it is important to Plato that the arts are imitative in some sense in which the other crafts are not; but to get our bearings on this important but elusive concept (or cluster of concepts), it is best to begin by considering the broadest use to which Plato puts it. For in this sense it is the heart of Plato's whole philosophy. There is not only the term *"mimesis,"* but three others that are often used in something approaching synonymity with, and even in apposition with, *"mimesis"*: *"methexis"* (participation), *"homoiosis"* (likeness) and *"paraplesia"* (likeness). The relation marked by these terms—the relation between an image *(eidolon)* and its archetype—is noted everywhere. Not only are objects imitated by pictures of them, but the essences of things are imitated by names *(Cratylus* 423–24), reality by thoughts, eternity by time *(Timaeus* 38b). The musician imitates divine harmony, the good man imitates the virtues, the wise legislator imitates the Form of the Good in constructing his state, the god (or the *demiourgos*) imitates the Forms in making the world of the mixed. Theaetetus speaks judiciously, then, in the *Sophist* (234b; trans. Cornford), when he remarks that the term "covers a very large variety."

In view of this diversity, any English word we might use to translate *"mimesis"* and its allied terms is bound to be misleading, for no English word that might serve has an equally unrestricted sense. "Representation" is possible, because it has several senses: the Senator represents his constituents, the picture represents the object, the trade-mark represents the product. *"Mimesis"* perhaps carries with it a stronger notion of copying, of being modeled upon; but this is present in "representation," too—even the Senator, when truly representative, may be said to mirror in his vote the will of those who put him into office. I adopt the usual term, "imitation," for Plato's *"mimesis,"* but try to safeguard it against misunderstanding by saying that it is to be used in a way close to "representation," in its multiple sense. And in the broadest sense, all productive craft, or making, involves representation. There is one curious passage in the last book of the *Republic* (597b; trans. Cornford), where Plato speaks of the Form of the bed as something "which exists in the nature of things and which, I imagine, we could only describe as a product of divine workmanship." But the suggestion that the god made the Forms is hardly reconcilable with the rest of Plato's metaphysics: for how then could they be eternal? And how could the making of them be an imitation unless there were super-Forms, or Forms of some other type, that the god could take as model?

The Form of an object, in this sense, is the essential nature of the object, which is its function, and also the ideal condition of the object if it were to fulfill that function perfectly (see

Republic 595–97). Consider, for example, a household knife. The function it shares with all knives, or knives of the same class, has an ontological status (as ideal archetype) which, according to Plato, is quite independent of the existence, or nonexistence, or change, of the physical knife itself. The ideal Form of the knife, which is eternal, immutable, and complete, can never be embodied completely in the physical knife. But in so far as the knife-maker makes a knife that can perform its function at all, or well, he is guided by some conceptual grasp of that function, hence of the Form of the knife. In this sense, the *actual* knife imitates its archetype (which is the "real" knife) ; and in a similar sense, the painter who draws a sketch of a knife imitates that physical object. In other language, the physical knife may be said to be an image (*eidolon*) of the ideal knife, and the picture an image of the physical knife.

In the course of his most sustained attempt to get at the special craft of the Sophist, if there really is one, Plato undertakes (in the *Sophist*) further subdivisions of the various products of productive craft in general. The first of these introduces a narrower meaning of "imitation," and comes closer to a theory of art. There is production (1) of actual objects—plants and elements by the god; houses and knives by men—and (2) of "images" (*eidola*)—reflections and dreams by the god; pictures by men (*Sophist* 266). The craft that produces images is the strictly "imitative craft." In this sense, a house is not an imitation, though its photograph is: "And what of our human art? Must we not say that in building it produces an actual house, and in painting a house of a different sort, as it were a man-made dream for waking eyes?" (266c; Cornford). Let us take "imitation" henceforth in the sense in which not all, but only some, productions are imitations.

Now it is essential to the notion of an image, or imitation, that it fall short in some way of its original; if the image were perfect—"expressing in every point the entire reality" of its object—it "would no longer be an image," but another example of the same thing (*Cratylus* 432; trans. Jowett). When one knife-maker copies a knife made by another, what he produces is not the image of a knife, but another knife; perhaps a little indirectly, but nevertheless genuinely, he is guided by the knife-Form. But a picture of a knife lacks the weight, the sharpness, the hardness of the actual knife, and it will not cut—it is an *objet manqué*. It is both true and untrue, has both being and nonbeing (*Sophist* 240c). Because it leaves out important properties, it is of a lower order of reality than its archetype. And this holds throughout Plato's metaphysics; the actual knife is less real than the ideal knife; time is less real than eternity; the government of a historical city-state less real than ideal Justice.

Now the "imitative art" may give rise to two sorts of thing: (1) The imitator may reproduce as accurately as possible the actual properties of the model, its true measurements and proportions and colors; in that case he produces a genuine likeness (*eikon*) (*Sophist* 235d). (2) The imitator may copy the way the object *looks*, as seen from some point of view; in that case he produces an apparent likeness, or a semblance (*phantasma*) (*Sophist* 236b). These sometimes coincide, when things look as they actually are, but painters, sculptors, and architects have found that in many cases they do not: if the temple columns are really equal all the way up, they will not look equal; to look equal, they must be wider at the top. Some degree of deliberate distortion is usually part of the process of semblance-making. And this is true whether the imitator produces the semblance by physical instruments (like a carver) or by his own body (the Eleatic Stranger calls this mimicry).

We now have a still narrower sense of "imitation" available: the making of *deceptive* semblances. When poets are spoken of disparagingly in the *Timaeus* as "a tribe of imitators" (19d), it is no doubt this sense that is present. And the attack on the painter in Book X of the *Republic* seems to narrow the term in the same way: the painter imitates the carpenter's bed not as it is but "as it appears" (597)—as it looks when seen from one point of view. Thus his painting is not as true as a blueprint or diagram that might be used to record and convey the actual structure of the bed, without regard to superficial similarity. Semblances are illusory, they are misrepresentations or false imitations, not only of reality, but even of actuality. That is why the painting of the house is "a man-made dream for waking eyes"—it belongs in the same class with actual dreams and perceptual illusions, which are all false appearances.

These reflections suggest another distinction important to Plato, which he makes sharp use of in other connections, when Socrates is battling the Sophists. The illusionist painter or architect has a purpose in making things look different from the way they actually are: he tries to make them look *better*, in order to please the beholder. He is in fact choosing between pleasure and truth. But in this respect he allies himself with certain others who make it precisely their business to deal with appearances rather than actualities. To make things seem better than they are is to flatter them. In the *Gorgias*, Plato distinguishes four pseudo crafts, or "arts of flattery," and contrasts them with the genuine. Thus gymnastics produces health, cosmetics the illusion of health; medicine tells us what is good for us, cookery produces what merely tastes good; there is genuine legislation of justice, and there is sophistic, which is a pretense at it; there is the administration of justice, and there is rhetoric, its ersatz (*Gorgias* 463–65).

If the argument hangs together so far, certain conclusions are inevitable. No doubt the expert on cosmetics must have what Plato calls "true opinion"—that is, some empirical information— to be a success at his trade; but he does not have knowledge (*epistemē*), in Plato's sense. At least, he doesn't have the sort of knowledge that he might be taken to have by the uncritical, for he doesn't really know how to produce health, but only the bloom of it. He does not have a craft, but a knack (*tribē*). Thus one criterion of a pseudo craft is that it is not based on knowledge, like the work of the carpenter or shipbuilder (*Euthydemus* 281). A second is closely connected with the first: the pseudo craftsman doesn't himself have a very clear idea what he is doing; it is impossible to give a rational account of his method (*Gorgias* 465ab).

But then are not the musician, the painter, and the composer in exactly the same situation? The painter, at any rate, seems to go in for deceptive semblances; the musician is perhaps chiefly an accomplice of the poet, when he sets the latter's words to music that will enable the singer to pretend to passions he doesn't really feel. But the poet is by all odds the most guilty. In that terse but slashing indictment of the tragic poets (including Homer) toward the end of the *Republic* (598–601), Plato seems

38   *Aesthetics from Classical Greece to the Present*

to deny them any claim to genuine knowledge (*epistemē*),
though their dangerousness arises precisely because many people
will think they do know what they are talking about. If they
really knew how to build ships and command troops, they would
do those useful things rather than write about people doing
them; if they knew the nature of a good life or a good state,
they would have had some influence on citizens and governments.
Lacking any philosophic grasp, and motivated as he is by the
desire to please the ignorant multitude and win their approval,
the poet does not even have true opinions (*doxa*, 601). "We may
conclude, then, that all poetry, from Homer onwards, consists in
representing a semblance of its subject, whatever it may be, including any kind of human excellence, with no grasp of the
reality" (600c). Hence their low status in the *Phaedrus*. When
the newly arrived souls, having beheld true being, sink into
various degrees of forgetfulness, and are placed on nine levels,
Socrates says "to the sixth [class] that of a poet or other imitative
artist shall be fittingly given" (*Phaedrus* 248e; trans. Hackforth).

The same conclusion may be drawn from a consideration of the
way the poet works. For when he writes, he is "out of his senses"
(*Ion* 534b; trans. Lamb)—and therefore "contradict[s] himself"
by depicting all sorts of people (*Laws* 719c; trans. Bury). He
works in a mad state, with the irrational part of his soul. Plato's
remarks about the mental condition of the poet are so often
exaggerated and ironic, or hovering on the verge of irony (as in
the reference to the poets as "our fathers, as it were, and con-
ductors in wisdom," [*Lysis* 214a; trans. Lamb]), that it is not easy
to piece together his doctrine. When it suits his purpose, he
attacks the nonrationality of the poet, who composes by a certain
"genius and inspiration" and does not even know the meaning
of what he has said (*Apology* 22; trans. Jowett); but as we shall
see later, this same line of thought easily passes over into the
suggestion that the nonrationality of the poet may not be beneath, but above, reason itself.

In any case, the conclusion of this present train of thought is
the denial of truth to the arts in general. The rhapsode Ion,
Socrates suggests (*Ion* 532c), can interpret Homer, but not other
poets, because he interprets without "art or knowledge." If he had
some general principles or method, he could interpret Hesiod as

well, but his interpretation consists in getting himself into a peculiarly aroused state in which he can declaim and emote most effectively, without having real knowledge of any of the things he talks about. Perhaps *mimesis* is not an art at all, but "a form of play, not to be taken seriously" (*Republic* 602b; trans. Cornford).

We have come, for the moment, to a rather paradoxical conclusion. For we began by trying to place the arts of music, painting, and poetry in a larger framework, to understand them as crafts of a special sort, with their own aims and methods. But now it appears that they may not be arts at all, but pseudo arts. This may be an overstatement; the painter (we might say) does not merely pretend to practice an art, but he practices an art that consists in pretending, in making things look like what they are not. Even so, the indictment is severe, as far as the cognitive aspect of art is concerned: art is, as Socrates says in the *Republic*, at one remove from actuality, and at a second remove from reality—the transcendental Forms that lie behind the actual (597, 602). In terms of Plato's four levels of cognition, as represented by the divided line (509–11), art belongs on the lowest (*eikasia*).

BEAUTY

Let us now turn to another property possessed by many works of art, and also shared by them with other objects, including objects of nature (*Republic* 400–1). This is the quality of beauty (*to kalon*). Individual things—statues, people, horses—exhibit this quality in variable ways: some are more beautiful than others, some lose their beauty after a time, some appear beautiful to one person but not to another (*Republic* 479a). But besides the changing beauties of the many concrete things in the world, there must be one Beauty that appears in them all (*Symposium* 210b, *Republic* 476, 479, *Phaedo* 78de, *Phaedrus* 250b). This is the essential Form of Beauty, absolute Beauty, not seen with the eyes but grasped conceptually by the "mind alone" (*Phaedo* 65, 75d).

Plato's reasons for believing that there must be a single transcendental Form of Beauty are the same as his reasons for believing in other Forms, such as Justice—though in the *Phaedrus*

Beauty is said to be easier of access through sensuous images (249bc). If the same term may be applied to many individuals, there must be a universal which they share. If an object changes, this change is best understood as a loss or gain in abstract properties that themselves do not change. If different things can embody Beauty more or less fully, then we must be able to conceive of perfect or complete Beauty, the ideal limiting point, which cannot be found in any concrete object, under the conditions of this world. "Now if a man believes in the existence of beautiful things, but not of Beauty itself, and cannot follow a guide who would lead him to a knowledge of it, is he not living in a dream?" (*Republic* 476c; Cornford).

The guide who can lead us to the knowledge of true Beauty is really leading us back to a home we have forgotten. This is Plato's (or Socrates') doctrine of recollection (*anamnesis*). "Now beauty, as we said, shone bright amidst these visions, and in this world below we apprehend it through the clearest of our senses, clear and resplendent" (*Phaedrus* 250d; Hackforth; cf. 251a). In the shock of birth, our souls, which beheld the Forms directly, repress this memory. But it can be recalled, and when recalled it constitutes true knowledge. The "beauty of this world" reminds us of "true beauty" (*Phaedrus* 249e). The question is: what is the role of the artist in this process of recollection?

Plato, in different dialogues, seems to think there are two ways back to the Forms. Perhaps they are complementary. Or perhaps we can usefully invoke Bertrand Russell's distinction between "knowledge by description" and "knowledge by acquaintance." By dialectical arguments, such as those sketched two paragraphs back, we can convince ourselves that the ideal Form of Beauty exists, or subsists, in a realm distinct from the empirical world, and has the same sort of Being as ethical ideals, like Justice, and mathematical entities, like numbers and perfect equality. But this conceptual knowledge is still abstract and detached. What we also want, and need, is a path that will bring us again into a direct apprehension of Beauty, in so far as this is possible while our souls are still in bodies; only in this way can the divine love (*eros*) within us be satisfied.

This is the theme of the *Symposium*, and especially the discourse of Diotima of Mantineia: we can progress from bodily beauty to beauty of mind, to beauty of institutions and laws and the sciences themselves (210–11)—finally, to "essential beauty entire, pure and unalloyed" (211e; trans. Lamb). We learn to love beauty, so to speak, in diluted form to start with—the physical beauty of man or woman—but having acquired the taste, or developed the perceptual skill to discern it clearly, we can go to higher and better beauties—with the promise, or at least the hope, that we may again behold Beauty in itself.

Strangely enough, Diotima and Socrates do not assign a role to the arts in this process of reawakening to Beauty, though it takes but a short step to do so, and this stopping on the verge has not prevented the *Symposium* from luring numerous readers, down to our own time, to press on. As long as we admit, as Plato clearly does, that melodies and paintings can be beautiful, some of them in a high degree, then, as part of the furniture of the earth, they embody, they participate in, and therefore they reveal, or exhibit, to some degree, the Form of Beauty. If we can become acquainted better with this Form by recourse to them, then to that extent they give us knowledge, or help us attain knowledge, of at least one of the Forms. Indeed, in the passage in the *Sophist* quoted earlier, where Plato is assigning the arts to the category of semblance-making, he says the artists, "leaving the truth to take care of itself, do in fact put into the images they make, not the real proportions, but those that will appear beautiful" (236a; Cornford)—when, for example, they distort the actual shapes of columns for visual effect. Is there a distinction between appearing beautiful and being beautiful? An artist who distorts shapes to make them "appear to be beautiful" might deserve from Plato a better treatment than he was given earlier: for he is working to embody to the highest degree the Form of Beauty in the things of sight (or sound). He is an imitator of the beautiful.

And from this point of view he could be said to belong with the greatest creator of all—the *demiourgos* who put the world together. In some of the more fanciful flights of rhetoric in the *Symposium*, extravagant things are said which we are not, perhaps, to take too seriously. Still, they may represent some of Plato's thinking. Agathon, for example, says that it was love (*eros*) that invented the arts, including those that yield beauty (*Symposium* 197b), and indeed "the gods contrived the world from a love of wonderful things" (201a; trans. Lamb).

What is beauty, then, if art is capable of bringing it into this world? Here is a question that Plato does not deal with very fully. His two main attempts are in the *Greater Hippias* and *Philebus*, where he leaves many questions unanswered. In the former, he is chiefly concerned to analyze various attempts to define beauty, and show why they will not do. The question has arisen, says Socrates, because when he was "finding fault with some things in certain speeches as ugly and praising other things as beautiful," someone—as though Socrates himself needed a Socrates!— asked, "How, if you please, do you know, Socrates, what sort of things are beautiful and ugly? . . . Could you tell me what the beautiful is?" (286cd; trans. Fowler). Socrates has (as often) a good deal of difficulty getting his interlocutor to understand that he does not want to know what is beautiful, but what the beautiful is. We must bear in mind, again, that *to kalon* can range more widely, in some contexts, than "beauty," to what is fair or fitting—Xenophon, in his *Memorabilia* (III, viii), even has Socrates claiming that objects are beautiful if well made to perform their function. But in the *Greater Hippias*, and still more plainly in the *Philebus*, Socrates is examining beauty in a sense pretty close to what the modern aesthetician is interested in. The functional concept of beauty, which makes the well-made pot a beautiful pot, is rejected; after all, as Heraclitus said, the most beautiful ape is not as beautiful as a man. Various proposals for defining beauty are offered and rejected, and the dialogue is inconclusive, though some part of the truth may be found in the idea that the beautiful is what is beneficial, and in the idea that it is what pleases through hearing and sight; perhaps beauty is "beneficial pleasure" (303e; cf. *Gorgias* 474d).

In the *Philebus*, Plato is prepared to say what sorts of things are beautiful, that is, what essential properties beautiful things have in common, without which, he thinks, they could not be beautiful. He is sure these properties are closely associated with beauty, as the conditions under which it is possible for the Form to become embodied in concrete particulars—but (he does not want to say that these properties *define* beauty, or constitute an analysis of it. And probably he means beauty itself to be a single simple property, not analyzable at all.)

If we take typical examples of complex beautiful things, from people to temples, what do we find? They exhibit certain ideal proportions in the relation of part to part; and indeed, in the construction of the temple, precise mathematical measurements are taken to insure these proportions (cf. *Timaeus* 87cd; *Politicus* 284a). We find that part answers to part, in a balance or opposition that gives the whole a dynamic stillness and self-completeness. In short, we find that "the qualities of measure (*metron*) and proportion (*symmetron*) invariably . . . constitute beauty and excellence" (*Philebus* 64e; trans. Hackforth). And so, when the list of classes of goods is drawn up at the end of the *Philebus*, the beautiful is assigned a high place. In the first class Socrates places "what is measured or appropriate," and in the second "what is proportioned and beautiful and what is perfect and satisfying" (66ab). The passage in which these distinctions are made is one of the most difficult and confusing in Plato's ethical writings, and he seems, at the very least, to have taken little pains to clarify these distinctions and relationships. But it is clear that he thinks of measure and symmetry as closely associated with beauty, and as essential for beauty—at least in complex things (cf. *Sophist* 228, where deformity is lack of proportion).

But there is also beauty in simple things—that is, elementary qualities of sense experience. "Audible sounds which are smooth and clear, and deliver a single series of pure notes, are beautiful, not relatively to something else, but in themselves" (*Philebus* 51d); and similarly with colors: pure white, not a large expanse of it, is "the truest of all white things, and the fairest too" (53ab). Moreover, simple geometrical figures—"something straight, or round, and the surfaces and solids which a lathe, or a carpenter's rule and square, produces from the straight and round" (51c)— are also absolutely and eternally beautiful.

What do all these have in common, then—the pure tone or hue, the straight line or regular polyhedron, the face and figure of Agathon or Alcibiades, the Greek krater or temple? They have unity, regularity, simplicity (whether or not imposed upon complexity)—something like the principle of "the same," employed by the *demiourgos* of the *Timaeus* (35a). This is what gives them ideal character, allies them with the One rather than the Many, and either constitutes, or, more probably, supports and sustains, their beauty.

If we now reconsider the artist and his creative power from

this new point of view, the irrationality that seemed so prominent in him considered as a fabricator of illusions may appear as a higher sort of wisdom, his madness as something approaching divine inspiration. The suggestions about this in the *Ion* are embedded in so ironic a context that we would not be sure from that dialogue alone whether Socrates is at all serious when he tells Ion that his undoubted gift is an "inspiration," that he is moved by a "divine power" as a magnet moves the iron (533d; trans. Lamb). "For all the good epic poets utter all those fine poems not from art, but as inspired and possessed, and the good lyric poets likewise" (533e; cf. 536b). "A sort of genius and inspiration," Socrates calls it in the *Apology* (22), and again it may be ironic. But the *Phaedrus* is more serious, and that is the classical location of the inspiration theory. The third kind of "possession or madness" (*mania*) distinguished by Socrates has its source in the Muses.

This seizes a tender, virgin soul, stimulates it to rapt passionate expression . . . But if any man come to the gates of poetry without the madness of the Muses, persuaded that skill alone will make him a good poet, then shall he and his works of sanity be brought to nought by the poetry of madness [245a; trans. Hackforth].

It may be difficult at times to distinguish the real craziness of the insane, and perhaps of the rhapsode, from the apparent wildness of one who is really inspired—like the philosopher who only seems mad because he is transported and reels at the sight of true beauty (249d). But Plato here seems to be assuring us that there is a difference; that the artist may have his own insight into the nature of ideal beauty, even though his effort to bring it to earth and establish it here may require an inspired state in which he does not fully know what he is up to, but is taken hold of and used, so to speak, by some creative forces poetically or conventionally called the Muses. So even if the poet (like the diviner) does not have knowledge of what he is doing (*Meno* 99c, *Timaeus* 71e–72a) he may have something valuable to say (cf. *Laws* 682a).

There is an interesting problem here, of reconciling these thoughts about inspiration with the thoughts about beauty. For the creation of order and symmetry by measure and proportion seems to be a cool and rational activity—the architect of the Parthenon certainly must know what he is doing every moment— and that is how it can plausibly be allied to virtue (especially if this is conceived as a mean in conduct, as Plato suggested before Aristotle). But the poet's creative frenzy seems to be of a very different nature. There are two ways of trying to fit these views together, though neither may succeed completely. The more radical one would be to say that implicit in all of Plato's writings about the arts there may be a fundamental distinction between two types of art. Beauty and measure are generally discussed in connection with visual arts; when he talks about poetry, he introduces madness and inspiration. There may be a difference in Plato's attitude here. Perhaps the second, and less far-reaching, suggestion is more plausible: though different arts (from, say, the architect's to the rhapsode's) may require more or less deliberate calculation, and though to analyze the beauties of a work once it is completed may require rational thought, still, wherever beauty is captured in sensuous form, some abandonment to the creative *eros*, some inspired access to ideal beauty, is involved.

This makes the artist an unreliable guide to the behavior of things in this world; he does not—or need not—have solidly based empirical opinions or productive skills, much less a rational grasp of basic logical and mathematical connections between the other Forms. But he does have knowledge, and of reality, in so far as he has access to beauty. And Plato at times gives him more. For in some kinds of art, beauty itself depends upon "correctness"; the composer, for example, cannot set the words to proper music unless he grasps their meanings and the Forms involved. Hence the third speech in the *Phaedrus* is the best—for it is based on truth. If we follow out this line of thought, we will have to say, not that all art is false or illusory, but that some works are true and some are not. Poetry by itself is not of great value (*Phaedrus* 277e), unless put to the test of dialectical argument (278), so a poet who really knows the truth is more than a poet—he is a philosopher. The problem in choosing materials for the early education of the guardians in the *Republic* (377) is that there is so little poetry that is true—not that it is impossible for poetry to tell the truth, but that the legislator must pick and choose.

Plato makes one further suggestion in the *Laws*—that art is to be judged by its correctness. Music, for example, he says, is "imitative and representative" (668b; trans. Bury), and so must correspond to something. (In Xenophon's *Memorabilia*, III, viii, Socrates tells Aristippus that music can imitate the invisible character of the soul; cf. *Republic* 400–1b). Sometimes it is hard to be sure what the composer or sculptor intended to imitate (668e)—when modern composers, says the Athenian Stranger, separate words from music, and have the lyre or flute play alone, "it is almost impossible to understand what is intended by this wordless rhythm and harmony, or what noteworthy original it represents" (669e). This difficulty, so casually noted as the consequence of a coarse and tasteless procedure, was destined to set up very important aesthetic problems later, when music liberated itself more fully from words: if it is hard to tell what pure music imitates, and judge its success, that may be because it imitates nothing. But in most cases, at least, Plato thinks, there is a special task for the competent judge. He must have "first, a knowledge of the nature of the original; next, a knowledge of the correctness of the copy; and thirdly, a knowledge of the excellence with which the copy is executed" (669ab).

MORALITY

Though the arts may impinge upon the lives of all cultured men, and though they may be of special technical interest to those trained to practice them, it is the statesman, in his role of legislator and educator, who should be most deeply concerned about them. He who practices the supreme art of statecraft must ask what role the arts of music, and painting, and poetry are properly to play in the social scheme; he must inquire into their effects upon their audience, their true value to the whole culture that produces them, the ultimate justification of their right to exist. Here again, we find in Plato divergent lines of thought, both of which must, however, be traced, for both have proved illuminating and fruitful in the later history of aesthetics.

Let us begin with what seems to be the simplest and easiest question: what is the peculiar nature of aesthetic enjoyment? We may be imputing to Plato too distinct a notion of the aesthetic, too sharp a separation of this from other interests, but let us put the question in the terms suggested in the *Philebus*. There one of the important issues is over the nature of pleasure, and its relation to the good; and this discussion calls for distinctions between different sorts of pleasure. "True pleasures" are those given by beauty of color and form, by certain odors and sounds, and by those geometrical constructions that were spoken of above (51bc). You may be walking along the street, for example, and catch a sudden odor from a flowering shrub. It comes unbidden, that is, it is not preceded by a hunger or a thirst; and it leaves behind no unwanted after-effect. Unlike the pleasure of scratching an itch, it is an unmixed blessing, and that constitutes its purity, in the Benthamite sense.

When we think of aesthetic pleasure—meaning in this context the pleasure of hearing music and poetry or seeing beautiful forms—in this way, it would seem to rank among the higher and finer pleasures open to a good man and a good citizen. There is one qualification. It is too simple to say that "the value of music consists in its power of affording pleasure" if that is taken, in Benthamite fashion, to mean that the greater the quantity of pleasure the greater the music (*Laws* 655c; trans. Bury). Quantity of pleasure is no test unless it be pleasure of the right audience; we ought to praise "that music which pleases the best men and the highly educated" (658e–659).

Unfortunately that is not the whole story. For many works of art, especially tragic and epic poetry, are imitations of human lives and fortunes, and derive much of their enjoyableness from the representation of people in highly emotional states, expressing their emotions violently, in a way that excites the emotions of the audience, too. The representation of calm, wise, self-controlled people does not make for very exciting drama, yet the hates and fears, the jealous rages and pitiful sorrows of a Medea, for example, appeal, not to the highest part of the soul, but to an inferior one. Such a play "stimulates and strengthens an element which threatens to undermine the reason" (*Republic* 605b; trans. Cornford). There is thus an important effect upon character to be considered, Plato thinks: the tendency to make people more emotional, less self-controlled—whether they are giving way to tears or to immoderate laughter. Drama "waters the growth of passions which should be allowed to wither away and sets them up in control, although the goodness and happiness of our lives depend on their being held in subjection" (606d). This is the other half of Plato's celebrated indictment of the arts, in Book X of the *Republic* (the first half being directed against their falsity). There is no question that dramatic poetry is enjoyable, but "we must take a lesson from the lover who renounces at any cost a passion which he finds is doing him no good," for the love of poetry is equally destructive to character and we must learn to get along without it (607a).

What Plato has said here does not seem to apply to all works of art, but only to those whose content is of a certain sort—yet that includes dance and song as well as drama and poetry. And usually when Plato speaks of "music," he is thinking of music combined with words or dance movement. Now, in this passage we see Plato introducing a new consideration, one we have not so far attended to: he is asking a moral question about the probable effects of art, that is, inquiring into its influence upon character and conduct.

A passage in the *Laws* makes this transition in a somewhat different way. There the Athenian Stranger concedes that certain "harmless pleasures," such as moderate wine-drinking, which cannot be judged by any higher standards (since they have, by hypothesis, no significant consequences), may be approved on hedonistic grounds alone. "Then we shall rightly judge by the criterion of pleasure that object only which, in its effects, produces neither utility nor truth nor similarity, nor yet harm, and which exists solely for the sake of the concomitant element of charm" (*Laws* 667de; trans. Bury). Plato might have made a distinction here between two sorts of art, representational and non-representational in some narrow sense. But if all art is imitation, then no art can be judged purely by its pleasure (667e). All are to be judged by the standard of truth (667–668)—not only truth as correspondence to actuality, but moral truth.

There are in Plato's dialogues, as we have seen, passages where he seems able to lay aside (or perhaps has not yet assumed) the role of the moralist, and can enjoy beauty for its own sake. But the dominant movement of Plato's thought about art, taking it all in all, is strongly moralistic, in a broad sense. That is, it is not always moralistic in the sense of requiring (as he finds it necessary to do when outlining the curriculum of studies for the guardians in their tender and formative years) that stories avoid any suggestion of the permissibility of immoral conduct. But it insists that the final evaluation of any work of art, and the statesman's decision whether it should be permitted to exist, must take into account the all-important ends and values of the whole society. To the common good, as Plato conceives it, private enjoyments will often have to yield—even the personal predilections of the guardians themselves (it is not for their benefit that we are constructing the state).

So it becomes very important to study carefully the effects, good and bad, that art may have upon the citizen. And in a characteristically paradoxical fashion, Plato manages to combine the severest criticism of art with the most extravagant claims for it. Yet here his approach is, in a way, more empirical than elsewhere, for he is not trying to derive some predictions of the inevitable effects of art from a general theory about it; he is trying to get hold of reliable psychological information about what works of art of different sorts may be expected to do to people.

It is fairly clear that we can distinguish between works of art with good tendencies and those with bad. Speaking in very general terms, "the postures and tunes which attach to goodness of soul or body, or to some image thereof, are universally good, while those which attach to badness are exactly the reverse" (*Laws* 655b). Note here the very important connection between imitating goodness and stimulating good behavior—to Plato these are inseparable. More specifically, when we consider dramatic poetry, we find that, unfortunately, nearly all existing works have an evil tendency, for by representing gods and heroes as immoral, they are bound to tempt the young into the imitation of vice (*Republic* 392–98). Allowing the young to take part in recitations has another deleterious side effect, for it habituates them to accept in themselves the traits of the miserable characters whose parts they have to play—railing, or sick, or boastful women, "men of a low type, behaving with cowardice," etc. (395). The only answer to this is to give young people dramatic poetry that represents noble characters doing admirable works, heroes that act like heroes and gods that act like gods. If such works are not on hand, no doubt they can be commissioned; and poets who won't write them must be escorted to the borders with polite firmness, and others found to do the job (398ab, 401bc).

When the art is right, its power to do good, to contribute to the health and order of society, is as great as its potential ill. The harmony of beautiful music imitates that virtue which is precisely the harmony of the soul (*Laws* 655a, *Protagoras* 326ab, *Republic* 432). How, then, could it fail to be a good influence on the character of the listener? There are dangers, for some of the modes, like the Lydian and Ionian, may induce certain weaknesses of character (398e), and too much exposure to the charms of music has a debilitating effect (411a). But music and poetry and dancing of the right sort are indispensable means of character education (*Laws* 653–54, 664, 672e). Music can make us better men (802cd, 812c; cf. 790e–791a).

If the arts are of such moment, then, in the life and education of the citizen, their regulation must be one of the important functions of the state. It seems inconceivable to Plato that people should be allowed freely to play with such dangerous things as tragic dramas and musical compositions (*Laws* 656c, *Republic* 377 ff). Art is too serious to be left to the artist. The legislator must supervise the composition of works of art, as he must supervise the making of fables and legends (*Laws* 664a), and Plato devotes two extended discussions to the nature of the regulations he would propose (*Republic* 376e–411, *Laws* 800–2). The poet must submit his works to censors and obtain their approval (*Laws* 801d). Moreover, once the proper rules are worked out, there is to be no innovation, on pain of severe punishment (*Republic* 423–24, *Laws* 798–99).

Few of Plato's many ideas, I suppose, have been so strongly attacked and so shamefacedly defended as these proposals for authoritarian governmental control over the artistic products, and through them the very thoughts, of the citizens. "And were I a legislator," says the Athenian Stranger (*Laws* 662bc; trans. Bury),

I should endeavor to compel the poets and all the citizens to speak in this sense; and I should impose all but the heaviest penalties on anyone in the land who should declare that any wicked men lead pleasant lives, or that things profitable and lucrative are different from things just.

One can point out, as a supposed reductio ad absurdum, that this would eliminate some of Plato's best dialogues, including the *Republic* itself, since Thrasymachus and Glaucon and Adeimantus could not be allowed to speak their minds, even for the sake of being refuted. There is no point, I think, in trying to minimize the force of Plato's position here, but it may leave a slightly unbalanced view of his whole aesthetics to have to make this the last word about him. So let us bear in mind that Plato's main point here is that art has its social responsibilities, and like any other source of pleasure or of ill (like liquor and psychodelic drugs, we might say), must find its rational place in the whole scheme of the citizen's life. And if Plato concludes that it must be censored and restricted, he (correctly or incorrectly) believes himself led to this position by rigorous logical inference from the nature of art and the nature of the good life.

Bibliography

Apology, trans. Benjamin Jowett, in *The Dialogues of Plato*, 5 vols. (3d ed., Oxford, 1893).

Cratylus, trans. Benjamin Jowett (op. cit.).

Greater Hippias, trans. H. N. Fowler (Loeb Library, London, 1926).

Ion, trans. W. R. M. Lamb (Loeb Library, London, 1925).

Laws, trans. R. G. Bury, 2 vols. (Loeb Library, London, 1926).

Lysis, trans. W. R. M. Lamb (Loeb Library, London, 1925).

Phaedrus, trans. R. Hackforth (Cambridge, 1952).

Philebus, trans. R. Hackforth as *Plato's Examination of Pleasure* (Cambridge, 1945).

Republic, trans. F. M. Cornford (Oxford, 1941).

Sophist, trans. F. M. Cornford as *Plato's Theory of Knowledge* (New York, 1935).

Rupert C. Lodge, *Plato's Theory of Art* (London, 1953).

Eric A. Havelock, *Preface to Plato* (Harvard U., 1963).

Raphael Demos, *The Philosophy of Plato* (New York, 1939), chs. 11–13.

G. M. A. Grube, *Plato's Thought* (London, 1935), ch. 6.

I. M. Crombie, *An Examination of Plato's Doctrines*, Vol. I (New York, 1962), ch. 5.

Constantin Ritter, *The Essence of Plato's Philosophy*, trans. A. Alles (London, 1933), Part II, ch. 5.

Ernst Cassirer, *Eidos und Eidolon—Das Problem des Schönen in der Kunst in Platons Dialogen* (Leipzig, 1924).

R. G. Collingwood, "Plato's Philosophy of Art," *Mind* N.S. XXXIV (1925): 154–72.

G. M. A. Grube, "Plato's Theory of Beauty," *Monist* XXXVII (1927): 269–88.

H. J. Paton, "Plato's Theory of EIKAΣIA," *Proc Arist Soc* N.S. XXII (1922).

W. C. Greene, "Plato's View of Poetry," *Harvard Stud Class Philol* XXIX (1918).

J. Tate, "'Imitation' in Plato's *Republic*," *Class Quart* XXII (1928): 16–23.

————, "Plato and 'Imitation,'" *Class Quart* XXVI (1932): 161–69.

————, "On Plato: *Laws* X 889cd," *Class Quart* XXX (1936): 48–54.

————, "Plato and Allegorical Interpretation," *Class Quart* XXIII (1929): 142–54, XXIV (1930): 1–10.

Edith Watson Schipper, "*Mimesis* in the Arts in Plato's *Laws*," *Jour Aesth and Art Crit* XXII (Winter 1963): 199–202.

Richard McKeon, "Literary Criticism and the Concept of Imitation in Antiquity," *Modern Philol* XXIV (1936–37): 1–35.

W. J. Verdenius, *Mimesis: Plato's Doctrine of Artistic Imitation and its Meaning to Us* (Leiden, 1949).

Katharine Gilbert, "The Relation of the Moral to the Aesthetic Standard in Plato," *Philos Rev* XLIII (1934): 279–94.

R. G. Steven, "Plato and the Art of His Time," *Class Quart* XXVII (1933): 149–55.

N. R. Murphy, *The Interpretation of Plato's Republic* (Oxford, 1951), ch. 11.

D. R. Grey, "Art in the Republic," *Philos* XXVII (1952): 291–310.

Craig LaDrière, "The Problem of Plato's Ion," *Jour Aesth and Art Crit* X (Sept. 1951): 26–34.

J. G. Warry, *Greek Aesthetic Theory* (New York, 1962), chs. 1–4.

Evanghélos Moutsopoulos, *La Musique dans l'oeuvre de Platon* (Paris, 1959).

E. Huber-Abrahamowicz, *Das Problem der Kunst bei Platon* (Winterthur, 1954).

Julius Walter, *Die Geschichte der Ästhetik in Altertum* (Leipzig, 1893).

THREE

Aristotle

The little book, or collection of lecture notes, that has come down to us as Aristotle's *Poetics* was probably written about 347–42 B.C., but revised at some later date either by Aristotle or by an apt pupil. Despite all the lacunae in the argument and all the corruptions of the text, its influence and authority in succeeding centuries has been out of all proportion to its length. Neither in this work nor in other passages in Aristotle's extant works where aesthetic and literary problems are discussed (he also wrote a dialogue *On Poets*, which has disappeared) is there anything that can be called a system of aesthetics. But from this one splendid model of what it is to give a theory of a literary genre, and particularly from Aristotle's implicit replies to the views of Plato and others, we can legitimately draw out some valuable suggestions toward fundamental aesthetic theories. No work in the entire history of aesthetics, it is safe to say, has presented so many problems of exegesis, or been so pondered over and disputed (the bibliography is enormous, and still growing), but even if we cannot always be certain what Aristotle himself meant, we know what he has been construed to mean, and which of his supposed ideas have been powerfully influential in the later history of aesthetics and literary criticism.

It is highly characteristic of Aristotle that, in opening up a new field of inquiry, he begins by mapping it as exactly as he can in terms of a system of classification. This is his general way of getting at the thing itself, its essential features, and when he turns to the art of poetry (*poietike*), he is determined to mark out boundaries and study the nature of that art quite independently of its moral and political connections. This is a separation that Plato could not make, or did not believe should be made, but that Aristotle evidently considers quite indispensable for a satisfactory understanding. What, he asks, is the genus to which the poetic art belongs—and what, in turn, are its species?

On several occasions, Aristotle makes use of a very fundamental distinction between three kinds of "thought"—knowing (*theoria*), doing (*praxis*), and making (*poiesis*) (see *Metaphysics* VI [E], i; *Topics* VI, vi). In this context, *poietike* would be the productive art in general, but in the *Poetics* it is taken in a narrower sense. Some, but not all, making is imitation, or representation, of objects and events (Aristotle seems to take this term quite straightforwardly). And the imitative art itself falls into two divisions: (1) the art of imitating visual appearances by means of color and drawing, and (2) the art of imitating human actions through verse, song and dance (*Poetics*, chs. 1, 25). The second is the art of poetry. Thus the art of poetry is distinguished from painting in terms of its medium (words, melody, rhythm) and from versified history or philosophy (the poem of Empedocles) by virtue of the object it imitates. Two of the species of the poetic art are of primary concern to Aristotle: drama (either tragic or comic) and epic poetry. Tragedy and epic are distinguished from comedy by the seriousness or gravity of their actions (chs. 2, 6), and from each other by their mode, or method, of treatment (dramatic vs. narrative).

When Aristotle inquires into the "nature" of something, his inquiry is likely to have two distinct aspects—or aspects which we find quite distinct (and have come, in the light of later philosophical developments, to want to keep separate), but which Aristotle sees as inherently connected. He asks: what is the nature of the poetic art? And the answer is both normative and descriptive. For it involves a set of categories that play a fundamental role in all his thinking: the "four causes," or four types of explanation (see *Physics* II, vii). These are not mentioned in the *Poetics* itself, but it is interesting that in the *Metaphysics* (V [Δ], ii) when he distinguishes the four causes, his example of the "material" cause is "the bronze of the statue"; the "formal" cause is the "pattern," or "formula of the essence"; the "efficient" cause is the productive agent (e.g. the sculptor and his activity); the "final" cause is "the end, i.e., that for the sake of which a thing is" (trans. Ross). To understand the poetic art, then, will require not only an objective investigation of the actual features of existing tragedies, but also a conclusion about what makes a *good* tragedy—"the causes of artistic excellence and the opposite" (ch. 26, 1462 b 17; trans. Else; cf. ch. 1). Aristotle, in short, is interested in the basis of critical judgment, the reasons that can be given in support of a comparative evaluation (why, for instance, he is justified in regarding Homer's epics and Sophocles' *Oedipus Rex* as the greatest of masterpieces)—and the excuses that might be given in reply to unfavorable criticism (see chs. 25, 26).

Since our concern here is with general aesthetics, rather than the details of critical theory, we need not review the six parts, or constituents of the tragic art, which Aristotle distinguishes (ch. 6) and goes on to analyze with some care. It is the logic of his method and the significance of his main ideas that we must be content to understand.

THE PROPER PLEASURE OF TRAGEDY

Suppose we have made a full empirical study of existing tragedies, and catalogued their various characteristics—those common to all, such as imitating an action (*praxis*), and those that vary from one to another. Still, our understanding will not be complete, nor will we be in a position to give an adequate definition of the species we are after, until we can state its function, or end (*telos*)—that is, its final cause. Aristotle is not at all explicit about his method, but it must be basically similar to that employed in the *Nicomachaean Ethics* to determine the end, or good, of man.

People go to see tragedies because they want to, not because they have to, and evidently derive enjoyment from this experience. And the perpetuation of the institution of tragic performance shows, too, that no substitute for it has been found—that it affords a unique sort of enjoyment. A study of tragedies in general should show what this enjoyment is like—what is the "proper pleasure" (*oikeia hedonē*) of tragedy (chs. 14, 23, 26), though it may be produced in different degrees by different works. Then we can say that it is the function of the tragic art to produce this particular sort of pleasure, we can ask how it does this, and we can discover what enables one tragedy to perform that function better than another.

The idea of approaching the problem of critical evaluation by looking for a particular kind of enjoyment that it is the function of a particular art, or genre of art, to give, is a very important one. And this seems capable of empirical investigation. What is it about serious drama, generally speaking, that draws us to it, that creates the demand? And what is the impulse that produces the supply? Aristotle asks the second question (ch. 4), but evidently thinks of his answer as also bearing on the first one. He makes two suggestions: (1) Imitation is natural to man, and the recognition of imitation is pleasurable; (2) "melody and rhythm" also come naturally to man—and so are presumably enjoyable. Each of these suggestions, though somewhat tersely and (especially the second one) casually made, leads to significant lines of thought. Let us take them up separately.

As rational animals, we take pleasure in imitation, because seeing an imitation and recognizing it as such (say, as a picture of a dog) is a special case of learning.

And since learning and admiring are pleasant, all things connected with them must also be pleasant; for instance, a work of imitation, such as painting, sculpture, poetry, and all that is well imitated, even if the object of imitation is not pleasant; for it is not this that causes pleasure or the reverse, but the inference that the imitation and the object imitated are identical, so that the result is that we learn something [*Rhetoric* I, xi, 1371b; trans. Freese].

The prevailing tenor of this remark is very different from Plato's denigration of the cognitive status of art. Though Aristotle does not seem to be saying something very different from what Plato said when he placed the arts on the lowest level of his divided line, in the context of Aristotle's general epistemology the difference is significant. He and Plato both agree that genuine knowledge is not of particulars, but of universals: recognizing the photograph as a picture of Lassie does not, for Aristotle, give knowledge in the important sense, like recognizing it as a picture of a dog (*Metaphysics* XI [K], i; VII [Z], xi). When the universals are thought of as transcendental Forms, they are remote from the works of the etcher or draftsman; but when they are thought of, in Aristotle's way, as existing only in substances, then the draftsman, who abstracts and reproduces in another medium certain dog-universals, is not doing something poles apart from, say, the taxonomist, who is abstracting and connecting other dog-universals. Art is knowledge, in not too bad a sense, or at least the pleasure it gives is, as far as one of its ingredients is concerned, of the same order as the pleasure of coming to know.

Even if tragedy pleases us as an imitation, it shares this value with other imitations, and so we have not yet found a *proper*, or peculiar, pleasure. But the differentia is to be sought in the *object* of imitation, for that is what is peculiar to tragedy (setting aside epic, at the moment). Thus Aristotle says the proper pleasure of tragedy "is the pleasure that comes from pity and fear by means of imitation" (ch. 14, 1453 b 14; trans. Else). The meaning of this statement is not perfectly clear. Perhaps Aristotle wants it to be taken in this way: this pleasure is the pleasure we derive from recognizing an imitation, when the imitation happens to be of fearful and pitiable events. Thus, as pleasure in imitation it belongs to a certain genus of pleasures, but there are species of imitation-pleasures, defined by the sort of object imitated, the subject matter. In so far as matters of human behavior are of greater moment to us than other actions, and the significant ("serious") actions of tragedy are most important of all, the pleasure of seeing an imitation of them—and in this sense learning about them—might be the most intense of all imitation-pleasures.

That is a possible view. But it leads immediately to a problem. For Aristotle clearly does not want to say only that the events of the tragedy are fearful and pitiable; he says they arouse emotions of fear and pity in the audience—and not only the theater audience, but those who just read the story or hear it told (see ch. 14). This specific combination, or pair, of emotions is unique to serious poetry—including both tragedy and epic, which Aristotle regards as having the same emotional effect, though he thinks that tragedy is capable of achieving it more fully than epic (ch. 26). But fear and pity are unpleasant emotions to feel, one would think. Indeed, in the *Rhetoric* (II, v, viii), they are defined as species of pain: pity, for example, is "a kind of pain excited by the sight of evil, deadly or painful, which befalls one who does not deserve it" (II, viii, 2). But then the question arises, How *can* there be a pleasure that "comes from pity and fear," even "by means of imitation"?

From our later vantage-point in the history of aesthetics, we might expect Aristotle to go on to show how emotions that are ordinarily painful can become pleasurable through the sort of imitation we have in tragedy. He might have said that the emotions, since they are directed at imaginary people or people who lived long ago, cannot trouble us (cf. *Rhetoric* II, viii: "the nearness of the terrible makes men pity"), or that something in the nature of the drama transmutes them, or removes their sting. But he does not say anything of the sort. And, indeed, his chief emphasis is on the importance of intensifying the fear and pity of the audience: the hero must be a man "like ourselves" (ch. 13), for example, so that we can pity him all the more readily and deeply. The closest Aristotle comes to resolving this paradox of the tragic pleasure is in his casual remark in Chapter 4 that "There are things we find painful to look at themselves, but of which we view the most accurate reproductions with pleasure: for example, replicas of the most unprepossessing animals, or of cadavers" (1448 b 11; trans. Else)—a claim made also in *Rhetoric* I, xi, and *De Partibus Animalium* I, v. Perhaps the point is simply that, however pitiable and fearful the events in the play, the painfulness of the emotions they arouse does not destroy the pleasure that comes simply because it is an imitation, and of important and interesting things.

Whether it is possible to make out in Aristotle's works a more specific solution to the tragic paradox is perhaps doubtful. One possibility, for which there is just the suggestion of a warrant, may be worth considering briefly. It is not the same events of the play that are both fearful and pitiable, but different ones, and indeed there is a natural order in which they would occur—at least in the ideal cases, as Aristotle conceives them. In *Oedipus Rex*, the events leading up to the climactic recognition scene are increasingly fearful, but when the climax comes our fears are over, for we have been through the worst, and it is at this point that we feel only pity for Oedipus. The tragic movement, it might be said, transforms fear into pity. But when pity is felt as a relief from fear, or other tense and painful feelings, such as horror or anger, it may become something like a pleasure—or the *transition* may be felt as a pleasure. When (like the Ancient Mariner) we experience a sudden opening of the channels of feeling, which have been dammed up by coldness of heart, by envy, or by self-centeredness, a strong sense of gladness may be mixed with the pity. Or suppose we are terrified that something bad will happen to someone, and it does, so that we can now pity instead of fear—or suppose we bitterly hate someone who suddenly becomes more understandable to us, so that we can pity him instead of hating—again there is a sense that we have been set free to some extent. According to one of Aristotle's accounts of pleasure (*Rhetoric* I, xi), it is "a certain movement of the soul, a sudden and percepti-ble settling down into its natural state" (trans. Freese), a restora-tion to "normal" condition. The end of the tragedy, when the hero is to be pitied, does not restore things to normal, but it brings things back much closer to an equilibrium, and this move-ment may be itself enjoyed.

Let us turn now to the second suggestion Aristotle makes (in ch. 4) about the pleasure of tragedy: that we enjoy melody and rhythm. It is a little startling that he should be so brief here (but the *Poetics* bristles with striking remarks that are left to us to follow up). Perhaps he did not think it would be questioned—at least by anyone familiar with Plato's *Philebus*—or did not at the time know where to go next. But it is tempting to ask, What *about* melody and rhythm makes them intrinsically pleasurable?— and to answer, It must be their beauty. For this move enables us to connect up this passage with other passages later in the *Poetics* in which Aristotle uses the term "beauty" (*to kalon*) or its cognates. To what extent we are warranted in taking this step is not clear, for Aristotle may simply be postulating a special pleasure in melody and rhythm, but it is worth considering.

As a possible connection between the two parts of the *Poetics*, we may consider Aristotle's most famous account of pleasure (*Nicomachean Ethics* X). Pleasures, he says, differ in kind accord-ing to the activity which they "complete"; each activity has its "proper pleasure." "Pleasures increase activities, and what in-creases a thing is proper to it" (X, v; trans. Ostwald). Sensing (for example, seeing a sculpture) and thought or contemplation (for example, reading or hearing Homer recited) are activities also, and have their proper pleasures.

All sense perception is actively exercised in relation to its object, and is completely exercised when it is in good condition and its object is the best of those that can be perceived by the senses. . . . From all this it follows that in any sense perception that activity is best whose organ is in the best condition and whose object is the best of all the objects that fall within its range, and this activity will be the most complete and the most pleasant [X, iv].

When the object experienced is "best" or "worthiest" (some translate "most beautiful"), the pleasure is greatest because the experience is most active. And this would describe the tragic experience above all. "A beautiful thing," says Aristotle suddenly in Chapter 7 of the *Poetics* (1450 b 35; trans. Else), "either a living creature or any structure made of parts, must have not only an orderly arrangement of these parts but a size which is not accidental—for beauty lies in size and arrangement . . ." (in the *Metaphysics* XIII [M], iii, "the chief forms of beauty are order and symmetry and definiteness"). And he goes on to apply this to tragedy. Now, there is a certain mystery in Aristotle's remarks about beauty—in some places in the *Poetics*, the term *kalliste* seems to be another name for "best" or "finest" or "artistically most excellent" (see, for example, ch. 13, 1452 b 31 and 1453 a 19, 23; cf. *kalos*, ch. 1, 1447 a 10). He is not necessarily thinking of beauty as a special quality distinct from, but capable of contributing to, artistic excellence—it may be that "beautiful tragedy" and "artistically good tragedy" are synonymous for him.

But *kalliste* is clearly an aesthetic value predicate, and applies to the tragedies that Aristotle deems worthy of praise. And he wants to point out that a good tragedy does have "orderly arrangement," with all that this can imply in the way of completeness, due proportion, and (if this is not too Platonic) measure. The epic, for example, must center about a complete action, "so that like a single whole creature (*zoön*) it may produce its proper pleasure" (ch. 23, 1459 a 20; trans. Else; the same analogy appears in Plato's *Phaedrus* 264c). This organic unity and order is something that the art of imitation can claim to offer—something that the art of serious poetry shares with the art of painting (and Aristotle here brings these arts closer together in his theory than Plato was able or willing to do), but perhaps achieves in its own way and degree, because the tragedy takes place in time and is itself an action that is complete, with a beginning, middle, and end (ch. 7).

ARISTOTLE'S ANSWER TO PLATO

From these conclusions about the end, or function, of tragedy, Aristotle derives his critical criteria, concerning those features of tragedy that are likely to enable it to fulfill that function most effectively. We will not be able here to give all the attention they deserve to the many penetrating suggestions that Aristotle has to offer, but some examples may be cited to illustrate his method. Since the wholeness of the tragedy is the curve of its movement to consummation, the plot (*mythos*), or "course of events," is basic and most important to get right; it is the (proximate) "end" or "as it were the soul of the tragic art" (ch. 6, 1450 a 39). Aristotle analyzes those features of the complex plot, peripety and recognition, that contribute most tellingly to the effect of fear and pity (chs. 9–11, 13). The play must be unified to have a single condensed impact (chs. 7, 8), and it must proceed with the greatest possible sense of inevitability. This means that the developments of the plot "must arise out of the very structure of the plot, in such a way that as a result of what has happened beforehand it follows either necessarily or probably that these particular things happen" (ch. 10, 1452 a 19; trans. Else).

It is in this context that we must understand some of Aristotle's most often quoted (and puzzling) remarks about probability and necessity. For example, he says "it is clear too that the poet's job is not to tell what has happened but the kind of things that *can* happen" (1451 a 36) and

that is why the writing of poetry is a more philosophical activity, and one to be taken more seriously, than the writing of history; for poetry tells us rather the universals, history the particulars. "Universal" means what kinds of thing a certain kind of person will say or do in accordance with probability or necessity, which is what poetic composition aims at . . . ; while "particular" is what Alcibiades did or had done to him [ch 9, 1451 b 6; trans. Else].

The remark about Alcibiades is the one to begin with, for to understand Aristotle's view of poetry by means of this comparison we must first understand his view of history. And it is clear that he thinks of history as a mere chronicle of distinct events that does *not* make any attempt to explain one event in terms of another, or show how one leads to another. This is certainly a very narrow concept of history, but it shows that we must not overstress the contrasting concept of poetry, for Aristotle's point is simply that to make a coherent and powerful plot, the poet must show how actions grow out of motives and motives out of circumstances. But this can be done only in terms of universals, or psychological laws (that a man under such-and-such circumstances would necessarily or probably act in such-and-such a way). Thus Aristotle is not saying that poetry is very philosophical, but only that it involves psychological knowledge (as, he thinks, history does not). We must not forget, of course, that this passage, quoted often out of context, has inspired many important theories about poetry and art as "imitations of universals or essences," and these theories must be considered in their place, whether or not Aristotle, when read with caution, can be said actually to have been their legitimate parent.

Nevertheless, it is clear that Aristotle is making an important point about the intellectual content of poetry here, and in this respect implicitly answering one of Plato's main objections to it. For though the poet can plausibly pretend to knowledge of shipbuilding or military strategy which he does not have, he cannot fake psychological knowledge—he must understand human nature. He must have true general knowledge of certain psychological mechanisms; for without these he cannot even make a good play. And, other things being equal, the better the play the more profound and extensive must the poet's knowledge be, for both the beautiful pattern of plot and the successful imitation of action depend upon it.

Hence there is an important cognitive element in Aristotle's critical theory, though he argues it, interestingly, as a consequence of his other critical principles. The assumed psychological laws must be true ones, because if they are not, the dramatic developments will not be inevitable, and the play will fall apart. Thus basically Aristotle is a structural critic: the business of the critic is to analyze aspects of structure to show what helps, and what hinders, the production of the tragic pleasure. Aristotle is also a textural critic, and shows the way—if not in Chapters 20–22 of the *Poetics* (which may not be by him at all), then in the *Rhetoric* —to the close and careful analysis of the verbal level in poetry. In both respects, in his intense interest in both structure and verbal texture, Aristotle's influence on the rhetoricians and critics of the Renaissance and early modern period was to be enormous.

There remains one line of thought to be considered—and the most difficult of all. This has to do with the famous concept of "catharsis." This term, in its verbal form (*katharsin*), appears but once in Aristotle's account of tragedy (*Poetics*, ch. 6, 1449 b 28), but over the centuries the translators and commentators have worked out an interesting theory which they find Aristotle sketching here, however briefly. And this interpretation is still the canonic one, though in recent years it has been challenged in a most fundamental way by Professor Gerald F. Else (see bibliography below). The issues are numerous and complex, but the difference between the two interpretations, and something of their support, must be reviewed briefly here.

The traditional interpretation is well expressed in Butcher's translation of the passage in Chapter 6 (1449 b 27): "through pity and fear effecting the proper purgation of these emotions" (*di eleou kai phobou perainousa tēn tōn toioutōn pathēmaton katharsin*). The general theory attributed to Aristotle, then, would be that tragedy, by arousing these emotions, has some sort of therapeutic effect upon the audience's mental health, giving a pleasurable sense of relief—"in calm of mind, all passion spent" (as Milton echoes this view in *Samson Agonistes*). The sparseness and ambiguity of the text and the plentifulness and ingenuity of the interpreters have combined to produce other subissues, without full resolution. For example, there has been much disagreement about whether *katharsin* is a medical metaphor, and implies the getting rid of noxious emotions in a way analogous to a physic, or whether it is a metaphor taken from religious ritual, and means a kind of "purification" of the emotions, but not their elimination. On behalf of the medical interpretation, which is dominant, it is argued that *katharsin* clearly has the purgative sense in Greek medical writings; and that the genitive form of *pathematon* often denotes the object removed (cf. Plato, *Phaedo* 69b). On behalf of the religious interpretation, it can be said that the genitive can also denote the object cleansed (cf. Plato, *Sophist* 227c). And it is noteworthy that in its only other occurrence in the *Poetics* itself (in the form *katharseos*; ch. 17, 1455 b 15), the word has to mean ritual purification (in this case of Orestes). And again, the puzzling grammatical construction (especially the phrase *ton toiouton pathematon*) has stimulated disagreement about whether Aristotle means that only these two tragic emotions, or emotions in general, are the ones that are purged or purified.

Professor Else, on the other hand, translates the passage as follows: "carrying to completion, through a course of events involving pity and fear, the purification of those painful or fatal acts which have that quality." The purgation, in his reading, is a purification, and it is not something that takes place in the spectator at all, but something that takes place in the *play*. It is carried out by the plot itself, in virtue of the fact that the plot consists of events of a certain sort. (Professor Else takes *pathematon* as tragic events, because *pathos* in later chapters means this.) The actions that have the most tragic quality, Aristotle says (ch. 14), are painful deeds "done to one another by persons who are bound by natural ties of affection," as "when a brother kills or intends to kill a brother, or a son a father" (trans. Else). These are acts evoking moral horror, to which the Greeks attached immemorial taboos—acts that were felt to require a "purification" because they carried (even to sophisticated Greeks of the fifth and fourth centuries, as can be seen in Plato's *Euthyphro*) a suggestion of blood-pollution, the curse on the house of Atreus, for example. But what makes it possible for the doer of the horrible deed, say of patricide, to be cleansed (and pitied) is that he did it in ignorance of some important fact, and therefore did not intend to murder his father and marry his mother. This, according to Professor Else, is the meaning of the so-called "tragic flaw" (*hamartia*), which he interprets as a "serious error." It would make possible the tremendous emotional impact of the "recognition" (for example, Oedipus' discovery of what he has done). Oedipus thus becomes pitiable, as it turns out he is free from pollution—the evil deed is purified in the course of the plot, because Oedipus' essential purity is revealed by his own horror at the discovery of his actions; his recognition shows that he deserves our pity.

According to this interpretation, the concept of catharsis is a *structural* concept—it belongs to the formal analysis of the drama itself—rather than a psychological one. There are many difficulties in making it fit the actual patterns of the tragedies Aristotle knew—even *Oedipus Rex*. Moreover, the traditional interpretation is strongly supported by Book VIII of the *Politics*. Here Aristotle discusses the place of music in education, echoing and developing some of the ideas that appeared in Plato's *Laws* (cf. 790c–791b). One of the benefits of music, he says, is "release of emotion" (as Barker translates *katharsis*, p. 412): we observe that certain people are

affected by religious melodies; and when they come under the influence of melodies which fill the soul with religious excitement they are calmed and restored as if they had undergone a medical treatment and purging (*katharsis*) . The same sort of effect will also be produced [i.e., by appropriate music] on those who are specially subject to feelings of fear and pity, or to feelings of any kind [*Politics* VIII, vii; trans. Barker].

It is natural to take Aristotle's side remark, after he introduces the term "release of emotion"—"the sense of that term will be explained more clearly in our lectures on poetics, but may be left to speak for itself at the moment"—as referring to some part of the *Poetics* that has disappeared. In that case, it becomes reasonable to carry over the catharsis theory that Aristotle undoubtedly held about music in the *Politics,* and make it into a theory about tragedy in the *Poetics.* Unfortunately, in the *Poetics* itself, there is little (besides the key clause in Chapter 6) on which to build such a therapeutic theory of catharsis—though also there is nothing to exclude it.

One of the strongest temptations to the traditional interpretation of the *Poetics* is that it imputes to Aristotle a direct answer to Plato's second main objection to poetry: that it could only feed and water the passions, and thus disrupt the harmony of the soul and the rationality of the citizen. According to this interpretation, Aristotle has an impressive rebuttal: no such thing; if we look only at the immediate frenzy, the audience's terror and weeping, it may seem that way, but if we look at the later and deeper psychological effects of going through the experience, the playgoer is like the religious enthusiast who feels cleansed and lightened and brightened by his emotional release. The play-going citizen, in the long run, is probably the calmest and the wisest, for he gets rid from time to time of those festering emotional irritations that poison the temperament and the mind.

Even if Aristotle never did, in fact, have any such theory about the indirect beneficial effects of the tragic experience, he nevertheless could be proposing a reply to part of Plato's objection. For, in the first place, as suggested earlier, he would be saying that the beauty of tragedy has a kind of purity like those beauties Plato speaks of in the *Philebus,* and is harmless and admissible. But, in the second place, he would be saying that the immorality of tragedy is not to be feared. Though there are various logical possibilities for the tragic reversal of fortune *(metabolē),* depending on whether the hero is good or not, and suffers good or ill fortune, the best tragedy, Aristotle thinks he can show, is one in which a man who is not wholly good, but enough like ourselves, suffers a misfortune he does not wholly deserve. What Plato feared most as a bad example for Athenian youth was the suggestion that good men are unhappy and that bad men prosper. Aristotle's reply might be understood in this way: there is no need to have a moral censorship of plays, but only an aesthetic one. For the play about the good man who becomes unhappy or the bad man who becomes happy will simply not be a very good tragedy; other things being equal, morality and justice will coincide with aesthetic excellence.

Bibliography

Gerald F. Else, *Aristotle's Poetics: The Argument* (Cambridge, 1957).

S. H. Butcher, *Aristotle's Theory of Poetry and Fine Art* (4th ed., London, 1923).

Ingram Bywater, *Aristotle on the Art of Poetry* (Oxford, 1909).

Lane Cooper, *The Poetics of Aristotle: its Meaning and Influence* (New York, 1927).

Metaphysics, trans. W. D. Ross, in *Works*, ed. J. A. Smith and W. D. Ross, Vol. 8 (Oxford: Clarendon Press, 1908).

Nicomachean Ethics, trans. Martin Ostwald (New York: Library of Liberal Arts, 1962).

Politics, trans. Ernest Barker (Oxford, 1948).

Rhetoric, trans. J. H. Freese (Loeb Library, London, 1939).

Gerald F. Else, "Aristotle on the Beauty of Tragedy," *Harvard Studies in Class Philol* XLIX (1938).

W. K. Wimsatt, "Aristotle and Oedipus or Else," in *Hateful Contraries* (U. of Kentucky, 1965).

R. P. Hardie, "The *Poetics* of Aristotle," *Mind* N.S. IV (1895): 350–64.

A. W. Benn, "Aristotle's Theory of Tragic Emotion," *Mind* N.S. XXIII (1914): 84–90.

Roman Ingarden, "A Marginal Commentary on Aristotle's Poetics," *Jour Aesth and Art Crit* XX (Winter 1961, Spring 1962): 163–73, 273–85.

John S. Marshall, "Art and Aesthetic in Aristotle," *Jour Aesth and Art Crit* XII (Dec. 1953): 228–31.

Katharine Gilbert, "Aesthetic Imitation and Imitators in Aristotle," *Philos Rev* XLV (1936): 558–73.

A. H. Gilbert, "The Aristotelian Catharsis," *Philos Rev* XXXV (1926): 301–14.

Richard McKeon, "Literary Criticism and the Concept of Imitation in Antiquity," *Mod Philol* XXXIV (1936): 1–35; reprinted in R. S. Crane, ed., *Critics and Criticism* (Chicago, 1952).

W. D. Ross, *Aristotle* (London, 1923; New York, 1959), ch. 9.

John Herman Randall, *Aristotle* (New York, 1960), ch. 13, § 1.

The Politics of Aristotle, ed. Franz Susemihl and R. D. Hicks (London, 1894), "A Note on *Katharsis*," pp. 641–56.

T. R. Henn, *The Harvest of Tragedy* (London, 1956), chs. 1, 2.

Whitney J. Oates, *Aristotle and the Problem of Value* (Princeton, 1963), ch. 8.

J. G. Warry, *Greek Aesthetic Theory* (New York, 1962), chs. 5–8.

FOUR

The Later Classical Philosophers

I t is remarkable that Aristotle's *Poetics* had practically no ancient history—that it does not seem to have been available to most of those who carried on the study of poetics in the next centuries. What was known of it by later Greeks and Romans came indirectly, for instance through the writings of Aristotle's favorite pupil, Theophrastus (about 372–287 B.C.). Of most of the latter's works (including his own *Poetics*) only a few fragments remain, but he evidently attempted some extension of Aristotle's theories. One of his proposals (reported by Dionysius of Halicarnassus) was a definition of verbal beauty as "that which gives pleasure to the ear or the eye or has noble associations of its own." But to explore the implications of this pregnant phrase would take us beyond what we can confirm by any text.

A somewhat later writer who seems to have known a good deal about the contents of the *Poetics* is the unknown author of the *Tractatus Coislinianus*, a compilation in Greek, probably from the first century B.C. It deals in some detail with the theory of comedy, and it not only follows characteristic Aristotelian methods but presents a definition of comedy that parallels very closely the definition of tragedy in Chapter 6 of the *Poetics*. For these reasons it has been taken as a report of the material supposed to be missing from Aristotle's work. One interesting departure from Aristotelian terminology is that poetry is said to be of two sorts, imitative and nonimitative: the former consisting of drama and epic (narrative), the latter of didactic (historical and educational) works.

[69]

From the entire period between Aristotle's *Poetics* and Horace's *Ars Poetica*, not one complete treatise on poetic theory has survived. We have plenty of evidence that a good deal of thinking and writing went on—we know a number of titles—but the actual remains are scanty. We possess extremely important scientific and philosophical works, for this was a period of intense intellectual activity. The Academy and the Lyceum continued to exist, and three major philosophical movements came to flower: Stoicism, Epicureanism, and Skepticism. Fortunately, a little can be said about the aesthetic theories connected with each of these.

HELLENISM AND ROMAN CLASSICISM

Among the Stoics there was a good deal of interest in poetry and the theory of poetry. The Stoics were deeply immersed in problems of semantics and logic and it was in this school that the allegorizing of Homer flourished most, after Plato's time. Treatises on poetics (no longer extant) were written by Zeno, Cleanthes, and Chrysippus—who also (according to Diogenes Laertius) wrote *Against the Touching up of Paintings* and *On the Right Way of Reading Poetry*. We know a little (from Philodemus) of a work on music by Diogenes of Babylon, and more (from Cicero's *De Officiis*) of a work on beauty by Panaetius. Apparently Diogenes held that the musician is concerned with sounds in quite a different way from ordinary perception: the latter deals with simple sense qualities, the former with "dispositions" of the qualities of perception (which may mean their harmonious and rhythmic relationships to each other). In a similar vein, Panaetius insists that the beauty of a visible object lies in the arrangement of its parts (*convenientia partium*, in Cicero's words), and requires a higher level of perception than that vouchsafed to animals.

In view of the basic Stoic doctrine that right action consists in conforming the individual reason (*logos*) with the universal *logos* of nature, it is not surprising to find Panaetius likening the beauty, or orderly arrangement, of objects to the rational order of the soul, and suggesting that the delight in beauty is connected with the virtue that expresses itself in an ordered life. Thus the notion of aesthetic harmony is bound up with the moral doctrine of decorum (*to prepon*), and a justification found, within the Stoic framework, for the pleasure of poetry. Considering the emphasis they placed on tranquillity and detachment (*ataraxia*), the effects of art might appear all too risky for the Stoics. But they seem to have made a distinction between two sorts of pleasure here: the pleasure (*hedone*) that is an irrational movement of the soul is not to be desired by the philosopher, for (like all forms of evil) it rests upon incorrect judgment or deceit; but one who is in the right frame of mind can derive from poetry another sort of pleasure (*chara*) which is a rational elevation of the soul.

Another interesting line of thought is attributed to Crates (probably a Stoic) by Philodemus. He raised the question whether there is more than one standard (*thema*) for judging a poem, and argued against certain unnamed relativists who held that there is no natural good (*physikon agathon*) in poetry. Apparently Crates argued that better and worse poems are distinguished by the ear, which does not employ a plurality of standards. That by itself does not show that the expression "a good poem" has a single meaning, or a single set of criteria of application. But it is significant, for, according to Stoic doctrine, perception is not merely sensation, but always involves a rational element of judgment. Thus to enjoy the pleasure of a poem is in part to judge it, for it is to grasp something in the poem that makes it good—i.e., its being composed according to the right principles of unity or harmony. Thus the pleasure of hearing it is not itself a standard, but a sign or indication, of the poem's goodness as a poem. It is not clear exactly what Crates thought the criteria of poetic goodness are, but he apparently emphasized the moral benefit of poetry as a final justification.

And from the Stoic Strabo (*Geography* I, i, 10; I, ii, 3) one gathers that the Stoics in general maintained this view—approving of the use of poems for moral teaching in schools, conceiving of poetry as a kind of allegorized philosophy and a vehicle (superior, it may be, to prose philosophic discourse, said Chrysippus) of the highest truths.

It has often been claimed that the Epicureans disapproved of music and of the pleasure to be derived from it. Apart from the report of Sextus Empiricus (*Against the Professors*; Book VI, *Against the Musicians*, § 27) that Epicurus denied that music contributes to happiness, the evidence for this view seems to be based on an interesting confusion. According to Plutarch (*That It is Not Possible to live Pleasurably According to the Doctrine of Epicurus*, 13), Epicurus

declares in his book called *Doubts* that the wise man is fond of shows and takes pleasure more than others in the Dionysiac recitals and spectacles; and yet he will not allow musical discussions and the learned inquiries of critics at parties.

All this proves is that Epicurus liked listening to music more than listening to music critics—which is surely a consistent position. As for poetry, we know this much, that Lucretius could think of no greater service to render to the immortality, not only of Epicurus but also of Epicureanism, than to put that philosophy into poetry.

Our most important source of information about Epicurean ventures in aesthetics is a remarkable writer of the first century B.C., Philodemus of Gadara, who spent much of his life in Italy. In papyri recovered from Herculaneum, there are (1) parts of Book IV of an essay *On Music* (*Peri Mousikes*), which suggest that—unless he was drawing heavily on a lost work of the same title by Epicurus himself—he took a fresh look at some important problems in musical aesthetics, and (2) parts of Book V of an essay *On Poems* (*Peri Poiematon*), which attacks with vigor some of the principles of other writers.

The Pythagorean theory that music (1) is capable of arousing and quieting the emotions and (2) is capable of exercising an influence on character, was, as we have seen, developed by Plato and accepted in modified form by Aristotle. After him, the Peripatetics, as well as the Stoics and Academics, continued to defend these propositions—though it is also worth noting that Aristoxenus (one of Aristotle's best pupils, whose book on the *Elements of Harmony* grasped the concept of music as an organic and dynamic system of sounds, and aimed to carry out a scientific analysis of music based on what is actually heard by the human ear) acknowledges that "one class of musical art is hurtful to the moral character, another improves it" only with the qualification, "—in so far as musical art can improve the moral character" (II, 31; trans. Macran).

It was these two propositions that Philodemus attacked, with arguments that sharply define one side in a recurrent dispute, as we shall see. He suggested that because the term *mousike* denoted poetry and dancing as well as what we would now call pure music, earlier theorists had been confused, and had attributed to the music itself effects that are (if they occur at all) due to the words. "*Qua* musicians they gave pleasure," he says of Pindar and Simonides, "and *qua* poets they wrote the words, and perhaps even in this capacity did not improve men, or at all events improved them only to a small extent" (trans. Wilkinson, *Class Quart* XXXII, 175). Music by itself cannot imitate character, and cannot have significant emotional effects.

No melody, *qua* melody, being irrational (*alogon*), either rouses the soul from a state of tranquillity and repose and leads it to the condition which belongs naturally to its character, or soothes and quietens it when it is aroused and moving in any direction. . . . For music is not an imitatory art (*mimetikon*), as some people fondly imagine, nor does it, as this man [Diogenes of Seleucia] says, have similarities to moral feelings which, though not imitative, yet express all ethical qualities such as magnificence, humbleness, courage, cowardice, orderliness and violence— any more than cookery [p. 176].

Philodemus's reasoning is that a sound cannot imitate things or abstractions, but only another sound—an evident insistence on using the term "imitate" in a restricted, and therefore clear, sense. Note that he is, however, not merely denying that music is imitative in this narrow sense; he is also denying that music can express (*epiphainesthai*) ethical qualities, even in some broader sense. And he bases this conclusion on the observation that different listeners (while they will no doubt all recognize the musical imitation of a thunderstorm) will respond very differently to the same piece of music, once it is separated from the words.

Both in the case of the Enharmonic and the Chromatic scale people differ, not in respect of the irrational perception, but in respect of their opinions (*doxas*), some, like Diogenes, saying that the Enharmonic is solemn and noble and straightforward and pure, and the Chromatic unmanly and vulgar and mean, while others call the Enharmonic severe and despotic, and the Chromatic mild and persuasive; both sides importing ideas which do not belong to either scale by nature [p. 177].

But if music cannot improve character by imitating virtue and arousing an impulse to follow, neither can it corrupt; being non-rational, its pleasure must be perfectly harmless.

The term *alogon* suggests the way in which this view of music was connected with the general Epicurean theory of perception. Against the Stoics, Epicurus held that sensation as such is devoid of cognitive value. Thus it would not be until *doxa* becomes connected with sensation that knowledge can occur, or any reference to the world. And not until there is knowledge, or reason, can the emotions be brought under control. "It is unthinkable that sounds which merely move the irrational hearing should contribute anything towards a disposition of soul capable of distinguishing the expedient and the inexpedient in our social relationships," says Philodemus (p. 178).

The book *On Poems,* or what remains of it, concentrates on another important thesis that cuts deeply into the controversies of that day. Philodemus holds that a great deal of critical theory rests upon a separation of two aspects of the poem, inspiration and technique, or (in Peripatetic language) matter (*pragmata*) and style (*lexis*). This is not only an untenable separation, for in the work itself they exist in a unity, but it leads to mistaken ideas about the real nature of poetic goodness (*to poiētikon agathon*). (1) Some insist that matter is the important thing, and argue that the primary function of poetry is to instruct and improve. But this is not so, for it is doubtful whether poetry can do these things at all, and, even if it can, it does not do them *qua* poetry, but only accidentally, as is shown by the fact that approved subject matter is neither a necessary nor a sufficient condition of poetic merit: "There is no good thought which, if the diction be poor, can make a piece of literature, as such, meritorious; nor any content essentially so trivial, that, if the form be good, the contrary effect is not produced" (trans. Wilkinson, *Greece and Rome* II, 150). But (2) others say that the form is the important thing, and argue that the primary function of poetry is to give pleasure. For example, Eratosthenes (we learn from Strabo, I, ii, 3) held that poetry aims, not at instruction (*didaskalia*) but at delight (*psychagogia*). Though an Epicurean, Philodemus rejects this too. Moreover, most subtly of all, he rejects the view that there are two functions of poetry, that its worth consists in a mere sum of the hedonic and cognitive (plus moral) values. We do not have enough information to know exactly how far Philodemus himself went toward formulating his own answer; it seems that he thought the goodness of a poem consists in a unity of form and content, and a consequent individuality contributed by the poet.

The Skeptics sought their ideal of tranquillity, or impassivity, through a renunciation of the irremediably painful philosophical thinking that aims at objective truth, and they attained this renunciation by leading thought into self-paralyzing paradoxes. We know a great deal about the sorts of argument they employed —many of them of the greatest philosophical value—from the works of Sextus Empiricus (second century A.D.). It may be that the Skeptical doubts about the possibility of knowing the nature of substance were partly responsible for their rejection of an imitative theory of art in either an Aristotelian or a Platonic sense, for this theory presupposes that we know something of substance and can grasp universals. Sextus questions whether poetry contains truth (Book I, entitled *Against the Grammarians*, of his work *Against the Professors*, § 297) and (along lines similar to the thinking of Philodemus) whether music has an *ethos* (Book VI, *Against the Musicians*). In Book VI, he presents a curious double argument against music. "Music," here, he is at pains to make clear in an initial distinction (§ 1), is to be understood as "a science dealing with melodies and notes and rhythm-making and similar things" (trans. Bury), not in its other two common senses, (a) instrumental skill (the "female harp-player" as a musician), (b) aesthetic merit (a "musical painting," meaning a good one). First, he lays out many examples supposed to prove the affective power of music, and analyzes them away, with counterarguments to show that music has no meaning ("It is not by nature that some are of this kind and others of that kind, but it is we ourselves who suppose them to be such," § 20) and no therapeutic value (like wine, it may distract the sufferer, who, however, relapses into his trouble when the music ends). Then Sextus turns to the more fundamental skeptical line of thought: there is no such thing as a science of music (§ 58) because in fact sound, melody, and rhythm do not really exist (§§ 39–67). (The Skeptical attacks on the reality of sense qualities need not be reviewed here.)

Many works on literary problems were produced during the

centuries of Roman ascendancy, and some of them are of great and lasting value. But it was not a period of very philosophical interest in the arts; much of the poetic and rhetoric was practical, pedagogical, or polemical. Even the two outstanding works, that by Horace (65–8 B.C.) and that attributed to Cassius Longinus (and certainly not by him, though possibly by a Greek named Longinus who lived during the first century A.D.), while they contain much of interest to the history of literary criticism, yield little that can be counted as a contribution to the progress of aesthetics.

Horace's *Epistle to the Pisos* (more widely known as *Ars Poetica*—the name given it by Quintilian) presents in marvelously terse and memorable language, but in loose order, certain practical principles of style and dramatic construction—and this work is supplemented by passages in his *Satires* and *Epistles*. A poem, he asserts, is the product of both Nature and Art; it must either please (*delectare*) or improve (*prodesse*), or, better, do both at once. The general spirit of the work is that poetry is something to be taken seriously, because it can serve an important moral and civic function.

One of Horace's most famous remarks, *"Ut pictura poesis"* (line 361), was destined (as we shall see) for a notable career in the modern period, when it became the text for various theories about the essential similarity of poetry and painting. In the context of the *Ars Poetica*, it was a casual introduction to some uncomplicated comparisons: "A poem is like a picture: one strikes your fancy more, the nearer you stand; another, the farther away . . . " etc. (trans. Fairclough). But this was not the first—or the last—aesthetic phrase to be abstracted from its context and made into a doctrine.

The lively book *On Elevation in Poetry* (*Peri Hypsous*, usually translated "On the Sublime") is another largely pedagogical work, brilliantly carried out. It evidently disappeared soon after it was written, and (except for some lost manuscript pages) it was rediscovered and published only in the sixteenth century; in the late seventeenth and eighteenth centuries its influence was enormous. "Longinus," the supposed author, is primarily interested in giving detailed advice about writing, and illustrating his suggestions with a wide variety of apt and nicely analyzed examples.

There is a certain quality that marks a great literary work, he says—*hypsous*. And the problem he sets himself is to show by what means, including stylistic devices, this is to be achieved.

The attempt to identify such a quality as the necessary and sufficient condition of literary greatness is not without interest, and some of the features of "Longinus's" method are worth noting. Is there, we might ask, just one such quality? "Longinus" discusses five features that contribute to this quality, of which the two most fundamental are (1) large and important ("full-blooded") ideas, and (2) vehement emotion. These he calls conditions or, sometimes, "constituents," of the "sublime" (VIII, 1). It is possible to have the "sublime" without emotion (VIII, 2), but "nothing makes so much for grandeur as genuine emotion in the right place. It inspires the words as it were with a fine frenzy and fills them with divine afflatus" (VIII, 4; trans. Fyfe). On the other hand, "a great style is the natural outcome of weighty thoughts" (IX, 3–4). When we now inquire what the quality of "sublimity" is, "Longinus" seems to hold that it can be defined only by its effects. He is impatient with aesthetic problems, and is satisfied to say that the "sublime" is what produces in the reader not mere pleasure or intellectual conviction, but transport (*ekstasis*): the sense of being carried away, as though by magic (I, 4). "The true sublime, by some virtue of its nature, elevates us: uplifted with a sense of proud possession, we are filled with joyful pride, as if we had ourselves produced the very thing we heard" (VII, 2). This doesn't tell us what the "sublime" is, but what it does. Indeed, just as "Longinus" sets up one aesthetic puzzle by not making a consistent distinction between the "sublime" and its conditions, so he sets up another by not keeping clear the difference between the "sublime" and its effects: note how objective, subjective, and affective terms are brought together when he says (XXXIV, 4) that Demosthenes "shows the merits of great genius in their most consummate form, sublime intensity, living emotion, redundance, readiness, speed—where speed is in season—and his own unapproachable vehemence and power." Much of what "Longinus" says can be interpreted either as showing how to move the reader deeply and yet nobly, or as showing how to make the work itself more intense and elevated in its qualities—for example, when he gives examples of collo-

quial phrases in Herodotus and says (XXXI, 2), "These come
perilously near to vulgarity, but are not vulgar because they are
so expressive *(semantikos)*."

The philosophy of Plato continued to be taught by his followers, during the first centuries of the Christian era, at Alexandria and Rome, and in the Academy at Athens, until it was
closed by the Emperor Justinian in 529, as a rival and threat to
Christianity. But in the hands of creative thinkers, like Philo
of Alexandria, at the beginning of the first century A.D., and
Numenius of Apamea, a century later, it evolved into a somewhat different system that became known as Neoplatonism. The
most distinguished and original of the Neoplatonists was Plotinus
(204/5–270 A.D.). Though his thinking ranged widely, and was
especially important in philosophy of religion, he also has a
significant place in the history of aesthetics.

Plotinus wrote fifty-four essays or "Tractates," which were
arranged and published in six "Enneads," or groups of nine, by
his pupil Porphyry in the first decade of the fourth century. The
text, as we have it today, is in quite good condition, but Plotinus's
terminology is idiosyncratic and often mysterious, so that some
parts of his elaborate and complex metaphysics are still subject
to doubt or dispute. In main outline, we may say this: Behind
the visible world, as its ultimate source and ground, is what
Plotinus calls "The One" *(to hen)* or "The First," which is, in
itself, beyond all conception and knowledge. Yet it can not un-
truthfully be described under certain aspects by certain terms,
if they are taken deeply enough: it is the Good, for example, and
the Infinite (Ennead II, Tractate ix, section 1). When we speak
of the One, we are taking ultimate reality in its first "hypostasis"
—a term for whose meaning one must rely on contextual speci-
fication, since no safe synonyms present themselves. The One has
also a second and a third hypostasis, which are identical to the
first, yet constitute different functions or, perhaps, roles. The
Second Hypostasis is Intellect or Mind, the Divine Knower
(nous), which is identical with what it knows *(noeta)*: the
Platonic Forms (or Ideas) that constitute the Intelligible World,

the ideal archetypes or patterns of the visible world. The Third Hypostasis is the All-Soul (*psyche*), or principle of creativity and life. Together, the three Hypostases make up a single transcendent Being, from which all other Reality proceeds by "emanation" (*tolma*), and to which all other Reality aspires to return as its primal source (the *epistrophe*). Emanation is not a temporal process, but timeless; from Plotinus's metaphors of Being as overflowing like a spring (V, ii, 1), and of a central source of light that grows dimmer with the distance from it (V, iii, 12), we may think of the various parts of reality, including nature and the visible world, as participating in the light of Being, but in various degrees, from the most real things of spirit and intellect down to the lowest grades of matter. The Platonic dualism of Being and Becoming is in one sense overcome by this conception of all things as ordered in a continuous degree of greater and lesser reality, but the contrast between the Visible World and the Intelligible World remains in the distinction between nature and the Forms of the Second Hypostasis.

A fully developed philosophy of beauty is central to this metaphysical system, and pervasive throughout the *Enneads*, though it is presented most systematically in three of the Tractates— principally in I, vi ("On Beauty"), but also in parts of V, viii ("On the Intellectual Beauty") and VI, vii ("How the Multiplicity of the Ideal-Forms came into being; and on the Good"). Its major inspiration is Plato's aesthetic theory, especially the *Symposium*, though it also owes a great deal to the *Phaedrus* and the *Timaeus*. Nevertheless, it strikes out on its own in some highly original ways. Plotinus's exposition is frequently obscure, and sometimes almost impenetrably so, but his attempt to preserve and deepen what he takes to be Plato's most important ideas, while giving the concept of beauty a new and most significant metaphysical status, is worth patient study.

The tractate "On Beauty" was the first one written, according to Porphyry's biography of Plotinus, and it does not develop all of the aesthetic theories characteristic of his mature thought. But it contains some important ideas, and since its argument is difficult, we may well begin our consideration of his aesthetics by tracing its thought with some care, supplementing it from time to time with material from other tractates.

Plotinus begins (I, vi, 1) by reviewing the variety of things that can possess beauty: most obviously things seen and heard, but also (for "minds that lift themselves above the realm of sense to a higher order") "beauty in the conduct of life, in actions, in character, in the pursuits of the intellect; and there is the beauty of the virtues" (trans. MacKenna and Page). The searching question is, "what, then, is it that gives comeliness" to all these things? "What . . . is this something that shows itself" in them? The first answer Plotinus formulates and rejects is

that the symmetry of parts towards each other and towards a whole, with, besides, a certain charm of color, constitutes the beauty recognized by the eye, that in visible things, as indeed in all else, universally, the beautiful thing is essentially symmetrical, patterned.

We cannot be sure whom he is referring to when he says that this is what "almost everyone declares," but he is clearly including the Stoics; the theory is a plausible misinterpretation of Plato's *Philebus*, and something close to it can be read from Aristotle's *Poetics*. In any case, Plotinus argues, it is false. His reductio ad absurdum argument has several parts. (1) "But think what this means. Only a compound can be beautiful, never anything devoid of parts . . ." In short, if symmetry is a *necessary* condition of beauty, then simple things cannot be beautiful. But (a) they must be beautiful, otherwise complexes, which are made up of simples, could not be beautiful either: "beauty in an aggregate demands beauty in details." And (b) some simple things clearly are beautiful: colors, single tones, the light of the sun, gold, night lightning, and so on. Moreover (c) spiritual qualities, such as "noble conduct, or excellent laws," can be beautiful, but what sense does it make to call them symmetrical? How, for example, could virtues be symmetrical? Finally (2) Plotinus inserts an argument that symmetry cannot be a *sufficient* condition of beauty, because an object that remains symmetrical can lose its beauty: "one face, constant in symmetry, appears sometimes fair and sometimes not"—and when the body becomes lifeless, it loses most of its beauty, though not its symmetry (VI, vii, 22).

Thus we come back to the original question: what is the "Principle that bestows beauty on material things" (I, vi, 2)? The answer of Plotinus is stated most fully in the tractate "On the Intellectual Beauty":

Suppose two blocks of stone lying side by side: one is unpatterned, quite untouched by art; the other has been minutely wrought by the craftsman's hands into some statue of god or man, a Grace or a Muse, or if a human being, not a portrait but a creation in which the sculptor's art has concentrated all loveliness.

Now it must be seen that the stone thus brought under the artist's hand to the beauty of form is beautiful not as stone—for so the crude block would be as pleasant—but in virtue of the Form or Idea introduced by the art. This form is not in the material; it is in the designer before ever it enters the stone; and the artificer holds it not by his equipment of eyes and hands but by his participation in his art. The beauty, therefore, exists in a far higher state in the art. . . . [V, viii, 1; p. 422].

It is, then, by virtue of matter's capacity to take and hold the Forms that "the Beauty of the divine Intellect and of the Intellectual Cosmos may be revealed to contemplation" (V, viii, 1; cf. VI, vii, 42). Nothing less than Being itself, as a mirror of the One and the Divine, can so stir the soul in contemplation. Since the One, in its second Hypostasis, is both the knowing Intellect and the knowable Forms, and it is form itself that makes the difference between a beautiful and an ugly object ("an ugly thing is something that has not been entirely mastered by pattern, that is by Reason, the Matter not yielding at all points and in all respects to Ideal-Form"), beauty is the mark, and the resultant, of this participation of the object in Ideal-Form.

But the experience of beauty, Plotinus also holds, is not the mere observation that matter is fit to receive Ideal-Form; this fitness is

something which the Soul names as from an ancient knowledge and, recognizing, welcomes it, enters into unison with it. . . .

Our interpretation is that the Soul—by the very truth of its nature, by its affiliation to the noblest Existents in the hierarchy of Being—when it sees anything of that kin, or any trace of that kinship, thrills with an immediate delight, takes its own to itself, and thus stirs anew to the sense of its nature and of all its affinity [I, vi, 2; p. 57].

In putting on beauty, then, matter acquires a deep "affinity" for the soul. And the soul takes joy in recognizing its own nature objectified, and in thus becoming conscious of its own participation in divinity. Here in Plotinus is the origin of the mystical and Romantic theories of art that we shall encounter later.

At first glance, it seems that Plotinus, having rejected symmetry as a necessary condition of beauty, now brings it in under another name, "pattern," and states his own conditions of beauty in a way that runs counter to his previous argument. How can the light of the sun be beautiful, if simple, and therefore incapable of pattern? But he has a different emphasis in mind.

> But where the Ideal-Form has entered, it has grouped and coordinated what from a diversity of parts was to become a unity: it has rallied confusion into cooperation: it has made the sum one harmonious coherence: for the Idea [i.e. the Form] is a unity and what it moulds must come to unity as far as multiplicity may.
>
> And on what has thus been compacted to unity, Beauty enthrones itself, giving itself to the parts as to the sum: when it lights on some natural unity, a thing of like parts, then it gives itself to that whole. Thus, for an illustration, there is the beauty, conferred by craftsmanship, of all a house with all its parts, and the beauty which some natural quality may give to a single stone.
>
> This, then, is how the material thing becomes beautiful—by communicating in the thought that flows from the Divine [I, vi, 2; p. 58].

It is unity, then, that is essential here. Speaking of a complex with heterogeneous parts, such as a house or painting, we can say that it becomes beautiful when and only when it is unified, and thus becomes a mirror of the One. But a single spread of color, or a sustained mellow tone, being homogeneous throughout, is unified by that very homogeneity, and so it too can be beautiful. Thus all beauty is the "outcome of a unification" (I, vi, 3).

> So with the perceptive faculty: discerning in certain objects the Ideal-Form which has bound and controlled shapeless matter, opposed in nature to Idea [i.e., Form], seeing further stamped upon the common shapes some shape excellent above the common, it gathers into unity what still remains fragmentary, catches it up and carries it within, no longer a thing of parts, and presents it to the Ideal-Principle as something concordant and congenial . . . [I, vi, 3; p. 58].

This explains sensuous beauties. "But there are earlier [i.e., logically prior] and loftier beauties . . ." (I, vi, 4)—"the beauty of noble conduct and of learning," seen not with the physical eye but with the eye of the soul. These are capable of thrilling and exulting us, too, and even more deeply (I, vi, 5). But how? There is "No shape, no color, no grandeur of mass," only the "hueless splendor of the virtues . . . loftiness of spirit; righteousness of life; disciplined purity"; and the like. To see what makes the virtuous soul beautiful, consider first, Plotinus suggests, the opposite: ugliness. The ugly soul is "dissolute, unrighteous: teeming with all the lusts; torn by internal discord; beset by the fears of its cowardice and the envies of its pettiness . . ." etc.—"What must we think but that all this shame is something that has gathered about the Soul, some foreign bane outraging it, soiling it . . ." In short, this "ugly condition is due to alien matter that has encrusted" the evil man, "and if he is to win back his grace it must be his business to scour and purify himself and make himself what he was."

According to this theory of evil as something "foisted" on the soul, the evil soul is impure and inwardly discordant (cf. III, vi, 2; I, viii, 13; V, viii, 13). Its moral discipline therefore consists in "purification" of the alien, harmonization of the discord—in a word, unification (I, vi, 6; cf. I, ii, 4; III, vi, 5; IV, vii, 10). So the spiritual beauty of the soul rests on exactly the same condition as the sensuous beauty of art or nature. "And it is just to say that in the Soul's becoming a good and beautiful thing is its becoming like to God" (I, vi, 6; cf. II, ix, 2). From this point of view, and considered in ideal terms, Beauty appears to be almost identical with Good. "We may even say that Beauty *is* the Authentic-Existents and Ugliness is the Principle contrary to Existence . . . and hence the one method will discover to us the Beauty-Good and the Ugliness-Evil." "The Good and The Beautiful," says Plotinus in another place (V, v, 12), "participate in the common source"; the goodness and beauty of the Forms derive from their ideal properties (VI, vi, 18), but in the hierarchy of Being, nevertheless, The Good has priority (I, viii, 2).

At this point (I, vi, 7), in the spirit of Plato's *Symposium*, Plotinus turns to a description of love—which is always, in every form, a love of beauty (cf. III, v, 1), and consequently a love of goodness and of being. Its hunger and its delight are directed, whether the soul knows it or not, toward the divine, which, in one aspect, is "the Beauty supreme, the absolute, and the primal . . ." (I, vi, 7; cf. VI, ii, 18; V, viii, 8–10). But by what path are we to rise to acquaintance with this absolute Beauty? Our experience of sensuous beauty gives us the foretaste, the intimation of what lies beyond, but to go beyond we must turn away from "material beauty" (I, vi, 8). "You must close the eyes and call instead upon another vision which is to be waked within you, a vision, the birth-right of all, which few turn to use." This means first fixing our attention, not on music and painting, but on "all noble pursuits, then the works of beauty produced not by the labor of the arts but by the virtue of men known for their goodness" (I, vi, 9). But even that is not enough: you must make yourself beautiful in spirit, morally excellent, to know perfect beauty.

When you know that you have become this perfect work, when you are self-gathered in the purity of your being, nothing now remaining that can shatter that inner unity, nothing from without clinging to the authentic man, when you find yourself wholly true to your essential nature, wholly that only veritable Light which is not measured by space, . . . when you perceive that you have grown to this, you are now become very vision: now call up all your confidence, strike forward yet a step—you need a guide no longer—strain and see.

This is the only eye that sees the mighty Beauty [pp. 63–64].

About this last progression, by which we ascend from the experience of sensuous beauty, through the contemplation of moral beauty, to truth itself, more can be added, from passages elsewhere in the *Enneads*, to make our account more accurate if, at the same time, less decisive. For the monism of Plotinus's system does not wholly heal or conceal something of the same ambivalence toward the arts and toward beauty that we discovered in Plato's philosophy.

What role, exactly, is played by the beauty of art, sensuous beauty, in the soul's passage to ultimate knowledge of, and immersion in, the full light of Being that the Plotinian philosopher craves? It is a path, says Plotinus: for when we recognize the beauty of a picture we are after all recollecting, however dimly, the eternal Beauty that is our home, and so, since

the sight of Beauty excellently reproduced upon a face hurries the mind to that other Sphere, surely no one seeing the loveliness lavish in the world of sense—this vast orderliness, the Form which the stars even in their remoteness display—no one could be so dull-witted, so immovable, as not to be carried by all this to recollection, and gripped by reverent awe in the thought of all this, so great, sprung from that greatness [II, ix, 16; p. 149].

But on the other hand, sensuous beauty may take us in a different direction:

Beauty is all violence and stupefaction; its pleasure is spoiled with pain, and it even draws the thoughtless away from The Good as some attraction will lure the child from the father's side [V, v, 12; p. 413].

Again, Plotinus distinguishes three ways to truth, those of the musician, the lover, and the metaphysician (I, iii, 1, 2). Being "exceedingly quick to beauty," the musician tends to respond sharply to "measure and shapely pattern";

This natural tendency must be made the starting-point to such a man; . . . he must be led to the Beauty that manifests itself through these forms; he must be shown that what ravished him was no other than the Harmony of the Intellectual world and the Beauty in that sphere, . . . and the truths of philosophy must be implanted in him to lead him to faith in that which, unknowing it, he possesses within himself [I, iii, 1–2; p. 37].

But on another occasion, Plotinus collapses the lover and the metaphysician into one hopeful and likely seeker after truth, who is "not held by material loveliness," and the path of the musician seems to disappear (V, ix, 2).

As the last quoted sentence suggests, the beauty of the visible world is its mirroring of the invisible, and Plotinus has much to say on behalf of natural beauty. "Even in the world of sense and part, there are things of a loveliness comparable to that of the Celestials" (II, ix, 17). The objects around us are expressions of Nature, and "the Nature . . . which creates things so lovely must be itself of a far earlier beauty" (V, viii, 2).

Thus there is in the Nature-Principle itself an Ideal archetype of the beauty that is found in material forms and, of that archetype again, the still more beautiful archetype in Soul, source of that in Nature [V, viii, 3; p. 424].

How easy would be the transition, then, from one to the other. Moreover,

The arts are not to be slighted on the ground that they create by imitation of natural objects; for, to begin with, these natural objects are themselves imitations; then, we must recognize that they give no bare reproduction of the thing seen but go back to the Reason-Principles from which Nature itself derives, and, furthermore, that much of their work is all their own; they are holders of beauty and add where nature is lacking [V, viii, 1; pp. 422–23].

Here is Plotinus's gentle answer to Plato's doubts about imitation: a tree and a picture of a tree share alike in the Form that bestows on each whatever beauty it may possess, and such is the freedom of the painter that his picture may in fact capture and exhibit that Form even more fully than the tree. "Thus Pheidias wrought the Zeus upon no model among things of sense but by apprehending what form Zeus must take if he chose to become manifest to sight"—a famous, and in a way revolutionary, statement. But even more significantly, and originally,

Any skill which, beginning with the observation of the symmetry of living things, grows to the symmetry of all life, will be a portion of the Power There which observes and meditates the symmetry reigning among all beings in the Intellectual Cosmos. Thus all music—since its thought is upon melody and rhythm—must be the earthly representation of the music there is in the rhythm of the Ideal Realm [V, ix, 11; p. 441].

Art need not be representational to be revelatory. (And for the full meaning of "the symmetry of all life" see III, ii, 16, 17; iii, 1.)

On the other hand, it must be remembered that Absolute Beauty itself is invisible: the "Authentic Beauty" is "Beyond-Beauty" (VI, vii, 33), since it surpasses shape and form, without which beauty cannot be experienced. Thus, paradoxically, to achieve absolute Beauty is not to see it; to know fully is to become the divine, no longer to be external to it, and he who is one with Beauty does not behold the beautiful (V, viii, 11). At this point, the argument has come full circle: or, in a perhaps now too familiar figure, the mystic, having climbed beyond the top of his ladder, kicks it away. Plotinus comes close to exalting Beauty at the expense of beauty, or Beauty at the expense of art; in the framework of his metaphysics, determined as he is to fix the transcendental Beauty as an essential aspect of ultimate reality, he sometimes carries the tension between sensuous and spiritual beauty to the snapping point—since the unseeable Beauty we are after will hardly satisfy the appetite aroused by the seeable beauty that sets us after it. But, on the whole, Plotinus means to bring the two orders of beauty together more closely than Plato could, and despite passages in the other direction he has had some success. For if Reality consists of a continuous series of planes, each farther from the central Light of Being, each in a way an imitation of those that are nearer, all beauties, however dim, must be connected ultimately with the Absolute Beauty that they allude to. And at all levels, as we have seen, some consciousness of its affinity with the divine is present in the soul.

Bibliography

Sextus Empiricus, *Against the Professors,* trans. R. G. Bury (Loeb Library, London, 1949).

Strabo, *Geography,* trans. Horace Leonard Jones (Loeb Library, London, 1949).

Aristoxenus, *The Harmonics,* trans. Henry S. Macran (Oxford, 1902).

Longinus, *On the Sublime,* trans. W. Hamilton Fyfe (Loeb Library, London, 1953).

W. Rhys Roberts, *Longinus on the Sublime* (Cambridge, 1899).

Phillip De Lacy, "Stoic Views of Poetry," *Am Jour Philol* LXIX (1948): 241–71.

L. P. Wilkinson, "Philodemus and Poetry," *Greece and Rome* II (1932–33): 144–51.

L. P. Wilkinson, "Philodemus on *Ethos* in Music," *Class Quart* XXXII (1938): 174–81.

A. Philip McMahon, "Sextus Empiricus and the Arts," in *Harvard Stud in Class Philol* (Cambridge, 1931).

Craig LaDrière, "Horace and the Theory of Imitation," *Am Jour of Philol* LX (1939): 288–300.

Horace: Satires, Epistles, and Ars Poetica, trans. H. R. Fairclough, (Loeb Library, London, 1929).

J. Tate, "Horace and the Moral Function of Poetry," *Class Quart* XXII (1928): 65–72.

G. M. A. Grube, "Notes on the *Peri Hypsous,*" *Am Jour of Philol* LXXVIII (1957): 355–74.

Plotinus, *The Enneads,* trans. Stephen MacKenna, rev. by B. S. Page (London, 1956).

E. R. Dodds, ed., *Select Passages Illustrating Neoplatonism* (London, 1923).

Émile Bréhier, *The Philosophy of Plotinus,* trans. Joseph Thomas (Chicago, 1958).

W. R. Inge, *The Philosophy of Plotinus* (London, 1918), Vol. II, pp. 210–18.

Philippus V. Pistorius, *Plotinus and Neoplatonism* (Cambridge, 1952), ch. 7.

Édouard de Keyser, *La Signification de l'Art dans les Ennéades de Plotin* (Louvain, 1955).

John P. Anton, "Plotinus' Refutation of Beauty as Symmetry," *Jour Aesth and Art Crit* XXIII (Winter 1964): 233–37.

FIVE

The Middle Ages

The early Fathers of the Christian Church were too deeply absorbed in their immense theological tasks to be drawn into speculative or analytical inquiries that could not be brought directly to bear on their immediate concerns. They had, first, to work out a viable theological system that would explain what can be explained of God and man's relations to God; and, second, to strengthen and defend Christian teaching, and the Church itself, against its enemies, especially pagan religion and philosophy. Neither of these tasks invited extensive study of the problems of aesthetics, though, as we shall see later in this chapter, the first one led into problems that, though only tangentially aesthetic at first, were to have important aesthetic consequences. Together, the two tasks left little time for original reflection on art and beauty. The outstanding exception among the early thinkers is St. Augustine, whose abundant energy and intellectual drive found occasion for some thought about everything that came his way. As the scholastic movement developed, in the later Middle Ages, the most powerful thinkers became fascinated by metaphysical and epistemological problems, and problems of ethics and social philosophy, and their aesthetic remarks tended to be brief and peripheral to their main thought. This is true even of St. Thomas. In its period of flourishing and triumph, scholasticism made but one contribution to the history of aesthetics comparable in significance to its work in other philosophical fields—and this in the philosophy of language and symbolism, which will be discussed in the section on interpretation below.

Yet even in the early period there was one aesthetic problem that the philosophers of Christendom had ultimately to come to terms with. That there is such a thing as beauty (however mysterious its nature and attraction), and especially in human bodies, could not be gainsaid, but what is the proper attitude toward it? Is it, so to speak, from Satan or from God—part of what the Christian must be prepared to turn away from and renounce, along with other tempting but unworthy things, or something he may embrace? Among the early Christians, Isaiah's words, "He hath no form or comeliness," were sometimes taken to be a repudiation of physical beauty in Christ. But it could not be forgotten, either, that according to *Genesis* man is made in the image of God.

From the beginning, the Church exhibited a similarly ambivalent attitude toward the arts, and for two basic reasons, which are Christian analogues of Plato's two great attacks on poetry in Book X of the *Republic*. First, and fundamentally, artistic activity is the sign of a strong interest in earthly things, which is necessarily, or at least can easily become, a rival to the true Christian's central and absorbing concern with salvation for another life. Second, and more specifically, the arts were closely associated with the cultures of Greece and Rome, from whose false religion Christianity was come to rescue the world. Some early Church leaders, such as Tertullian (writing around the beginning of the third century), wished to renounce all secular learning and profane studies. This counsel did not prevail, and the later acceptance of the trivium and quadrivium—the seven liberal arts—as the basis of education, meant that important parts of classical learning, or what remained of it, were acknowledged to be legitimate stages in the individual's progress toward theological knowledge.

Tertullian characterized literature as "foolishness in the eyes of God" (*De Spectaculis* xvii; cf. x, xxiii), and his condemnation was echoed in other terms by Jerome, Gregory, Augustine, and Boethius in his *Consolations of Philosophy* (I, i)—though in his *De Musica*, number and proportion are said to be the principles of reality, through which music expresses the divine. In some of these writers, especially Jerome and Augustine, there was also a contrary strain—an appreciation of classical literature and a sense that it may have a positive use in education. This favorable view was expressed by Origen, by Clement of Alexandria, by Basil the Great. And on the whole poetry was victorious, though not the drama: the Church remained for a long time strenuously opposed to acting and playgoing—which Augustine also attacks in several of his works.

Since the chief classical productions of visual art with which the early Christians were acquainted represented gods or self-deified Roman emperors, and were thus the objects of a hateful idolatry, visual art itself came under suspicion, and there were some who believed that the introduction of any images into churches would tempt the Christian worshiper into a similar idolatry. Much later on, this attitude was revived by the Iconoclastic movement, which developed in the Eastern Church in the eighth and ninth centuries. But the alternative view prevailed. Gregory, in the sixth century, was defending pictures as necessary for religious instruction, especially with illiterate people, and as legitimate if they are not themselves worshiped, but only used to lead the mind to God. Though a synod under Constantine V, meeting at Constantinople in 754, condemned the attempt to depict in visual terms the nature of the incarnate Logos, a General Council at Nicaea in 787, under Constantine VI, reversed the condemnation and declared that "honorable reverence" is due to religious pictures, as to the cross and the Gospels. "For the honor which is paid to the image passes on to that which the image represents, and he who shows reverence to the image shows reverence to the subject represented in it."[1] The mainstream of Christian thought became, as time went on, more and more open to sensuous aids of religious worship—plainsong and then polyphony, statues and paintings, the great architectural triumphs of the cathedral age.[2]

[1] See Williston Walker, *A History of the Christian Church* (New York, 1918), p. 163.
[2] See S. R. Maitland, *The Dark Ages* (London, 1845), pp. 171–87; Henry Osborn Taylor, *The Classical Heritage of the Middle Ages* (New York, 1903), pp. 107–35.

ST. AUGUSTINE

In the course of his agonized review of the moral and intellectual pitfalls into which he had fallen before his conversion to Christianity—a cross-section of the evils and errors of his age, as he looks back upon them—St. Augustine (354–430) tells us that when he was about twenty-six or twenty-seven years old he wrote a treatise (of two or three books, "I think"), *On the Beautiful and the Fitting* (*De Pulchro et Apto*), in which he tried to answer certain aesthetic questions:

> Do we love anything but the beautiful? What, then, is beautiful [*pulchrum*]? And what is beauty [*pulchritudo*]? What is it that allures and unites us to the things we love; for unless there were a grace and beauty [*decus et species*] in them, they could by no means attract us to them? And I marked and perceived that in bodies themselves there was a beauty from their forming a kind of whole [*et videbam in ipsis corporibus aliud esse quasi totum et ideo pulchrum*], and another from mutual fitness [*aliud autem, quod ideo deceret, quoniam apte accommodaretur alicui*], as one part of the body with its whole, or a shoe with a foot, and so on [*Confessions* IV, xiii; trans. Pilkington, with one correction].

From Augustine's sketchy description of its contents, we may guess that this early work would be of more interest to us than it was to him in his later years—for he reports its loss with little apparent regret (since the treatise reflected a greater interest in the mutable beauties of the visible world than in the immutable glory of God). His remarks are tantalizingly brief. He seems clearly to have distinguished, for example, between the question, What is beautiful?, and the question, What is beauty?, and between the question, What is beauty?, and the question, How does beauty attract us? The distinction between the fair (*pulchrum*) and the fitting (*aptum*), he says, was a distinction between that which is beautiful "in itself," and that which is beautiful in virtue of being applied (*adcommodatum*) to something else (IV, xv). There are two grounds for the predication of beauty. First, a complex may be said to be beautiful in that it is a kind of whole (*totum*), and beauty is a property of the whole; or, second, a part—a patch of color or bit of sound—which is not by itself beautiful may be called beautiful if it is made a part of a complex that is beautiful in the first use of the term. Or perhaps there is a utilitarian notion involved in the *aptum*—the shoe must "fit" the foot. This is all that can be offered by way of explication, since unfortunately Augustine does not recall any of the "corporeal examples" that were supplied, he says, in the original treatise.

That Augustine thought of beauty as a property of heterogeneous wholes is further indicated by his statement that "the beauty of the course of this world is achieved by the opposition of contraries" (as is grace of style through antitheses), "arranged, as it were, by an eloquence not of words, but of things" (*City of God* XI, xviii; trans. Dods, Wilson, and Smith). Again, David's love of music, because he used it to praise God, was proper and admirable: "the rational and well-ordered concord of diverse sounds in harmonious variety suggests the compact unity of the well-ordered city" and can even be a "mystical representation" of the divine (XVII, xiv). In one of his most succinct characterizations of beauty, Augustine echoes Cicero (*Tusculanarum Disputationum* IV, xiii) almost word for word: "All bodily (corporeal) beauty consists in the proportion of the parts (*congruentia partium*), together with a certain agreeableness (*suavitas*) of color" (XXII, xix; cf. XI, xxii). But the Ciceronian formula has a good deal more meaning in St. Augustine, who, at various places in his works, sketches a highly formalistic account of the "congruence of parts," with ideas derived from Pythagoras, Plato, and Plotinus, as well as others, though combined in his own way. The main discussions are in *Concerning Order* (*De Ordine*), written in 386; in *De Musica*, a treatise on meter written about 388–91; and in some sections (especially xxix, 52, to xli, 77) of *Concerning True Religion* (*De Vera Religione*), written about 390.

The key concepts in Augustine's theory of beauty are unity, number, equality, proportion, and order. They turn up frequently in relation to each other. From the scattered references, attesting to the great importance he attached to these concepts and to beauty itself, it is difficult to piece together a single doctrine. But the leading interconnections among them can perhaps be reported with some confidence. Unity is basic in all of reality, for in order to be at all, anything must be one (*De Moribus*

Ecclesiae Catholicae et Manichaeorum II, vi). But unity is also a matter of degree, for some beings (and God most supremely) have more of it than others. A second very fundamental concept is that of equality or likeness (see *De Musica* VI, xiv, 44). The existence of individual things as units, the possibility of repeating them and comparing groups of them with respect to equality or inequality, gives rise to proportion, measure, and number (*De Libero Arbitrio* II, viii, 22; *De Musica* VI, xvii, 56).

Number exercised a great fascination for Augustine, who followed the suggestions he found in Plato's *Timaeus* and regarded number as the fundamental principle in God's creation of the world. Everything depends on number. Objects are what they are—participate in the Forms that exist in the mind of God—through their numerical properties. Number is fundamental both to being and to beauty:

> Suppose there is no actual work in hand and no intention to make anything, but the motions of the limbs are done for pleasure, that will be dancing. Ask what delights you in dancing and number will reply: "Lo, here am I." Examine the beauty of bodily form, and you will find that everything is in its place by number. Examine the beauty of bodily motion and you will find everything in its due time by number . . . [*De Libero Arbitrio* II, xvi, 42; trans. Burleigh].

Number is the underlying principle of order, which consists in the arrangement of equal and unequal parts into an integrated complex in accordance with an end (*City of God* XIX, xiii, 1; cf. *De Musica* VI, xiv, 46; xv, 47; *De Ordine* II, xv, 42). "Everything is beautiful that is in due order" (*De Vera Religione* xli, 77).

Besides the elementary unity that is presupposed by number and order, there is a higher unity that is the consequence or resultant of them. An elementary thing is unified because of its lack of internal diversity, but a complex and heterogeneous thing is unified in spite of its diversity, and this is the sort of emergent unity we experience in art and nature. Composites become wholes only when they are harmonized or given symmetry, and harmony or symmetry consists in the likeness of one part to another (*De Vera Religione* xxx, 55; xxxii, 59, *De Genesi ad Litteram, Liber Imperfectus* x, 32; xvi, 57–59). The more likeness or equality among the parts, the greater the unity (*De Musica* VI, xvii, 58;

De Quantitate Animae). Augustine sums up the connections among several of his leading ideas in this Socratic passage:

> If I ask a workman why, after constructing one arch, he builds another like it over against it, he will reply, I dare say, that in a building like parts must correspond to like. If I go further and ask why he thinks so, he will say that it is fitting, or beautiful, or that it gives pleasure to those who behold it. But he will venture no further . . . But if I have to do with a man with inward eyes who can see the invisible, I shall not cease to press the query why these things give pleasure . . . He transcends it and escapes from its control in judging pleasure and not according to pleasure. First I shall ask him whether things are beautiful because they give pleasure, or give pleasure because they are beautiful. Then I shall ask him why they are beautiful, and if he is perplexed, I shall add the question whether it is because its parts correspond and are so joined together as to form one harmonious whole [*De Vera Religione* xxxii, 59; trans. Burleigh].

Beauty, then, proceeds from unity, proportion, order (*De Musica* I, xiii, 28)—and shares their admirable immutability. Thus it exists in various degrees up to the beauty of the universe as a whole (*De Ordine* I, ii, 3; *Confessions* X, vi) and the beauty of God (see *Confessions* I, iv; III, vi; IV, xvi). Ugliness, on the other hand, is simply the inverse of beauty, "a privation of form" (*De Immortalitate Animae* viii, 13). And it is this Plotinian continuity between the lowest and highest beauty that enables Augustine to give beauty a role even in the soul's religious journey. For aesthetic experience at its highest passes into religious wisdom (*De Vera Religione* xxix, 52; *De Libero Arbitrio* II, ix, 25–27). Beauty is not brought in adventitiously, because the unity that is basic to beauty is also basic to being, and things are therefore beautiful to the degree to which they really are (*De Vera Religione* vii, 13).

The judgment of beauty, then, involves a grasp of order. And from this thesis Augustine derives two further conclusions. Since order involves number and connection, it has a rational character; reason is involved in the cognition of order and in the pleasure it affords. This kind of pleasure is limited to those senses ("the ocular and the auricular") that perceive order; pleasure in sheer quality, as in tastes and smells, is radically different, and of a lower sort. It makes sense, Augustine argues at some length, to say that "something formed with well-fitting parts . . . appears reasonably [fashioned]," or that a melody "sounds reasonably [harmonized]. But anyone would be laughed at if he should say that something smells reasonably or tastes reasonably" or if he should enter a garden, pluck a rose, and remark, "How reasonably sweet it smells!" (*De Ordine*, trans. Russell, pp. 133–35).

Augustine's second theorem concerns the nature of judgment. The grasp of order is normative: the orderly object is perceived and understood as being what it ought to be, and the disordered object as falling short, in some way, of what it ought to be. This enables the painter to correct and improve as he goes along, to see what requires to be done at each stage. And it enables the critic to judge that the painting is flawed or flawless (*De Vera Religione* xxxii, 60). But this sort of perceptual rightness or wrongness cannot be given in sensation alone (*De Musica* VI, xii, 34); it presupposes that the spectator bring with him a concept of ideal order and unity which is never exhibited in the corporeal world. He possesses this concept by a "divine illumination," by which God's light enables the mind to grasp the Forms in the mind of God. It follows that when the spectator judges the beauty of a painting, he does it by unalterable objective—because a priori— standards; there is no relativity in beauty (*De Trinitate* IX, vi, 10; *De Libero Arbitrio* II, xvi, 41).

Another question on which Augustine throws new light is that old one concerning the cognitive status of literature. Augustine is thinking of Plato's argument, and he says (*City of God* II, xiv) that, while Plato was not (as some claimed) divine, he was a good deal closer to the divine, in virtue of having banished the poets and playwrights, than those who would let them stay. Augustine is quite as severe as Plato on the likelihood that moral laxity will be promoted by the theater, but comes to a different conclusion when he turns to the question whether poetry is lies. This occurs in his *Soliloquies*, a dialogue between himself and Reason, written in 387—his first work after his conversion. Book II is concerned with the nature of the false or fallacious and the conditions under which it can be deceptive. The false, in the pejorative sense, must be different from the true, and yet it must be like the true in some way, also, or it could not mislead. There is nothing "that we may justly term false," suggests Reason, "except that which feigns itself to be what it is not, or pretends to be when it does not exist" (II, ix, 16; trans. Burleigh).

The difference between the fallacious and the mendacious is that the former all wish to deceive while the latter do not all wish to do so. Mimes and comedies and many poems are full of lies, but the aim is to delight rather than to deceive. Nearly all who make jokes lie. But the fallacious person, strictly speaking, is he whose design is to deceive.

Now what of the class of things that "pretend" to be when they are not? For example, says Reason: the bent oar, the mirror-image, dreams, and delusions.

Don't you think that your image in the mirror wants to be you but is false because it is not? . . . And every picture, statue, or similar work of art tries to be that on which it is modelled [II, ix, 17].

So the painter is a kind of liar, it would seem. What, then, is the distinction between perceptual illusions on the one hand and those "poems and jests and other fallacious things"?

It is one thing to will to be false and another not to be able to be true. We can classify comedies, tragedies, mimes and the like with the works of painters and sculptors. The picture of a man, though it tries to be like him, cannot be a true man any more than a character in the books of the comedians. These things are false not from any will or desire of their own, but from the necessity of following the will of their authors [II, x, 18; cf. 19].

The bent oar could be straight, and therefore is illusory; the painted representation of a man is necessarily nonhuman, and is not therefore strictly an illusion. Paradoxically, since the false is what is false to what it tends toward and ought to be, that which ought to be false, and is so, is not so. The actor is most true (to himself and to his art) when he is most deceptive, because playing a part: "On the stage Roscius wants to be a false Hecuba, but by nature he is a true man. By so wanting, he is also a true tragedian, so far as he fulfils the part" (II, x, 18).

It is for this reason that "the fables of the grammarians and poets" are much better than the doctrines of the Manicheans; for when Augustine was young, he recalls bitterly (*Confessions* III, vi), though he sang the "Medea Flying," he did not believe a word of it, and was not injured; but when he lent credence to the Manichean heresies he was dragged down to the very edge of Hell. Augustine seems indeed to have worked out a fuller and more sophisticated concept of fiction than his predecessors, and he has taken a long step away from the classic doctrines of imitation. Art is not imitation, he says, since animals imitate, but have not art (*De Musica* I, iv, 5–7). When he refers to poems, stories, fables, he does not speak of them as imitations, but as inventions, as products of the imagination:

> Therefore it is possible for the mind, by taking away, as has been said, some things from objects which the senses have brought within its knowledge, and by adding some things, to produce in the exercise of imagination that which, as a whole, was never within the observation of any of the senses; but the parts of it had all been within such observation, though found in a variety of different things: *e.g.*, when we were boys, born and brought up in an inland district, we could already form some idea of the sea, after we had seen water even in a small cup; but the flavor of strawberries and of cherries could in no wise enter our conceptions before we tasted these fruits in Italy [Letter VII, iii, 6, to Nebridius, 389 A.D.; trans. Cunningham].

ST. THOMAS AQUINAS

Nine centuries lie between the greatest of the Church Fathers and the greatest of the Schoolmen. It is generally considered a mark of sophistication in a historian when he can see continuities where others find only gaps or breaks, and of course twentieth-century historiography has taught us to be wary of apparently abrupt transitions. Certainly medieval culture did not start off completely on its own, with no legacy from the classical world. St. Augustine and his contemporaries felt that classical culture was all about them, though crumbling, and they had firsthand acquaintance with Greek and Latin works. Platonism was a living force, still being taught at Athens and Alexandria and Rome. But a fundamental break occurred in the centuries that immediately followed; many remains of classical culture that were later to be of decisive influence disappeared for centuries, and found their way back only by a long and indirect route into the intellectual current of medieval and Renaissance thought.

One important step was taken in the middle of the third century when Latin replaced Greek as the official liturgical language. Practically all that Plato, Aristotle, Plotinus, and others had accomplished in aesthetics, as well as the greatest masterpieces of Greek literature, became inaccessible. Meanwhile, a great deal of Roman literature and poetics also passed from view. There was a violent and systematic suppression of paganism in the fifth century under Theodosius, and during the ensuing centuries of social and political upheavals much was lost sight of. It was not until the hitherto unknown dialogues of Plato, the metaphysical and physical works of Aristotle, and other important classical documents, were brought forth once again in the eleventh and twelfth centuries, that medieval thinkers could give stimulus and challenge to their own thinking by drawing on the Greeks.

In the meantime, the central ideas of St. Augustine's aesthetics were taken up and kept alive by other thinkers, who continued to reflect on some of his key terms—unity, equality, number, order—and refine or enrich their meaning. Four especially deserve mention: John Scotus Eriugena, or Erigena (ninth century), in his commentary on the *Hierarchie Celeste* of Dionysius the pseudo-Areopagite (he translated the latter's four principal works into Latin); Hugh of St. Victor, (twelfth century), in his *Didascalicon*, and also his followers in the school of St. Victor; Alexander of Hales (early thirteenth century), in his *Universae Theologiae Summa*; and St. Bonaventure (thirteenth century), in various passages of his commentary on the *Sentences* of Peter Lombard. Though all of these thinkers may be placed in the Augustinian tradition, as far as their theories about beauty and its ontological and mystical significance are concerned, they also occasionally touched on interesting special problems: for example, John Scotus Eriugena's description of the different responses to a beautiful vase by a good man and by a man who is a prey to his desires, suggesting that the proper response to beauty is disinterested (see *De Divisione Naturae* IV, 16; in Migne's *Patrologiae*, vol. 122, col. 828B); or Hugh of St. Victor's classification of types of beauty (*species*), and his opinion that all of man's senses find appropriate aesthetic qualities to enjoy in the natural world—suggesting that there are beautiful tastes and smells (see *Eruditionis Didascalicae* VII, 1, 9–13; Migne, vol. 176, cols. 812C–813A, 819–22).

Considering the vast number of difficult and fundamental problems that are dealt with so extensively in the greatest system of scholastic philosophy, that of St. Thomas Aquinas (1225–74), it is perhaps surprising that he is so short with aesthetics. But what he says is penetrating, and its significance is out of ordinary proportion to its length.

Fundamental to Thomistic metaphysics is the Aristotelian concept of being (*ens*), which has three modes; for every being is one (*unum*), true (*verum*), and good (*bonum*)—Thomas sometimes adds two others, *res* and *aliquid*. These terms are "transcendental"—because they transcend the Aristotelian categories, being predicable of everything real—and hence are "convertible" with being. But they are not predicable in the same way of every being—they are "analogical terms" (see *Summa Theologica* I, Q. 13, Art. 5). This concept derives from Aristotle (for example, his remark in the *Metaphysics* IV [Γ], ii, that things may be said to be, or exist, in many different ways). Objects, Thomas holds, may be named either univocally or equivocally. Thus, to use Aristotle's examples (*Categories* i) an ox and a man are both called "animal"; here the signification of "animal" is the same in both cases, so they are named univocally. On the other hand, a man and a picture of a man are both called "animal," but here the signification of "animal" is different in the two cases; they have not a common genus, are not animals in the same sense, and so are named equivocally. The Scholastics introduced a further distinction between two types of equivocation, that in which the two objects equivocally named have no common property that is signified by the name (as when a tree and a traveler are both said to possess a "trunk"), and that in which the two objects have an important property in common that is part of what the word signifies (as in Aristotle's example of the man and his picture, which are similar in shape). Terms predicated in the latter way are analogical. One kind of analogical predication is that in which a term signifies different degrees of some property in different contexts (an "intelligent man," an "intelligent ox").

Unity is being that is considered as distinct from other things, for everything is either simple (hence undivided) or composite, but in the latter case it does not have being unless the parts compose a whole of some sort (I, Q. 11, Art. 1). In a homogeneous whole, "the whole is made up of parts having the form of the whole; as, for instance, every part of water is water," but in a heterogeneous whole "every part is wanting in the form belonging to the whole; as, for instance, no part of a house is a house, nor is any part of man a man" (Art. 2). Truth is being that is considered in relation to thought. "Truth is the equation [*adequatio*] of thought and thing," and belongs to beings as to thought (Q. 16, Art. 1; see also *De Veritate*, Q. 1, Art. 1), for "everything, in as far as it has being, so far is it knowable" (Art. 3). Goodness is being that is considered in relation to desire. The good is defined (in Aristotle's terms) as "what all things desire." Now

a thing is desirable only in so far as it is perfect; for all desire their own perfection. But everything is perfect so far as it is actual. Therefore it is clear that a thing is perfect so far as it exists. . . . Hence it is clear that goodness and being are the same really [Q. 5, Art. 1; see also *De Veritate*, Q. 21, Art. 1].

The good is further divided by Thomas, following the lead of St. Ambrose, into the "befitting," the "useful," and the "pleasant," or delightful. Since "everything is good as far as it is desirable, and is a term of the movement of the appetite," a distinction can be made between different manners in which the good terminates the movement of appetite (or desire). When the object desired terminates appetite as a means, in relation to something else, it is the useful; when "sought after as the last thing," for its own sake, it is the "virtuous"; "but that which terminates the movement of appetite in the form of rest in the thing desired, is called the pleasant." And it is this sort of goodness (not strictly a species, since "good" is not predicated univocally, but analogically, of the three sorts) that beauty has (Q. 5, Art. 6). (On the nature of delight, or enjoyment, see Part I–II, Q. 11, Arts. 1, 4.)

Beauty, says Thomas, in a discussion of the question whether goodness may be considered to be a final cause, is to be defined succinctly as "what pleases when seen," or contemplated. "Beauty and goodness in a thing are identical fundamentally; for they are based upon the same thing, namely, the form . . . But they differ logically," since

beauty relates to the cognitive faculty; for beautiful things are those which please when seen [*pulchra enim dicuntur quae visa placent*]. Hence beauty consists in due proportion; for the senses delight in things duly proportioned, as in what is after their own kind—because even sense is a sort of reason, just as is every cognitive faculty. Now, since knowledge is by assimilation, and similarity relates to form, beauty properly belongs to the nature of a formal cause [Q. 5, Art. 4].

This passage is condensed, and the reference to Aristotle's formal cause is abrupt. First, we must bear in mind that "seeing" is to be taken over metaphorically from "the noblest and most trustworthy of the senses" to "knowledge obtained through the intellect," as Thomas points out in the course of his argument that the word "light" is not used literally when applied to spiritual things (Q. 67, Art. 1). The proportion referred to is a feature of the object that lends itself to clear and ready grasp—in the case of a visible object, for example, that makes it accommodating to the sight. Sight responds to the eminently seeable as the intellect responds to what is intelligible in the world, for both seeing and understanding are cognitive acts. Cognition or knowing consists essentially in abstracting the form that makes a thing what it is, and so beauty (since it provides immediate contemplative pleasure) must be connected with the form of the object, that is, its formal cause (cf. the commentary on the *Divine Names*, iv, 5). Appetite or desire "tends to the beautiful inasmuch as it is proportioned and specified in itself" (*De Veritate*, Q. 22, Art. 1; trans. R. W. Schmidt).

We can now see the implications of another highly significant passage in which Thomas discusses beauty:

The beautiful is the same as the good, and they differ in aspect only. For since good is what all seek, the notion of good is that which calms the desire; while the notion of the beautiful is that which calms the desire, by being seen or known. Consequently those senses chiefly regard the beautiful, which are the most cognitive, viz., sight and hearing, as ministering to reason; for we speak of beautiful sights and beautiful sounds. But in reference to the other objects of the other senses, we do not use the expression *beautiful*, for we do not speak of beautiful tastes, and beautiful odors. Thus it is evident that beauty adds to goodness a relation to the cognitive faculty: so that *good* means that which simply pleases the appetite; while the *beautiful* is something pleasant to apprehend [*id cujus ipsa apprehensio placet*] [Part I–II, Q. 27, Art. 1].

Three points may be noted here. (1) The distinction, on cognitive grounds, between the higher and the lower senses is somewhat modified elsewhere (e.g., I, Q. 91, Art. 3: "man alone takes pleasure in the beauty of sensible objects for its own sake," which seems to broaden the application of beauty). (2) It is difficult to read into this passage, as some have done, an anticipation of the notion that the experience of the beautiful is disinterested or desireless: the "calming of desire" referred to here is that which is given by any good when attained. (3) The experience of beauty is definitely given a cognitive status, but not, in the Platonic or Plotinian sense, a transcendental one; what we know in seeing the statue or painting is precisely its shapes and colors.

The most famous remark about beauty in the *Summa Theologica* appears in the course of a discussion of attempts by Augustine to identify the persons of the Trinity with some of his key concepts—for example, the Father with unity, the Son with equality, the Holy Ghost with "the concord of equality and unity." In an effort to sort out these notions and decide how best to construe them, Thomas says,

Species or beauty has a likeness to the property of the Son. For beauty includes three conditions: *integrity* or *perfection* [*integritas sive perfectio*], since those things which are impaired are by that very fact ugly; due *proportion* or *harmony* [*debita proportio sive consonantia*]; and lastly, *brightness*, or *clarity* [*claritas*], whence things are called beautiful which have a bright color [I, Q. 39, Art. 8; clarity and proportion are also referred to in II–II, QQ. 145, Art. 2; 180, Art. 2].

The terms used by Thomas in this passage have a long history, and are rich in suggestiveness; this richness, combined with his terseness, have tempted numerous commentators to venture beyond the role of explicator and develop their own Thomistic (or neo-Thomistic) aesthetic out of them.[1] But I shall be more cautious.

What Thomas means by his first condition (integrity or perfection) is plainly enough indicated by his example: an object that is broken is said to be lacking in this condition. Integrity is wholeness: being all there. "Due proportion or harmony" is a little less obvious. Thomas's application of this concept to the theological problem before him helps to fix its meaning: the Son, he says, has harmony in that he is the "express image" of the

---

[1] The speculations of Stephen Dedalus in Joyce's *Portrait of the Artist as a Young Man* are best known; see William T. Noon, S.J., *Joyce and Aquinas* (Yale, 1957), pp. 11–12 and ch. 2.

Father. "Proportion," says Thomas in another place (I, Q. 12, Art. 1), has a narrower and a broader sense. In the narrower sense "it means a certain relation of one quantity to another, according as double, treble and equal are species of proportion"; in the broader sense,

every relation of one thing to another is called proportion. And in this sense there can be a proportion of the creature to God, inasmuch as it is related to Him as the effect to its cause, and as potentiality to its act; and in this way the created intellect can be proportioned to know God.

Proportion, in this double sense, plays an important role in Thomas's thinking about the relation between man's knowledge and God; it is possible, in his terminology, to speak of proportions between the parts of the work of art, as we would now take it (cf. his commentary on the *Divine Names*, viii, 4, and ix, 2, 3), but it is the relation of the work to its model, of the statue to the human being, that Thomas seems to have primarily in mind.

It is easy to make much of Thomas's third condition, clarity, or brilliance, though his casual reference to "bright color" does not perhaps invite a very fancy reading. "Claritas" has important associations. We can connect it with the medieval Neoplatonic tradition of light symbolism—the idea of light as the symbol of divine truth and beauty (as, for example, in Robert Grosseteste, his commentary on the *Hexaëmeron* and his book *De Luce*—and see also ch. 4 of the *Divine Names* of the pseudo-Areopagite). Clarity can be connected, too, with that "splendor of form [*resplendentia formae*] shining upon the proportioned parts of matter" in the opusculum *De Pulchro et Bono* (I, vi, 2), written either by the young Thomas or by his teacher Albertus Magnus. "The third [condition]," Thomas says, "agrees with the property of the Son as the Word, which is the light and splendor of the intellect," and something like, or of, this splendor must be involved in beauty, or the analogy would not hold.

There remains a question, not decisively answerable from the texts, about the relation between beauty and its three "conditions." "Tria requiruntur," three things are required, says Thomas, introducing them. But elsewhere, "Beauty *consists* of due proportion," etc. Does he mean to distinguish two things, or three? There is certainly the psychological response, pleasure taken in direct perception or intellectual grasp. There are, second, the necessary and sufficient conditions of beauty, the three properties of objects in which beauty is to be found. Is "beauty" another name for these conditions, collectively—are they what the pleasure is taken *in*? Or is beauty a third thing, distinct from its conditions, though dependent on them? It is clear (and important) that for Thomas beauty is everywhere different. Being a form of good, it is predicated analogously of beings; each object is said to be beautiful in its own way. "The beauty of one [body] differs from the beauty of another" (Commentary on the *Psalms*, Psalm xliv, 2; cf. the *Divine Names*, iv, 5). There is not a single beauty common to all beautiful things, but a whole family of qualities, each to be prized wherever it is found. If integrity, proportion, and clarity are univocal, universally the same, then beauty cannot be identical with them; but it may be that these properties are also analogical, and constitute beauty in each of its endlessly varied forms.

THE THEORY OF INTERPRETATION

As we have seen, medieval philosophers had important and interesting things to say as a result of their reflections on the nature of beauty, and some of their ideas were to bear further fruit in modern aesthetics. They did not much concern themselves with working out a theory of art, in our modern sense, however. "Art" in the middle ages meant either (1) the "mechanical" or "servile" arts, that is, practical technology; or (2) the "liberal arts" (the trivium: grammar, rhetoric, dialectic; the quadrivium: music, arithmetic, geometry, and astronomy); or (3) the "theological arts." Painting and architecture belonged among the mechanical arts, poetry with rhetoric in the trivium, music in the quadrivium, and the problem of beauty was part of theology. There was no special concept to group together the fine arts, and no sense that they constitute, as such, a distinctive philosophical problem.

Nevertheless, a theory of beauty has, of course, a direct bearing upon the nature of art, and it was not only beauty in nature or in man that aroused the interest and intellectual curiosity of those philosophers. And in another direction, the Christian experience, and the peculiar nature of the Christian message, opened up a line of thought that was of great moment for the later history of aesthetics. Three of the radically new ideas that Christianity brought into view were of special importance in this development.

First, there was the Christian theory of creation, the theory that God created the natural universe out of nothing—not giving birth to it in some way, or molding or carving, or fashioning prime matter after the Forms, but simply making something where before there was nothing. This theory raised difficult theological and metaphysical problems, of course, and especially it called for a new conception of the relation between the visible world and its invisible cause. The universe became the work of God in a more fundamental sense than hitherto, and might be expected to show in its nature the marks of its origin, to reflect, however dimly or remotely, the goodness and beauty of its maker. It would be possible for some Christian thinkers, of course, to think of matter as opposed to spirit; but since matter itself, in the creation theory, is not eternal or inherently resistant to divine workmanship, nature might more naturally be interpreted as in some sense a living symbol of divinity.

Second, the central notion of Christianity was the Incarnation: the Word becoming flesh, giving a meaning to history. In this profound mystery, requiring the subtlest thinking of the Fathers to be made intelligible to reason, there is already another concept of the symbol: the bodily vehicle, or vessel, that takes and carries the divine Truth, the *Logos*, but is yet somehow distinct from it. Some of the early Fathers tried to assimilate this relationship to the Platonic form-matter relationship, but new concepts were going to be needed.

Third, Christianity acknowledged a double set of divine texts, posing complex problems of their own. As sacred writings, the books of the Bible required the development of a method and system of interpretation to be made understandable and acceptable. Moreover, after the early Christians evolved their theory that the events of the New Testament were prefigured in the Old, the problem was how to read the Old Testament so as to make this anticipation clear. And because the sacred writings were fundamentally different from secular writings (the pagan poems and plays and histories), this difference had to be explained and defended.

The earliest Fathers, and notably Clement and Origen, were taken up with this third problem, of interpreting the Biblical texts and forging from them a theological doctrine that could answer doubts and refute heresies. Much work was required to carry out this exegetical purpose: obscure Biblical texts must be clarified and illuminated; apparently contradictory passages must be reconciled and harmonized; bare and sketchy remarks on important points of doctrine must be elaborated into fuller theories. Historical scholarship, textual criticism, philological speculation, might go some way toward solving these problems, but a more flexible and fruitful method was also needed, and this was found in the allegorical method of Philo Judaeus of Alexandria (first century A.D.).

It was remarked in Chapter 1 that the allegorizing of Homer and Hesiod was practised at least as early as the sixth century B.C., and, despite the objections of Plato and others, it was carried further by the late Stoics. The Jewish rabbis also used this method to expound their Scriptures, and the Jewish and Greek traditions came together in Philo. His aim was partly to construe the Old Testament books in harmony with his elements of Platonism, and partly to universalize their spiritual truths by abstracting them from their specific historical situation. Allegorizing was also a way of purifying sacred truth, by transmuting what was barbarous or scandalous into something higher. Origen gratefully adopted Philo's allegorical method, and from Alexandria it was introduced to the West by Ambrose and by Hilary of Poitiers. Jerome, Augustine, and Gregory used it in their own ways, and it was finally accepted by the Middle Ages as the standard method of Biblical exegesis. Meanwhile, it was also applied to secular writings, and in fact made it possible for Vergil and others to be accepted as suitable reading for Christians—already by Augustine's time, for example, Vergil's Fourth *Eclogue* (lines 6–7) was interpreted as a prophecy of the coming Messiah, and the *Aeneid* was given a detailed Christian construction.

The allegorical method was reasonable to accept. Divine truth could not be expected to transmit itself perfectly, without losses or distortions, through human language, and some way had to be found to go behind the text. There was, however, a methodological problem. Once it was understood that any Biblical character, object, or event might be taken as standing for some abstract quality or Christian truth, how could correct interpretations be distinguished from incorrect ones? Philo's allegories were sometimes very free-wheeling, and there was some fear among the early Christian Fathers that this procedure might be carried too far. It was not clear how one is to decide which passages are to be taken literally, and which allegorically; and, of the allegorical ones, how remote and abstract the meaning is allowed to be.

Origen followed Philo and Clement in holding that all Scriptural passages have a deeper meaning than that which first appears. It is not merely that the Biblical interpreter is to look in the Old Testament for things that can usefully be allegorized—for example, the Red Sea signifying baptism. The task is to bring out into the open the higher sense of every event. For the Biblical language is like a cloak that conceals from the casual eye—but not from the Christian initiate—the inner and better truth. In some Biblical passages, Origen said, there are three kinds of meaning, literal, moral, and spiritual (or mystical). Thus, for example, the little foxes in the *Song of Songs* (he says in his commentary) can be understood literally as foxes, or morally as sins besetting the individual, or spiritually as heresies attacking the Church. In some passages there is no moral meaning, and in some not even a literal meaning—as when the words are too absurd when taken literally: "If thine eye offend thee pluck it out" (*De Principiis* IV, i, 16, 18, 20). But there is always a spiritual meaning, for any object (since it comes from God) can stand for a spiritual quality or truth, and Scripture, being divinely inspired, would not miss the highest possible meaning. Or, to put it another way, just as Jesus spoke in parables, and gave the fig tree and the talents a spiritual signification, so everything in the Old Testament as well is a sort of divine parable, whether or not it can be taken as history or as ethical example.

St. Augustine took up this problem in *De Doctrina Christiana* (written about 397). It is crucial for the Biblical interpreter, he says, to be clear about the difference between the letter and the meaning (*sententia*), which is far more important, just as the soul is more important than the body. The words are the "fleshly robes" in which the meaning is concealed, waiting to be "unwrapped," as he says in *De Catechizandis Rudibus* ix, 13 (trans. Huppé, *Doctrine and Poetry*, p. 8). The process of interpretation, of laying open what is concealed, is for Augustine the source of a kind of special aesthetic pleasure in reading Christian literature; there is a difficult beauty in revealed truth that comes because the mind must penetrate a certain obscurity of language: "The more they [i.e., the Prophets] seem to be obscure by the use of figurative expressions, the more pleasing they are when their meaning has been made clear" (*De Doctrina Christiana* IV, vii, 15; trans. Sister Thérèse Sullivan).

The problem is to ascertain whether a given text is "literal" or "figurative," and Augustine proposes an interesting solution to this problem. The function of scripture is to promote Christian charity—the movement of the spirit toward love of God for his own sake and of one's neighbor for the sake of God. It follows that the correct meaning of Scripture is always what will fulfill this function.

In all cases this is the method: whatever in Scripture cannot literally be related to purity of life or to the truth of faith, may be taken as figurative. . . . In regard to figurative passages, a rule like the following shall be observed: *what is read must be diligently turned over in the mind until an interpretation is found that promotes the reign of charity* [*De Doctrina Christiana* III, x, 14; xv, 23; trans. Huppé, p. 19].

The true underlying meaning of the text (*sententia veritatis*; III, xxiv, 34) will always emerge for the properly prepared reader: he must come in the right spirit, and he may find that the knowledge of the rhetorical tropes and figures, as well as scientific knowledge of nature, are indispensable.

It was apparently John Cassian (360–435) who first formulated the fourfold distinction between levels of Scriptural meaning that was to become more or less standard in the Middle Ages—and gave the classic example. In his *Collationes* (xiv, 8; Migne, vol. 49, cols. 963–64) he says that Jerusalem, in the Old Testament, makes a "historical" reference to a city of the Jews; on the "allegorical" level (or what was also called the "typical" level, the level on which the Old Testament refers prophetically to the New) it refers to the Church of Christ; on the "tropological" or moral level, to the individual soul; and on the "anagogical" level to the heavenly city of God. The distinctions (along with the example) are repeated in the *De Schematibus et Tropis* of the Venerable Bede.

Two points about this scheme were further clarified by Hugh of St. Victor. First, there is the relation between the literal and the other levels. Hugh criticizes those who have exalted the three allegorical levels at the expense of the literal level. All other levels are a function of the literal level, he insists—if you don't know what "lion" literally means, you can't know that it can allegorically mean Christ (*De Scripturis et Scriptoribus Sacris* v, cols. 13–15A; cf. *Eruditionis Didascalicae* VI, 4, cols. 804–5; 8–11, cols. 806D–809A). Second, there is the scope of the literal meaning. "Literal" is not here opposed to "metaphorical" or "figurative," but simply means going by the words, rather than seeking symbolic intimations in the object denoted. The literal reading includes what can be derived from the language, diction, syntax, metaphors, and similes. Hugh distinguishes "letter," "sense," and "sentence"—the "sense" is the intention of the writer, and the "sentence" is the deeper meaning extracted from letter and sense.

St. Thomas argued for the appropriateness, and even the necessity, of metaphors in Holy Scripture, because all knowledge originates from sense, and it is natural for man to attain to concepts of spiritual things via material things (*Summa Theologica* I, Q. 1, Art. 9), though he makes clear that the essence of God cannot be seen through a material likeness (see Q. 12, Art. 2; Q. 13, Art. 5). He introduces the convenient term "spiritual senses" for the three nonliteral senses, and, following Hugh of St. Victor, emphasizes the point that the literal sense includes "parabolical" (i.e., figurative) meaning: "Nor is the figure itself, but that which is figured, the literal sense. When Scripture speaks of God's arm, the literal sense is not that God has such a member, but only what is signified by this member, namely, operative power" (I, Q. 1, Art. 10; trans. Dominican Fathers).

The most famous allusion to the four levels of meaning is in the letter to Can Grande (1319) that Dante put as a preface to the *Paradiso* (assuming that Dante wrote it, which has been questioned). Though Dante makes the distinctions and illustrates them by the interpretation of a Biblical passage (sec. 7), he proceeds to treat the allegorical, moral, and anagogical meanings together under the general heading of "allegorical," and he does not distinguish all four levels when he refers to the allegorical meaning of the *Divine Comedy* (secs. 8, 11: the allegorical subject is man as meriting reward and punishment). Indeed, the application of the scheme to poetry, even religious poetry, would require some modifications, since the "typical" meaning would drop out. St. Thomas had in fact said explicitly (*Quaestiones Quodlibetales* VII, Q. 6, Art. 16) that poetry could have only literal, not spiritual, meaning.

As a method of Scriptural interpretation, the fourfold scheme could of course come to be applied mechanically—in the schools of the twelfth and thirteenth centuries, dictionaries were drawn up for object-names, "bed," "rock," "lamb," etc., in which each of the four levels was described and illustrated from Scripture, and sometimes several variant examples were given of each level. For our purposes here, we need not trace this decline in the theory of Biblical exegesis; nor can we follow another trail, the development of allegory as a conscious and deliberate poetic method, as in the *Divine Comedy*, *The Faerie Queene*, and *Pilgrim's Progress*. We can only consider in a general way the ground that was laid for a general conception of literature and art: the suggestions in the direction of a theory of symbolic forms, a view that every literary work of art, and perhaps every non-verbal work as well, is a kind of symbol. To fill out this picture, we must consider, at least briefly, a medieval development that was parallel with, and closely related to, the one already considered—the growth of a conception that not only the sacred written word, and the objects referred to in Scripture, but all of the material world, is to be construed as a symbol waiting to be interpreted.

The chief source of medieval inspiration on this matter was the work of the late-fifth-century (or early-sixth-century) writer mistakenly believed by the Middle Ages to be Dionysius the Areopagite, and now called the pseudo-Areopagite or the pseudo-Dionysius. In his writings—and chiefly the *Celestial Hierarchy*, the *Ecclesiastical Hierarchy*, and the *Divine Names*—Christian, Greek, Jewish, and oriental materials are brought together in a solution saturated with the Neoplatonism of Plotinus and Proclus, and a remarkable mystical system emerges. The various orders of mundane and supramundane beings are described in picturesque detail, and sometimes with exalted ardor. The structure of relationships within society and the Church is paralleled by the echelons of angelic beings.

The pseudo-Areopagite was preoccupied with the problem of religious language, and he put this problem in its classic form for Western theology. What can meaningfully be said, affirmatively or negatively, of God and the divine nature? If all words we use must be learned in earthly contexts, and must therefore have empirical referents, how can our language reach so far as to apply truly to transcendent being? In the *Celestial Hierarchy* (ch. 2), the pseudo-Areopagite explains how humble objects, animals for example, can stand for divine things; he argues that the very incongruity, on the surface, of calling Christ a lamb or a shepherd, for example, shocks us into seeking, and finding, a deeper meaning. In the *Divine Names*, he analyzes the various Scriptural predicates applied to God, and argues for their legitimacy if taken in metaphorical or analogical senses. He speaks of

that loving kindness which in the Scriptures and the Hierarchical Traditions, enwrappeth spiritual truths in terms drawn from the world of sense, and super-essential truths in terms drawn from Being, clothing with shapes and forms things which are shapeless and formless, and by a variety of separate symbols, fashioning manifold attributes of the imageless and supernatural Simplicity [ch. 1; trans. Rolt, p. 58].

The idea that everything in the visible universe is in some way a counterpart of something invisible is, of course, a derivation from the Platonic doctrine of Forms, by way of the Plotinian doctrine of emanation. Visible things are, says John Scotus Eriugena in *De Divisione Naturae* (I, iii, col. 443), signs of the invisible. The investment of the corporeal world with an incorporeal symbolic meaning took on sacramental depth in the Christian context. It dominated medieval thinking in almost every area, and though in eclipse during the Enlightenment, it remained alive to blossom again in the Idealism and Romanticism of the nineteenth century.[1]

[1] See Erwin Panofsky, "Abbot Suger of St.-Denis," in *Meaning in the Visual Arts* (Garden City, 1957), for a most interesting account of the way in which Abbot Suger drew upon the ideas of Scotus and the pseudo-Areopagite for justification of the lavish sensuous beauties with which he furnished St.-Denis.

Something of this spirit can be seen in St. Francis's mystical empathy with nature, and it is worked out even more fully by that later Franciscan, St. Bonaventure. The order that interpenetrates his universe is constituted by the endless analogies between its parts, great and small; everything has, directly or indirectly, this kind of connection with everything else—it might almost be called an aesthetic connection, though he thinks of it as a special sort of logical one. The relationship between God and his creation is to be understood in these terms, for "It is clear," he says (*Collationes in Hexaëmeron* II, 27; *Opera Omnia*, 1882–1902, V, 340), "that the whole world is like a mirror, bright with reflected light of the divine wisdom; it is like a great coal radiant with light" (trans. Wimsatt, *Literary Criticism*, p. 147). Although the degrees of distance between created things and God are infinite and continuous, St. Bonaventure thinks it reasonable and helpful to distinguish three degrees in which objects reflect and represent their creator. A "shadow" is a distant and confused representation of God, by means of certain properties but without specifying the type of causal relationship God has to it. A "vestige" is a distant but distinct representation of God; the vestige is a property of the created being that is related to God as its efficient, exemplary, or final cause. An "image" is a representation that is both distant and close; it is a property that acknowledges God not only as its cause but also as its object (see his *Commentary on the Sentences* III, i, 1, Q. 2; III, 72).

The essence of every material object shows that God created all things according to order, measure, and weight (*Commentary on the Book of Wisdom* xi, 21), which are primary vestiges of God. Creation, viewed as a whole, is like a picture or a statue representing divine wisdom (*quoddam simulacrum sapientiae Dei et quoddam sculptile*; *In Hexaëmeron* xii, 14; V, 386). Or, the visible universe is a holy book, of which individual creatures are words; and like a sacred book written in a difficult language, it lies there to be made understandable, so its Author will be revealed (ibid. II, 20; V, 340). Natural objects can be considered either as things (*res*) or as signs (*signa*)—and the methods used to interpret Scripture can be applied to nature as well: above all, we must not miss its spiritual significations (*Sentences* I, iii, 3,

Q. 2; I, 75). Farther toward a universal semiotic, the application of the category of symbol to all existence, it would not be possible to go.

Bibliography

Edgar de Bruyne, *Études d'esthétique médiévale*, 3 vols. (Brugge, 1946).

Frederick A. Norwood, "Attitude of the Ante-Nicene Fathers Toward Greek Artistic Achievement," *J Hist Ideas* VIII (1947): 431–48.

Edgar de Bruyne, "Esthétique païenne, esthétique chrétienne," *Rev Int de Philos* No. 31 (1955): 130–44.

St. Augustine, *De Libero Arbitrio, De Vera Religione, The Soliloquies*, in *The Library of Christian Classics*, Vol. VI, trans. John H. S. Burleigh (Philadelphia, 1953); *De Trinitate* and *The Spirit and the Letter*, in ibid., Vol. VIII, trans. John Burnaby (Philadelphia, 1955).

St. Augustine, *De Immortalitate Animae*, trans. George G. Leckie (New York, 1938).

St. Augustine, *De Doctrina Christiana*, Book IV, trans. Sister Thérèse Sullivan (Catholic U., 1930).

St. Augustine, *De Ordine (Divine Providence and the Problem of Evil)*, trans. Robert P. Russell (New York, 1942).

St. Augustine, *Letters*, trans. J. G. Cunningham in *A Select Library of the Nicene and Post-Nicene Fathers*, Vol. I (Buffalo, 1886).

St. Augustine, *Confessions*, trans. J. G. Pilkington; *City of God*, trans. M. Dods, G. Wilson, and J. J. Smith, in *Basic Writings of St. Augustine*, 2 vols., ed. Whitney J. Oates (New York, 1948).

W. F. Jackson Knight, *St. Augustine's De Musica: a Synopsis* (London, 1949?).

Emmanuel Chapman, *Saint Augustine's Philosophy of Beauty* (New York, 1939).

K. Svoboda, *L'esthétique de Saint Augustin et ses sources* (Brno, 1933).

Kathi Meyer-Baer, "Psychologic and Ontologic Ideas in Augus-·tine's De Musica," *Jour Aesth and Art Crit* XI (March 1953) : 224–230.

Joseph A. Mazzeo, "The Augustinian Conception of Beauty and Dante's *Convivio*," *Jour Aesth and Art Crit* XV (June 1957): 435–448.

Carl Johann Perl, "Augustine and Music," *Musical Quart* XLI (1955): 496–510.

D. W. Robertson, Jr., *A Preface to Chaucer: Studies in Medieval Perspectives* (Princeton U., 1962), ch. 2.

Leo Schrade, "Music in the Philosophy of Boethius," *Musical Quart* XXXIII (1947): 188–200.

St. Thomas Aquinas, *Summa Theologica*, trans. by the Dominican Fathers, Vol. 6 (2d ed., London, 1927).

St. Thomas Aquinas, *Truth (Quaestiones Disputatae De Veritate)*, 3 vols., trans. R. W. Mulligan, J. V. McGlynn, and R. W. Schmidt, S.J. (Chicago 1954).

Basic Writings of St. Thomas Aquinas, ed. Anton C. Pegis, 2 vols. (New York, 1945) .

Jacques Maritain, *Art and Scholasticism*, trans. J. F. Scanlan (London, 1930), esp. ch. 5.

Maurice de Wulf, *Études historiques sur l'esthétique de S. Thomas d'Aquin* (Louvain 1896).

M. C. D'Arcy, S.J., *Thomas Aquinas* (London, 1930), pp. 134–42.

Leonard Callahan, *A Theory of Esthetic According to the Principles of St. Thomas Aquinas* (Catholic U., 1927).

John Duffy, *A Philosophy of Poetry Based on Thomistic Principles* (Catholic U., 1945).

Mortimer Adler, *Art and Prudence* (New York, 1937), ch. 3.

Gerald Phelan, "The Concept of Beauty in St. Thomas," in *Aspects of the New Scholastic Philosophy* (New York, 1932).

F. J. Kovach, *Die Ästhetik des Thomas von Aquin* (Berlin, 1961).

J. W. H. Atkins, *English Literary Criticism: the Medieval Phase* (New York, 1943) , ch. 2.

Henry Osborn Taylor, *The Classical Heritage of the Middle Ages* (New York, 1903), pp. 82–106.

Beryl Smalley, *The Study of the Bible in the Middle Ages* (Oxford, 1952), esp. chs. 1, 3, 5.
Bernard F. Huppé, *Doctrine and Poetry* (N.Y. State U., 1959), chs. 1, 2.
Dionysius, the Pseudo-Areopagite, *The Divine Names,* trans. C. E. Rolt (London, 1950).
H. Flanders Dunbar, *Symbolism in Medieval Thought* (Yale U., 1929), pp. 263–81, 497–99.
Henry Osborn Taylor, *The Medieval Mind,* 2 vols. (London, 1927), Book V.
J. Huizinga, *The Waning of the Middle Ages* (London, 1924), chs. 15, 16.
Étienne Gilson, *The Philosophy of St. Bonaventure,* trans. Dom Illtyd Trethowan and F. J. Sheed (New York, 1938), ch. 7.
Murray Wright Bundy, *The Theory of Imagination in Classical and Medieval Thought,* U. of Illinois Studies in Language and Literature (Urbana, 1927), chs. 8–12.
T. F. Torrance, "Scientific Hermeneutics, According to St. Thomas Aquinas," *Jour Bibl Stud* N.S. XIII (1962): 259–89.
Robert Grinnell, "Franciscan Philosophy and Gothic Art," in F. S. C. Northrop, ed., *Ideological Differences and World Order* (Yale U., 1949).
Paul Frankl, *The Gothic* (Princeton, 1960), ch. 1, §§ 7, 10.
Cyril Barret, "Medieval Art Criticism," *Brit Jour of Aesth* V (1965): 25–36.

SIX

The Renaissance

During the two hundred years that may, somewhat arbitrarily, be marked off as the Renaissance—say, from the birth of Nicholas of Cusa (1401) to the death of Giordano Bruno (1600)—there was no great philosopher to turn his mind to the problems of aesthetics, and no single thinker made systematic contributions to its progress. This may (or may not) be surprising, in view of the tremendous flowering of creative energy in the plastic arts, in poetry, and in music, the results of which were not only to enrich the Western world so greatly, but also, in good time, to give rise to deeper and broader reflection on the nature and importance of art.

The mature systems of scholastic philosophy—those of Thomas, Scotus and Occam—had reached a stage of consolidation, rather than enterprise, and there was a gradual hardening of arteries in the academically dominant Aristotelianism. The new and hopeful philosophy during this period was a revived Platonism, or Neoplatonism, learned and taught with poetic enthusiasm, and developed in novel speculative and practical directions. What the Renaissance Platonists discussed and believed was often highly fanciful, especially where they were most original. But some of their leading ideas did much to enhance the freedom and joy of Renaissance culture, and their general philosophy had—as in its classical form—important affinities with aesthetics. To get some notion of the sort of question they were preoccupied with, and to make an estimate of their contribution to the progress of aesthetic philosophy, let us consider two philosophers who may, in a broad sense, be placed in this tradition. Of these, Marsilio Ficino was the greatest of the self-styled followers of Plato, but the spirit and concepts of Neoplatonism also permeate the philosophy of Giordano Bruno.

NEOPLATONISM

The moving spirit of Renaissance Neoplatonism was undoubtedly Marsilio Ficino (1433–99), first translator of Plotinus into Latin and of the complete works of Plato, and founder of the new Academy in 1462, when Cosimo de' Medici set him up in a villa with some Greek manuscripts to interpret and teach the Platonic philosophy. In his *Commentary on Plato's Symposium* (originally *De Amore*; written 1474–75, published 1484), and in some of the later books of his principal work, the *Theologia Platonica* (1482), Ficino discusses metaphysical problems that bear upon aesthetics. For the most part, his philosophy is a compound of ideas taken enthusiastically from Plato, Plotinus, Aristotle, St. Augustine, the pseudo-Areopagite, and others, but espoused with a new fervor and sometimes connected in novel ways. This philosophy was to become widely known, and widely held, in the sixteenth century.

Early in his *Commentary*, Ficino describes the divinely created world: "This composite of all the Forms and Ideas we call in Latin a *mundus*, and in Greek, a *cosmos*, that is, *Orderliness*. The attractiveness of this *Orderliness* is Beauty" (I, iii; trans. Jayne, p. 128). Love is then defined as "the desire for Beauty" (p. 130)— it consists in being drawn to the Good under the aspect of beauty. Now, the charm that is beauty is found in the harmony of elements: in the harmony of the virtues in the soul, of colors and lines in visible things, of tones in music. "That of the soul is perceived by the mind; that of the body, by the eyes; and that of sound, by the ear alone" (pp. 131–32; cf. p. 166).

Ficino argues (V, iii–vi) that beauty must be incorporeal—in the same way, he holds, that light is incorporeal (pp. 170–71)— since it is a property of virtues, as well as of sights and sounds. He rejects, with Plotinian arguments, attempts to analyze beauty in physical terms. It is not, for example, "a disposition of parts, or . . . size and proportion together with a certain agreeableness of colors" (V, iii; p. 168), because then only composite things (not, say, gold) could be beautiful. Yet on the other hand, it is true that until a complex bodily thing has been prepared by "Arrangement, Proportion, and Adornment" (p. 173), it is not ready to receive beauty. Consider a human being, for example:

What, then, is the beauty of the body? Activity, vivacity, and a certain grace shining in the body because of the infusion of its own idea. This kind of glow does not descend into matter until the matter has been carefully prepared [V, vi; p. 173].

The "infusion of its own idea" is this: when we walk along the street and encounter a person who at once attracts us, it is because "the appearance and shape of a well-proportioned man agrees most clearly with that concept of mankind which our soul catches and retains from the author of everything" (V, v; p. 171). There is in the mind a Platonic Form of the "true Idea of man" (p. 172), which is matched with the actuality and thus discerned in it.

Ficino does not explain how all the various kinds of beauty can be accounted for in this way; but it seems clear that he finds a transcendental element in all beauty. And it is through this element, as his *Commentary* goes on to tell in profuse detail, that beauty can lure love to its highest aspirations, and make a path to the contemplation of the divine.

Though the love of beauty has, in Ficino, a more markedly dynamic character than in some of his predecessors, he also sketches a theory of contemplation, based on Plato's *Phaedo*, that is important to his religious epistemology as well as his aesthetics. Contemplation consists in the withdrawal, or disassociation, in some degree, of the soul from the body, and from concern with corporeal things. In the resulting inward experience, the Forms are attended to in a purely rational consciousness, in which the knower, surrounded by eternal order, becomes calm and serene. Now, Ficino finds his experience in all creative activity, because a certain inward concentration, an attention to what does not yet exist, except as an ideal or future thing, is required in every art ("art" being taken here in the wide medieval sense of "craft"). Such a concentration involves a certain freeing of the soul from the body. Man, being more capable of contemplation than the animals, becomes master of nature because he can exercise a variety of arts, mechanical and political, whereas spiders that spin webs, and birds that build nests, have only a single art.

Similar themes, variations on the *Symposium* and the *Enneads*, run through *De gl' Eroici Furori* (translated as *The Heroic Enthusiasts*) of Giordano Bruno (1548–1600)—it dimly reflects the contrast between sensuous beauty and the pure absolute beauty; the danger that those who are addicted to the former will be kept away from the latter; the assurance that those who approach the lower beauty in the right spirit can use it as the stepping-stone to love of the higher (see, for example, I, ii, 11; I, iii, 12, 15; I, v, 29; II, i, 41). In this strange and rather enigmatic book, which Bruno dedicated to Sir Philip Sidney (whose acquaintance he had made in England), the discussion is carried on in a dialogue that takes the form of a commentary on successive passages of a long poem. There is hardly any philosophical analysis or argument, but there is a frequently eloquent development of a Neoplatonic religion of art. Beauty is characterized in fairly familiar terms:

Thus that which causes the attraction of love to the body is a certain spirituality which we see in it, and which is called beauty, and which does not consist in major or minor dimensions, nor in determined colors or forms, but in harmony and consonance of members and colors [I, iii, 13; trans. Williams].

It is this that appears to the senses, but also and more importantly is given to the mind,

Because it sees that all which it possesses is only a limited thing, and therefore cannot be sufficient of itself, nor good of itself, nor beautiful of itself; because it is not the universal nor the absolute entity; but contracted into being this nature, this species, this form, represented to the intellect and present to the soul. Then from the beautiful that is understood, and consequently limited, and therefore beautiful through participation, it progresses towards that which is really beautiful, which has no margin, nor any boundaries [I, iv, 20].

Bruno's book is a kind of celebration of the poet and the artist, going farther than pre-Renaissance Platonists could ever have gone in the direction of making beauty a way of life, a religion. In this it reflects an important development of the Renaissance, when the artist was coming into new relationships with others.

The artist is judged a superior man, with a unique genius that goes beyond rules, a hero who needs freedom and scope, who stamps his individual personality on his work, so that it is interesting and valuable partly (or even largely) because it is *his* work.

THEORY OF PAINTING

The highflying speculation and highpitched emotion of the Neoplatonists show us one side of Renaissance aesthetic thought; but for the other side we must turn from the philosophers to the theoretical practitioners (or empirically equipped theorists) of the arts themselves. For not only were great works created in profusion, but a great deal of thinking was going on about the principles involved—about the criteria of artistic worth and about the right methods for attaining it. These thinkers were not philosophical aestheticians, but they were dealing in part with aesthetic problems, and more importantly they were striking out in directions that would lead to fundamental changes in the prevailing Western assumptions about, and attitudes toward, the arts. Taking first the visual arts, we can obtain a fairly adequate notion of what was new and important if we consider the thought of three art theorists of this period, Leon Battista Alberti, Leonardo da Vinci, and Albrecht Dürer.

Setting to one side the architectural achievements of Alberti (1409–72), his place in the history of art theory rests on three works, two of which were of the greatest historical importance: *On Painting* (*Della pittura*, in three books; Latin 1435, Italian 1436) ; *On Sculpture* (*Della statua*, in one book; written in 1435); and *On Architecture* (*De re aedificatoria*, in ten books; presented to Pope Nicholas V, in an early version, 1452, first published 1485). What is perhaps most impressive (and what was fresh) about these works is their remarkable combination (so anticipatory of the spirit of Galileo) of careful empirical inquiry with systematic interest in theory.

The empiricism is pervasive. To compensate for his lack of genius, Alberti says in the *Architecture*, "I was continually searching, considering, measuring and making Draughts of every Thing I could hear of" (VI, i; trans. Leoni, p. 112; cf. his commendation of the Greeks, VI, iii). The canon of proportions for the human figure worked out in the *Sculpture* was derived from the measurement of many actual individuals. And there is his straightforward approach to painting, in terms of what the eye actually sees. At the very beginning of Book I Alberti begs to be considered, not as a mathematician (since "Mathematicians measure with their minds alone the forms of things separated from all matter") but as a painter using "a more sensate wisdom." Thus:

I call a figure here anything located on a plane so the eye can see it. No one would deny that the painter has nothing to do with things that are not visible. The painter is concerned solely with representing what can be seen [*On Painting*; trans. Spencer, p. 43].

And Alberti keeps his eye on the object throughout. When he says, later on, that the painter must know about bones and muscles, he remarks, "Here someone will object that I have said above that the painter has only to do with things which are visible. He has a good memory." But there is no contradiction, for the existence of the bone beneath the flesh is visible, even though the bone is not: "So in painting the nude we place first his bones and muscles which we then cover with flesh so that it is not difficult to understand where each muscle is beneath" (p. 73).

The distinction between the painting considered as a visual design and the painting considered as a representation is not yet sharply made, but it is emerging with some clarity in Alberti's treatise. For the instructions to the painter have to be given in terms of the figures, lines, colors; but they themselves do not constitute the painting. Alberti's relation to past and future is interestingly suggested in his laconic definition of a painting, at the beginning of Book III:

I say the function of the painter is this: to describe with lines and to tint with color on whatever panel or wall is given him similar observed planes of any body so that at a certain distance and in a certain position from the center they appear in relief and seem to have mass. The aim of painting: to give pleasure, good will and fame to the painter more than riches [p. 89].

The concept of a painting as inherently representational is traditional; the emphasis on visual verisimilitude (mass and depth), and the lack of insistence on any higher symbolic aim, are comparatively new, and thoroughly in the spirit of the Renaissance.

During the Middle Ages the picture was conceived as an opaque two-dimensional surface covered with lines and colors which were to be interpreted as tokens or symbols of three-dimensional objects. In the Renaissance, a picture was conceived as a "window through which we look out into a section of the visible world," to quote Leon Battista Alberti.[1]

The most important feature of a painting is what Alberti calls its *"istoria,"* which I take to be dramatic subject, or scene. "The greatest work of the painter is the *istoria"* (p. 70; cf. p. 72)—the actions, expressed emotions, themes involved in what is going on. And to be a good *istoria*, it must, first, avoid incongruities (a vase of wine still standing amidst a tumult; a dog that looks as big as a horse, etc.), and also move the soul through a wealth and variety ("copiousness") of people and actions, though with "dignity and truth" (p. 75; cf. p. 95).

In Alberti's defense of painting, at the beginning of Book II, we find several themes that are characteristic of the Renaissance, and appear again and again. Painting and sculpture were being distinguished from the other manual and technical crafts, and earning a place among the "liberal" arts. It was a long struggle— not until the middle of the sixteenth century were painting, sculpture, and architecture grouped together as *"Arti di disegno"*; and it was only gradually that these artists were fully accepted as first-class citizens of the Humanist society, along with men of literary learning. Alberti's arguments are significant. First, painting and sculpture are difficult, and require special talent and skill, which ought to lend them dignity and add to the pleasure of seeing them. Indeed, in this respect painting is superior to sculpture, though "related and nurtured by the same genius," since the painter "works with more difficult things"—he has to create the illusion of depth, for example, without actual depth (p. 66). Second, a good painter (because of what is required by the *istoria*) needs a liberal education, a knowledge of human affairs and of higher things (p. 89), and so it was well that the Greeks forbade slaves to learn painting, "for the art of painting has always been most worthy of liberal minds and noble souls" (p. 66). But third, since the painter should represent correctly

---

[1] Erwin Panofsky, *The Codex Huygens* . . . (London: The Warburg Institute, 1940), p. 92. Cf. Alberti, *On Painting*; trans. Spencer, p. 56.

the way things actually appear to sight, he must understand the laws of nature; he must be a scientist. The close connection between the growth of painting and the growth of empirical science in the Renaissance, and the intertwining of these two interests—today so widely separated—in such a man as da Vinci, has often been remarked. The logic is straightforward. To depict an arm, especially in motion, one must observe actual arms with the greatest accuracy and care; to show how it looks when it moves, one must know how it moves, what makes it move, where the muscles and joints are; and so the painter (da Vinci, Michelangelo, Dürer) must dissect, and penetrate to the hidden secrets of nature.

It is this third line of thought that leads to the painter's concern with mathematics, after all—at least with applied mathematics. And especially in two forms, which dominated thinking about the fine arts during the Renaissance: the theory of linear perspective, and the theory of proportion. Alberti's *Painting* was the first book to present a theory of one-point perspective (though Brunelleschi had probably anticipated him in thought); his *Sculpture*, as I have said, contained a theory of proportions. The same mathematical method is to be followed in architecture, as it was followed by the Ancients, who studied Nature ("as the greatest Artist at all Manner of Compositions") to learn her laws (IX, v, p. 195). Alberti is

convinced of the Truth of Pythagoras's Saying, that Nature is sure to act consistently, and with a constant Analogy in all her Operations: From whence I conclude, that the same Numbers, by means of which the Agreement of Sounds affects our Ears with Delight, are the very same which please our Eyes and our Minds [IX, v, pp. 196–97; cf. *Painting*, p. 72].

This principle was basic to Renaissance architectural theory and practice: that the same universal order expresses itself in the mathematical ratios of auditory and visual consonance and harmony. The three fundamental ratios discussed in Plato's *Timaeus* and brought into prominence by Ficino's commentary on the *Timaeus*—the arithmetic, geometric, and harmonic means —were pervasive in the work, for example, of Palladio (see his *Quattro libri dell'architettura*, 1570). Alberti's book includes an elaborate discussion (IX, v–vii) of these proportions in the relation of length to width of room, etc.

For it is beauty, he says, that is the highest aim of the architect. Translating the three criteria of Vitruvius[2]—buildings should be "accommodated to their respective Purposes, stout and strong for Duration, and pleasant and delightful to the sight"—he adds that the third "is by much the most Noble of all, and very necessary besides" (VI, i, p. 112). Alberti explicates beauty with an original turn: "I shall define Beauty to be a Harmony of all the Parts, in whatsoever Subject it appears, fitted together with such Proportion and Connection, that nothing could be added, diminished or altered, but for the Worse" (VI, ii, p. 113). He adds that this perfection is seldom to be expected, in nature or art—for it is perfect beauty, rather than just beauty, that he seems to be defining here. Distinct from beauty is what he calls "ornament": "a Kind of an auxiliary Brightness and Improvement to Beauty" (p. 113). Beauty is a quality "which is proper and innate, and diffused over the whole Body, and Ornament somewhat added or fastened on, rather than proper and innate"—a sort of local or adventitious beauty. Since beauty and ornament are a function of harmony and proportion, they are not relative or variable (though some say they are). Alberti returns to the subject later (IX, v), to inquire again, more definitely, "what that Property is which in its Nature makes a Thing beautiful" (p. 194). His answer:

The Number, and that which I have called the Finishing and the Collocation. But there is still something else besides, which arises from the Conjunction and Connection of these other Parts, and gives the Beauty and Grace to the Whole: Which we will call Congruity, which we may consider as the Original of all that is graceful and handsome. The Business and Office of Congruity is to put together Members differing from each other in their Natures, in such a Manner, that they may conspire to form a beautiful Whole: So that whenever such a Composition offers itself to the Mind, either by the Conveyance of the Sight, or any of the other Senses, we immediately perceive this Congruity [p. 195].

This last point, the immediate perception, is another original feature of the account. In the last analysis, Alberti doesn't see how our recognition of beauty, or our delight in it, can be explained in terms of anything else, and he postulates a special

---

[2] *Utilitas, firmitas, venustas* (see Vitruvius, *On Architecture*, I, iii, 2).

sense of beauty to receive it. He speaks of "that natural Instinct or Sense in the Mind by which . . . we judge of Beauty and Gracefulness" (IX, vii, p. 201)—"for, indeed, the Eye is naturally a Judge and Lover of Beauty and Gracefulness, and is very critical and hard to please in it" (IX, viii; p. 203).

Alberti's concern to establish the dignity and intellectual status of painting is paralleled in the large collection of manuscript notes left by Leonardo da Vinci (1452–1519), his preparation for a definitive work on the art of painting. The famous Codex Urbinas Latinus 1270, in the Vatican Library, discovered and published in 1817, was put together from Leonardo's notes by his friend and pupil, Francesco Melzi, about 1550. Another selection, gathered a century later, was published in 1651 by Raphael Du Fresne, with illustrations by Poussin, and exercised enormous influence through its successive reprintings. So Leonardo's thinking may be taken as indicating not only Renaissance ideas on painting but also assumptions underlying later work.

As is evident throughout the *Treatise on Painting,* despite its unfinished condition, Leonardo's aim was to systematize the science of painting, considered as representation of natural objects. He begins with an argument that painting is a branch of natural philosophy, or what we would call empirical science. Leonardo rejects the traditional medieval distinction between "mechanical" and "scientific" knowledge, knowledge from experience vs. knowledge independent of experience (McMahon ed., I, 11), and insists that both empirical observation and formal thinking are involved in painting, just as in any worthwhile field, such as music or astronomy (p. 12).

That painting is most praiseworthy which conforms most to the object portrayed. I put this forward to embarrass those painters who would improve on the works of nature, such as those who represent a child a year old, whose head is a fifth of his height while they make it an eighth; and the breadth of the shoulders is similar to that of his head, and they make it half the breadth of the shoulders; and thus they proceed reducing a small child a year old to the proportions of a man of thirty [p. 161; cf. pp. 48, 158–59, and his statement that "The mirror, above all, should be taken as your master," p. 160].

Hence the *Treatise on Painting* deals exhaustively with the most accurate observations of light, shadows, smoke, trees, and the workings of the human body and countenance. Painting, says Leonardo, is a science because (1) the principles of representation are capable of systematic formulation (p. 4); (2) "it treats of the motion of bodies and the rapidity of their actions" (p. 5); and (3) it is mathematical, since it "treats of all continuous quantities as well as the proportions of shadow and light" (p. 9; cf. p. 4)—though it is even greater than arithmetic and geometry, because it includes qualities as well as quantities. Since "all visible things are born of nature, and painting is born of these . . . we rightly call painting the grandchild of nature and related to God" (p. 5) ; or painters may be called "the grandchildren of God" (p. 19).

There is another kind of knowledge that the painter must possess as well, and that is knowledge of man—though, in the extant notes, Leonardo does not give this so much attention (see pp. 149–57). "Make the motions of your figures appropriate to the mental conditions of those figures" (p. 151), he says: and to do this you must know how people express their emotions and their intentions in their faces and gestures and bodily movements (p. 149). The painter is to acquire this knowledge by careful observation of life: he is not to draw a weeping figure from one who pretends to weep, but keep his eyes open for people who are actually in sorrow, and sketch them on the spot (p. 151). The doctrine—which was to dominate the thought of painters and theorists in the seventeenth century—that painting exists to represent, not primarily nature, but *human* nature (and nature in relation to man), can be found in germ here.

On such premises, it is easy enough for Leonardo to develop his argument that painting is superior to both poetry (pp. 12–30) and music (pp. 15, 25–32). This discussion, extending throughout most of Book I, is a curious medley of arguments on startlingly different levels of importance. It is best to think of it, it seems to me, as primarily an answer to invidious comparisons, so that many of his remarks, while proving nothing of themselves, might be considered legitimate rebuttals to equally silly arguments—for example, his point that painting can deceive animals, while poetry cannot (p. 20), or that paintings last longer than musical notes (p. 26). Most serious, however, is the claim that painting "represents the forms of nature's works with more truth than does the poet," and that the works of nature are nobler than the works of man (p. 20). But Leonardo seems of two minds on this point. "With justified lamentation, painting complains that she has been driven from the number of the liberal arts, though she is a true daughter of nature and appeals to the noblest of senses," and "gives heed not only to the works of nature but to an infinite number of things that nature never created" (p. 17). (He does not exalt sculpture, however, since it does not require so much intelligence, and "brings sweat and bodily fatigue"— see pp. 34–35.)

The two mathematical problems of representation—linear perspective and proportion—occupied Albrecht Dürer (1471–1528) throughout his artistic life, as we can see in his surviving memoranda, his numerous illustrative studies, and his two theoretical works, the *Course in the Art of Measurement with Compass and Ruler* (1525) and the *Four Books on Human Proportion* (1528). (Two passages of prime importance are the drafts of 1512–13 and the "aesthetic excursus" appended to Book III of the *Four Books*; see Conway, pp. 176–80, 243–50.) In his thinking it is very clear how the mathematical laws sought for in these two branches of study meant to the Renaissance theorist a reconciliation between two fundamental demands in painting: for accuracy of representation, and for visual order or harmony. A method of disposing objects in deep space so that their relative sizes and positions can be clearly read, and a method of depicting the parts of human and animal figures accurately, not only make the painting realistic, in this plain sense, but also define systems of relationships within the picture space, and give the painting a new unity, unknown to the earlier Renaissance, that enables it to be taken in as a whole all at once. Representation is primary: "The more closely thy work abideth by life in its form, so much the better will it appear" (trans. Conway, p. 247; cf. Panofsky, p. 243). "The attainment of true, artistic, and lovely execution in painting is hard to come unto," Dürer remarks (Conway, p. 177), suggesting that these three properties—verisimilitude, skill, and beauty—go together.

Dürer's interest for our present history does not lie in any very well worked out aesthetic theories that he is able to come up with; indeed, he confesses himself exceedingly puzzled.

But Beauty is so put together in men and so uncertain is our judgment about it, that we may perhaps find two men both beautiful and fair to look upon, and yet neither resembleth the other, in measure or kind, in any single point or part; and so blind is our perception that we shall not understand whether of the two is the more beautiful, and if we give an opinion on the matter it lacketh certainty [p. 248].

What is important for us to notice is his candid facing of difficulties, even if he cannot resolve them satisfactorily; the questions he raises show the puzzles of his age. First, there is the general question about the nature and conditions of beauty. He thinks that beauty lies in a mean between extremes (pp. 179, 243), that perhaps "Use is a part of beauty," and that "The accord of one thing with another is beautiful, therefore want of harmony is not beautiful. A real harmony linketh together things unlike" (p. 180). But he is impressed with the variability of opinion (p. 244), and says, "What Beauty is I know not, though it dependeth upon many things" (p. 179; cf. 244–45). Second, there is the problem of circularity in verifying any theory about beautiful proportions. Suppose we measure a number of women to determine, say, the mean proportion of leg to torso or of hips to waist, in order to discover ratios of ideal beauty. We cannot measure any woman who comes along, but only beautiful ones— so we are in danger of imposing our a priori notions of beauty on nature, rather than extracting it from nature (see Panofsky, pp. 278–79). Third, there is the problem whether there is only one ideal set of proportions. Alberti's method of determining proportions was to divide the length of the body into 600 units; Leonardo turned from this metrical system to the search for equalities or correspondences (the width of the wrist is equal to the length of the thumb, etc.); Dürer looked for ratios between various divisions of the body and the length of the whole, a flexible system which he carried out in detail to fractions like 1/30 and 2/19. Most importantly, he was led to abandon the notion of a single set of ideal proportions for human beauty, and to accept the idea of a variety of attractive human types. "There are many causes and varieties of beauty" (Conway, p. 180; cf. pp. 245, 241, 243). And as he worked it out, his canon of proportions became, in effect, a canon of expressiveness: an exploration of ratios that would make a figure look melancholy or sanguine, timid or cheerful, noble or rustic (see Panofsky, pp. 264–66). Fourth, there is the problem of the nature of the artist's creative imagination, of novelty and originality. The figure of the artist's mind as a mirror (which Dürer also uses, p. 177) explains how he can copy nature, but what explains his evident capacity to invent? It is an important development in the Renaissance, and part of its general humanism, that the artist's powers are thought of less in relation to divine inspiration,[3] in a Platonic-Christian sense, and more as a genius innate in man, capable of development by training. Man, having this power, is himself like a God (p. 177); given many hundred years to live, the painter could spin out of his mind countless figures that nature itself has never thought of producing (p. 243); he can "pour forth that which he hath for a long time gathered into him from without" (p. 247; cf. Panofsky, pp. 279–81). But the link between what he gathers and what he pours—the power of imagination—remains to be inquired into.

MUSIC AND POETRY

The same concern with faithfulness of representation, or imitation in a broad sense, that we have found in the theorists of visual art also permeates the treatises on music theory that were written during the sixteenth century. In creative ferment and permanent achievement, of course, music was no less noteworthy in the Renaissance than painting—this was the age of the madrigal, the motet, and the great polyphonic mass, in which Italy and the Netherlands (then including Belgium and Northern France) were dominant. Composers revealed, in their actual work, radical musical thinking, and significant new concepts of music were emerging also in the textbooks of musical practice.

The two principal ideas from which music has since the sixteenth century drawn its inspiration, music as expression, as painting in tones, and music as structure based on thematic work, both originated in the Renaissance.[4]

---

[3] The characteristic medieval view may be seen in the Preface to Book III of the *De Diversis Artibus,* by the pseudonymous Theophilus (probably first half of twelfth century), trans. C. R. Dodwell (London, 1961).

[4] Edward E. Lowinsky, "Music in Renaissance Culture," *Jour Hist Ideas* XV (1954): 542.

The Renaissance music theorists, like the Humanists in other fields, were excited by the idea of reviving all that could be revived of classical culture, and, though they knew even less than we do of Greek music, they found in Plato, Aristotle, Plutarch, and others many descriptions of Greek music that had a decisive influence on their concept of what music is and ought to be. The first point that impressed them was the close co-operation of poetry and music in ancient Greece, the combination of these arts in the same individuals, the conception of *mousike* (like St. Augustine's *musica*) as word and melody together. The second point was the considerable stress which ancient authors, as we have seen, put upon the ethical effects of music; it seemed to the Renaissance theorists that the existence of music can be justified, in keeping with the authority of Plato and Aristotle, only if it is placed in the service of character and virtue.

The ethical function of music was supported strongly by a number of theorists. For example, Vincenzo Galilei, in his *Dialogo della Musica antica e della moderna* (Venice, 1581) says that

if the musician has not the power to direct the minds of his listeners to their benefit, his science and knowledge are to be reputed null and vain, since the art of music was instituted and numbered among the liberal arts for no other purpose [trans. Strunk, p. 319].

And Marin Mersenne, in his *Quaestiones Celeberrimae in Genesim* (Paris, 1623), whose work, though written later, may be taken to represent some of the best of sixteenth century thinking, emphasizes the same point, citing the authority of Plato's *Laws* and Aristotle's *Politics*—even to the *katharsis* (Q. 57, Art. 1). In general, these theorists accepted the most extreme claims for the effects of ancient music, and their hope for contemporary music was that it could rise to an equal level—as their complaint was often that

neither its novelty nor its excellence has ever had the power, with our modern musicians, of producing any of the virtuous, infinitely beneficial and comforting effects that ancient music produced [Galilei; trans. Strunk, p. 306].

From these two premises was derived a most important conclusion. The question was, How are the required emotional and ethical effects of music to be produced? For one thing, by an increase in musical resources: a richer harmonic language, mixtures of modes, modulations from one mode to another, the introduction of new instruments with wider tonal ranges, etc. But more importantly, through a subjection of music to its text. Since words are obviously the best means of arousing passions and conveying ideas, they must be given primacy in the song; the music must be made to follow the meaning of the words, to underline and intensify the moods they express. The emotional resources of melody, harmony, and rhythm exist to increase the affective language of the poet. The implications of this view were ably argued by one of the foremost musical theorists, Gioseffe Zarlino, in his *Instituzioni Armoniche* (Venice 1558).

> For if in speech, whether by way of narrative or of imitation (and these occur in speech), matters may be treated that are joyful or mournful, and grave or without gravity, and again modest or lascivious, we must also make a choice of a harmony and a rhythm similar to the nature of the matters contained in the speech in order that from the combination of these things, put together with proportion, may result a melody suited to the purpose [IV, 32; trans. Strunk, p. 256].

And he says of the composer:

> Thus it will be inappropriate if in a joyful matter he uses a mournful harmony and a grave rhythm, nor where funereal and tearful matters are treated is he permitted to use a joyful harmony and a rhythm that is light or rapid, call it as we will. On the contrary, he must use joyful harmonies and rapid rhythms in joyful matters, and in mournful ones, mournful harmonies and grave rhythms, so that everything may be done with proportion.
>   . . . In so far as he can, he must take care to accompany each word in such a way that, if it denotes harshness, hardness, cruelty, bitterness, and other things of this sort, the harmony will be similar, that is, somewhat hard and harsh, but so that it does not offend. In the same way, if any word expresses complaint, grief, affliction, sighs, tears, and other things of this sort, the harmony will be full of sadness [IV, 32; trans. Strunk, pp. 256–57].

Zarlino goes on to explain the musical means for creating joyful and mournful compositions: major sixths and thirteenths are naturally harsh, semitones sweet, "swift and vigorous" rhythms joyful, "slow and lingering movements" sad.

Zarlino's emphasis on the primacy of the text led him to propose that the Gregorian melodies be revised so that they would

follow the words more exactly—a remarkable suggestion, considering that in the Middle Ages it was believed that these
melodies had been dictated to Gregory I by the Holy Ghost.
(The reform was ordered by Gregory XIII in 1577, and Palestrina
was engaged to supervise it.) And not only was the language of
poetry adopted by the sixteenth-century composer as his main
musical inspiration, but the range of texts, of subjects and attitudes and moods, was enormously widened. The whole of the visible world of nature and of the inner psychological world became
the composer's domain, and its accurate and faithful representation the aim of his art.

This program would evidently give rise to many theoretical
and practical problems, some of them hinted at in the quotations
above. First, there might be a conflict between the ethical and
the realistic purposes, when the composer is given a "lascivious"
poem, for example, to set. The old moral problem would recur:
should he be faithful and immoral, or moral but false to the text?
Second, there might be a conflict between expressive adherence
to the text and musical structure (note Zarlino's phrase: "so that
it does not offend"). For example, should the composer follow
the individual words, changing his mode and harmony constantly
with the text, or would this not produce musical nonsense? And,
again, since these theorists, in keeping with their basic thesis,
insisted that the words should be clearly audible in singing
(which is why some of them attacked counterpoint in favor of
monody) and that the musical rhythms should not distort the
natural rhythms of speech (which suggests that a kind of recita-
tive would be best), would not the most faithful music be poorest
as music? Third, there might be a conflict between expressiveness
and beauty. Galilei defends a kind of musical puritanism on this
point. He objects to purely instrumental music because it only
exists to give pleasure in its sound; he objects to polyphony
(which he considers to be a degeneration of instrumental music)
and to consonances. Pleasure taken in the beauty of musical
sounds is bound to distract from the true function of expressing
emotions. Speaking of his contemporaries, he says scornfully,

They aim at nothing but the delight of the ear, if it can truly be called
delight. They have not a book among them for their use and convenience that speaks of how to express the conceptions of the mind and of

how to impress them with the greatest possible effectiveness on the minds of the listeners . . . In truth the last thing the moderns think of is the expression of the words with the passion that these require, excepting in the ridiculous way that I shall shortly relate . . . Their ignorance and lack of consideration is one of the most potent reasons why the music of today does not cause in the listeners any of those virtuous and wonderful effects that ancient music caused [Galilei; trans. Strunk, pp. 312–13; cf. p. 314].

A fourth problem concerns the nature of imitation itself. The "ridiculous way" of setting the words is explained by Galilei with many apt examples. He says it is silly to write rapid music to illustrate words like "to flee" or "to fly," or to make the melody descend or rise when the text speaks of going to hell or aspiring to the stars, or (worst of all) to use black or white notes with allusions to dark or blond hair. A fifth problem is barely touched upon: how far can these principles be extended to nonvocal music? Apart from dance music, purely instrumental music in the sixteenth century was still in an early form, and these theorists were thinking almost exclusively of vocal music. Galilei and Mersenne acknowledged that the Greeks, including Aristotle, admitted the ethical and affective force of instrumental music, but they did not pursue the matter. Mersenne's view was that the effects of instrumental music are due to the melody's reminding us of some other melody that has already been set to words.

A new encouragement to work in the theory of poetry was given by the printing of Aristotle's *Poetics* in Latin (1498) and Greek (1508); there followed many treatises, and some memorable literary controversies. The most intense activity was in Italy, where much of the most serious thinking revolved around four problems, some of them taken over essentially unchanged from Aristotle and Plato, but attacked with new vigor in relation to sixteenth-century literature. First, there was the problem of the "rules," whether, for example, tragedy must conform to certain necessary conditions in order to be good. Aristotle, of course, had emphasized the importance of unity of action, and had touched on the unity of time. In the sixteenth century arose the doctrine of the "three unities," space, time, and action, pleading Scriptural authority in Aristotle, but defended with a zeal and rigor new in the history of critical theory. Julius Caesar Scaliger for-

mulated them in his *Poetics* (*Poetices Libri Septem*, 1561), and
Lodovico Castelvetro championed them in his *Poetics of Aristotle
Translated and Annotated* (*Poetica d'Aristotele Vulgarizzata et
Sposta*, 1570). But other theorists—a good example is Torquato
Tasso, in his *Discourses on the Heroic Poem* (*Discorsi del Poema
Eroico*, 1594), Book III (see Gilbert, pp. 492–502)—defended a
broader and more fundamental concept of unity, in relation to
variety. Second, there was the closely related problem of genres.
The power and success of the Italian epics, Dante's *Divine
Comedy*, Ariosto's *Orlando Furioso*, Tasso's *Jerusalem Delivered*,
and other poetic productions that did not fit the classical categories—that had forms not sanctioned by Vergil and Horace—
provoked violent disputes. Though accepted and enjoyed by
many readers, such works had to be defended against the cavils
of theorists who insisted on strict adherence to known genres. A
number of the outstanding sixteenth-century treatises on critical
theory had this aim: Giraldi Cinthio's *Discourses* (1554), Jacopo
Mazzoni's *Defenses* (1572, 1587), Tasso's *Discourses on the Heroic
Poem*.

Third and fourth, the Platonic challenge against the cognitive
value and morality of poetry was taken up again by various
writers. It was an age of apologies for poetry, beginning with
Book XIV of Boccaccio's *Genealogia Deorum Gentilium* (finished
in the 1360s). The best Renaissance thought on these matters is
evidenced in Sir Philip Sidney's *Defense of Poesie* (also entitled
An Apologie for Poetrie), published in 1595 after having been
widely circulated in manuscript. Though it is considered to be,
in its occasion, a reply to the Puritan attack on poetry and drama
in Stephen Gosson's *School of Abuse* (1571), it is a kind of summary, often in language that is still quotable, of the best that the
thinkers of his day could say in reply to Plato's *Republic*. The
inventive and creative power of the poet is said to rank him high
among men, and his works above all other works except Holy
Scripture. The poet combines philosophy (which teaches by
precept) and history (which teaches by example); poetry deals
with the universal, but in vivid and understandable shape. If the
poet illustrates his universals by fables, it must be remembered
that the fables are a make-believe: "the poet . . . nothing affirms
and therefore never lieth" (Gilbert, p. 439). As to the moral
objection "that [poetry] is the nurse of abuse, infecting us with

many pestilent desires" (p. 438)—that "the lyric," for example, "is larded with passionate sonnets" (p. 440) —it must be granted that poetry can do much harm when it is abused, and so can anything that can also do much good when used rightly: medicine, law, even the Bible. These objections do not touch the essential nature of poetry, and the capacity for much evil only proves the capacity for much good. "Truly, a needle cannot do much hurt, and as truly (with leave of ladies be it spoken) it cannot do much good. With a sword thou mayest kill thy father, and with a sword thou mayest defend thy prince and country" (p. 441).

In general, Renaissance poetics rested on two broad assumptions. The first (derived from Plato and Aristotle) was that poetry is in some sense an imitation of action. The exact nature of this imitation was the subject of a great deal of discussion. It was given diverse interpretations and sharply criticized—as by Francesco Patrizi in the second volume of his *Poetics* (*Della Poetica*, 1586). But it remained the central concept around which most discussion of genres and rules revolved. The second (derived from Horace) was that the twin functions of poetry are to delight and instruct. There was much debate about the meaning of the Aristotelian *katharsis*, and about Plato's real position on the effects of poetry. Some of it contributed permanently to our understanding of these topics; some of it was carried on in a spirited style of personal polemics that did not foster very constructive argument. The Renaissance theorists were generally able to keep both functions of poetry in view, though they could seldom make a genuine synthesis. Presentiments of an impending split appeared in some quarters. For example, Castelvetro, one of the better theorists, denied explicitly that poetry has the aim to teach, and, depending on the authority of Aristotle as well as on his own arguments, insisted that pleasure is its sole purpose:

The poet's function is after consideration to give a semblance of truth to the happenings that come upon men through fortune, and by means of this semblance to give delight to his readers; he should leave the discovery of truth hidden in natural or accidental things to the philosopher and the scientist, who have their own way of pleasing or giving profit which is very remote from that of the poet [op. cit.; trans. Gilbert, p. 307; cf. pp. 348–49, 353].

Bibliography

Marsilio Ficino, *Commentary on Plato's Symposium*, trans. Sears Reynolds Jayne, U. of Missouri Studies, XIX, No. 1 (Columbia, Mo., 1944).

Paul O. Kristeller, *The Philosophy of Marsilio Ficino*, trans. Virginia Conant (Columbia U., 1943), esp. 263–69, 304–9.

N. Ivanoff, "La Beauté dans la Philosophie de Marsile Ficin," *Humanisme et Renaissance* III (1936) : 12–21.

Giordano Bruno, *The Heroic Enthusiasts*, trans. L. Williams (London, 1887–89), 2 vols.

Nesca A. Robb, *Neoplatonism of the Italian Renaissance* (London, 1935), ch. 7.

Erwin Panofsky, *Idea: Ein Beitrag zur Begriffsgeschichte der Älteren Kunsttheorie* (2d. ed., Berlin, 1960).

Leslie P. Spelman, "Calvin and the Arts," *Jour Aesth and Art Crit* VI (March 1948): 246–52.

Leslie P. Spelman, "Luther and the Arts," *Jour Aesth and Art Crit* X (December 1951): 166–75.

Leon Battista Alberti, *On Painting*, trans. John R. Spencer (Yale U., 1956).

Leon Battista Alberti, *On Architecture*, trans. James Leoni (1726), Facsimile ed. (London, 1955).

Edward R. deZurko, "Alberti's Theory of Form and Function," *Art Bulletin* XXXIX (1957): 142–45.

Leonardo da Vinci, *Treatise on Painting*, trans. A. Philip McMahon, 2 vols. (Princeton U., 1956).

Erwin Panofsky, *The Codex Huygens and Leonardo da Vinci's Art Theory* (London, 1940).

Kenneth Clark, *Leonardo da Vinci* (Cambridge U., 1940), ch. 4.

Milton C. Nahm, "Leonardo da Vinci's Philosophy of Originality" *Bucknell Review* VIII (1958): 1–16.

Erwin Panofsky, *The Life and Art of Albrecht Dürer* (4th ed., Princeton U., 1955), ch. 8.

William M. Conway, *The Writings of Albrecht Dürer* (title in 1889: *Literary Remains of Albrecht Dürer*) (New York, 1958).

Rensselaer W. Lee, "*Ut Pictura Poesis*: The Humanistic Theory of Painting," *Art Bulletin* XXII (1940): 197–269.

Anthony Blunt, *Artistic Theory in Italy, 1450–1600* (Oxford, 1940).

Rudolf Wittkower, *Architectural Principles in the Age of Humanism* (London, 1949), esp. Part IV.

Rudolf Wittkower, "Individualism in Art and Artists: A Renaissance Problem," *Jour Hist Ideas* XXII (1961): 291–302.

D. Mahon, *Studies in Seicento Art and Theory*, Studies of Warburg Inst. XVI (London, 1947).

Otto Benesch, *The Art of the Renaissance in Northern Europe* (Harvard U., 1947).

Robert J. Clements, *Michelangelo's Theory of Art* (New York, 1961).

I. L. Zupnick, "The 'Aesthetics' of the Early Mannerists," *Art Bulletin* XXXV (1953): 302–6.

Arnold Hauser, *The Social History of Art* (New York, 1950), Vol. I, Part V, chs. 1, 3.

Elizabeth Gilmore Holt, ed., *Literary Sources of Art History* (Princeton, 1947), Part II.

J. Huizinga, *The Waning of the Middle Ages* (London, 1924), chs. 19–23.

Edward E. Lowinsky, "Music in the Culture of the Renaissance," *Jour Hist Ideas* XV (1954): 509–53.

D. P. Walker, "Musical Humanism in the 16th and Early 17th Centuries," *Music Rev* II (1941): 1–13, 111–21, 220–27, 288–308; III (1942): 55–71.

William Oliver Strunk, ed., *Source Readings in Music History* (New York, 1950).

Claude V. Palisca, "Girolamo Mei: Mentor to the Florentine Camerata," *Musical Quart* XL (1954): 1–20.

Bernard Weinberg, *A History of Literary Criticism in the Italian Renaissance,* 2 vols. (Chicago U., 1961).

Baxter Hathaway, *The Age of Criticism: The Late Renaissance in Italy* (Cornell U., 1962).

Allen H. Gilbert, ed., *Literary Criticism: Plato to Dryden* (New York, 1940), pp. 199–533.

Vernon Hall, Jr., *Renaissance Literary Criticism* (Columbia U., 1945).

H. B. Charlton, *Castelvetro's Theory of Poetry* (Manchester U., 1913).

Harold S. Wilson, "Some Meanings of 'Nature' in Renaissance Literary Theory," *Jour Hist Ideas* II (1941): 430–48.

SEVEN

The Enlightenment:
Cartesian Rationalism

I t is no doubt a little ironic that we must begin our examination of seventeenth- and eighteenth-century aesthetics by
recalling the philosophy of Descartes, whose volumes of
writings nowhere present even the sketch of an aesthetic
theory. Apart from his early *Compendium Musicae* (1618),
Descartes hardly refers to beauty or the arts. Yet in aesthetics,
as in nearly every other branch of philosophy during these two
centuries, his philosophical ideas were highly influential. Where
we cannot demonstrate that certain aesthetic theories were in
fact derived indirectly from his principles and methods, we can
at least show that, logically speaking, they belong to a family of
ideas for which the period was notable, and of which Descartes
was the outstanding philosophical representative, if not the
actual progenitor.

The ideals of knowledge that Descartes formed by reflection
upon arithmetic and geometry, and promised a universal application, stamped themselves indelibly upon the consciousness of his
age. Though the uncompleted *Regulae ad Directionem Ingenii*
(written about 1628) were not published until after his death,
the *Discours de la Méthode* (1637) was one of the most memorable epistemological manifestoes. As regards concepts, Descartes
proposed by analysis to discover the essentially simple, and therefore utterly clear and distinct, ideas, which should be the basic
ingredients of knowledge. And as regards propositions, he took

intuition and deduction as his sources of necessary truth, an intuition being "the undoubting conception of an unclouded and attentive mind" that "springs from the light of reason alone"[1]— and a deduction being, in effect, a chain of intuitions. One of Descartes' most important claims was to have discovered a method that anyone can use to get at indubitable and universal truth— universal both in that it would be valid for all rational beings and in that it would hold of everything, or everything in a given field of inquiry.

Thus Descartes' method was a priori and abstract. The kind of knowledge he was after could not be expected from an empirical investigation of nature; it had to rest on innate concepts and propositions that commend themselves directly to the "natural light." And its security as knowledge would be attested not only by its evident clearness but by its deductive systematization, with the more fundamental and less fundamental propositions arranged so as to exhibit their logical dependences. The ideal of a Cartesian knowledge spread across Europe, and the hope of attaining it arose in many fields, including the study of the arts. It is true that Descartes himself, in the *Discours* (Part I), said he thought that Poetry and Eloquence were "gifts of the mind rather than fruits of study" (p. 85), native talents rather than rational arts; nevertheless, theorists who were closer than he to the actual problems of poets, painters, composers, or critics were moved to see whether even these refractory subjects (however hopelessly unmethodical they might seem) could be conquered by Reason.

POETICS

L'art poétique (1674) of Nicolas Boileau-Despréaux is perhaps the most perfect expression of the Cartesian spirit in poetic theory. Reason, good sense, intelligibility—these are essential and basic, he tells the poet:

> Love reason then: and let what e'er you Write
> Borrow from her its Beauty, Force, and Light.
> [Canto I, lines 37–38; trans. Soame]

[1] *Rules for the Direction of the Mind*, Rule III, in *Philosophical Works*; trans. Haldane and Ross (Cambridge U., 1911), I, 7.

Aimez donc la Raison—yes. But also: *Que la Nature donc soit vostre étude unique*:

> You then, that would the Comic Lawrels wear,
> To study Nature be your only care
> [Canto III, lines 359–60]

And this holds for the tragic as well as the comic, art. Nature is the universal underlying the particular, the reality behind the appearance. Nature, in this sense, and Reason are intrinsically allied; the rules of following either are the same.

> Would you in this great Art acquire Renown?
> Authors, observe the Rules I here lay down.
> In prudent Lessons every where abound,
> With pleasant, joyn the useful and the sound.
> [Canto IV, lines 85–88]

In the same spirit, René Le Bossu began his *Traité du poème épique* (1675) by remarking:

The arts have this in common with the sciences, that the former like the latter are founded on reason and that in the arts one should allow himself to be guided by the lights which nature has given us [Book I, ch. 1].

And "Nature" is again the key word in Pope's *Essay on Criticism* (1711), the most concentrated statement of neoclassical critical theory.

> First follow NATURE, and your judgment frame
> By her just standard, which is still the same:
> Unerring NATURE, still divinely bright,
> One clear, unchang'd, and universal light,
> Life, force, and beauty, must to all impart,
> At once the source, and end, and test of Art.
>   .   .   .
> Those RULES of old discovered, not devis'd,
> Are nature still, but Nature methodiz'd:
> Nature, like Monarchy, is but restrain'd
> By the same Laws which first herself ordain'd.
> [Part I, lines 68–73, 88–91; cf. 130–40]

The subtleties and complexities of these two concepts, Nature and Reason, as they permeated the thinking of the Enlightenment, are enormously difficult to unravel, and only an outline of the story can be given here. The high point of Aristotle's prestige, and of the respect accorded his doctrines, came in the seventeenth century, but the seventeenth-century theorists were, in general, no longer content to cite him as an authority; they believed that his conclusions could be rationally justified, and indeed given more solid support than was provided in the extant passages of the *Poetics*. One principle (or definition) was taken as axiomatic: that poetry is an imitation of human action. But this idea had now to be developed and systematized, with the help of the emerging concept of Nature. The clue was taken from the *Poetics*: poetry is universal, whereas history is particular.

Reason, said Aristotle, grasps the universal in the particular, which is to say it begins to understand when it locates the individual thing in the class, or species, to which it properly belongs—for a class is identified by the universal which its members share. Taking "nature" in its broadest sense, for all that confronts us, including human and nonhuman creatures and things, what strikes us most of all, it was argued, is the way in which they fall into distinct and definite groups. Each group has not only its defining universals, constituting the "nature" of its members, but it also has typical or ideal or unusually representative members: the first-rate horse who exhibits better than others the character of its species. Thus a number of important ideas come to be mingled together in the concept of Nature: the statistically frequent, the essential, the fundamental, the typical, the characteristic, the normal, the ideal. Of these notions, the statistically frequent is not central in the thinking of the neoclassical theorists: when Boileau advises the comic writer to study the mores of men, he does not mean just what they usually do, though that is perhaps part of it; the poet must "discern the hidden secrets of the heart" and depict

> The Jealous Fool, the fawning Sycophant,
> A Sober Wit, an enterprising Ass
> [Canto III, lines 363–4]

or in Boileau's words,

> un Prodigue, un Avare,
> Un Honneste homme, un Fat, un Jaloux, un Bizarre

—essential types of common humanity, not individuals remarkable for their uniqueness.

This is Aristotle's principle of universality in its neoclassical transformation: the aim of the poet is to provide, in Samuel Johnson's words, "just representations of general Nature" (*Preface to Shakespeare*, 1765). The pervasiveness of this principle in neoclassical theory can be copiously illustrated, but for our purpose that is not necessary. Its implications are best revealed in the words of Johnson, who gave it one of its latest—and most forceful—formulations. Johnson's best-known passage is from *Rasselas* (1759):

The business of a poet . . . is to examine, not the individual, but the species; to remark general properties and large appearances: he does not number the streaks of the tulip . . . [ch. 10].

Shakespeare's characters are praised for their universality, not their individuality (*Preface to Shakespeare*), and Cowley is censured because he "loses the grandeur of generality" by his "scrupulous enumeration" (*Life of Cowley*, pars. 58, 133; cf. *Rambler* No. 36).

"The grandeur of generality" is a significant phrase. To deal, in poetry or drama, with a universal trait of human nature, or a trait typical of a certain class of men (however the class may be defined) is at once to reveal something importantly true about human nature and to bring it forcibly and movingly to mind, in a way that would be weakened by detailed dwelling upon idiosyncratic features. And it is also to touch the common springs of humanity in a wide audience, and thus please and instruct most successfully. This is the neoclassical theory that accords generality its poetic power.

Because the end of poetry can be exactly stated, the neoclassical theorists held, there can be a science of its means. It should be in principle possible to discover and draw up a set of general rules by reference to which a good poem can be successfully constructed and a faulty poem be proved bad—perhaps even a "poetical scale" of measurement such as Goldsmith later attempted (Roger de Piles had made a similar scale for paintings). The doctrine of the rules—especially the three alleged Aristotelian rules of tragedy, as formulated by Scaliger—came into its own in the seventeenth century. And it brought into the heart of aesthetics the epistemological conflict of the Enlightenment: between the rival claims of reason and experience. As this controversy was carried on by the theorists of poetry, it seldom rose to a very high level; they did not, on the whole, learn enough from the philosophers, and there were too many vested interests, personal and national, as well as mixed loyalties (to Aristotle, to the Muse, to the box office), to make for easy and rational discussion.

Consider, for example, the three *Discourses* of Corneille (1660), which did a great deal to give a seventeenth-century stamp of official approval to the unities. "It is necessary to observe unity of action, place, and time; that no one doubts," says Corneille in the first *Discourse* (*De l'utilité et des parties du poème dramatique*). Why? Because "A dramatic poem is an imitation, or rather, a portrait of human action; and it is beyond question that portraits are more excellent as they better resemble the original" (trans. Clara W. Crane; in Gilbert, pp. 575, 578). In his Dedicatory Epistle to *La Suivante* (1634), written much earlier, he says, "I love to follow the rules, but far from being their slave, I enlarge them or narrow them down according to the demands of my subject," and even "break without scruple" for the sake of beauty (trans. Crane; Gilbert, p. 575). The fascination with space and time as basic dramatic principles no doubt owed something to the fact that intervals of space and time can be defined quantitatively (we can, in Descartes' terms, have clear and distinct ideas of them). However, a general rule like "unity of place" is vague, and could be made flexible when the playwright found that a narrow interpretation would force him to leave out something necessary for the "unity of action." Thus Corneille, in his third *Discourse*, on the Unities, confesses that he succeeded in bringing only three of his plays under the space rule, if rigorously interpreted, but defends himself on a somewhat querulous note:

It is easy for critics to be severe; but if they were to give ten or a dozen plays to the public, they might perhaps slacken the rules more than I do, as soon as they have recognized through experience what constraint their precision brings about and how many beautiful things it banishes from our stage [trans. Elledge and Schier, p. 131].

Few had the temerity to speak out so boldly as Molière did through the mouth of Dorante, in his play *The Critique of the School for Wives*:

If plays written in accordance with the rules do not please, whereas those which please are not in accordance with the rules, then it necessarily follows that the rules were badly made. Let us therefore disregard this quibbling whereby public taste is restricted, and let us consider in a comedy merely the effect it has upon us [*La critique de l'école des femmes* (1663), vi].

Most of the theorists were united on the a priori approach. "Every art has certain rules which by infallible means lead to the ends proposed," says George de Scudéry (in his Preface to *Ibrahim* [1641]; trans. Crane; in Gilbert, p. 580). "I know that there are certain eternal rules, grounded upon good sense, built upon firm and solid reason, that will always last," says Charles de St.-Évremond (essay on tragedy [1672]; trans. Olga M. Perizweig; in Gilbert, p. 665)—but he adds, "yet there are but few that bear this character." When faced with an apparent conflict between experience and the rules (as in a dull play that followed the rules, or a moving one that did not), the theorists were apt to argue either that a play that "pleases" must really follow the rules, when they are conveniently reinterpreted, or that no one ought to be pleased by it.

But of course a purely a priori approach to the problem of critical standards was not quite realizable, and the arguments by which even the most rigidly classical critical judgments were supported were bound to contain some empirical premises. As for the major premise, that poetry is an imitation of human action, its logical status was not firmly fixed by most of the rather unphilosophical theorists who took it as basic. The nearest that critical theory could be brought to a Cartesian system is perhaps indicated in some passages of Dryden. For if the formula "poetry is imitation" can be taken as a *definition* of poetry, and in that sense independent of experience, then some principles of metacriticism, if not of criticism, might actually be demonstrated. In his *Defense of an Essay of Dramatic Poesy* (1668), Dryden reaffirms his definition of a play as "a just and lively image of human nature, &c," and adds: "for the direct and immediate consequence is this; if Nature is to be imitated, then there is a rule for imitating Nature rightly; otherwise there may be an end, and no means conducing to it" (*Essays*, ed. Ker, 1926, I, 123; cf. John Dennis, *The Grounds of Criticism in Poetry*, 1704, ch. 2).

It is clear that Dryden thought it demonstrable that there are *some* general rules defining standards of criticism; he is quite explicit that "taste" alone, the uncritical response of liking or disliking, cannot be all there is to criticism.

> The liking or disliking of the people gives the play the denomination of good or bad, but does not really make or constitute it such. To please the people ought to be the poet's aim, because plays are made for their delight; but it does not follow that they are always pleased with good plays, or that the plays which please them are always good [ibid., I, 120–21].

Dryden adds—and this is one of the points of his originality—that though it is certain that there are rules, the rules themselves are only *probable* (I, 123), for in the end they rest upon experience, however analyzed, co-ordinated, and refined. It is in this spirit that Johnson later rejected the unities of space and time—they "arise evidently from false assumptions" about the dramatic experience—though he considered unity of action "essential to the fable" (*Preface to Shakespeare*).

Another part of this story, which cannot be told here, is of course the celebrated quarrel between the "ancients" and the "moderns," or rather between their seventeenth century partisans. The widely-held view that the rules of art are best studied in the classical writers, because they provide the greatest models, implied the conclusion that in poetry (and no doubt the other arts, if we knew more about them) progress does not occur, or cannot be counted on. And this conviction, in contrast with the emerging intellectual optimism of the Baconian scientists, who were convinced that human knowledge becomes progressively greater, helped to bring about the separation, now so familiar to our thinking, of the arts from the sciences. Yet, at the same time, the view that the rules do not depend merely on authority (as seemed to have been so often taken for granted in the sixteenth century), but can be rationally justified, when this view combines with the recognition that empirical knowledge will be required for some of the premises of that justification, leads in turn (as we shall see in the following chapter) to the conclusion that a kind of progress can occur in the arts, after all, since not all the possibilities of excellence have been explored.

THEORY OF PAINTING AND MUSIC

Despite La Fontaine's reminder that "Eyes are not ears," that "Words and colors are not alike," the prevailing theory of painting and music in the Enlightenment paralleled closely the theory of poetry. Every applicable principle of Horace and Aristotle was seized upon to make painting a serious and intellectual art, comparable to tragedy and epic, even when liberated from its earlier subservience to a religious end. The function of painting, the theorists held, is (in the Horatian formula) to please by teaching, or to teach by pleasing. Nature is the object, and the painting is an imitation of Nature. As Charles Du Fresnoy says in his *De arte graphica* (translated into French by Roger de Piles and first published 1668; translated by Dryden, 1695),

> The principal and most important part of Painting, is to find out, and thoroughly to understand what Nature has made most Beautiful, and most proper to this Art; and that a Choice of it may be made according to the Taste and Manner of the Ancients [Precept I, trans. Dryden; in E. G. Holt, p. 396].

In the late fifteenth and early sixteenth century, as we saw, the painter had been admonished to imitate Nature, but in a realistic way, with attention to the sensuous show of things. Gradually this view was supplanted by another one, which became dominant in the seventeenth century, and reached its peak of emphasis in the French Academy: what may be called the theory of "ideal imitation," where "ideal" combines in varying proportions the essential, characteristic, and admirable. (The theory of realistic imitation and of ideal imitation are sometimes found cheek by jowl in the same writer.)

Ideal imitation meant, as it did in literary theory, the representation of the general rather than the individual. A vivid illustration of this concept is provided in the report left to us by Guillet de Saint Georges of the discussion in the French Royal Academy of Painting and Sculpture, on January 7, 1668, after the lecture by Philippe de Champaigne on Poussin's painting *Rebecca and Eleazer*. Champaigne remarked "that it seemed to him that M. Poussin had not handled the subject of the picture with complete truth to history, for he had omitted the camels which the Scripture mentions" (trans. E. G. Holt, p. 391). The reasons given for and against this criticism in the ensuing debate were remarkable in several respects. For example, "the Academy argued . . . whether a painter could remove from the principal subject of his picture the bizarre and embarrassing circumstances with which history or legend had endowed it" (p. 394), and something of a consensus in the affirmative seems to have been reached. "Not what Alcibiades did and suffered," said Aristotle; no more than the poet need the painter "number the streaks of the tulip."

The basic ideas of neoclassical theory in the fine arts were set forth in definitive form, with clarity and grace and judicious qualification, by Sir Joshua Reynolds, in his *Discourses on Art* (delivered at the English Royal Academy from 1769 to 1790; the first seven published in 1778). In these lectures to students and friends of the Academy (and especially in the third *Discourse*), Reynolds reflected on the nature and function of painting, and the problems of the painter and the teacher. One of his recurrent themes is the role of reason in art: to what extent can the art of painting be verbally taught; what is the place of rules in the training of the painter and in the judgment of his work? "REASON, without doubt, must ultimately determine every thing; at this minute it is required to inform us when that very reason is to give way to feeling" (XIII; Wark ed., p. 231). If painting is an art at all, it must have principles; but what can be the nature of principles in such a field as this?

Reynolds defines the aim of painting in this way:

> THE ART which we profess has beauty for its object; this it is our business to discover and to express; but the beauty of which we are in quest is general and intellectual: it is an idea that subsists only in the mind; the sight never beheld it, nor has the hand expressed it: it is an idea residing in the breast of the artist, which he is always laboring to impart, and which he dies at last without imparting; but which he is yet so far able to communicate, as to raise the thoughts, and extend the views of the spectator [IX, p. 171].

This sounds a little as though Reynolds were poised between the Neoplatonic transcendentalism of the Renaissance and the Romantic view of the tragic artist. But he does not strictly belong to either school, for his main emphasis is on the "just representation of general Nature." "For perfect beauty in any species must combine all the characters which are beautiful in that species" (III, p. 47): the reason that "sight never beheld" beauty is not that it is so remote; it is just that no actual individual can possess (in the way a painter can make one possess) all the important and characteristic beauties of which its species is capable. So the beauty of a man, or of a child, or of a virgin, is something that the painter must construct, or reconstruct, himself—but from the materials of his observation, including (of course) the works of the ancients (see III, p. 49, and *passim*).

ALL the objects which are exhibited to our view by nature, upon close examination will be found to have their blemishes and defects. The most beautiful forms have something about them like weakness, minuteness, or imperfection. . . [The painter's] eye being enabled to distinguish the accidental deficiencies, excrescences, and deformities of things, from their general figures, he makes out an abstract idea of their forms more perfect than any one original [III, p. 44].

In this fashion "he, like the philosopher [i.e., the natural philosopher, such as a botanist] will consider nature in the abstract, and represent in every one of his figures the character of its species" (III, p. 50)—he will paint "the general forms of things" (III, p. 52; cf. Johnson, *Idler*, Nos. 79, 82, written by Reynolds). For example, Bernini is to be reproved because in his statue of David, "he has made him biting his under-lip. This expression is far from general, and still farther from being dignified" (IV, p. 61). And again, the historical painter does not "debase his conceptions with minute attention to the discriminations of Drapery. . . . With him, the cloathing is neither woolen, nor linen, nor silk, sattin, or velvet: it is drapery; it is nothing more" (IV, p. 62). This is almost a parody of Locke's famous example of an "abstract idea" (*Essay Concerning Human Understanding*, IV, vii, 9).

Reynolds' discussion of the place of rules in art honestly reflects his awareness of the difficulty of the problem. On the one hand, there must be rules, because there must be general laws that would, if we only knew them, explain the effects of painting. "Every object which pleases must give pleasure upon some certain principles" (III, p. 46); "it cannot be by chance, that excellencies are produced with any constancy or any certainty," so that "even works of Genius, like every other effect, as they must have their cause, must likewise have their rules" (VI, pp. 97–98). But

"GENIUS is supposed to be a power of producing excellencies, which are out of the reach of the rules of art; a power which no precepts can teach, and which no industry can acquire" (VI, p. 96; cf. *Idler*, No. 76, written by Reynolds). "Could we teach taste or genius by rules, they would be no longer taste and genius" (III, p. 44). How can these ideas be reconciled? Perhaps genius "begins, not where rules, abstractedly taken, end; but where known vulgar and trite rules have no longer any place" (VI, p. 97). And perhaps the real rules are more subtle than is usually thought. "As the objects of pleasure are almost infinite, so their principles vary without end" (III, p. 46). "There are many beauties in our art, that seem, at first, to lie without the reach of precept, and yet may easily be reduced to practical principles" (III, p. 44). But there are no doubt many others that, so to speak, depend on so many variables, or involve such subtle discriminations, that they cannot well be formulated in words. "Unsubstantial, however, as these rules may seem, and difficult as it may be to convey them in writing, they are still seen and felt in the mind of the artist" (VI, p. 98; see also p. 162).

It was not only Descartes' epistemology that played a decisive role in neoclassical theory of painting. In the early days of French Academicism a certain part of his metaphysics found important application also. If painting, like poetry, is taken as the imitation of human beings in action, historical painting becomes the archetypal genre, and the essential problem of representation is to make the bodily motions that the painter can alone depict express the states of mind and soul that are the real subject of the art. Unlike the poet, the painter cannot say that Achilles is sulking or that Pharaoh's daughter is delighted by the baby in the bulrushes; he must show these things. This is what is called "expression" in seventeenth-century theory, for example in the leading textbook of Charles Le Brun, co-founder in 1648 of the French Royal Academy: his *Méthode pour apprendre à dessiner les passions proposée dans une conference sur l'expression générale et particulière* (1698), a synthesis of his very influential teachings over the years. Whatever may be done to formulate principles for the combining of colors, for composition, and for the depiction of objects, the art of painting will not be regularized, that is, rendered subject to rule, unless there is a method of managing expression. This method was found in Descartes' treatise on the *Passions of the Soul* (*Traité des passions de l'âme*, 1649).

The passions of the soul are defined by Descartes as "the perceptions, feelings, or emotions of the soul which we relate specially to it, and which are caused, maintained, and fortified by some movement of the spirits" (I, xxvii; trans. Haldane and Ross, op. cit.). In this treatise he attempted to give systematic definitions, rational analyses, of the emotions—of love, hate, wonder, veneration, cowardice, and so on. And he went on to analyze their physiological manifestations, "How joy causes us to flush" (II, cxv), "How sadness causes paleness" (II, cxvi), "Of tremors" (II, cxviii) and "Of swooning" (II, cxxii). Quintilian, in his *Institutes of Oratory* (XI, iii), had given examples of external behavior by which the effects are exhibited, and through which they might be depicted, and the seventeenth-century painters read him with care. But Descartes provided a theory of expression: an account of how light coming from the object (the Crucifixion, for example) would strike the sense organs, arousing the ever-restless "animal spirits," which in turn can activate (1) the emotions of the soul (pity), through the pineal gland, and at the same time (2) the movements of the body that constitute the expression of this emotion (weeping, or paleness, a drawn face, a drooping mouth, a bent head). Thus he allowed a threefold correlation between the external event, the psychological state, and the physical movement or gesture (II, xxxv, xxxvi, xxxviii). But he also explained how there might be a one-many relation, in that the same external cause might excite varying emotions in people of varying sorts—the men standing about the Crucifixion showing, variously, pity, anger, wonder, fear, curiosity (II, xxxix).

The Academicians were often indefatigable in distinguishing and classifying the details of physiological expression for the sake of the fledgling painter:

But behind the categorical exactitude with which they formulated the visible manifestations of these invisible states of the soul lay not only the rational thoroughness of the Cartesian method, but also the central concept of the Cartesian physics that the whole universe and every individual body is a machine, and all movement, in consequence, mechanical. Hence the exhaustively precise nature of Le Brun's anatomy of the passions which treats the body as a complex instrument that records with mechanical exactitude the invariable effects of emotional stimuli rather than as the vehicle of a humanly significant emotional life.[2]

It is tempting to draw general lessons from this little chapter in the history of art theory—for example, concerning the effects of too narrow a psychology (for that was the operative part of Descartes' theory) upon painting. But the cultural and social conditions were somewhat special. And two ideas of some lasting consequence emerged out of even this low ebb of Academicism. First, there was the lively confidence, which even the silliness of extreme expression theory could not make futile, that general principles to explain the goodness and badness of painting might be found. This confidence, we have seen, was still felt by Reynolds. And second, there was the more specific theory (taken over from the Renaissance theorists, but given a new Cartesian justification) about the unity of the dramatic content of the painting itself: the principle of the appropriateness of the gestures to the situation, and the unification of diverse gestures in terms of the central emotional object.

In a sense, a certain degree of rationalism had been, from the time of Pythagoras, at the heart of music theory, because of the known connection between mathematics and consonance. But the practical musicians of late medieval times were not much troubled by these highly abstract considerations, and made their discoveries about melody and harmony on largely empirical grounds. In the Renaissance, partly because of the influence of Neoplatonic ideas, there was a greater attempt to legislate practice on theoretical grounds. Zarlino, for instance, in his *Harmonic Institutions* of 1558, had made mathematical proportion the basis of his whole theory of composition. His approach was somewhat numerological, since he felt that a priori justifications were required for the use of harmonic relations based on a given proportion—e.g., the minor third, based on 6/5, is acceptable because six is a perfect number, being equal to both the sum and the product of its divisors ($1 \times 2 \times 3$). In the later sixteenth and early seventeenth centuries, when theoretical issues were forced into the open by the daring experiments of actual composers, a new

[2] Rennselaer W. Lee, "*Ut pictura poesis*: The Humanistic Theory of Painting," *Art Bulletin* XXII (1940): 221–22.

conflict between empirical and rational bases of musical theory emerged.

Music theory during this period was concerned with several problems, including that of consonance and dissonance: which harmonic intervals are permissible in music? Some would obviously reply: do what sounds right. Others were far from satisfied by this simple appeal to experience. Just as Galileo Galilei, in his first investigation into the laws of dynamics, felt that these laws should not only correspond to experience but should also be derivable from self-evident principles—a view that came to be embodied in Descartes' physics—so music theorists believed that the laws of harmony should be deduced as well as induced. It is interesting to observe some of the positions in this controversy. Galileo's father, Vincenzo Galilei, in his *Dialogue Concerning Ancient and Modern Music* (1581), was inclined toward empiricism: if the question is raised whether parallel fifths are to be admitted in a particular composition, let the ear be the judge. Descartes, in the letters he wrote to Mersenne, in 1629–30, defended a distinction between (1) mathematical simplicity, or theoretical concordance, and (2) pleasantness of actual sound— and he argued that these might not necessarily coincide. But he thought that the ultimate decision ought to be based on *"demonstrations très assurées"* (see *Oeuvres*, I [1897], pp. 227–28).

Leibniz's few remarks on the subject of harmony, fascinating as they are in themselves, may also reflect an interest in reconciling the parties to this issue, though he did not say enough for us to be sure. Taking advantage of his metaphysical theory that most of each monad's, or soul's, perceptions are *petites perceptions*, below the threshold of consciousness, he suggested, in his essay on "The Principles of Nature and of Grace," that

even sensuous pleasures are really confusedly known intellectual pleasures. Music charms us, although its beauty only consists in the harmonies of numbers and in the reckoning of the beats or vibrations of sounding bodies, which meet at certain intervals, reckonings of which we are not conscious and which the soul nevertheless does make. The pleasures which sight finds in proportions are of the same nature; and those caused by the other senses amount to almost the same thing, although we may not be able to explain it so distinctly.[3]

[3] "Principles of Nature and of Grace" (1714), §17, trans. George Martin Duncan, *The Philosophical Works of Leibniz* (New Haven, 1908), pp. 306–7.

That is, the soul, listening to music, unconsciously counts the beats of the tones, compares their mathematical ratios, and finds them acceptable because the ratios are simple; and what is actually an appreciation of mathematical relationships—a "secret arithmetic [*un Arithmétique occulte*]"[4]—appears, on the confused conscious level, as sensuous enjoyment. The aesthetic enjoyment of painting is no doubt explainable in the same way, says Leibniz —and even the pleasure of taste and smell, though the mathematical theory is yet lacking, so that "we may not be able to explain it so distinctly."

With the help of Descartes' theory of the emotions, the earlier Renaissance speculations about the emotional effects of music were developed into a full-fledged "Affect Theory" (*Affectenlehre*) in the seventeenth century. A number of music theorists contributed to this development, which also had an influence upon musical practice. A good example of their thinking is to be found in *Der vollkommene Capellmeister* (1739) of Johann Mattheson. Basing his approach explicitly upon Descartes, Mattheson undertakes a detailed analysis of the effective resources of music —that is, the capacity of music to arouse specific emotions. The elementary emotions are easy to correlate with music: for example, since joy is an expansion of the vital spirits, "it follows sensibly and naturally that this affect is best expressed by large and expanded intervals" (I, iii, 56; trans. Lenneberg, *Jour Mus Theory* II, 52). The opposite is true for sadness. Complex emotions are to be analyzed into their constituents, for which musical correlatives are available. Thus:

76. Music, like poetry, occupies itself a great deal with jealousy. Since this state of emotion is a combination of seven passions, namely, mistrust, desire, revenge, sadness, fear, and shame, which go along with the main emotion, burning love, one can easily see why it gives rise to so many kinds of musical invention. All of these, in accordance with nature, must aim at restlessness, vexation, anger, and mournfulness [II, 55].

Mattheson also analyzes the affective character of various musical genres—the minuet, gavotte, bourrée, etc. (II, xiii)—of rhythms (II, vi), and even "musical punctuation" (II, ix). (The specific feelings of keys are treated in an earlier work.)

4 "Remarks on an Extract from Bayle's Dictionary" (1703), in C. J. Gerhardt, ed., *Philosophischen Schriften*, 7 vols. (Berlin, 1880), IV, 550.

As in the theory of painting, music theory, in the early eighteenth century, tended to insist on rigorous rules. This may be seen, for example, in the *Gradus ad Parnassum* (1725) of Johann Joseph Fux, who in the first exercise of the first lesson of Book II points out "that the legislators of any art have ordained nothing needless or not founded on reason" (trans. Alfred Mann, in Strunk, p. 541). But the greatest Cartesian in music theory was undoubtedly Jean-Philippe Rameau, who made the most extensive attempt to apply scientific method to the solution of musical problems, in his *Traité de l'harmonie réduite à ses principes naturels* (1722). The insistence on reason as the warrant of any acceptable theory is here very strong:

> Music is a science which ought to have certain rules; these rules ought to be derived from a self-evident principle; and this principle can scarcely be known to us without the help of mathematics [Preface, trans. Strunk, p. 566].

Experience may be admitted as confirmation and illustration of the principles (see e.g., Book II, ch. 18, Article 1), but "the consequences we derive from it are often false, or leave us at least with a certain doubt that only reason can dispel" (Strunk, p. 565). That doubt seems to be a Cartesian doubt—the kind that can only be dispelled by theorems rigorously deduced from self-evident truths.

TOWARD A UNIFIED AESTHETICS

Though, as we have seen, the Cartesian standards of truth can be extended, mutatis mutandis, over the work of artist and critic, that does not make a complete Cartesian aesthetics. Neither Descartes nor his two great successors, Leibniz and Spinoza, were drawn to aesthetic problems, though they contributed enormously to progress in other branches of philosophy. The implications of Descartes' philosophy in the field of art (or one possible set of implications) were first worked out by Alexander Gottlieb Baumgarten, who coined the term "aesthetics" for a special branch of study, in his *Reflections on Poetry* (*Meditationes philosophicae de nonnullis ad poema pertinentibus*, 1735). In this work, and in his unfinished *Aesthetica* (1750, 1758), Baumgarten attempted an aesthetic theory (chiefly of poetry, but extensible to the other arts) based upon Cartesian principles and using the rationalist deductive method, with formal definitions and derivations. The object of logic, he said, is to investigate the kind of perfection proper to thought, in other words to analyze the faculty of knowledge; the object of aesthetics (exactly coordinate with logic) is to investigate the kind of perfection proper to perception, which is a lower level of cognition but autonomous and possessed of its own laws (*Reflections*, §§ 115–116). Aesthetics is "the science of sensory cognition" (*scientia cognitionis sensitivae*; *Aesthetica*, § 1).

From the Cartesian point of view, a science of perception is paradoxical: for perception is just what does not submit to exact and systematic treatment. As we have seen, many philosophers had held that the arts give us some kind of truth, but they did not have Descartes' idea of truth; they did not judge it by the criteria of clearness and distinctness, of mathematical rigor, which he proposed (*Meditations*, 1641, Part III). And these criteria make it hard to understand how poetry, for example, can have anything worthy of being called truth, just as they make it hard to understand how we could hope for anything in the way of exact truth about poetry. It was Baumgarten's purpose to provide this understanding.

Though Descartes' formula, "clear and distinct ideas," is often repeated like a single idiom, he actually meant two different things by these terms. In the *Principles of Philosophy* (1644, Part I, xlv–xlvi), Descartes says, "I term that clear which is present and apparent to an attentive mind. . . But the distinct is that which is so precise and different from all other objects that it contains within itself nothing but what is clear."[5] Thus a sharp pain, though clear, is not distinct, since the feeling itself is confused with the judgment that it has a bodily cause. Leibniz took over these terms, and in his *Discourse on Metaphysics* (1686) gave them an expanded definition:

When I am able to recognize a thing among others, without being able to say in what its differences or characteristics consist, the knowledge is confused. Sometimes indeed we may know clearly, that is without being in the slightest doubt, that a poem or a picture is well or badly done because there is in it an "I know not what" [*je ne sais quoi*] which satisfies or shocks us. Such knowledge is not yet distinct. It is when I am

[5] Trans. Haldane and Ross, Vol. I, p. 237.

able to explain the peculiarities which a thing has, that the knowledge is called distinct. Such is the knowledge of an assayer who discerns the true gold from the false by means of certain proofs or marks which make up the definition of gold.[6]

In short, ideas may be clear or unclear (obscure), and clear ideas may be either distinct or confused. Distinct ideas are abstract thoughts, mathematical and philosophical; confused ideas are sensations: colors, sounds, smells. For they are the blurred blending of our infinite percepts, which at any instant correspond to the percepts of all the infinite other monads in preëstablished harmony with us. Sense perceptions are like the roar of the sea, which is really a mass of little sounds, some of them even below the threshold of hearing.[7] Thus, in its own way each sensation has a hidden formal structure, like every other perspective upon the universe, and, as a unification of complex diversity, is like a miniature work of art.

A *discourse (oratio)*, says Baumgarten (§ 1) is "a series of words which designate connected representations" (trans. Aschenbrenner and Holther, p. 37), and a *sensate discourse* (§§ 3, 4) is a discourse involving representations, or ideas, which are sensuous, i.e., confused. "By *perfect sensate discourse* we mean discourse whose various parts are directed toward the apprehension of sensate representations" (§ 7; p. 39). "By *poem* we mean a perfect sensate discourse, by *poetics* the body of rules to which a poem conforms, by *philosophical poetics* the science of poetics, by *poetry* the state of composing a poem, and by *poet* the man who enjoys that state" (§ 9; p. 39). Finally: "By *poetic* we shall mean whatever can contribute to the perfection of a poem" (§ 11; p. 40).

Evidently Baumgarten is making the most determined effort

___

[6] *Discourse on Metaphysics,* xxiv, op. cit., p. 43; cf. "Thoughts on Knowledge, Truth, and Ideas" (1684). Leibniz's *"je ne sais quoi"* became a familiar phrase in the later debates over the nature of taste. Thus, for example, Berkeley, in the third dialogue of *Alciphron* (1752), where he is attacking Shaftesbury, connects it with the theory of the "moral sense" (*Works,* ed. Luce and Jessop, 9 vols. [London, 1948–57], III, 120)—he goes on to make Alciphron concede that beauty consists in "symmetry or proportion pleasing to the eye" (III, 123), and argues that it cannot therefore be perceived by sight alone, and "is an object, not of the eye, but of the mind" (III, 124).

[7] *Discourse,* xxxiii. Cf. Leibniz's Preface to his *New Essays on Human Understanding,* trans. A. G. Langley (Chicago, 1916), p. 47.

thus far made to distinguish between two fundamentally different types of discourse: the clear and distinct, or abstract, discourse of science, and the confused, though more or less clear, discourse of poetry, which exists to render and realize sense experience. We must say "more or less clear," because this is where the task of poetic theory comes in. Good poetry is clear, but poor poetry is obscure.

In obscure representations there are not contained as many representations of characteristic traits as would suffice for recognizing them and for distinguishing them from others, and as, in fact, are contained in clear representations (by definition). Therefore, more elements will contribute to the communication of sensate representations if these are clear than if they are obscure. A poem, therefore, whose representations are clear is more perfect than one whose representations are obscure, and clear representations are more poetic than obscure ones [§13; p. 41].

Degree of clarity in an idea is "intensive clarity"; Baumgarten also introduces a concept of "extensive clarity": an idea that contains more ideas within it, so long as they are clear (though confused), is extensively clearer (§ 16). Given these basic principles, he proceeds, with admirable terseness, to show how various lower-order rules, concerning diction, meter, plot, theme, etc., can be derived; they specify the poetic devices that increase extensive clarity, which determines poetic goodness (§ 41).

Baumgarten's philosophically refined and sophisticated concept of "sensate discourse," for all the questions that can be raised about it, deserves to be regarded as a forward step toward a fundamental aesthetic theory. It is a technical version of the reigning theory of art as imitation, but a version that takes this theory out of its cruder form. Once poetry and painting came to be widely regarded as "sister arts," as they were often called in the seventeenth century (see, for example, the opening of Du Fresnoy's *De Arte Graphica*), and this conjunction supported by the catch phrase taken out of context from Horace (*ut pictura poesis*), it was natural enough to inquire whether the principles of both arts could not be derived from the same fundamental principles. Aristotle had called them both "imitations" in his *Poetics*. The Renaissance theories of musical imitation, still flourishing in the Baroque era, suggested that music is basically the same. Hence there grew up a very widespread attitude, expressed so well and perhaps even unconsciously caricatured in the book by the Abbé Charles Batteux, *Les beaux arts réduits à un même principe* (1746), where the "single principle" to which all the fine arts are to be "reduced" is the principle that art is the imitation of "beautiful nature." Batteux included poetry, painting, music, sculpture and dance, and was perhaps the first to define the "beaux arts" as a special category. Parts of his system, much improved, became part of the conceptual scheme underlying the great *Encyclopédie ou dictionnaire raisonée des sciences, des arts, et des métiers* (1751), as explained by D'Alembert in the *Discours préliminaire*.

This monistic view of the arts was being questioned, even while it was dominant, and even by those who accepted its basic premise that, in some sense or other, all the arts belong together as imitations. Before a more profound and adequate unifying theory could be achieved, not only the similarities of the arts, but also their differences—the special powers and potentialities of each medium—needed to be explored. For example, the Abbé Jean Baptiste Dubos, a thoroughgoing imitationist, noted, in his *Réflexions critiques sur la poésie et la peinture* (1719), that painting can ·imitate an object only at a single moment, while poetry can describe a process. Similar points were made by James Harris, in his *Three Treatises, the First Concerning Art, the Second Concerning Music, Painting, and Poetry, the Third Concerning Happiness* (1744). Moses Mendelssohn, in *Über die Quellen und die Verbindungen der schöne Kunste und Wissenschaften* (1757), developed a distinction, already suggested by others, between natural and conventional symbols, on which important differences between the visual and the literary arts could depend.

These tendencies of thought reached a kind of consummation in the little book by Gotthold Ephraim Lessing, *Laokoon, oder über die Grenzen der Malerei und Poesie* (1766), a book whose clarity and vigor had a profound impact upon later eighteenth-century thinking about the arts. Essentially, Lessing called attention to the distinctiveness of the medium in each art, or, as he put it, the "signs" (*Zeichen*) it uses for imitation. He did not question that the arts exist to imitate, but he asked, for the first time with such directness and explicitness, what a given art *can* imitate, and what it can imitate most successfully.[8]

But I will try to prove my conclusions by starting from first principles.

I argue thus. If it be true that painting employs wholly different signs or means of imitation from poetry,—the one using forms and colors in space, the other articulate sounds in time,—and if signs must unquestionably stand in convenient relation with the thing signified, then signs arranged side by side can represent only objects existing side by side, or whose parts so exist, while consecutive signs can express only objects which succeed each other, or whose parts succeed each other, in time.

Objects which exist side by side, or whose parts so exist, are called bodies. Consequently bodies with their visible properties are the peculiar subjects of painting.

Objects which succeed each other, or whose parts succeed each other in time, are actions. Consequently actions are the peculiar subjects of poetry.

All bodies, however, exist not only in space, but also in time. They continue, and, at any moment of their continuance, may assume a different appearance and stand in different relations. Every one of these momentary appearances and groupings was the result of a preceding, may become the cause of a following, and is therefore the center of a present, action. Consequently painting can imitate actions also, but only as they are suggested through forms.

Actions, on the other hand, cannot exist independently, but must always be joined to certain agents. In so far as those agents are bodies or are regarded as such, poetry describes also bodies, but only indirectly through actions.

Painting, in its coexistent compositions, can use but a single moment of an action, and must therefore choose the most pregnant one, the one most suggestive of what has gone before and what is to follow.

Poetry, in its progressive imitations, can use but a single attribute of bodies, and must choose that one which gives the most vivid picture of the body as exercised in this particular action. . . .

I should place less confidence in this dry chain of conclusions, did I

[8] An interesting anticipation of Lessing's position is found in Diderot's *Lettre sur les Sourds et Muets* (1751): "I have remarked that each art of imitation had its hieroglyphic, and that it is much to be wished that some informed and discriminating writer would undertake to compare them" (*Oeuvres Complètes*, 20 vols. [Paris, 1875–77], I, 391; see pp. 385–92 for Diderot's reply to Batteux, including an interesting comparative analysis of the ways in which the subject of a dying woman might be represented by poet, painter, and composer).

not find them fully confirmed by Homer, or, rather, had they not been first suggested to me by Homer's method [*Laocoon*, xvi, trans. Ellen Frothingham, pp. 91–92].

Lessing's method of argument, and his central principles, are revealed in these paragraphs. He believes painting best equipped to render "beautiful shapes in beautiful attitudes," and, despite his doctrine of the "pregnant moment," does not care to have this human beauty, of proportion and harmony, sacrificed to expressiveness—to violent action and emotion, which, after all, poetry can handle better. And if anyone cites (as a counter-example to his view of what is primary in poetry) the Homeric description of the shield of Achilles, so much admired in antiquity and in the Renaissance, Lessing replies with ingenuity and cogency that Homer succeeds by describing, not the finished shield, but the *process* of creating it, the successive pictures as laid on by the master craftsman (see xviii, p. 114).

Some of Lessing's specific theories of poetry and painting were found open to objection: he had a limited conception of what painting, especially, should be. But to understand his contribution to aesthetics in a true light, we must, I think, note that he set a new standard of clarity and exactness in aesthetic argument, trying to set forth his premises and his reasoning for all to inspect and discuss. And his work was an open invitation to others to be equally scrupulous and plain in asking precisely what poetry and painting, and music and sculpture, are good for, and how they actually work.

The *Laocoon* was the only segment of a projected three-part work that Lessing actually finished. But in some of his notes and letters we can see his thought moving one step further in a direction that is of some special interest in view of twentieth-century aesthetic theories. He distinguishes natural signs from conventional or artificial (*willkürlichen*) signs, and makes this suggestion:

As the power of natural signs consists in their similarity with things, metaphor introduces, instead of such a similarity, which words do not have, another similarity, which the thing referred to has with still another, the concept of which can be renewed more easily and more vividly [trans. René Wellek, *History*, I, 165].

If a painting signifies in virtue of a similarity between its forms
and those of actual objects—if it is, in Charles Peirce's terms, an
"iconic sign"—then the question is whether poetry can be said to
contain iconic signs as well. Words, being conventions, have
no such capacity. But in metaphor, where one object is made to
stand for, or represent, another which it resembles in some way
(as the "walking shadow" and "poor player" in Macbeth's speech
might be called iconic signs of life), poetry also becomes a sort
of natural sign, or comes close to it. Something like this seems
to be Lessing's theory here; and if it is, we have more than the
hint of a system of the arts that would later lift the imitation
theory to a new level of significance.

Bibliography

Émile Krantz, Essai sur l'Esthétique de Descartes (Paris, 1882).
Brewster Rogerson, "The Art of Painting the Passions," Jour
    Hist Ideas XIV (1953): 68–94.
Scott Elledge and Donald Schier, eds., The Continental Model:
    Selected French Critical Essays of the Seventeenth Century
    (Minneapolis, 1960) .
Nicolas Boileau-Despréaux, L'art poétique, trans. Sir William
    Soame and John Dryden, 1683 (Paris, 1952).
Marcel Hervier, L'art poétique de Boileau (Paris, 1949).
Scott Elledge, "The Background and Development in English
    Criticism of the Theories of Generality and Particularity," Pub
    Mod Lang Assoc LXII (1947): 147–82.
A. O. Lovejoy, " 'Nature' as Aesthetic Norm," Mod Lang Notes
    XLII (1927): 444–50.
J. E. Spingarn, ed., Critical Essays of the Seventeenth Century
    (Oxford, 1908).
Hoyt Trowbridge, "The Place of Rules in Dryden's Criticism,"
    Mod Philol XLIV (1946–47): 84–96.
Meyer H. Abrams, The Mirror and the Lamp (Oxford U., 1953),
    chs. 1, 2.

Samuel Hynes, ed. *English Literary Criticism: Restoration and 18th Century* (New York, 1963).

Rensselaer W. Lee, "*Ut pictura poesis*: The Humanistic Theory of Painting," *Art Bulletin* XXII (1940): 197–269.

Lawrence Lipking, "The Shifting Nature of Authority in Versions of *De arte graphica*," *Jour Aesth and Art Crit* XXIII (Summer 1965): 487–504.

Rémy G. Saisselin, "*Ut pictura poesis*: DuBos to Diderot," *Jour Aesth and Art Crit* XX (Winter 1961): 145–56.

James S. Ackerman, "Science and Visual Art," in H. H. Rhys, ed., *Seventeenth Century Science and the Arts* (Princeton U., 1961).

Sir Joshua Reynolds, *Discourses on Art*, ed. Robert R. Wark (San Marino: Huntington Library, 1959).

Walter J. Hipple, Jr., "General and Particular in the *Discourses* of Sir Joshua Reynolds: A Study in Method," *Jour Aesth and Art Crit* XI (March 1953): 231–47.

Michael Macklem, "Reynolds and the Ambiguities of Neo-classical Criticism," *Philol Quart* XXXI (1952): 383–98.

Frances B. Blanshard, *Retreat from Likeness in the Theory of Painting*, 2d. ed. (Columbia U. 1949), chs. 1, 2.

André Fontaine, *Les Doctrines d'Art en France* (Paris, 1909).

Louis Hourticq, *De Poussin à Watteau* (Paris, 1921).

Samuel H. Monk, *The Sublime: a Study of Critical Theories in XVIII-Century England*, rev. ed. (Michigan U., 1960), ch. 9.

Frank P. Chambers, *The History of Taste* (Columbia U., 1932), chs. 3–5.

Claude V. Palisca, "Scientific Empiricism in Musical Thought," in H. H. Rhys, ed., *Seventeenth Century Science and the Arts* (Princeton U., 1961).

Glen Haydon, "On the Problem of Expression in Baroque Music," *Jour Am Musicological Soc* III (1950): 113–19.

Hans Lenneberg, "Johann Mattheson on Affect and Rhetoric in Music," *Jour Mus Theory* II (1958): 47–84, 193–236.

Gretchen L. Finney, "Ecstasy and Music in Seventeenth-Century England," and " 'Organical Musick' and Ecstasy," *Jour Hist Ideas* VIII (1947): 153–86, 273–92.

Arthur W. Locke, "Descartes and Seventeenth-Century Music," *Musical Quart* XXI (1935): 423–31.

Herbert M. Schueller, "Literature and Music as Sister Arts: An Aspect of Aesthetic Theory in Eighteenth-Century Britain," *Philol Quart* XXVI (1947): 193–205.

Louis I. Bredvold, "The Tendency toward Platonism in Neoclassical Esthetics," *ELH: A Jour of Eng Lit Hist* I (1934): 91–119.

John Hollander, *The Untuning of the Sky: Ideas of Music in English Poetry, 1500–1700* (Princeton U., 1961).

Cicely Davis, "Ut pictura poesis," *Mod Lang Rev* XXX (1935): 159–69.

Karl Aschenbrenner and William B. Holther, trans., *Reflections on Poetry: Alexander Gottlieb Baumgarten's Meditationes Philosophicae* (California U., 1954).

Frederic Will, Jr., "Cognition Through Beauty in Moses Mendelssohn's Early Aesthetics," *Jour Aesth and Art Crit* XIV (Sept. 1955): 97–105.

Gotthold Ephraim Lessing, *Laocoon: An Essay upon the Limits of Painting and Poetry*, trans. Ellen Frothingham (Boston, 1910).

Gotthold Ephraim Lessing, *Laocoön: An Essay on the Limits of Painting and Poetry*, trans. Edward A. McCormick (New York, 1962).

William G. Howard, "Burke among the Forerunners of Lessing," *PMLA* XXII (1907): 608–32.

Irving Babbitt, *The New Laokoon* (Boston and New York, 1910), Part I.

Paul O. Kristeller, "The Modern System of the Arts," *Jour Hist Ideas* XII (1951): 496–527, XIII (1952): 17–46.

Ernst Cassirer, *The Philosophy of the Enlightenment*, trans. Koelln and Pettegrove (Princeton U., 1951), ch. 7.

George Boas, "The Arts in the '*Encyclopédie*,'" *Jour Aesth and Art Crit* XXIII (Fall 1964): 97–107.

EIGHT

The Enlightenment: Empiricism

Valid objections can no doubt be raised against an over-tidy imposition of the rationalism-empiricism dichotomy upon the fluid and complex movements of modern thought. And certainly it is a serious mistake to use this distinction as a kind of spatula for separating two groups of thinkers, since it is tendencies of thought, rather than individuals (who may have divided tendencies) that ought to be marked by these terms. But when we undertake a relatively brief survey of the philosophy of the Enlightenment—and if we put ourselves on guard against too rigid an interpretation of what we are doing—it must be confessed that the terms are quite helpful. In the preceding chapter, I have grouped together a number of ideas that seem to me (as they have seemed to others) closely connected with the Cartesian methodology and theory of knowledge, though few of the thinkers I discussed can be summed up or dismissed by general labels—and their ideas are often worthy of careful consideration quite apart from any affinity for Descartes' philosophy. In the present chapter, I shall discuss together several lines of inquiry opened up by those philosophers whose main contribution to modern philosophy has been the development of an empiricist theory of knowledge. It was, on the whole (though not at all exclusively), the British philosophers who promoted the important thinking that was done during this period on the psychological causes and effects of works of art. I do not mean that they were merely psychologists, of course, for in this period psychological questions and questions of (what was then called) moral philosophy had not yet been separated, or even clearly distinguished. And from their discoveries, or seeming discoveries, about such processes as creative imagination and aesthetic enjoyment, the empiricist aestheticians drew many conclusions of considerable historical—and ᵓme of permanent—significance.

As Descartes, no doubt with some arbitrariness, is often placed at the fountainhead of modern rationalism, so Sir Francis Bacon, with perhaps less solid claim, is generally regarded as the first-mover, or at least the herald and pilot projector of modern empiricism. There is, at least, no question of the impetus he gave to empirical lines of inquiry in all fields of thought.

Neoclassical rationalism and formalism, as we saw it in the preceding chapter, claimed to derive its logical force from the analysis of the essential nature of the arts. And the rationalistic method retained a large a priori, and (in Kant's sense) "dogmatic," element, even though in fact it could not really deduce the rules of correctness and the principles of genres without employing any empirical premises at all. The Baconian tradition, on the other hand, called attention from the start to the need for empirical study of the psychological processes involved in art, and in the seventeenth and eighteenth centuries the British school concentrated its main, and most fruitful, effort on this task.

Part of what was needed was a freeing of the arts from criticism, a kind of Declaration of Independence that would, like many such declarations, be contagious—that would free criticism itself from its own shackles of unexamined, or insufficiently examined, aesthetic theory. For example, we find the British critic, John Dennis, in *A Large Account of the Taste in Poetry* (1702), speaking out in a new way for the poet, and insisting "that for the judging of any sort of Writings, those talents are in some measure requisite, which were necessary to produce them." And George Farquhar, in the same year, argued forcefully that "Aristotle was no poet, and consequently not capable of giving instructions in the art of poetry" (*Discourse upon Comedy*; Elledge, p. 90). Such a principle might have far-reaching implications. As one scholar has remarked,

Criticism was becoming self-conscious and examining the scope, the assumptions and the methods of its own work, and it was from this increase of self-consciousness that the study of aesthetics was born in England.[1]

Close studies of individual works became more usual than hitherto. And the authority of general rules, both of composition and criticism, began to be challenged more firmly. There arose the concept of the poet as "genius," who (in Pope's words) can "snatch a grace beyond the reach of art"—that is, who produces great work by defying the rules. Addison, in his *Spectator*, No. 291 (1712), for example, observes that

the productions of a great genius, with many lapses and inadvertencies, are infinitely preferable to the works of an inferior kind of author, which are scrupulously exact and conformable to all the rules of correct writing.

The authority of the classics—to imitate which is to follow nature, reason, and the rules—was undermined by the same criticism. A hard blow was struck by Edward Young (an admirer and follower of Bacon) in his *Conjectures upon Original Composition* (1759). "A GENIUS differs from a *good* UNDERSTANDING," he said, "as a Magician from a good Architect" (p. 26). One of his main points was that until we cease to imitate the ancients—who were lucky to have no one to imitate—we cannot free ourselves to surpass them. Though not given much attention in England, the *Conjectures* were enthusiastically read in Germany, where many of Young's ideas fitted in well with, and strengthened, some tendencies in German aesthetic theory that we shall come to later.

IMAGINATION AND ARTISTIC CREATION

The concept (or concepts) of the imagination first came into the forefront of thinking in the seventeenth century. It had been, of course, a commonplace that the mind somehow has the capacity to rearrange the materials of its experience, at least within limits set by logical consistency, but seventeenth-century thinkers began to take seriously the possibility that a more exact and searching study of this process might throw light on a number of problems about the arts, particularly literature, and especially the relation between art and other enterprises of civilized man,

[1] R. L. Brett, *The Third Earl of Shaftesbury* (London, 1951), p. 127.

such as science, and religion. If, as the central classical tradition maintained, poetry can teach, as well as delight, one might obtain a clearer notion of just what sort of truth it has to teach (as well as a more solid backing of its claim to truth) and a fuller explanation of its delight, by asking what faculties of the mind it proceeds from, and how these faculties connect with others.

The philosophers of the Cartesian tradition generally were not attracted to this inquiry, because they conceived of imagination as playing a very subordinate role, along with sensation, in the acquisition of genuine knowledge. Giving his definition of "intuition" in the *Regulae* (Rule III), Descartes says emphatically that he does not refer to "the fluctuating testimony of the senses, nor the misleading judgment that proceeds from the blundering constructions of imagination" (trans. Haldane and Ross, p. 7). Later on (Rule XII) he cites "understanding, imagination, sense, and memory" as the "four faculties" of the mind involved in cognition, and allows that the imagination may be of some service to the understanding (p. 35). But in the *Principles of Philosophy* (I, lxxi–lxxiii) the data of the "senses and imagination" are contrasted with the concepts of the primary qualities, which reason can grasp but of which no images can be formed. This distinction is also elaborated at the beginning of the sixth *Meditation*, which asserts that imagination "inasmuch as it differs from the power of understanding, is in no wise a necessary element in my nature, or in my essence" (trans. Haldane and Ross, p. 186). In Descartes, the term "imagination" wavers between two senses: it means the passive image-forming faculty, registering the deliverances of the senses; it also means the semi-active power of recombination. But the distinction is not sharply made, and the latter is not emphasized. In the *Recherche de la Vérité* (1674) of Descartes' successor, Malebranche, all of Book II is devoted to a proof that imagination is the source of manifold illusions and delusions, from which we can be protected only by reining it in severely and keeping reason in control.

A rather different status was assigned to imagination by Bacon (1561–1626). His *Two Books of the Proficience and Advancement of Learning, Divine and Humane* (1605), which afterward he amplified in a Latin version, the *De Dignitate et Augmentis Scientiarum* (1623), constituted his call to the new age, and he undertook not only to review the current state of human knowledge, classifying and systematizing it, but to prophesy what the future held in store if proper methods were applied. The classification at the beginning of Book II was to count heavily with later thinkers:

The parts of human learning have reference to the three parts of Man's Understanding, which is the seat of learning: History to his Memory, Poesy to his Imagination, and Philosophy to his Reason [see *Works*, III, 329].

And further:

POESY is a part of learning in measure of words for the most part restrained, but in all other points extremely licensed, and doth truly refer to the Imagination; which, being not tied to the laws of matter, may at pleasure join that which nature hath severed, and sever that which nature hath joined, and so make unlawful matches and divorces of things [III, 343].

Poetry, says Bacon, is "Feigned History," which exists to "give some shadow of satisfaction to the mind of man in those points wherein the nature of things doth deny it"; it improves upon nature, "by submitting the shews of things to the desires of the mind," in contrast to reason, which "doth buckle and bow the mind unto the nature of things" (I, 343–44). But if the dignity of poetry is properly manifested by its being made coordinate with history and philosophy, that does not make it one with those disciplines, "for imagination hardly produces sciences; poesy (which in the beginning was referred to imagination) being to be accounted rather as a pleasure or play of wit than a science," as Bacon added in the Latin version (IV, 406).

In these few but carefully meditated remarks, Bacon posed a problem for the seventeenth century: What is the imagination, and exactly how does it work to produce poetry (and painting and sculpture)? By separating off the imagination as a special active power in its own right, Bacon opened up a new field of inquiry; but his suggestion that "imagination hardly produces sciences" prophesied that when the imagination was better understood, poetry would turn out to be something rather different from what had long been supposed.

Bacon's challenge may be said to have been taken up by Thomas Hobbes (1588–1679), who devoted the first chapters of his *Leviathan* (1651)—and also sections of other works—to a careful account of imagination (or fancy, as he often calls it) and its relation to sense. The aim of all his work was to establish the lawfulness of human behavior, individual and social—to treat man naturalistically, and on that basis solve pressing problems of religion and government. His theory of the imagination was a part of the general system, and despite his reputation as a dangerous thinker, he did much to advance, as well as to stimulate, scientific psychology.

"There is no conception in a man's mind, which hath not at first, totally, or by parts, been begotten upon the organs of sense," Hobbes tells us (I, i; ed. Molesworth III, 1), thus rejecting all innate or a priori ideas, and giving every idea the character of an image—either a sensible quality, or a group of them. The physiology of sensation consists of motions, whose appearance to us is "fancy" (I, i), or imagination (I, ii). When the physical motions cease, these images, or phantasms, remain: "IMAGINATION therefore is nothing but *decaying sense*" (I, ii; p. 4). Sense does not decay by simply fading away; it is obscured or covered up by later and more vivid images, as the light of the stars is by that of the sun, or "as the voice of a man is in the noise of the day" (p. 5). When the sense is "fading, old, and past, it is called *memory*" (p. 6).

So much may be said of "simple imagination," but there is also "compound imagination,"

as when, from the sight of a man at one time, and of a horse at another, we conceive in our mind a Centaur. So when a man compoundeth the image of his own person with the image of the actions of another man, as when a man imagines himself a Hercules or an Alexander, which happeneth often to them that are much taken with reading of romances, it is a compound imagination, and properly but a fiction of the mind [I, ii; p. 6; cf. *Elements of Philosophy* IV, xxv].

So much had often been noted, but Hobbes faced more directly than others the evident next question: how does this compounding take place? What laws explain why certain combinations (centaurs, for example) occur and not others? Hobbes notes (I, ii) that some philosophers have thought that such novel images arise purely spontaneously, without cause; or that they are inspired by God or devil—but he insists that a naturalistic explanation can be given.

Hobbes sketches his answer in the following chapter, "Of the Consequence or Train of Imaginations" (I, iii), and it is an early version of the association theory;

When a man thinketh on anything whatsoever, his next thought after, is not altogether so casual as it seems to be. . . . But as we have no imagination, whereof we have not formerly had sense, in whole, or in parts; so we have no transition from one imagination to another, whereof we never had the like before in our senses [p. 11].

Because, in sensation, a given image may be followed by a variety of other images on different occasions, the same image becomes capable of giving rise to the same variety in imagination: but it can never give rise to any other image except one that has been associated with it in sensation. Such is Hobbes's account. He goes on to distinguish "unguided" trains of thoughts—free association, a "wild ranging of the mind"—from those that are "regulated" by the dominance of desire or need, as when the desire of an end leads to thoughts about appropriate means (I, iii).

When Hobbes turns a little later (I, viii) to further psychological observations, he makes another distinction that was to pass (via Locke) into wide critical currency. When men compare their images, they may find similarities and differences among them: those who are good at discerning similarities "are said to have a *good wit*; by which, in this occasion, is meant a *good fancy*" (p. 57). Those who are good at detecting differences "are said to have a good Judgment." Both of these capacities are required in composing poems, "But the fancy must be more eminent; because they please for the extravagancy; but ought not to displease by indiscretion" (p. 58). It is fancy that gives rarity of invention, richness of metaphorical adornment. This same point Hobbes had developed in his Answer to Davenant's Preface to *Gondibert* (1650): "Judgment begets the strength and structure, and fancy begets the ornaments of a poem" (IV, 449; cf. the preface to his translation of the *Odyssey*, 1675). The ornamental view of imagination's contribution is to be noted, but it is perhaps given more depth in this statement, also from the Answer:

All that is beautiful or defensible in building; or marvellous in Engines and instruments of motion; whatsoever commodity men receive from the observations of the heavens, from the description of the earth, from the account of time, from walking on the seas; and whatsoever distinguisheth the civility of Europe, from the barbarity of the American savages; is the workmanship of fancy but guided by the precepts of true Philosophy [IV, 449–50]

—where "Philosophy," of course, means empirical science.

It is imagination, according to Hobbes, that primarily gives poetry the power to arouse the passions. Hobbes can find within his general system a justification of poetry in terms of its emotional effects. Each man he sees as a bundle of desires and aversions, or (as we might say now) drives, tied together by that fundamental and incessant urge toward self-preservation which makes life in the state of nature a hell and drives men to political organization. Living is essentially desiring, and satisfying desire by voluntary actions whose motive power and accompaniment is emotion. "To have no desire, is to be dead" (*Leviathan* I, viii; p. 62). Hobbes distinguishes sensual pleasures from "pleasures of the mind," among which one of the greatest is the satisfaction that is afforded by new experience and new knowledge. "Because curiosity is delight, therefore also all novelty is so" (*Elements of Law*, I, ix, 18)—and it is precisely novelty that the compounding imagination exists to give.

In his great, and quietly revolutionary, inventory of the resources and capacities of the human mind, the *Essay Concerning Human Understanding* (1690), John Locke (1632–1704) nowhere discusses the imagination under that name. He does, at one point, in his discussion of memory, say that in the mind's ability to furnish readily the "dormant ideas" of memory "consists that which we call invention, fancy, and quickness of parts" (II, x, 8), but the term "fancy" does not figure much in the work, either. Nevertheless, one of his major aims is to show how the understanding, though its sources are limited to the simple ideas of sensation and reflection, can so operate upon them as to produce all the complex ideas that we have, even those (like infinity and power) that had been regarded by the Rationalists as incapable of being traced to experience. One of the important activities of understanding that is needed to explain our complex ideas is composition: the combining of simple ideas of the same or of diverse sorts (II, xi, 6). "In this faculty of repeating and joining together its ideas, the mind has great power in varying and multiplying the objects of its thoughts, infinitely beyond what sensation or reflection furnished it with" (II, xii, 2). Here, apart from the limits imposed by original experience, the emphasis is on the freedom of the mind to assemble ideas—even inconsistent ideas, so long as the inconsistency is not noted.

If Locke were concerned to work out a theory of artistic creation, it would begin here, with this faculty; we must take note of his words because of what they meant to others. Locke is interested in what he considers to be far more important operations of the understanding, by which it constructs knowledge. Knowledge consists in the comparison of ideas, in the search for genuine connections. For some time, Locke meditated a line of thought that finally took shape in a new chapter, added to the fourth edition (1700), "Of the Association of Ideas" (II, xxxiii). Here he distinguishes between a *"natural* correspondence and connection" that ideas sometimes have with each other, which "it is the office and excellency of our reason to trace," and "another connection of ideas wholly owing to *chance* or *custom."*

Ideas that in themselves are not all of kin, come to be so united in some men's minds, that it is very hard to separate them; they always keep in company, and the one no sooner at any time comes into the understanding, but its associate appears with it; and if they are more than two which are thus united, the whole gang, always inseparable, show themselves together [II, xxxiii, 5].

The examples by which Locke illustrates this association of ideas are in themselves of great interest to the history of psychology, and also of education, for he has a pedagogical intent. Thus, for example, he points out how the "ideas of goblins and sprites," which "have really no more to do with darkness than light," can become associated with darkness in the mind of a child, by the tales of a "foolish maid," so that the child will ever afterward be terrified of the dark (II, xxxiii, 10). Other examples are given, and the lesson is that we must take utmost care to avoid "this wrong connection in our minds of ideas in themselves loose and independent of one another" (9)—for it "is the foundation of the greatest, I had almost said of all the errors in the world" (18; cf. *Of the Conduct of the Understanding,* 1762, § 41). In Locke's view, then, the association of ideas is the source of error, superstition, and prejudice—totally opposed to the kind of orderly process of thinking that may be expected to eventuate in truth. It would be only a step to suggest that these unnatural associations are more characteristic of poetry than of philosophy.

Though Locke does not take this step, he has another train of thought that moves toward the same general conclusion. This begins with his very famous distinction between "wit" and "judgment":

For *wit* lying most in the assemblage of ideas, and putting those together with quickness and variety, wherein can be found any resemblance or congruity, thereby to make up pleasant pictures and agreeable visions in the fancy; *judgment*, on the contrary, lies quite on the other side, in separating carefully, one from another, ideas wherein can be found the least difference, thereby to avoid being misled by similitude, and by affinity to take one thing for another. This is a way of proceeding quite contrary to metaphor and allusion; wherein for the most part lies that entertainment and pleasantry of wit, which strikes so lively on the fancy, and therefore is so acceptable to all people, because its beauty appears at first sight, and there is required no labor of thought to examine what truth or reason there is in it [II, xi, 2].

The difference between this passage and Hobbes goes deeper than the substitution of "wit" for "fancy": here there is a quite un-Hobbesian separation and opposition of the two supposed faculties. It is suggested not only that the same person is not likely to be good at both, but that they lead away from each other, one by an easy and pleasant path to entertainment, the other by a difficult discipline to knowledge.

Moreover, the contrast is explicitly referred to language, as though wit (or fancy) and judgment (or reason) must have different ways of speaking, at least when they are at their best. Not only is fancy a "court-dresser," a flatterer "that studies but to please" (*Conduct of the Understanding*, § 33; cf. §§ 32, 42), but its "figurative speeches and allusion in language" are to be classified among the primary abuses of language. Fancy is no fault when we have pleasure in view, but figures of speech are "perfect cheats" when "we would speak of things as they are" (III, x, 34). Locke here expresses one of the most powerful new ideas about language that the seventeenth century brought forth: that when language is used as a tool in the acquisition and teaching of well-confirmed empirical knowledge, it must meet certain standards of professional plainness, clarity, and precision—and that these standards are radically different from the standards that language must meet when it is used to the fullest advantage in poetry. Hobbes had taken a similar stand briefly (*Leviathan*, I, viii). The definitive statement of this point of view was that of Thomas Sprat, in his *History of the Royal Society* (1667), where he argued for new criteria of style suited to the needs of empirical science. "Who can behold, without indignation, how many mists and uncertainties, these specious *Tropes* and *Figures* have brought on our Knowledg?" (p. 112). The members of the Royal Society, says Sprat, have cultivated "a close, naked, natural way of speaking; positive expressions; clear senses; a native easiness: bringing all things as near the Mathematical plainness as they can" (p. 113). A widespread distrust of the imagination itself, in the latter part of the seventeenth century, went along with this suspicion of its characteristic language. Samuel Parker, in his *Free and Impartial Censure of the Platonick Philosophy* (1666), went so far as to say this:

Now to Discourse of the Natures of Things in Metaphors and Allegories is nothing else but to sport and trifle with empty words, because these Schemes do not express the Natures of Things, but only their Similitudes and Resemblances . . . All those Theories in Philosophy which are expressed only in metaphorical Termes, are not real Truths, but the meer products of Imagination, dress'd up (like Childrens *babies*) in a few spangled empty words. . . . Thus their wanton and luxuriant fancies climbing up into the Bed of Reason, do not only defile it by unchaste and illegitimate Embraces, but instead of real conceptions and notices of Things, impregnate the mind with nothing but Ayerie and Subventaneous Phantasmes [1667 ed., pp. 78–79].

In this kind of logical positivist thinking, launched by Locke, we see emerging the concept of two distinct languages, the metaphorical language of poetry and the literal language of science. But this distinction reflects a deeper conflict over the nature of knowledge itself. The Horatian injunctions, that poetry should please and instruct, now for the first time seem in danger of being split apart: for if the language that serves one of these ends best is destructive of the other, it would seem that they cannot both be done (well, at least) by the same discourse. It will be necessary to specialize. This does not necessarily mean that poetry must be assigned quite so low a role as Locke casually assigns it, and in any case the implications of this distinction would take time to be felt. Poetry would still be widely thought of as a vehicle of knowledge; but it would also be thought of as something that exists to give an experience, a special kind of pleasure, quite apart from any claim to inform or prove.

Meanwhile, the theory of the association of ideas developed into a systematic psychological theory that pervaded the thinking of the eighteenth century (especially in England, but also in France), and in the nineteenth century led to the founding of modern experimental psychology. David Hume (1711–76) undertook in his *Treatise on Human Nature* (1739–40) a Newtonian inquiry into the workings of the human mind, and in his system the propensity of the mind to associate ideas became one of the cardinal principles of explanation (I, i, 4). He distinguished ideas from impressions, the former being the fainter copies of the latter that remain after them, and he asked how certain ideas tend to follow or accompany one another in the mind. His answer consisted in postulating a kind of psychological "attraction," or gravitation of ideas, a "gentle force, which commonly prevails," by which ideas tend to associate according to their resemblance, causal connection, and the spatial and temporal contiguity of their original impressions. In the first edition of his *Enquiry Concerning Human Understanding* (1748; Section 3), Hume illustrated these principles of association in an interesting passage (omitted from later editions) in which he discussed the problem of unity of action in epic and dramatic poetry.[1]

It was David Hartley (1705–57), however, who worked out the elaboration of this psychology, and provided, in his *Observations on Man, His Frame, His Duty, and His Expectations* (1749), what became the definitive associationist psychology until the Mills a century later, though its principles and particular explanations were worked over and added to by many other eighteenth-century thinkers. Hartley simplified Hume's scheme, in certain respects, but he gave associationism its classic form. Association reduces essentially to contiguity, and his law of association predicts that the mere repetition ("a sufficient number of times") of sensations in conjunction will give each of them the power to call to mind the corresponding ideas. In terms of this principle he explained both successive and simultaneous association—

---

[1] For this passage see Antony Flew, ed., *Hume on Human Nature and the Understanding* (New York, 1962), pp. 39–46.

sequences of thoughts as well as compounded ideas, such (he said) as "beauty, honor, moral qualities, etc." Locke (*Essay* II, xii, 5) had also classified beauty as a complex idea, because "consisting of a certain composition of color and figure, causing delight in the beholder," but he had not explained his complex ideas by the associative mechanism.

One interesting modification of pure associationism was suggested by later eighteenth-century thinkers, and ought to be remarked here, even though it did not become highly influential until the coming of Romanticism. This was the theory that emotion also plays an important role in determining the mind's bringing together of associated ideas. Alexander Gerard, for example, in his associationist *Essay on Genius* (1774), pointed out that a strong passion reaches out like a magnet, to draw toward itself all the ideas that might gratify it, or feed it, or that are associated with its causes or effects. Hence the poet, in the grip of such an emotion, finds almost miraculously the unity of his material; relevant ideas are suggested, irrelevant ones are shunted aside, by the mind that is under the control of emotion. Evidently a new conception of artistic creation, very different from that of the Rationalist aesthetics appears here.

THE PROBLEM OF TASTE: SHAFTESBURY TO HUME

A psychological approach to art invites at least a preliminary distinction between two lines of inquiry, however much they may turn out to overlap. There are problems about the origin, or genesis, of art: the psychology of the creative process. And there are problems about the effects of art: the psychology of aesthetic enjoyment. Though the thinkers in the empiricist aesthetic movement did not always make this distinction very definitely, their work can, without serious distortion, be so divided. Most of their theories about imagination, for example, bear upon the genetic problem—though Addison, as we shall see, in his writings on the "pleasures of the imagination," was really concerned with the experience of the appreciator, rather than the artist. In the present section I turn from the genetic or causal theories to the affective or experiential theories.

And, despite his lack of sympathy with Hobbesian and Lockean psychology, it is that seminal though unsystematic thinker, the Third Earl of Shaftesbury (1671–1713), with whom we must begin. (His *Characteristics of Men, Manners, Opinions, Times,* was published in 1711, revised 1714.) Shaftesbury's general metaphysics, which permeates all of his writings, was a reinvigorated Neoplatonism. God is conceived as exercising a continually creating power in nature, which is then itself the greatest of all works of art. The central notions in Shaftesbury's aesthetics are all implicit in the following passage, which we may take as our first text:

Is there then, said he, a natural beauty of figures? and is there not as natural a one of actions? No sooner the eye opens upon figures, the ear upon sounds, than straight the beautiful results and grace and harmony are known and acknowledged. No sooner are actions viewed, no sooner the human affections and passions discerned (and they are most of them as soon discerned as felt) than straight an inward eye distinguishes, and sees the fair and shapely, the amiable and admirable, apart from the deformed, the foul, the odious, or the despicable. How is it possible therefore not to own "that as these distinctions have their foundation in Nature, the discernment itself is natural, and from Nature alone?" [*Moralists* (1709), III, 2; *Characteristics*, ed. Robertson, II, 137].

The Plotinian spirit of this passage (and, more directly, its echo of the Cambridge Platonists) is evident, but in Shaftesbury's hands (because he abhorred systems, was not too proud to learn from anyone, and thought everything over in his own individual style) the ideas take on new forms. Harmony is one of the central themes—the harmony of the natural world, as created by God, reflecting itself in the virtuous character, in which traits and impulses are balanced and integrated, and also in works of art. Thus beauty and goodness are identical (see II, 128, and *Miscellany* III, 2), and are grasped in the same way, by the same faculty. The theory of this "inward eye," to which Shaftesbury gave the name "moral sense," was his contribution to eighteenth-century ethical theory, and at the same time to aesthetics. For the faculty that is called a moral sense when applied to human actions and dispositions is the sense of beauty when applied to external objects, of nature or art (see *An Inquiry Concerning Virtue or Merit* [1699], I, ii, 3; I, 251). Its essential feature is that it grasps its object immediately, without reasoning, but its grasp involves a comparison of the object with an a priori concept of harmony. It is not sensuous, but intuitive (see *Moralists*, III, 2). The human action (or the painting) must, of course, be sensuously perceived before the moral (or aesthetic) sense can come into play, but what that inner sense reports has something of the character of G. E. Moore's "non-natural quality." Harmony, under the name of goodness or beauty (see II, 63; I, 251), is not a sense quality, but a transcendental one (see II, 144).

The question whether we possess a special faculty by which we appreciate, or "relish," beautiful objects, was one that had already turned up in seventeenth-century thinkers, and was to have a high priority among the topics of eighteenth-century aesthetic empiricism. The name "taste" had already been given to this capacity, by analogy with the sense that delivers the most immediate and decisive verdicts of liking and disliking. "Taste" came to cover a good deal of ground, since its ambiguities could be exploited in many different directions. For one very significant chapter in aesthetic history it seemed like a fruitful concept, a clarifying aid in posing questions about the effects and values of works of art. The split between relativistic and absolutistic tendencies developed quite early, for taste could easily be analyzed as simply subjective response. Shaftesbury, though his theory of the aesthetic sense did a great deal to develop the concept of taste, made it clear that he did not think of taste as relative (see *Soliloquy, or Advice to an Author* III, iii). The aesthetic sense, like the moral sense, permits, he held, universal standards of judgment. When he came to discuss these standards, in his essays on painting (*Second Characters,* ed. Rand, 1914), he often fell back upon fairly conventional rationalistic principles, and never reconciled them with the theory of the aesthetic sense which, it might seem, would have no use for any rules.

Locke's "new way of ideas," his analysis of experience as built up out of simple ideas, was one of the most decisive and pervasive philosophical influences upon eighteenth-century thought, in all departments. Even those philosophers who, like Shaftesbury, resisted the implications of that epistemology, were turned in the same direction. Just as he was led to face directly the question by what faculty beauty is apprehended, so Shaftesbury also took a closer look at the phenomenology of that apprehension, and in doing so he helped to formulate a notion that was to have a long and significant later history. He got into the problem of what is now often called the "aesthetic attitude" by reflecting on the theory of psychological egoism, which was so much in the air around the turn of the century. Are all human actions selfish? Hobbes, for one, said they were; and it took some very acute analyses by Bishop Butler and David Hume to show what subtle equivocations were required for a defense of this proposition. Shaftesbury saw clearly one of the important points: the fact that a person actually gets pleasure out of a particular action does not entail that the action was selfish. In certain satisfactions of the mind, no self-reference at all is involved, said Shaftesbury:

And though the reflected joy or pleasure which arises from the notice of this pleasure once perceived, may be interpreted a self-passion or interested regard, yet the original satisfaction can be no other than what results from the love of truth, proportion, order and symmetry in the things without [*Characteristics* I, 296].

The enjoyment of beauty, especially, is completely separate from the desire of possession:

Imagine then, good Philocles, if being taken with the beauty of the ocean, which you see yonder at a distance, it should come into your head to seek how to command it, and, like some mighty admiral, ride master of the sea, would not the fancy be a little absurd? . . . Let who will call it theirs, . . . you will own the enjoyment of this kind to be very different from that which should naturally follow from the contemplation of the ocean's beauty [II, 126–27].

Here disinterested aesthetic contemplation is clearly contrasted with the practical interest.

There is one other important eighteenth-century achievement in which Shaftesbury was something of a pioneer: that widening of the scope of the aesthetic that came in with the recognition of other valuable aesthetic qualities besides beauty. Of these others, the sublime was to be the most discussed. This concept, or cluster of concepts, has itself a most complex history, which we must drastically oversimplify here. It begins with the pseudo-Longinian *Peri Hypsous*, and one of its astonishing features is that this work should have reached its long-delayed peak of popularity and influence in the early decades of the eighteenth century. In "Longinus," the sublime was partly a stylistic concept, though the "elevated style" commended by "Longinus" was not separated in his mind from elevated thoughts and passion strongly stirred. Reflections upon the Longinian sublime were given a boost by

Boileau's famous translation (1674), and subsequent commen-
taries, which multiplied rapidly; and this development played
an important part in producing more fundamental and valuable
concepts of the sublime. But another important stimulus came
with the emergence, in the late seventeenth century, of a powerful new feeling for nature and for natural beauty, as we see it
expressed, for example, in Shaftesbury (and, about the same
time, in John Dennis[1]).

There is something new in Shaftesbury's taking nature as
an object of aesthetic contemplation, along with art. Since he
thought of nature as produced by the greatest of all artists, it is
understandable that nature was to him more than an object
to be manipulated for maximum utility. The willingness to enjoy
the look and feel of nature opened the eye to the delights of its
more wild and fearsome aspects: rugged cliffs, chasms, raging
torrents—and the appalling vastness of interstellar space. Out of
this broadening of appreciation grew the deeper concept of the
sublime. True, the world contains vast deserts and seas, cold
wastes, jungles, and rocks; but "they want not their peculiar
beauties" (II, 122; see all of *Moralists* III, 1). The basic principle of this new sort of contemplative delight—which he does
not contrast with beauty, but places under it—Shaftesbury found
in the size of the object, in relation to the human mind. Thomas
Burnet, in his *Sacred Theory of the Earth* (1681), had already
suggested the idea:

The greatest objects of Nature are, methinks, the most pleasing to
behold: and next to the great Concave of the Heavens, and those
boundless Regions where the Stars inhabit, there is nothing that I look
upon with more pleasure than the wide Sea and the Mountains of the
Earth. There is something august and stately in the Air of those things
that inspires the mind with great thoughts and passions; we do naturally
upon such occasions think of God and his greatness, and whatsoever
hath but the shadow and appearance of INFINITE, as all things have that
are too big for our comprehension, they fill and overbear the mind with
their Excess, and cast it into a pleasing kind of stupor and admiration [I, xi].

[1] The transformation of feeling toward mountains, and the accompanying
theological controversies, have been well told and documented by Marjorie
Hope Nicolson in *Mountain Gloom and Mountain Glory: The Development
of the Aesthetics of the Infinite* (Cornell U., 1959).

These are the themes that Shaftesbury develops. The vastness of nature, in certain aspects, its being "too big for our comprehension," or for our apprehension, makes it a reminder of the Infinite that created it. This religious experience becomes the aesthetic experience of the sublime.

The concept of the sublime was next taken up, though not under that name, by Joseph Addison (1672–1719), in the stimulating series of papers on the "Pleasures of the Imagination" which he wrote for the *Spectator* in June and July 1712 (Nos. 409, 411–21). These papers, written in his liveliest and most provocative manner, hardly formulated a systematic aesthetics, or pursued any problem very deeply, but they lived up to the author's claim to originality (see No. 409) by posing most of the topics of eighteenth-century British aesthetics. In the paper announcing the series (No. 409), Addison promises to "give some account" of "a fine taste in writing," which he defines as "that faculty of the soul which discerns the beauties of an author with pleasure, and the imperfections with dislike" (ed. Aitken; VI, 63). He commends "Longinus" as one of the few to have noted that in great poetry the rules and unities do not take one far, and that "there is still something . . . that elevates and astonishes the fancy, and gives a greatness of mind to the reader"—something he finds pre-eminently in "those rational and manly beauties which give a value to that divine work," Milton's *Paradise Lost* (No. 409; VI, 66; this poem is discussed in a number of essays, beginning with No. 267).

The Pleasures of the imagination (or fancy), says Addison, are "such as arise from visible objects, either when we have them actually in our view, or when we call up their ideas into our minds by paintings, statues, descriptions, or any like occasion" (No. 411; VI, 72), the pleasures from present objects being "primary," those from remembered or fictitious ones being "secondary" (VI, 73). And the problem he sets himself is the empirical problem of discovering "from whence these pleasures are derived" (No. 411; VI, 76). The primary pleasures, "I think, all proceed from the sight of what is great, uncommon, or beautiful" (No. 412; VI, 76).[2] "Greatness" is his word for the sublime—

---

[2] Cf. Longinus (xxxv, 3; trans. Fyfe): "Look at life from all sides and see how in all things the extraordinary, the great, the beautiful stand supreme."

the largeness of a whole view, considered as one entire piece. Such are the prospects of an open champian country, a vast uncultivated desert, of huge heaps of mountains, high rocks and precipices . . . with that rude kind of magnificence which appears in many of these stupendous works of Nature. Our imagination loves to be filled with an object, or to grasp at anything that is too big for its capacity. We are flung into a pleasing astonishment at such unbounded views, and feel a delightful stillness and amazement in the soul at the apprehension of them [No. 412; VI, 76–77].

Uncommonness is novelty, which "fills the soul with an agreeable surprise, gratifies its curiosity" (No. 412; VI, 78) .

But there is nothing that makes its way more directly to the soul than beauty, which immediately diffuses a secret satisfaction and complacency through the imagination, and gives a finishing to anything that is great or uncommon. The very first discovery of it strikes the mind with an inward joy, and spreads a cheerfulness and delight through all its faculties" [VI, 79].

Beauty is not opposed to the great, or sublime; Addison says in fact (No. 369) that parts of *Paradise Lost* "are beautiful by being sublime, others by being soft, others by being natural."

Here Addison's conclusions raise many doubts, which were to be seized upon by his successors, but his method is simple enough. He is trying to give a phenomenological description of a certain species of pleasure (which was not yet called "aesthetic pleasure"), and he is trying to discriminate the chief varieties or sources of this pleasure in terms of the qualities to which it is a response. The secondary pleasures he treats in a somewhat different way, and much less clearly. All the arts are capable of giving such pleasures, he says, even music, for "there may be confused, imperfect notions of this nature raised in the imagination by an artificial composition of notes" (No. 416; VI, 99). The mind compares "the ideas arising from the original objects, with the ideas we receive from the statue, picture, description, or sound that represents them" (VI, 99)—and here suddenly Addison adds that "it is impossible for us to give the necessary reason why this operation of the mind is attended with so much pleasure." But granting that it is so, we can explain many things: the enjoyment of representational art, of mimicry, of wit (VI, 99), and the pleasure we take in "apt description" of things not themselves delightful, such as a "dunghill." In such cases, it is not "the image that is contained in the description," but "the aptness of the description to excite the image" that pleases (No. 418; VI, 107–8).

Addison's work invited, and to some extent exemplified, a new approach to the problems of art and beauty. The first modern essay in philosophical aesthetics was *An Inquiry concerning Beauty, Order, Harmony, and Design*, the first half of *An Inquiry into the Original of our Ideas of Beauty and Virtue*, which Francis Hutcheson published in 1725. Hutcheson was in part a disciple of Shaftesbury, from whom he took the concept of a moral sense, which he introduced in the *Inquiry* and developed further in his *Essay on the Nature and Conduct of the Passions and Affections, with Illustrations of the Moral Sense* (1728).[3] Because of its originality and clarity, the *Inquiry* was much read, respected, and reprinted.

Hutcheson begins with a Lockean review of sensation, of simple and complex ideas, of primary and secondary qualities, then turns to beauty.

Let it be observ'd that in the following papers, the word *beauty* is taken for the idea rais'd in us, and a *sense* of beauty for our power of receiving this idea. *Harmony* also denotes our pleasant ideas arising from composition of sounds, and a *good ear* (as it is generally taken) a power of perceiving this pleasure [*Inquiry*, sec. 1; 2d ed., p. 7; capitalization and italicization modernized].

Hutcheson's aim is to discover "what real quality in the objects ordinarily excites" these ideas (beauty in the case of vision, or its analogue, harmony, in the case of hearing). He holds that "It is of no consequence whether we call these ideas of beauty and harmony, perceptions of the external senses of seeing and hearing, or not" (p. 8) —that is, whether they are (in Locke's terms) ideas of sensation or reflection. But he "should rather chuse to call our power of perceiving these ideas, an *internal sense*," for several reasons. First, because many people have excellent vision and hearing but get little or no pleasure from music, architecture, etc.—which suggests that they lack some other sense, or "taste" (pp. 8–9). Second, because beauty can be perceived in cases "where our external senses are not much concern'd," such as mathemati-

---

[3] He also wrote three essays on humor, *Reflections on Laughter* (1725), criticizing Hobbes's theory.

cal theorems and the virtues (p. 9). Hutcheson compares the idea
of beauty briefly with those of other sense qualities. Cold, heat,
sweetness, bitterness, are sensations in the mind, which do not
correspond to the primary qualities of external objects; and so is
beauty, except that, since beauty and harmony are excited by
sensations involving "figure and time," which are primary qualities, beauty and harmony have a closer resemblance or at least
relation to external objects than cold and sweetness (pp. 14–15).

The capacity to perceive beauty may correctly be called a
"sense" because the pleasure it produces does not arise from
"any knowledge of principles, proportions, causes, or of the usefulness of the object" (p. 11). The idea of beauty strikes us
immediately and directly. Further knowledge about the object
may "superadd" distinct pleasures, intellectual or practical, but
can neither augment nor diminish that pleasure peculiar to the
perception of beauty. Associations of ideas, for example, may
affect the sense of beauty, but it is antecedent to custom, habit,
education, prospect of advantage, or association of ideas (sec. 7;
cf. *Essay on the Passions*, Treatise I, sec. 6; 1st ed., pp. 171–72).
And this is evident because, though association of ideas might
explain how certain objects become able to excite the idea of
beauty by accompanying other objects that already do, association explains nothing unless some objects afford the idea independently of any other objects.

We should note also Hutcheson's proposed distinction (sec. 1)
between "absolute or original beauty," which objects have independent of comparison with other objects, and "comparative or
relative beauty"—"that which we perceive in objects, commonly
considered as imitations or resemblances of something else"
(p. 15). Comparative beauty is founded on a "kind of unity between the original and the copy" (p. 40), and the original doesn't
have to have beauty in itself (sec. 4).

An inductive survey of beautiful objects—beginning with simple geometrical figures—reveals, according to Hutcheson, the common characteristics on which the perception of beauty depends:

What we call beautiful in objects, to speak in the mathematical style,
seems to be in a compound ratio of uniformity and variety: so that
where the uniformity of bodys is equal, the beauty is as the variety;
and where the variety is equal, the beauty is as the uniformity [p. 17].

Mathematical theorems that cover an infinite set of figures or curves, and principles that are rich in explanatory power, also derive their beauty from the same feature (sec. 3). The generalization holds in nature as in art; Hutcheson discusses the beauties of plants and animals. The sense of beauty may therefore be redefined as "a passive power of receiving ideas of beauty from all objects in which there is uniformity amidst variety" (p. 82; sec. 6). Though not all men possess this sense in the same degree, wherever it exists it operates by the same laws. Thus is laid the ground of a nonrelativistic standard of aesthetic judgment (almost indeed of a method of numerical grading). It is not denied, however, that actual judgments sometimes differ (sec. 6). Deformity is "the absence of beauty, or deficiency in the beauty expected in any species" (p. 73)—not a positive thing in itself, but relative to expectations or demands, and hence varying somewhat with experience, even where the beauty actually perceived is the same. Moreover, various associations of ideas give to objects a kind of agreeableness or disagreeableness that is easily confused with beauty and ugliness (pp. 83–85).

Perhaps Hutcheson's most fruitful influence was that upon David Hume, whose moral philosophy (including the philosophy of criticism) especially owes something to Hutcheson's work, despite its original features. Hume's earliest concern with problems about beauty is reflected in his *Treatise of Human Nature* (Books I, II, 1739; Book III, 1740), where they are treated subordinately to other problems, as illustrations of his general explanatory principles, rather than for their own sake.

If we consider all the hypotheses, which have been form'd either by philosophy or common reason, to explain the difference betwixt beauty and deformity, we shall find that all of them resolve into this, that beauty is such an order and construction of parts, as either by the *primary constitution* of our nature, by *custom*, or by *caprice*, is fitted to give a pleasure and satisfaction to the soul [*Treatise* II, i, 8; ed. Selby-Bigge, p. 299].

Since "beauty like wit, cannot be defin'd, but is discern'd only by a taste or sensation, we may conclude, that beauty is nothing but a form, which produces pleasure, as deformity is a structure of parts, which conveys pain" (p. 299).[4] This is the essence of beauty and deformity, which are therefore sometimes referred to as "sentiments." Hume also divides feelings, or impressions of reflection, into the "calm" and "violent," and places under the first heading "the sense of beauty and deformity in action, composition, and external objects" (*Treatise* II, i, 1; p. 276; cf. pp. 438, 472).

Now, "a great part of the beauty, which we admire either in animals or in other objects, is deriv'd from the idea of convenience and utility" (p. 299)—and to a large extent is proportioned to fitness (p. 577). Of this Hume gives several illustrations. "The top of a pillar shou'd be more slender than its base . . . because such a figure conveys to us the idea of security, which is pleasant" (p. 299). And "When a building seems clumsy and tottering to the eye, it is ugly and disagreeable; tho' we be fully assur'd of the solidity of the workmanship." "The *seeming tendencies* of objects affect the mind," as well as their "*real consequences*," even when these are opposed, as when the enemy's fortress fortifications "are esteem'd beautiful upon account of their strength, tho' we cou'd wish that they were entirely destroy'd" (III, iii, 1; pp. 586–87; cf. 576). Like the disinterested pleasure we take in utility in general, our pleasure in beauty, as far as that pleasure is derived from association with utility, is explained by Hume's basic principle of sympathy. This is what enables us to admire the beauty of a house or swift vessel (p. 576), even when it does not belong to us (cf. 584). It is important to note that Hume never *reduces* beauty to utility; he argues that within certain limits we transfer our pleasure in beauty from things that have it in themselves to things that have a capacity to serve some human end. But, like Hutcheson, Hume acknowledges (in the phrase "primary constitution of our nature") that this explanation presupposes that some enjoyment of beauty must arise as a natural response to the "order and construction of parts" in what we observe.

It is this primary sentiment of beauty that raises the epistemological problems about critical judgment. It can be argued that

---

[4] That beauty is not a quality is also argued in the essay "The Sceptic" ("Euclid has fully explained every quality of the circle, but has not, in any proposition, said a word of its beauty")—but Hume is not speaking in his own voice here, and need not subscribe to all that the skeptic says.

a moral judgment expresses the speaker's pleasure in what he sees, and "as that pleasure or pain cannot be unknown to the person who feels it, it follows, that there is just so much vice or virtue in any character, as every one places in it" (III, ii, 8; p. 547)—and Hume indicates in his footnote that the same argument might be made for the judgment of beauty or ugliness. And so the problem is "in what sense we can talk either of a *right* or a *wrong* taste in morals, eloquence, or beauty." When he came to rewrite Book III of the *Treatise,* in the form of his *Inquiry Concerning the Principles of Morals* (1751), Hume was ready to suggest a distinction between (1) those "species of beauty" which "on their first appearance command our affection and approbation," so that "it is impossible for any reasoning to redress their influence or adapt them better to our taste and sentiment," and (2) "many orders of beauty, particularly those of the finer arts," where "it is requisite to employ much reasoning in order to feel the proper sentiment; and a false relish may frequently be corrected by argument and reflection" (sec. 1; ed. C. W. Hendel, p. 6). It is this problem to which he addressed himself directly and carefully in his chief work in aesthetics, the essay "Of the Standard of Taste." This essay first appeared[5] in the *Four Dissertations* (1757), and was later included among the *Essays and Treatises on Several Subjects.*

Hume begins his essay by remarking that the diversity of taste prevailing in the world is obvious at a glance, but turns out to be even greater on close inspection, since those who agree, for example, in "applauding elegance, propriety, simplicity, spirit in writing" and in "blaming fustian, affectation, coldness, and a false brilliancy," are found to mean rather different things when their judgments are examined in detail (Elledge II, 811). Nevertheless,

It is natural for us to seek a "standard of taste," a rule by which the various sentiments of men may be reconciled, at least a decision afforded, confirming one sentiment and condemning another [II, 813].

Now, there is one philosophical position that regards this aim as hopeless.

---

[5] Along with the essay "Of Tragedy," which deals ingeniously with the problem of explaining our pleasure in viewing painful events.

The difference, it is said, is very wide between judgment and sentiment. All sentiment is right, because sentiment has a reference to nothing beyond itself, and is always real wherever a man is conscious of it. But all determinations of the understanding are not right, because they have a reference to something beyond themselves, to wit, real matter of fact [II, 813].

A sentiment "only marks a certain conformity or relation between the object and the organs or faculties of the mind" (II, 813). "Beauty is no quality in things themselves. It exists merely in the mind which contemplates them, and each mind perceives a different beauty." There is no "real" beauty, any more than there is a "real sweet or real bitter." Nevertheless, says Hume, though common opinion may accept this view, and repeat that there is no disputing about tastes, it is also strongly inclined to acknowledge an opposite view. For "Whoever would assert an equality of genius and elegance between Ogilby and Milton, or Bunyan and Addison, would be thought to defend no less an extravagance than if he had maintained a molehill to be as high as Teneriffe, or a pond as extensive as the ocean" (II, 814). Where objects are nearly equal, the "principle of the natural equality of tastes" seems plausible; where objects are widely different in beauty, it is a "palpable absurdity."

Now, it is evident, says Hume, that critical principles, or "rules of composition," are not a priori, but based upon experience; they can only be established by induction from many observations of the actual effects that poems and paintings have upon the beholder, and to generalize from these observations supposes (and there is adequate evidence for) common dispositions of human nature to be pleased or displeased by certain things. This does not mean that all men will actually be moved in the same way:

Those finer emotions of the mind are of a very tender and delicate nature, and require the concurrence of many favorable circumstances to make them play with facility and exactness according to their general and established principles. . . . When we would make an experiment of this nature and would try the force of any beauty or deformity, we must choose with care a proper time and place and bring the fancy to a suitable situation and disposition. A perfect serenity of mind, a recollection of thought, a due attention to the object, if any of these circumstances be wanting, our experiment will be fallacious, and we shall be unable to judge of the catholic and universal beauty" [II, 815].

"It appears, then, that amidst all the variety and caprice of taste there are certain general principles of approbation or blame" (II, 816)—namely, general propositions about which forms and qualities, in which relations and combinations, will give immediate pleasure to the qualified percipient. In the light of these general propositions, a person who judges of beauty or ugliness can correct his judgment, can discover that he lacks sufficient perceptual discrimination, or "delicacy of imagination" (II, 817), or has formed his opinion in haste or from a bias. He discovers that "the fault lies in himself" (II, 818), and in this sense he was mistaken. To be a "true judge" is rare and admirable: "Strong sense, united to delicate sentiment, improved by practice, perfected by comparison, and cleared of all prejudice, can alone entitle critics to this valuable character; and the joint verdict of such, wherever they are to be found, is the true standard of taste and beauty" (II, 823).

Hume has, then, the concept of a Qualified Observer, in terms of which critical disputes are resolvable within limits, since some judgments can be disqualified or overruled on various grounds—insensitivity, inattention, prejudice, inexperience. Hume's system thus has a nonrelativist basis: "The general principles of taste are uniform in human nature" (II, 824). Yet there is room for a good deal of explainable variability, since different works of art will appeal to different temperaments or at different stages of life. Hence there is a residual range of unresolvable disagreements:

It is plainly an error in a critic to confine his approbation to one species or style of writing and condemn all the rest. But it is almost impossible not to feel a predilection for that which suits our particular turn and disposition. Such preferences are innocent and unavoidable and can never reasonably be the object of dispute, because there is no standard by which they can be decided [II, 825].

THE AESTHETIC QUALITIES: HOGARTH TO ALISON

In the eighteenth century's determined effort—particularly in England—to understand and explain our experience of art, we can trace two fundamental lines of interest, labeled on the one hand "taste," and on the other "beauty, the sublime, etc." They are distinct because one question calls for an investigation into the nature of the critic's verdict, and ultimately of his judgment and its justification, and so involves a normative inquiry, while the other invites an analysis, or at least a full description, of the predominant aesthetic qualities, as these thinkers identified them. Of course the two problems are closely related, and hence frequently intermingled, but at this point in our history we change emphasis for the moment, when we come to the seventeen-fifties and two writers who did much to develop and clarify the concepts of beauty and the sublime.

William Hogarth's *Analysis of Beauty, Written with a View of Fixing the Fluctuating Ideas of Taste* (1753) aimed

> to shew what the principles are in nature, by which we are directed to call the forms of some bodies beautiful, others ugly; some graceful, and others the reverse; by considering more minutely than has hitherto been done, the nature of those lines, and their different combinations, which serve to raise in the mind the ideas of all the variety of forms imaginable [Intro.; Burke ed., p. 21].

The single-mindedness and definiteness of the method, and the simplicity of the main conclusions, laid this book open to a good deal of criticism and ridicule, but it nevertheless left its mark upon later writers.

Hogarth begins by simplifying the problem of visual beauty; he argues that solids and shapes, as seen, can be reduced to lines of various sorts, and that if we can analyze beauty of line, that will explain all visual beauty. Six characteristics cooperate in producing linear beauty: fitness, variety, uniformity,, simplicity, intricacy, and quantity, or size (p. 31). Fitness is principally important in defining species of beauty—the beauty of a race horse is not that of a war horse (ch. 1, p. 33). Variety and intricacy are closely associated; uniformity and simplicity are thought of as their limits or ordering factors; quantity makes for intensification. Hogarth constructs and proposes a kind of line that optimally embodies these criteria, the wavy line that is "the line of beauty," and its three-dimensional serpentine counterpart, "the line of grace," which adds grace to beauty (ch. 10; p. 68). These lines are distinguished from those that are "mean and poor" because they lack sufficient variety and intricacy (curvature) and those that are "gross and clumsy" because they lack sufficient uniformity and simplicity—they are too twisted and bulged (ch. 9; p. 65). All sorts of beautiful paintings, quite different from each other (as, say, Raphael from Botticelli) can be explained, Hogarth believed, as variations on these fundamental linear relationships.

The most famous investigation into the nature of the aesthetic qualities is that published by the young Edmund Burke in 1757, *A Philosophical Enquiry into the Origin of Our Ideas of the Sublime and Beautiful.* Because of its ingenuity and originality of argument, as well as its fresh and vigorous style, this work became very popular, at least among the general public. Though Burke did not make many converts among the aestheticians, partly because he was opposing the dominant associationism by a new combination of physiological and phenomenological methods, his theories had to be reckoned with.

One of Burke's aims, explained in the "Introduction on Taste" which he added to the second edition (1759), was to discover an intersubjectively valid standard of taste—meaning by this term "no more than that faculty, or those faculties of the mind which are affected with, or which form a judgment of the works of imagination and the elegant arts" (*Enquiry*, ed. Boulton, p. 13). He thought that if various confusions and ambiguities in the conceptions of the aesthetic qualities, the sublime and the beautiful particularly, could be cleared up, and aesthetic satisfactions more sharply discriminated from other enjoyments, it would be found probable "that the standard both of reason and Taste is the same in all human creatures", and that a kind of "logic of Taste, if I may be allowed the expression" (pp. 11–12), might be worked out as a basis for criticism. Noting that the human mind deals with external objects through the senses, imagination, and judgment, he offers evidence to show that the principles operating in the production of the satisfactions we get through taste and judgment are probably universal, and that differences in preference among different people derive "either from a greater degree of natural sensibility, or from a closer and longer attention to the object" (p. 21). In other words, Taste may be the same always, but some have more of it than others, and some exercise what they have more carefully than others. But Burke also points out that it is a mistake to overlook the complexity of Taste.

On the whole it appears to me, that what is called Taste, in its most general acceptation, is not a simple idea, but is partly made up of a perception of the primary pleasures of sense, of the secondary pleasures of the imagination, and of the conclusions of the reasoning faculty, concerning the various relations of these, and concerning the human passions, manners and actions [p. 23].

The basis of Burke's distinction between the beautiful and the sublime is his distinction between two types of agreeable sensation: positive "pleasure," and "the removal or diminution of pain" (Part I, Section 3; p. 33), which he calls "delight." He first emphasizes this difference, and then makes a brief "attempt to range and methodize some of our most leading passions" (p. 52), according to a scheme recapitulated in I, 18: the passions connected with self-preservation "turn on pain and danger"; "they are delightful when we have an idea of pain and danger, without being actually in such circumstances. . . . Whatever excites this delight I call *sublime*." The social passions, on the other hand, are of two main types. The first is love of female beauty, which is mixed with lust; and "beauty" is to mean "all such qualities in things as induce in us a sense of affection and tenderness, or some other passion the most nearly resembling these." The pleasure of love is positive. The second social passion is sympathy, whose nature is "to put us in the place of another in whatever circumstance he is in, and to affect us in like manner," giving us either pain or pleasure or delight (pp. 51–52). In terms of this scheme, Burke hopes to explain the aesthetic feelings without postulating any autonomous faculty of taste or inner sense.

Burke's method of investigation is quite clearly marked out; he is one writer who knows what he is doing. Consider the sublime. There is, first, a certain emotion to be identified and analyzed. This he calls "astonishment"—"that state of the soul, in which all its motions are suspended,—with some degree of horror," a sense of the mind's being filled with what it contemplates, held and transfixed. The lower grades of this feeling of sublimity are "admiration, reverence and respect" (II, 1; p. 57). Thus fear—of pain or death—is closely connected with this experience, and is indeed a precondition of it.

Whatever is fitted in any sort to excite the ideas of pain, and danger, that is to say, whatever is in any sort terrible, or is conversant about terrible objects, or operates in a manner analogous to terror, is a source of the *sublime*; that is, it is productive of the strongest emotion which the mind is capable of feeling [I, 7; p. 39].

Note the three things distinguished here, and the qualification in the term "source." In order for an object to excite the feeling of sublimity, either it must be terrible, or it must be connected with actually terrible things, or it must have certain properties by which it "operates in a manner analogous to terror." Terribleness (immediate, indirect, or analogical) arouses the feeling of sublimity, and its peculiar delight, when its painfulness is controlled and diminished by safety.

The second step is to inquire into those sensible qualities of things that make objects terrible, or make them seem terrible, or enable them to affect us in a manner analogous to terrible things. And here Burke is very specific. Obscurity is necessary to terribleness, because fear is increased by ignorance (II, 3). Power (II, 5), privation and emptiness (II, 6), and greatness of dimension (II, 7) also contribute strongly to sublimity. Burke even attempts finer discriminations: "I am apt to imagine likewise, that height is less grand than depth; . . . but of that I am not very positive" (p. 72). Greatness that approaches, or seems to approach, infinity is sublime in a high degree (II, 8), and this is closely connected with obscurity, since "to see an object distinctly, and to perceive its bounds, is one and the same thing. A clear idea is therefore another name for a little idea" (p. 63)—but infinity has no bounds. Burke notes also that "The eye is not the only organ of sensation, by which a sublime passion may be produced" (p. 82), for there is loud music (I, 17); "Smells, and Tastes, have some share too, in ideas of greatness; but it is a small one" (II, 21; p. 85); and, of course, there is sublime poetry, which Burke discusses in Part V, concluding with a theory that poetry produces its effects by a kind of emotive language (see V, 7).

The analysis of beauty is parallel to that of the sublime: Burke investigates "that quality or those qualities in bodies by which they cause love, or some passion similar to it" (III, 1; p. 91), the response to female beauty (minus lust) being taken as the paradigm here, as was the response to the terrible (minus actual fear) in the case of sublimity. Burke analyzes with great care, and rejects, two familiar answers to this question: that beauty consists in "proportions of parts"—an examination of vegetables and animals reveals no set of proportions either necessary or sufficient for beauty (III, 2–5)—and that beauty is caused by, or consists of, fitness (III, 6–7). The qualities that cause beauty are smallness (III, 13), smoothness (14), gradual variation (15), delicacy (16). Burke adds, incidentally, brief analyses of two other aesthetic qualities, distinct from beauty, namely gracefulness (III, 22) and elegance (III, 23). And he has a little to say of beauty in touch (III, 24) and sound (III, 25). The final conclusion is that beauty and sublimity are opposed in many of their conditions, but a complex work of art may have some of both, though it is not likely to have either so strongly as a work that concentrates on one or the other.

It is an important methodological feature of Burke's inquiry that he attempts two levels of explanation (see IV, 1, 5). If we ask what causes the feelings of beauty and sublimity, the answer will be in terms of sensible qualities, as we have seen. If we ask, on the other hand, what causes these qualities to produce those feelings, the answer will be a physical one. If actual terror produces "an unnatural tension and certain violent emotions of the nerves" (p. 134), then anything else that produces such a (physiological) tension may be expected to produce passions similar to terror. Mere induction has shown us that certain qualities produce sublimity; it remains to be shown how these qualities (or their physical counterparts) operate upon the body in a manner analogous to terror, and so produce sublimity. Burke's explanations here are highly speculative, of course; two will serve as examples. Why does greatness of dimension contribute toward sublimity? Because the light coming from so vast an object must tax the eye, which, "vibrating in all its parts must approach near to the nature of what causes pain" (IV, 9; p. 137). Again, why do smooth, small, delicate objects make us feel love? Because they have a similar effect upon the organism: "beauty acts by relaxing the solids of the whole system" (IV, 19; pp. 149–50). Similar explanations are given for the other qualities. They may not be found very helpful today, but here is an important idea with some novelty in the history of aesthetics: that the explanation of aesthetic enjoyment is to be sought on the physiological level.

It is impossible, in a short history, to do justice (in the sense of rendering every man his due) to all those who contributed to the development of aesthetic theory in the eighteenth century—

a period that probably ranks below only our own in the intensity and variety of its creative thinking about fundamental aesthetic problems. In this chapter, we have considered the leading ideas of the most seminal thinkers in England, where, before Kant, the greatest ferment was going on. The developments they initiated, or gave definitive shape to, continued in a steady line through the middle of the nineteenth century. There was, for one thing, a continuous growth in the associationist theory, the attempt to explain more and more aesthetic phenomena, more subtly and completely, in terms of the association of ideas. There was a further widening of the aesthetic categories, one of the prime achievements of the eighteenth century. It may be true, as Professor Monk has said, that in the eighteenth century, the term "sublime" "grew more and more into a catch-all for elements in art that the Cartesian aesthetic had suppressed or had not accounted for,"[6] though to some extent the broadening of the concept of the sublime entailed a narrowing and a sharpening of the classical concept of beauty, too. Nevertheless, the upshot of this development was a recognition that other qualities than beauty, even though the latter be taken broadly, were capable of affording direct aesthetic satisfaction. And the introduction, toward the end of the century, of a new category of the "picturesque" (as, for example, in William Gilpin's essay *On Picturesque Beauty*, 1792), despite some odd features in this notion, led to the exploration of new ranges of aesthetic response.

The psychological study of aesthetic feelings, and the enthusiasm—in the third quarter of the century, especially—for the sublime (reflected in new tastes in poetry and nature), gave the final blow to the neoclassic system of criticism. The concept of decisive rules and canons gave way to the emphasis on taste (personal, or interpersonal, or cultivated); with the welcome to stronger and less controlled emotions came the admiration of genius (Michelangelo supplants Raphael as the sublimest of painters), a pre-Romantic emphasis on imaginative or intuitive truth, as something perhaps superior to reason.

Many other thinkers played a part in this whole movement, and the names of some of them should be recorded, even though

---

[6] Samuel H. Monk, *The Sublime, A Study of Critical Theories in XVIII-Century England* (Ann Arbor, 1960), p. 233.

their contributions can only be touched upon. Dr. John Baillie's *Essay on the Sublime* (published posthumously in 1747) echoed "Longinus," but aimed to improve on him. The necessary condition of sublimity, for him, is vastness, either directly presented in nature, or indirectly brought into literature and painting (and architecture and music) by association. "Where an Object is *Vast*, and at the same Time *uniform*, . . . the Mind runs out into *Infinity*," and the sublime is experienced as "one simple, grand *Sensation*," which fills the mind to the exclusion of all else, and gives the soul a feeling of elevation and serenity that enlarges and dilates it (pp. 8–11). Alexander Gerard's *Essay on Taste* (written by 1756; published 1759; enlarged in 3d ed., 1780) analyzes taste into seven "internal senses," or "powers of imagination," which perceive novelty, sublimity, beauty, imitation, harmony, ridicule, and virtue. Each of these is further analyzed; for example, the pleasure obtained from beauty is resolved into "the pleasure of facility, that of moderate exertion, and that which results from the discovery of art and wisdom in the cause" (III, i; p. 147). His concept of the sublime follows that of Baillie; he explains the sublimity of passions by association with their objects, causes, or effects (universal benevolence is sublime, rather than beautiful); and works of art become sublime either through their subjects or through the passions they evoke. Gerard's discussion of the standard of taste is also interesting: while acknowledging the actual diversity of aesthetic preferences, he holds that an inductive study of the effects of various objects on the human perceiver can provide at least general principles of criticism by which, within limits, divergences of taste can be reconciled (3d ed., III, iii)—"that a standard may be found, to which even they whose relish it condemns, may find themselves obliged to submit. The person who *feels* in a certain manner . . . may yet be convinced that he feels amiss, and yield readily to a *judgment* in opposition to his feeling" (3d ed., IV, ii).

Another large and systematic treatise, partly concerned with aesthetics, was the *Elements of Criticism* written by Henry Home, Lord Kames (1762). The range of this book is wide: it is concerned, in part, to answer the skeptical views of Berkeley and Hume concerning the self and the external world, and the general method of reply consists in postulating a variety of "senses," by which intuitive assurance of things can be obtained. Like his predecessors, Kames searches out general rules of art, "drawn from human nature, the true source of criticism" (Intro.; 4th ed., 1769, p. 13). He bases them on the general and persistent preferences among civilized nations (xxv). Beauty is analyzed into regularity and simplicity, as properties of a whole, and uniformity, proportion, and order as properties of the parts (iii, xviii). Grandeur is distinguished from sublimity; the former is produced by great magnitude, the latter by great elevation: "A great object makes the spectator endeavor to enlarge his bulk. . . . An elevated object produces a different expression: it makes the spectator stretch upward, and stand a-tiptoe" (iv; p. 210)—an early and interesting version of empathy.

Hugh Blair's *Lectures on Rhetoric and Belles Lettres*, given at the University of Edinburgh from 1759 on, and published in 1783, define taste as "the power of receiving pleasure from the beauties of nature and of art" (ii; I, 20). He holds that "mighty force or power, whether accompanied with terror or not, . . . has a better title, than anything that has yet been mentioned, to be the fundamental quality of the Sublime" (iii; I, 71). He distinguishes beauty by its brisker, gayer, more soothing, more serene emotion, but reminds us that a great number and variety of visually pleasing qualities are comprehended under the term "beauty," some of which have nothing in common save the "agreeable emotion which they all raise" (v; I, 102).

The discussion was continued by Thomas Reid, the leader of the school of "Scottish philosophy," in the last of his *Essays on the Intellectual Powers of Man* (1785). He criticizes a subjective analysis of the judgment of taste, the view that "when I say Virgil's 'Georgics' is a beautiful poem, I mean not to say anything of the poem, but only something concerning myself and my feelings"; he appeals to ordinary language, which furnishes a more direct and appropriate idiom for saying, "I like it" when that is all we mean (viii, 1; *Works*, ed. Hamilton, 8th ed., 1882, p. 492a). Reid holds that "original" beauty is found in those mental qualities that deserve love, "the whole train of the soft and gentle virtues" (viii, 4; I, 502b), and the beauty of shapes, colors, sounds, etc., is derived from this original source. We take pleasure in the concord of music (Reid suggests that "concord" applies literally to human conversation and only metaphorically, or analogously, to music), and in the regional qualities of paintings (grace, harmony, dignity, etc.) because we see in them analogues of moral qualities. Sublimity (which Reid calls "grandeur") is similarly analyzed: the grandeur we admire in created works or in nature is admirable because it reflects the creative mind behind.

Another noteworthy essay, especially in its penetrating discussion of music, is Adam Smith's essay *Of the Nature of that Imitation which Takes Place in what are Called the Imitative Arts* (1795). He shows clearly how music, alone among the arts, can be said to imitate only what may be indicated by accompanying words or gestures—we would not know from the music itself that it "represents" a battle, or the rocking of a cradle (as in Corelli's *Christmas Concerto*). The effects of absolute music are direct and immediate:

instrumental Music does not imitate, as vocal Music, as Painting, or as Dancing would imitate, a gay, a sedate, or a melancholy person; . . . it becomes itself a gay, a sedate, or a melancholy object [*Works* (1811), V, 287].

Music, adds Smith, in words that anticipate later well-known remarks:

seldom means to tell any particular story, or to imitate any particular event, or in general to suggest any particular object, distinct from that combination of sounds of which itself is composed. Its meaning, therefore, may be said to be complete in itself, and to require no interpreters to explain it. What is called the subject of such Music . . . is altogether different from what is called the subject of a poem or a picture, which is always something which is not either in the poem or in the picture. . . . [V, 301].

Even this sketchy account of several subordinate thinkers has had to leave out others with serious, though lesser, claim to notice: for example, Joseph Priestley's *Course of Lectures on Oratory and Criticism* (1777), a defense of associationism; Richard Payne Knight's *Analytical Inquiry into the Principles of Taste* (1805), which included a severe criticism of Burke, a defense of beauty independent of association, and a subtle analysis of sublimity in terms of the concept of energy; Dugald Stewart's

Philosophical Essays (1810); and numerous others. Philosophers, divines, landscape gardeners, architects, painters, rhetoricians, and poets were teased and excited by the problem of analyzing beauty and sublimity, explaining their effects and causes, justifying judgments about them.

A more extensive history would also have to deal with a parallel, and often interacting, development on the Continent. The Swiss aesthetician Jean Pierre Crousaz, in his *Traité du beau* (1714), argued that aesthetic judgments are not propositions, but expressions of our immediate feeling for beauty. But he insisted that beauty depends on uniformity and variety. The Abbé Jean Baptiste Dubos, in his *Réflexions critiques sur la poésie et sur la peinture* (1719; trans. into English 1748), a notable and influential work, held a similar Hutchesonian notion of the sense of beauty (we know immediately whether music is melodious or a stew is tasty). He went on to justify aesthetic pleasure as a relief from the monotonies of ordinary existence. A similar view of the judgment of taste as a sudden discernment, not requiring reflection or thought, was presented in Voltaire's *Temple du goût* (1733). The *Essai sur le beau* of Père Yves-Marie André (1741) was Cartesian in its foundations, and Platonic and Augustinian in its conclusion that beauty is a transcendental perfection, but this set of lectures was influential, even on the empirically minded Diderot, who borrowed from it and discussed it in his essay on beauty in the *Encyclopedia*.

Among his multifarious projects, Denis Diderot gave more—and more systematic—thought to aesthetic problems than most of his French contemporaries. His famous essay, *Le Paradoxe sur le comédien* (a fragment of which was published in 1770, but the whole not until 1830) dealt subtly with the problem of the relation between the actor's emotions and the role he is playing: artistic creation, in acting or poetry, is far removed, he argued, from mere emotional self-expression. He wrote on painting with much enthusiasm in his *Salons* and in his *Essai sur la peinture* (first published 1796). And he was especially interested in poetics. The heart of his poetic theory is explained in his *Lettre sur les sourds et muets* (1751). The poet's problem, he says, is that he must convey a complex psychological state through a medium—language—that is a product of reason, suited to logical analysis, and hence inherently discursive—words have to be laid down in sequence, one idea at a time. Poetry overcomes this limitation by metrical devices, by syntactical inversions that jam ideas together, and by figurative language. The term "hieroglyph" came to Diderot, via Condillac, from Warburton's writings on the Egyptian hieroglyph, which Warburton believed to be a picture that compresses and expresses many meanings all together. So poetic discourse, says Diderot,

is no longer only a linking together of strong terms that set forth the thought nobly and forcibly, but a fabric of closely interwoven hieroglyphs that picture it (*un tissu d'hiéroglyphes entassés les uns sur les autres qui la peignent*). I might say that in this sense all poetry is emblematic [trans. M. Gilman, *The Idea of Poetry*, p. 79].

Diderot's *Encyclopedia* article on beauty, *Recherches philosophiques sur l'origine et la nature du beau* (1751), discusses critically some earlier writers, including Crousaz and Hutcheson, and attempts a definition that will at least avoid excessive narrowness. The qualities that are the condition of beauty, says Diderot, must be common to beautiful things of all varieties, must be such that without them there is no beauty, and such that when they change, the degree of beauty changes. There is only one concept that will serve, the concept of *rapports*, or relationships—not simply relationships in the logical sense, but relationships involving some sort of connection or mutual fitness or conformity. Whatever "awakens in my understanding the idea of *rapports*" is to be called beauty. No special inner perception need be postulated here; the ideas of order, symmetry, proportion, etc., that enter into various sorts of beauty are those with which we are familiar in our practical experience, for, Diderot says, we are born with needs that we must learn to satisfy by experimenting with the world, and these constant experiments acquaint us with the manifold ways in which things fit together and work upon each other. We are glad to perceive, in great art, the congruence of multiple relationships all at once, and the more *rapports*, the more beautiful the work. Since beauty has many varieties, depending on the species or class of things considered, our grasp of beauty is refined by a close study of natural objects: thus Diderot tries to give a clearer meaning to the maxim of Batteaux and others that art is "the imitation of beautiful nature."

As a final measure of the distance that empiricist aesthetics (and particularly associationist aesthetics) had come since, say, Hobbes or Addison, we may conclude this chapter by noticing a little more fully the work of Archibald Alison, who represents one of the high points of achievement in this movement, a culmination and exemplification of much of what was best and most fruitful in it. His *Essays on the Nature and Principles of Taste* went almost unnoticed when first published at Edinburgh (1790), but the second and expanded edition (1811) came to be acknowledged as a most important systematic work, distinguished by the care and subtlety of its arguments, and by the interesting implications of its attempt to explain the "pleasures of the imagination" on completely associationist principles. We can consider only a part of his argument, and briefly, but it is an important part.

Alison's first main thesis is that the pleasures of taste, that is, the enjoyment of beauty and sublimity in nature or art (see Intro.), occur "when the Imagination is employed in the prosecution of a regular train of ideas of emotion" (Essay I, Conclusion, 4; 6th ed., I, 172). The first argument, then, is to show that for an object to be aesthetically enjoyed (in this sense), it must initiate a train of associated ideas. The argument is inductive, and it is both thorough and exact. First, "when we feel either the beauty or sublimity of natural scenery—the gay lustre of a morning in spring," etc., "we are conscious of a variety of images in our minds, very different from those which the objects themselves can present to the eye" (I, i, 1; I, 5). Second, when the object is prevented from initiating an associative chain, as when we are occupied with grief or with practical business, or when we are taking the role of art critics rather than appreciators, or if we are people of limited imaginative capacity—then the aesthetic enjoyment is not felt (I, i, 2). Third, the intensity of aesthetic enjoyment varies concomitantly with the number and variety of associations aroused by the object (I, i, 3).

The train of imaginations is a necessary condition of aesthetic enjoyment, but not sufficient: the ideas must also be "productive of Emotions"; and the train itself must be characterized by a single "principle of connection" so that the whole chain is bound together, not just connected by separate associative links (I, ii). Again, careful inductive arguments are drawn out to prove both points: "That no objects, or qualities in objects, are, in fact, felt as beautiful or sublime, but such as are productive of some simple Emotion" (I, ii, 2; I, 81)—*any* simple emotion—and that in successful works of art there is a dominant quality or emotion that makes them wholes. The conclusion is that "the pleasure . . . which accompanies the Emotions of Taste, may be considered not as a simple, but as a complex pleasure" (I, Conclusion; I, 169).

It follows also "that the qualities of matter are not to be considered as sublime or beautiful in themselves, but as being the signs or expressions of such qualities as, by the constitution of our Nature, are fitted to produce pleasing or interesting emotion" (II, Conclusion; II, 416). Alison does not deny that colors and sounds of themselves, and even Hogarth's curves, may produce "agreeable sensations," but he holds that the beauty of colors arises from their expressiveness, and their expressiveness from association (II, iii, 1). "Purple, for instance, has acquired a character of Dignity, from its accidental connection with the Dress of Kings" (I, 298). And he argues by ingenious experimental comparisons that even Hogarth's principle is not fundamental, for when his lines are beautiful their beauty is not purely formal, but depends on expression (II, iv, 1, Part II).

The associationist analysis of beauty was developed still further by later British writers. For example, Francis Jeffrey, in his essay on *Beauty* (*Edinburgh Review*, 1811; later in the 8th edition of the Encyclopaedia Britannica), after some good criticisms of his predecessors, such as Hutcheson, Diderot, Knight, Stewart, and Alison (whom he admires), proposes that a beautiful object is one that is

associated either in our past experience, or by some universal analogy, with pleasures, or emotions that upon the whole are pleasant, and that these associated pleasures are instantaneously suggested, as soon as the object is presented, and by the first glimpse of its physical properties; with which, indeed, they are consubstantiated and confounded in our sensations [par. 12].

A significant feature of Alison's system is that it represents an abandonment of the persistent attempt to discover a neat formula for the perceptual conditions of beauty, and opens up the possibility of an indefinite range of beauties. Jerome Stolnitz has remarked that "By the closing decades of the century, discouragement over the possibility of finding a successful formula of objective beauty, has turned into despair."[7] Alison concluded that the attempt was "altogether impossible" (I, 316). Even more interestingly, Dugald Stewart suggested that this failure might be explained if we would abandon the "prejudice, which has descended to modern times from the scholastic ages;—that when a word admits of a variety of significations, these significations must all be *species* of the same *genus*" (*Philosophical Essays*, 1810, p. 214) —and would allow that the objects to which "beautiful" applies have only a "family resemblance" (in Wittgenstein's term) to one another.

One further consequence that Alison draws from his arguments recalls the neoclassic discussions of the preceding chapter. Since a work of art provides the genuinely aesthetic pleasure by the coherence of the association chain it provokes, it is essential for the work of art to preserve its "Unity of character or expression" (I, 133), which, in the drama for example, "is fully as essential as any of those three unities, of which every book of Criticism is so full" (I, 152). From this follows a general principle of critical evaluation:

In all the Fine Arts, that Composition is most excellent in which the different parts most fully unite in the production of one unmingled Emotion; and that Taste the most perfect, where the perception of this relation of objects, in point of expression, is most delicate and precise [I, 157].

From this generalization, in turn, particular critical rules might be derived. Alison seeks an empirical warrant for objective criticism—which had been on the agenda since Hutcheson and Hume. It is perhaps a bit startling to find that, when he ventures into the illustration of his principles by specific examples, his condemnation of Shakespeare's mixtures of tragic and comic elements in the same play is as severe as could be wished by the most rigorous neoclassicist. However, what is philosophically significant in the long run, in any field of human endeavor, is, of course, not what people believe but what reasons they have for believing it.

[7] " 'Beauty': Some Stages in the History of an Idea," *Jour Hist Ideas* XXII (1961): 199.

Bibliography

Sir Francis Bacon, *Works,* ed. Spedding, Ellis, and Heath, 3 vols. (London, 1870).

M. W. Bundy, "Bacon's True Opinion of Poetry," *Stud in Philol* XXVII (1930): 244–64.

Thomas Hobbes, *English Works,* ed. Molesworth, 11 vols. (London, 1839–45).

Clarence DeWitt Thorpe, *The Aesthetic Theory of Thomas Hobbes* (Ann Arbor, 1940).

Donald F. Bond, "The Neo-classical Psychology of the Imagination," *ELH: A Jour of Eng Lit Hist* IV (1937): 245–64.

John Locke, *An Essay Concerning Human Understanding,* ed. A. C. Fraser, 2 vols. (Oxford, 1894).

John Locke, *Of the Conduct of the Understanding,* in *Works,* 12th ed., 9 vols. (London, 1824), Vol. II.

Martin Kallich, "The Association of Ideas and Critical Theory: Hobbes, Locke, and Addison," *ELH: A Jour of Eng Lit Hist* XII (1945): 290–315.

George Williamson, "The Restoration Revolt Against Enthusiasm," *Stud in Philol* XXX (1933): 571–603.

Walter Jackson Bate, "The Sympathetic Imagination in Eighteenth-Century English Criticism," *ELH: A Jour of Eng Lit Hist* XII (1945): 144–64.

Donald F. Bond, " 'Distrust' of Imagination in English Neo-classicism," *Philol Quart* XIV (1935): 54–69.

Shaftesbury, *Characteristics of Men, Manners, Opinions, Times, etc.,* ed. J. M. Robertson, 2 vols. (London, 1900).

R. L. Brett, *The Third Earl of Shaftesbury: A Study in Eighteenth-Century Literary Theory* (London, 1951).

R. L. Brett, "The Aesthetic Sense and Taste in the Literary Criticism of the Early Eighteenth Century," *Rev of Eng Stud* XX (1944): 199–213.

Jerome Stolnitz, "On the Significance of Lord Shaftesbury in Modern Aesthetic Theory," *Philos Quart* XI (1961): 97–113.

Joseph Addison, *The Spectator*, ed. G. A. Aitken, 8 vols. (London, 1898).

Francis Hutcheson, *An Inquiry into the Original of Our Ideas of Beauty and Virtue*, 2d. ed. (London, 1726).

Clarence D. Thorpe, "Addison and Hutcheson on the Imagination," *ELH: A Jour of Eng Lit Hist* II (1935): 215–34.

Marjorie Grene, "Gerard's *Essay on Taste*," *Mod Philol* XLI (August 1943): 45–58.

David Hume, *Treatise of Human Nature*, ed. L. A. Selby-Bigge (Oxford U., 1888).

David Hume, *Inquiry Concerning the Principles of Morals* (New York, 1957).

Martin Kallich, "The Associationist Criticism of Francis Hutcheson and David Hume," *Stud in Philol* XLIII (1946): 644–67.

William Hogarth, *The Analysis of Beauty*, ed. Joseph Burke (Oxford U., 1955).

Edmund Burke, *A Philosophical Enquiry into the Origin of our Ideas of the Sublime and Beautiful*, ed. J. T. Boulton (London and New York, 1958).

Martin Kallich, "The Argument against the Association of Ideas in Eighteenth-Century Aesthetics," *Mod Lang Quart* XV (1954): 125–36.

Dixon Wecter, "Burke's Theory of Words, Images and Emotions, *PMLA* LV (1940): 167–81.

David O. Robbins, "The Aesthetics of Thomas Reid," *Jour Aesth and Art Crit* I (Spring 1942), No. 5, pp. 30–41.

Archibald Alison, *Essays on the Nature and Principles of Taste*, 6th ed. (Edinburgh, 1825), 2 vols.

Martin Kallich, "The Meaning of Archibald Alison's *Essays on Taste*," *Philol Quart* XXVII (1948): 314–24.

Margaret Gilman, *The Idea of Poetry in France from Houdar de la Motte to Baudelaire* (Harvard U., 1958), ch. 2.

Yvon Belaval, *L'esthétique sans paradoxe de Diderot* (Paris, 1950).

James Doolittle, "Hieroglyph and Emblem in Diderot's *Lettre sur Les Sourds et Muets*"; Otis E. Fellows, "The Theme of Genius in Diderot's *Neveu de Rameau*"; and Margaret Gilman,

"Imagination and Creation in Diderot"; in Otis E. Fellows and Norman L. Torrey, eds., *Diderot Studies* II (Syracuse U., 1952).

Margaret Gilman, "The Poet According to Diderot," *Romanic Rev* XXXVII (1946): 37–54.

Eleanor M. Walker, "Towards an Understanding of Diderot's Esthetic Theory," *Romanic Rev* XXXV (1944): 277–87.

Thomas J. Durkin, "Three Notes to Diderot's Aesthetic," *Jour Aesth and Art Crit* XV (March 1957): 331–39.

Wladyslaw Folkierski, *Entre le classicisme et le romantisme* (Krakow and Paris, 1925).

Scott Elledge, ed., *Eighteenth-Century Critical Essays*, 2 vols. (Cornell U., 1961).

Walter Jackson Bate, *From Classic to Romantic: Premises of Taste in Eighteenth-Century England* (Harvard U., 1946).

Ernest Lee Tuveson, *The Imagination as a Means of Grace: Locke and the Aesthetics of Romanticism* (California U., 1960).

Richard F. Jones, "Science and Criticism in the Neo-classical Age of English Literature," *Jour Hist Ideas* I (1940): 381–412.

Jerome Stolnitz, " 'Beauty': Some Stages in the History of an Idea," *Jour Hist Ideas* XXII (1961): 185–204.

Jerome Stolnitz, "Locke and the Categories of Value in Eighteenth-Century British Aesthetic Theory," *Philosophy* XXXVIII (1963): 40–51.

Jerome Stolnitz, "On the Origins of 'Aesthetic Disinterestedness,' " *Jour Aesth and Art Crit* XX (Winter 1961): 131–43.

H. A. Needham, *Taste and Criticism in the Eighteenth Century* (London, 1952), Introduction.

Walter John Hipple, Jr., *The Beautiful, the Sublime, and the Picturesque in Eighteenth-Century British Aesthetic Theory* (Southern Illinois U., 1957).

Samuel H. Monk, *The Sublime: A Study of Critical Theories in XVIII-century England* (rev. ed., Michigan U., 1960).

Herbert M. Schueller, "The Pleasures of Music: Speculation in British Music Criticism, 1750–1800," *Jour Aesth and Art Crit* VIII (March 1950): 155–71.

Rémy G. Saisselin, "Critical Reflections on the Origins of Modern Aesthetics," *Brit Jour of Aesth* IV (1964): 7–21.

NINE

German Idealism

The great flowering of German thought in the latter part of the eighteenth and early nineteenth centuries had a profound effect upon the history of aesthetics. Rich in epistemological and metaphysical explorations on the one hand, and in practical and theoretical criticism on the other, it gave, out of the fruitful convergence of these intellectual activities, a new direction and a new impetus to the subject.

The aesthetic theories that took form in this period were not all of a piece, and in this short history they are treated in three groups. First, I have discussed Baumgarten and Lessing, two of the earlier thinkers, in connection with Rationalist aesthetics, as bringing to a head certain problems that had long been meditated. Second, there is philosophical idealism, especially the Critical Idealism of Kant and the Objective Idealism of Schelling and Hegel. This movement will be reviewed in the present chapter, along with the work of some other thinkers who shared important ideas with the idealists or are easiest understood in connection with them. Third, there are other thinkers who belong, it seems to me, most closely to the history of Romanticism, which in the course of its development introduced, or at least newly featured, certain special aesthetic doctrines. These are to be given attention in the following chapter. Among the later and important developments of Romanticism are the voluntarist philosophies of Schopenhauer and Nietzsche. Although the former is a metaphysical idealist in certain respects, and develops directly out of Kant (from whom it is therefore somewhat artificial to separate him), he seems to me more illuminatingly discussed with a different orientation, as will presently appear.

Nowhere in the history of Modern Philosophy is the Parable of the Talents better illustrated than in the achievement of Kant (1724–1804): it is astonishing that a thinker who turned the course of metaphysical, epistemological, and ethical inquiry irrevocably in new directions should also have been capable of working out an aesthetic theory which, in its originality, subtlety, and comprehensiveness, would mark a turning point in this field as well. Kant did not start from scratch. He was widely and well acquainted with the developments we have been surveying in the past two chapters, and he conceived of his own work not only as a capstone to his system but as a much-needed answer to questions raised by his predecessors. Most especially, he hoped to provide a theory of the aesthetic judgment that would justify its apparent claim to intersubjective validity, and escape the temptations of skepticism and relativism; and he believed this could be accomplished only by giving a deeper interpretation of art and of its values, by establishing for it a more intimate connection with the basic cognitive faculties of the mind. He thus became the first modern philosopher to make an aesthetic theory an integral part of a philosophic system. Despite the complexities and obscurities of his thought, he opened up, or opened more widely, several channels whose later exploration has proved to be of immense value.

Kant's early *Observations on the Feeling of the Sublime and the Beautiful* (1764) already shows evidence of much thinking about the problems of aesthetics, but his main and significant position is that set forth in the first part of his *Critique of Judgment* (1790), the work that completed his great trilogy of Critical Idealism. The relation between this third *Critique* and its two fellows cannot be succinctly stated without risk of being misleading, and of course we will not be able to explore all its aspects in this short account. One of Kant's ways of putting the matter is that man has three modes of consciousness, knowledge, desire, and feeling, and that it was the task of the *Critique of Pure*

Reason to study the first, and of the *Critique of Practical Reason* to study the second, leaving the third for the *Critique of Judgment*. Again, he says (in the Introduction) that the third *Critique* aims to reunite the worlds of Nature and Freedom sundered by the other two. For our purposes—and without raising unnecessary questions about the extent to which the third *Critique* was foreseen during the composition of the first—it will be sufficient to suppose that having explored the varieties of both empirical and a priori propositions in the first two *Critiques*, Kant discovered that there remained on his hands two rather puzzling kinds of proposition whose cognitive status he had not yet cleared up: aesthetic judgments (especially of the sublime and the beautiful), and teleological judgments (judgments of purpose). The third *Critique* undertakes this assignment, approaching the problems through a further examination of the faculty of judgment (*Urteilskraft*) itself. In the first *Critique*, this faculty is explained as the capacity to subsume particular sense-intuitions, or "representations," under general concepts, and thus bring the manifold of sense to the categories of the understanding (*Verstand*): or, in other words, to mediate between the understanding, as the faculty of concepts, and the imagination (*Einbildungskraft*), as the faculty that brings together in a synthesis the manifold of sense.

The second part of the *Critique of Judgment*, which deals with the teleological judgment, we shall have to ignore. In the first part, Kant follows as far as he can the general scheme of transcendental philosophy, as worked out earlier: there is to be an Analytic of the aesthetic judgment, in which it is clarified and validated by the examination of its presuppositions, and a Dialectic, in which its antinomy is exposed and resolved. The analysis of the aesthetic judgment begins with the discrimination of its four "moments," or logical aspects, in terms of the table of forms of judgment introduced in the first *Critique*. With these and other architectural niceties we shall not be able to concern ourselves very much, not because they are uninteresting, or unimportant to a full grasp of Kant's philosophy, but because they require, to be understood, more space than this little history affords.

Another general distinction is needed before we turn to the

text itself: Kant has a theory of the beautiful (*das Schöne*) and a theory of the sublime (*das Erhabene*), which he takes up separately, beginning with beauty, the predicate of the "judgment of taste."

As to its *quality*, the judgment of taste (*Geschmack*) is characterized by means of two distinctions. First, the class of "aesthetic judgments" is distinguished from the class of "logical judgments." A logical judgment ("This is red") refers a representation (*Vorstellung*) to an object, as its property. An aesthetic judgment refers the representation to "the subject, and its feeling of pleasure or pain" (§ 1; trans. Bernard, p. 45) ; it is a judgment "whose determining ground can be *no other than subjective*" (pp. 45–46). Second, most aesthetic judgments are simply reports of pleasure, or satisfaction ("This is pleasant," "This is delightful"), but some aesthetic judgments are judgments of taste, defined as "the faculty of judging the beautiful" (p. 45 n). The distinguishing feature of the judgment of taste is that the satisfaction it reports is "disinterested" (§ 2). Kant adapts this important concept from the empiricists, to make it the cornerstone of his aesthetic system. When the satisfaction we get from an object is bound up with a desire that it exist, or a desire to possess it, that satisfaction is called "interest."

Now when the question is if a thing is beautiful, we do not want to know whether anything depends or can depend on the existence of the thing either for myself or for anyone else, but how we judge it by mere observation (intuition or reflection) [p. 47].

In this important respect, judgments of taste are entirely different from judgments of pleasurableness and judgments of the good (§§ 3, 4), for pleasure excites an inclination, and the good involves the concept of a purpose, of what the object judged good ought to be, while when we find an object beautiful we need have no definite concept of it. The judgment of taste, Kant insists, is "merely *contemplative*"; it is not a cognitive judgment, for it does not formulate or connect concepts at all (§ 5; p. 53). The satisfaction in the beautiful "is alone a disinterested and *free* satisfaction" (p. 54).

As to its *quantity*, the judgment of taste has a kind of universality. When we judge an object beautiful, we speak as though beauty were a property, though actually the judgment is subjective, since it connects the object with aesthetic satisfaction. But since such a satisfaction does not depend on any individual peculiarities or preferences (being disinterested), it is natural for us to suppose that we have found in the object a ground of *anyone's* satisfaction—something that can be enjoyed in that way universally. We therefore impute the same judgment to everyone (p. 60). That is why we use the impersonal mode of speech, and say "This is beautiful" rather than "This gives me a disinterested satisfaction." The judgment of beauty, being conceptless, cannot claim the objective universality of a logical judgment, but it lays "title to subjective universality" (§ 6; p. 56).

This claim to interpersonal validity is a crucial mark of judgments of taste, for Kant, and it is fundamentally what gives rise to the necessity of a third *Critique* (at least the first part). As always, the transcendental question is, "How are such judgments possible?" How can judgments that rest upon a purely subjective enjoyment, and do not involve the categories of the understanding, still command universal assent? Not that they will *get* universal assent, of course—the claim to universality does not rest on any empirical generalizations about human preferences (§ 7; p. 58)—but that when people disagree about the beauty of an object, each is claiming correctness for his judgment, and at least one of them must be mistaken. In this respect, the judgment of taste is very different from, say, judgments of delight in colors or sounds, in sense qualities, which may vary from person to person— "To one violet color is soft and lovely, to another it is faded and dead" (p. 57); "A smell which one man enjoys gives another a headache" (p. 154). On such things people are content to differ, without feeling that they are contradicting each other. But it makes no sense to say "This object . . . is beautiful for *me*" (p. 57), and let it go at that.

Kant introduces a special term (*Gemeingültigkeit*) for the peculiar interpersonal validity (or "common validity") of judgments of taste (§ 8). Universal logical judgments have this property on objective grounds, since to connect concepts universally, as in "All roses have petals," is clearly to claim that this holds true for all reasonable persons. But such judgments can be supported by reasons, and their common validity is therefore not hard to understand; they are subject to public discussion and logical tests. A judgment of taste, however, is essentially a singular judgment, "immediately accompanying . . . intuition" (p. 233)—having the form, "This rose is beautiful." (Out of a set of such singular judgments, a general one, "Most roses are beautiful," can be framed, but this is now a logical judgment, not an aesthetic one). Since such a singular judgment, in its pure form, uses the concept of "rose" only to identify the representation judged (and even here is not interested in the rose as such, as an object, but only as a sense-quality), and does not subsume the particular under any general concept, it cannot be defended by reasons. "There can be no rule according to which any one is to be forced to recognize anything as beautiful" (p. 62).

If a man reads me a poem of his or brings me to a play, which does not after all suit my taste, he may bring forward in proof of the beauty of his poem *Batteux* or *Lessing* or still more ancient and famous critics of taste, and all the rules laid down by them; certain passages which displease me may agree very well with rules of beauty (as they have been put forth by these writers and are universally recognized) : but I stop my ears, I will listen to no arguments and no reasoning; and I will rather assume that these rules of the critics are false, or at least that they do not apply to the case in question, than admit that my judgment should be determined by grounds of proof *a priori* [pp. 157–58; § 33].

We can, in the end, only confront the work itself, or get others to confront it, for this is where the judgment is made. Yet, strangely enough, when the judgment is made, it purports to be true for all people. How can this be? "The solution of this question," says Kant, "is the key to the Critique of Taste" (§ 9; p. 63).

If aesthetic satisfaction, the enjoyment of beauty, can be traced back to, or grounded in, some condition of the mind that we know to be universally possible, then the claim to universality in the judgment of beauty can be vindicated. Only some connection with knowledge will serve—not with any particular knowledge, but knowledge in general. Here Kant draws upon the conclusions of his first *Critique*, which sorted out the various cognitive faculties. All rational beings are capable of cognition, which requires the connectibility of two faculties, imagination (to gather together the manifold of sense-intuition) and understanding (to unify these representations by means of concepts). Particular acts of cognition involve the connection of particular representations with particular concepts—they require determinate relationships between imagination and understanding. But these acts presuppose an *indeterminate* general relationship—an underlying harmony of the two cognitive faculties. Now, when they are idling, so to speak, not seriously directed to the pursuit of knowledge, these faculties can play at knowledge, in a sense, enjoying the harmony between them without being tied down or bound by particular sense-intuitions or particular concepts. There arises a state of mind in which there is "a feeling of the free play of the representative powers in a given representation with reference to a cognition in general" (p. 64). In this state, the mind takes intense pleasure or satisfaction in the harmony of the two cognitive faculties. This pleasure is precisely the experience of beauty. The object we judge beautiful is one whose form, or principle of order, causes a "more lively play of both mental powers" and a keen awareness of their harmony (p. 66). Since all rational beings are capable of achieving this state of mind, under these conditions, beauty is shareable by all.

The third aspect of the judgment of taste—when it is considered as *relation*—leads to a further analysis of the principle of order, just referred to, that enables an object to provide that special disinterested and universally accessible satisfaction. When the concept of an object exists before the object, and enters into its production, that object is a *purpose* (or end), says Kant (§ 10; cf. § 65 and Introduction, pp. 20 ff, 30 ff).

But an Object, or a state of mind, or even an action, is called purposive, although its possibility does not necessarily presuppose the representation of a purpose, merely because its possibility can be explained and conceived by us only so far as we assume for its ground a causality according to purposes, *i.e.*, a will which would have so disposed it according to the representation of a certain rule [p. 68].

Then we have, in Kant's famous phrase, "purposiveness without purpose" (*Zweckmässigkeit ohne Zweck*). In this formulation of the distinction, there are puzzles; it comes close to a contradiction: the object doesn't necessarily require to have been purposed, though we can conceive it only as having been purposed. But there is a distinction.

We can say that it is one thing to believe that an object has a purpose, and another to regard it (for explanatory purposes) *as if* it had a purpose—for example, we might get a lead to important discoveries about an organ of the body if we began our study of it by asking about its function. Or we can say that the object doesn't have a purpose, but its harmony and wholeness make it *look* as though it were purposefully made, though we can't say what for (the Milky Way or the Great Stone Face). At least, it looks as though it were somehow made to be *understood*. Now, the judgment of taste is intimately connected, Kant thinks, with purposiveness, but it is not, of course, concerned at all with particular purposes, for then it would be conceptual and it would not be disinterested. What gives us aesthetic satisfaction "is the mere form of purposiveness in the representation by which an object is *given* to us, so far as we are conscious of it" (§ 11; pp. 69–70).

It is the experience of formal purposiveness in a representation that evokes the free harmonious play of the two cognitive faculties. But there is a difficulty here which Kant recognizes and discusses in the "General Remark" appended to the exposition of beauty: if we are intent upon the object, in aesthetic perception, how can the imagination have that free play? The concept of purposeless purposiveness supplies the solution: there is conformity to law without a law:

Although in the apprehension of a given object of sense [the imagination] is tied to a definite form of this Object, and so far has no free play (such as that of fancy [*wie im Dichten*]) yet it may readily be conceived that the object can furnish it with such a form containing a collection of the manifold, as the Imagination itself, if it were left free, would project in accordance with the *conformity to law of the Understanding* in general [p. 96; cf. Cassirer, p. 217 n, for the meaning of "*Dichten*"].

That is, the imagination recognizes an expression of itself in the formally satisfying object—something it might itself have made, or would wish to have made, out of freedom, though in harmony with the lawfulness (but not any particular law) of understanding.

Thus the form of the object is connected a priori with the feeling of the harmony of the two cognitive faculties; and the feeling of this harmony is precisely the disinterested (aesthetic) pleasure itself (§ 12; p. 71; cf. Introduction, pp. 27 ff). Though such a mental state gives rise to a special kind of interest, the desire to maintain it, to *"linger* over the contemplation of the beautiful, because this contemplation strengthens and reproduces itself" (p. 71), it does not follow that our aesthetic pleasure has anything to do with the pleasures of charm and emotion. Sensuous enjoyment (as of colors in painting, § 14), may contribute to aesthetic pleasure, but not constitute it, since the latter is concerned with form, not quality (§ 13). Form is either *"Gestalt,"* the structure of visual objects, or *"Spiel"* (play), the structure of temporal processes, like music (p. 75). This does not mean, however, that there can be an objective formal rule that will distinguish beautiful objects from those that are not:

To seek for a principle of taste which shall furnish, by means of definite concepts, a universal criterion of the beautiful, is fruitless trouble; because what is sought is impossible and self-contradictory [§ 17; p. 84; cf. §§ 33–34].

If aesthetic pleasure were merely empirical, the stimulation of an inner or outer sense, as the empiricists thought, this inquiry might be feasible, though the criterion found would only be probable, not necessary. Or if aesthetic pleasure were dependent upon a concept of some kind, as the rationalists thought, then such a criterion might be determined a priori, and applied by reason to mark out beautiful objects and demonstrate their beauty. However, aesthetic pleasure is neither sensuous nor intellectual, but something else (cf. § 58).

The fourth aspect of the judgment of taste is its *modality*: and that is necessity. "The beautiful we think as having a *necessary* reference to satisfaction" (§ 18; p. 91). This necessity is not apodictic, for no one who makes a judgment of taste can guarantee that all others will agree. Kant calls it "exemplary"—a particular judgment invites universal assent: it "claims that every one *ought* to give his approval to the object in question and also describe it as beautiful" (§ 19; p. 92). But it also promises agreement on the part of all those who correctly relate the object to their own cognitive faculties. The necessity, or obligatoriness, implicit in the judgment of taste presupposes a "common sense"—the state of mind "resulting from the free play of our cognitive powers"

(p. 93)—in all men. Do we have any reason for presupposing such a common sense? Yes, because it is a necessary condition of the shareability ("communicability") of knowledge itself, and this is assumed by all philosophical inquiry that is not skeptical (§ 21; cf. § 32). But this question really looks forward to the Deduction (see below).

The Second Book of the Analytic presents Kant's "transcendental exposition" of the sublime. Beauty and sublimity have two things in common: they can both be predicates of aesthetic judgments that are singular in logical form and claim universal validity, and they afford in themselves a pleasure that does not depend on sense or on a definite concept of the understanding. But beauty and sublimity are contrasted in two respects: that the former is connected with the form, hence the boundedness, of an object, while the latter involves an experience of boundlessness; and that the former depends upon the purposiveness of an object, making it seem "as it were, pre-adapted to our judgment" (§ 23; p. 103), while the latter is aroused by objects that seem "as it were to do violence to the imagination." The purposiveness we observe and call beautiful enriches our very concept of nature, by suggesting that it is not mere mechanism, but "something analogous to art" (p. 104); but it is wildness, chaos, disorder and desolation that excite sublimity, and therefore "the concept of the sublime is not nearly so important or rich in consequences as the concept of the beautiful."

The analysis of sublimity—one of Kant's most difficult undertakings—requires a further distinction between the mathematical sublime, which is evoked by objects that strike us as maximally huge, and the dynamical sublime, which is evoked by objects that seem to have absolute power over us.

"We call that *sublime* which is *absolutely great*" (§ 25; p. 106), which is such that in comparison with it everything else is small (p. 109). The judgment of absolute greatness (unlike judgments of comparative magnitude) is nonconceptual and noncognitive. Nothing observed by the senses permits this description, only something within, namely, the Ideas of Reason (*Vernunft*), which reach beyond all possible experience.

When we estimate magnitudes through numbers, that is, conceptually, the imagination selects a unit, which it can then repeat indefinitely. But there is a second kind of estimation of magnitudes, which Kant calls "aesthetic estimation," in which the imagination tries to comprehend or encompass the whole representation in one single intuition. There is an upper bound to its capacity. An object whose apparent or conceived size strains this capacity to the limit—threatens to exceed the imagination's power to take it all in at once—has, subjectively speaking, an absolute magnitude: it reaches the felt limit, and appears as if infinite. "Nature," says Kant, is "sublime in those of its phenomena, whose intuition brings with it the Idea of their infinity" (p. 116; § 26). When this Idea is aroused, Reason demands that it be given as a completed totality, that it be presented as a possible experience. This was just the demand that led to the antinomies in the first *Critique*, and it cannot be satisfied. But in straining to satisfy it, the imagination reaches its maximum capacity, shows its failure and inadequacy when compared to the demands of Reason, and makes us aware, by contrast, of the magnificence of Reason itself. The resulting feeling is the feeling of the sublime.

The joy and elevation felt in the presence of the sublime is the natural human pleasure of being reminded that we have *"a faculty of the mind surpassing every standard of Sense"* (p. 110). The feeling of the sublime contains a pain, the awareness of the disparity between imagination and Reason, but it is transformed into pleasure by its reflection of Reason's greatness. Thus we are moved by the sublime, not set to *"restful* contemplation," as by beauty (p. 120; § 27); and our feeling has some similarity to our respect for the moral law. The "sublime" object, though utterly nonpurposive and even antipurposive itself, makes us conscious of "a subjective purposiveness in the use of our cognitive faculty" (p. 108), that is, the supersensible faculty of Reason —bearing in mind here that Reason does not, of course, actually give us supersensible knowledge, but exercises a regulative function over the operations of understanding upon sense by demanding a completeness in the system of our knowledge that could be attained only by going beyond appearance to things in themselves. It is our own greatness, as rational beings, that we celebrate and enjoy in sublimity.

It is interesting to notice in this theory a piece of Kant's elaborate architectonic: the faculty of judgment generates the feeling of beauty out of the *harmony* it finds in relating the imagination, in its free play, to the understanding, in its general character; it generates the feeling of the sublime out of the *conflict* it creates by relating the imagination, even in its fullest exertion, to the Reason and its transcendent Ideas (see p. 117).

Nature is judged to be *dynamically* sublime when its overwhelming might makes it appear fearful, under circumstances when we are actually secure. Lightning and thunder, for example, hurricanes and volcanoes,

raise the energies of the soul above their accustomed height, and discover in us a faculty of resistance of a quite different kind, which gives us courage to measure ourselves against the apparent almightiness of nature [p. 125; § 28].

The sense of our impotence, as physical creatures, brings home to us the awareness of our infinite superiority as moral beings, our spiritual inviolability in the midst of natural perils. "Thus, humanity in our person remains unhumiliated, though the individual might have to submit to this dominion" (p. 126). It is the sublimity of our "destination" that we actually admire.

For Kant, this account of the dynamical sublime is not empirical psychology (like that of Burke, whom Kant praises), but transcendental philosophy, because, he holds, the judgment of sublimity (like the judgment of taste) claims universal validity, and thus rests upon an a priori foundation. True, the feeling for the sublime is rarer than the sense of beauty, and requires more cultivation, but because it comes out of a relation between imagination and Reason, which can exist in any man, and presupposes only the moral feeling that has been shown by the second *Critique* to be universal, we are justified in holding that all are obliged to agree with us (cf. pp. 149–50).

But there is a problem here that Kant leaves in a not wholly satisfactory state. He insists in several places that, properly speaking, sublimity is not predicated of objects of nature, but only of subjective states. In the judgment, "This is sublime," then, what does "this" refer to? If it refers to the speaker's own feelings, the judgment has no general claim to validity at all. If it refers to the Ideas of Reason, so that the judgment means either "Infinity is sublime" or "Man's moral nature is sublime" (or perhaps "Reason is sublime"), then it can claim universal validity, but all judgments of sublimity mean the same. The man who says (elliptically) that the waterfall is sublime, and the man who says the raging sea is sublime, are both talking about the same thing, namely man's moral nature or Reason. If sublimity-judgments are to be interesting as well as universally valid, they must make some external reference. And Kant's considered definition seems to allow this:

We may describe the Sublime thus: it is an object (of nature) *the representation of which determines the mind to think of the unattainability of nature regarded as a presentation of Ideas* [p. 134].

In the case of sublimity, the mind does more work, so to speak, than in the case of beauty. Both please immediately, but formal purposiveness, when freshly perceived, calls attention at once to the harmony of imagination and understanding, while the vast and terrible aspects of nature are only a kind of raw material that imagination and Reason can *use* to initiate activities that show up their own incommensurability. Judgment is more passive before beauty. Nevertheless, the judgment of sublimity is universal; to say the waterfall is sublime is to say that it can be used in that way by any being that possesses Theoretical and Practical Reason.

Thus there is an important logical difference between judgments of beauty and sublimity. The judgment of beauty claims a close and necessary connection between the object and disinterested aesthetic pleasure—that anyone who properly perceives the object will necessarily feel that pleasure. The judgment of sublimity claims a conditional or potential connection, which still has an indirect necessity: it is a necessary truth that if an object can be used by one rational being to evoke a feeling of the grandeur of reason or of man's moral destiny, it can be freely used by all who properly prepare themselves (see § 29, p. 131). It will not necessarily be so used by all. In the case of beauty, there is, then, a double aspect to Kant's argument: he must first reveal, by analysis, what is involved in the meaning of the judgment of beauty; then he must go on to prove its a priori necessity, to show by a transcendental argument that there is a necessary connection between beauty and aesthetic pleasure. This second argument is called "the deduction of pure aesthetic judgments," and Kant turns next to that task. No such deduction, he says, is required for the sublime, for there is no such direct necessary connection: when analysis has shown (as he thinks it has shown) that everything requisite for the sublime is necessarily present in all rational beings, no more can be done, or need be done, to justify the claim to universal validity (§ 30).

The problem of the deduction Kant states this way:

How is a judgment possible, in which merely from *our own* feeling of pleasure in an object, independently of its concept, we judge that this pleasure attaches to the representation of the same Object *in every other subject,* and that *a priori* without waiting for the accordance of others? [p. 163; § 36].

The way toward the solution has already been prepared: the synthetic a priori judgment of taste is legitimized if he can prove that its subjective condition, as we find it in ourselves, can be ascribed to every man. This is simply the general cooperativeness of two cognitive faculties. Since the judgment of taste does not subsume any particular representation under any particular concept, but only the general faculty of representations (the imagination) under the general faculty of concepts (understanding), the only subjective condition of the judgment of taste is the very faculty of judgment itself (§§ 35–36), and the universality of this faculty is shown by the simple fact that knowledge is shareable, or "communicable" (*mitteilbar*) (§§ 38–39; cf. p. 64).

In the last sections of the Analytic, Kant turns from his main argument to more discursive reflections on a number of topics: art and nature, the classification of the arts, genius, and humor. He has interesting and provocative things to say about all of them, and in these sections are some passages destined to be of considerable influence upon the aesthetics of Romanticism. Kant's analysis of genius picks up earlier reflections, but advances them considerably: through genius, "Nature gives the rule to Art" (p. 188; § 46): the genius has a talent for producing that for which no rule can be given; originality is his essential property; he does not imitate, though he may be inspired by examples; his manner of working eludes scientific description. Genius is also the faculty of *"aesthetical Ideas"* (p. 238).

By an aesthetical Idea I understand that representation of the Imagination which occasions much thought, without, however, any definite thought, *i.e.*, any *concept*, being capable of being adequate to it; it consequently cannot be completely compassed and made intelligible by language [p. 197; § 49].

In a manner analogous to that in which Reason, reaching beyond all possible experience, evolves its transcendent Ideas, to which no sense-intuition can be adequate, Imagination, freeing itself from the laws of association of ideas, works experience up into something new, "creating another nature, as it were, out of the material that actual nature gives it" (p. 198), and creates the aesthetic Ideas (cf. "Remark I," pp. 235 ff). Imagination "emulates the play of Reason"—the poet, for example, tries to realize or actualize in sensuous terms abstract rational concepts like heaven, hell, eternity. The representations in which imagination "binds up" (p. 238) or concentrates a great many ideas—Kant cites symbols like the eagle and the peacock—"arouse more thought than can be expressed in a concept determined by words" (p. 199). They are too rich for the understanding.

In the Dialectic, the second and final division of the Critique of Aesthetic Judgment, Kant presents the antinomy of taste. The puzzle that Kant exposes here arises from an apparent dialectical conflict between two propositions about taste that are not only implicit in widely accepted proverbs, but commend themselves directly to Reason. First, it seems clear that there can be no logical proofs of judgments of taste, and hence no logical method for resolving conflicts of judgment, as when two critics make incompatible judgments of a work. The first proposition is that "there is no disputing about taste" (§ 56)—where disputation (*disputieren*) is understood to include the claim that the difference of opinion can (in principle) be decided. Second, it also seems clear that we do in fact quarrel (*streiten*) about tastes, that is, issue judgments that are apparently incompatible, since one who praises a work of art feels rebuffed when another condemns it, and no one can comfortably say that a given work of art is both excellent and poor. But quarreling, in this sense, cannot occur unless the parties mean, by their judgments, to claim the assent of others. These two propositions, says Kant, lead to a contradiction, when we ask again the earlier question, whether the judgment of taste is based upon concepts. The antinomy is, then, this: (1) *Thesis*: the judgment of taste is *not* based upon concepts; for if it were, it would permit disputation, since logical arguments could be brought to bear (this contradicts the first proposition above). (2) *Antithesis*: the judgment of taste *is* based upon concepts; for if it were not, even quarreling would not be possible, since general assent could not be demanded (and this contradicts the second proposition).

There is no doubt some artificiality in this antinomy, as in those of the earlier *Critiques*, but it helps to bring out certain features of Kant's aesthetic theory quite sharply. The reconciliation consists in showing that "the concept to which we refer the Object in this kind of judgment is not taken in the same sense in both maxims of the aesthetical Judgment" (p. 231; § 57). The judgment of taste cannot be disputed because it is not based on *determinate* concepts of understanding; it can be quarreled about because it is based on the *indeterminate* concept, "the mere pure rational concept of the supersensible [the thing in itself] which underlies the object (and also the subject judging it)" (p. 233).

The main drive of Kant's philosophy of art is to establish the autonomy of the aesthetic, its independence of desire, of moral duty, and of knowledge—just as in the earlier *Critiques* he had striven to show that the understanding in its a priori activity is independent of sense, and that the moral law is independent of utility. But this is not the whole substance of his final thought, for once his distinctions are made, he always looks for a higher level on which connections can be re-established. Thus, the beautiful and the good have affinities after all. "I maintain," says Kant, "that to take an *immediate interest* in the Beauty of Nature (not merely to have taste in judging it) is always a mark of a good soul" (p. 177; § 42). This is not true of an interest in the beauty of art, he adds, curiously enough, for that may be contaminated with vanity. But to enjoy the beauty of nature we must find in nature a purposiveness and harmony that we recognize as the expression of a cosmic Reason akin to that within us which expresses itself in the moral law. Thus beauty can be taken as a symbol of the moral order (*Sittlichkeit*), and this is the true source of its capacity to make the mind "conscious of a certain ennoblement and elevation above the mere sensibility to pleasure received through sense" (p. 251; § 59). Like the other functions and faculties that make up the Kantian mind, aesthetic taste, precisely in following its own bent, plays its role in the larger economy of Reason.

OBJECTIVE IDEALISM

Difficult and highly individual philosophical theories like Kant's usually have to wait some time for converts. But Kant's aesthetics almost immediately took hold of a mind admirably equipped to grasp its fundamentals and develop them in new and interesting directions. After his early burst of creativity, the dramatic poet Friedrich Schiller (1759–1805) turned for a time to the study of history and philosophy. He read Kant carefully and well. He found in the third *Critique* the epistemological framework, and the basic theory of beauty and its relation to the cognitive faculties, that he needed to resolve the general problems about man and culture and freedom that he was pondering. These Kantian ideas he was able to connect with other influences—the educational and moral philosophy being thought out by his friend Fichte, and the metaphysical speculations of his close companion, Goethe. During the period from 1792 to 1796, before he wrote the last great dramas, he was preoccupied with aesthetic problems; and he produced, out of the extraordinary energy and vitality of his mind, a series of essays on various aesthetic subjects—the sublime, tragedy, "On Naïve and Sentimental Poetry" (1795)—several poems on art, and, most important of all, the *Letters on the Aesthetic Education of Man (Briefe über die ästhetische Erziehung des Menschen*, 1793–95).

In this work—so rich in ideas despite its brevity, and so full of the humane spirit, the concern for man and for men, that breathes through all of his works—Schiller asked a question that no one had put so profoundly since Plato: what is the ultimate role of art in human life and culture? To give his answer, he brought together his own Kantian conception of the cognitive faculties, his deep reflections on the history of culture and civilization, and his strong sense of living in a time of cultural crisis, for which a constructive resolution was needed.

Schiller begins by comparing two states of man: the natural, or sensuous, state, in which he first appears; and the state of reason, or morality, which he must make himself, out of his freedom (Letter 3). The relations between these states are developed with great subtlety. In certain respects they are antithetical, yet the highest morality to which man aspires cannot be achieved by negating his sensuous nature, but only by carrying it into a higher synthesis. To achieve humanity in himself (that is, his ideal nature) the individual man must find a harmony of his diverse powers, just as the state must find a harmony of its discordant wills—without mere suppression in either case (Letter 4). But it is just this harmony that Schiller finds so lacking when he looks about him. It seems that the idea of political freedom, of inalienable rights, has spread to the point where man at last can govern himself—yet a pervasive moral apathy refuses to seize the opportunity (Letter 5). Moreover, the very growth of culture itself has brought a deep split into human nature (Letter 6). Civilization could not develop without specialization of function, divergences of talent and desire: "There was no other way of developing the manifold capacities of Man than by placing them in opposition to each other" (Snell trans., p. 43). But the consequences can be severe (and Schiller describes them in words that could easily be put into the mouth of John Dewey, nearly a century and a half later):

State and Church, law and customs, were now torn asunder; enjoyment was separated from labor, means from ends, effort from reward. Eternally chained to only one single little fragment of the whole, Man himself grew to be only a fragment; with the monotonous noise of the wheel he drives everlastingly in his ears, he never develops the harmony of his being, and instead of imprinting humanity upon his nature he becomes merely the imprint of his occupation, of his science [p. 40].

The problem is how this fragmentation of society, and of the self, is to be overcome. Schiller's thought is so compact and suggestive that any summary must do him a considerable injustice, but we shall have to take the risk here of noting only the central theses, however abstract and unpersuasive they may seem by themselves. The character of the individual and the character of the state are so intimately connected, he says, that it may seem hopeless to try to break into the circle, to mend both together.

We should need, for this end, to seek out some instrument which the State does not afford us, and with it open up well-springs which will keep pure and clear throughout every political corruption.

. . . This instrument is the Fine Arts, and these well-springs are opened up in their immortal examples [pp. 50–51; Letter 9].

This, Schiller is aware, is a great deal to claim for art, and for beauty. He recalls that a considerable amount of historical evidence can be brought to cast doubt upon this claim. Beauty may attract the attention to surface and appearance rather than reality, to pleasure rather than active social commitment; moreover

It must indeed set us thinking when we find that in almost every epoch in history when the arts are flourishing and taste prevails, humanity is in a state of decline, and cannot produce a single example where a high degree and wide diffusion of aesthetic culture among a people has gone hand in hand with political freedom and civic virtue . . . [p. 58; Letter 10].

But these are merely empirical considerations, and may reflect contingent facts. They can be rebutted only by a transcendental study: by searching (as Kant did) for the a priori foundations of the "pure *rational concept* of Beauty" (p. 59).

It must therefore be sought along the path of abstraction, and it can be inferred simply from the possibility of a nature that is both sensuous and rational; in a word, Beauty must be exhibited as a necessary condition of humanity [p. 60].

Because of man's dual nature, which lives in the ever-changing world of sensation but preserves an inward self-identity that organizes sense-materials into law (Letter 11), man has two basic drives, or impulses: the sensuous impulse (*Stofftrieb*), which binds us to Nature, in the stream of time, pressing "for reality of existence, for some content in our perceptions and for purpose in our actions" (p. 65; Letter 12); and the formal impulse (*Formtrieb*), the demand of man's free rational self "to bring harmony into the diversity of his manifestation" (p. 66). These two drives are opposed, but seem to be exhaustive of the self. "How then are we to restore the unity of human nature?" (p. 67; Letter 13)— and in a way that preserves the importance of both? For man does not realize his humanity if either is sacrificed to the other.

But if there were cases when he had this twofold experience at the same time, when he was at once conscious of his freedom and sensible of his existence, when he at once felt himself as matter and came to know himself as spirit, he would in such cases, and positively in them alone, have a complete intuition of his humanity, and the object which afforded him this vision would serve him as a symbol of his accomplished destiny. . . . [p. 73–74].

The impulse that combines both the sensuous and the formal impulses, in a synthesis in which each is overcome by being lifted to a higher plane (*aufgehoben*; p. 88; Letter 18), is what Schiller calls the play impulse (*Spieltrieb*). And since the sensuous impulse seeks out life as its object, and the form impulse shape, the play impulse responds to "living shape" (*Lebensform*), or, in a more familiar term, beauty (Letter 15).

Beauty is thus, for Schiller, an objective quality. In a letter to Körner (Feb. 8, 1793) he described it as "freedom in the appearance" (*Freiheit in der Erscheinung*), the air of self-determination in the sensible object. Kant's insistence upon the subjectivity of beauty was one of the things that troubled him from his first study of Kant, and he had been searching for an account that would give it more objectivity. Later (in a letter to Goethe, July, 1797) he was to wonder whether the term "beauty" should not after all be "dismissed from circulation," because its meaning has been too narrowed and emptied, and the field of the aesthetic consequently too restricted.

When Schiller speaks of play, as his discussion and examples show, he is thinking first of the kind of harmony of cognitive faculties that Kant described, but he gives this a great deal of content. He does not intend to reduce art to play in the ordinary sense, man's sports and games—but he finds in these activities (in that peculiar combination of freedom and necessity that comes in the voluntary submission to rules for the fun of it) intimations of that higher spiritual synthesis that marks the aesthetic. "Man plays only when he is in the full sense of the word a man, and *he is only wholly Man when he is playing*" (p. 80). Thus "It is through Beauty that we arrive at Freedom" (Letter 2, p. 27), and through Beauty that we realize, as far as may be, our humanity (that is, our ideality as men). "As soon as [Reason] issues the command: a humanity shall exist, it has thereby proclaimed the law: there shall be a Beauty" (p. 77).

About the nature of the experience itself, in which the play impulse is evoked by Beauty, Schiller has a number of important things to say. In the complete aesthetic experience "we find ourselves at the same time in the condition of utter rest and extreme movement, and the result is that wonderful emotion for which reason has no conception and language no name" (p. 81, Letter 15); but since it has "at the same time a relaxing and a tightening effect" (p. 82; Letter 16), some experiences will tend more toward the "melting" and others toward the "energizing" pole. "That art alone is genuine which provides the highest enjoyment," he says in the introduction to his play *The Bride of Messina* (trans. Ungar, p. 167). "The highest enjoyment, however, is freedom of spirit in the vivacious play of all its powers." This is the aesthetic experience.

We can now see very clearly a deep ambivalence in Schiller's aesthetic theory, which he never resolved: whether the aesthetic condition, as he calls it (Letter 20), is merely transitional or truly final. The cultural question with which he began was: How can man pass from the sensuous to the rational (moral) condition? And one of his main arguments is that art makes this possible, by providing a via media, an intermediate condition in which both are combined. Art makes this possible, in part, by teaching "contemplation" (Letter 25), which makes reflection possible; for art encourages a delight in appearance (*Schein*), a detachment from the world of sense without a repudiation of it: "When therefore we discover traces of a disinterested free appreciation of pure appearance, we can infer some such revolution of his nature and the real beginnings in him of humanity" (p. 132; Letter 27). The beautiful "paves the way for mankind to a transition from sensation to thought" (p. 92; Letter 19); "there is no other way to make the sensuous man rational than by first making him aesthetic" (p. 108; Letter 23). From this point of view, beauty has only one function, to free man for the realization of his higher self (see Letter 21). But, as the argument has developed, and the play impulse become more concrete, the aesthetic condition has emerged, not just as a step toward the highest state of man, but as a *constituent* of it. Only in this condition are both the sensuous and the intellectual sides of man kept in free harmonious relationship, and only through a continuous experience of beauty is the political system able to combine order with freedom.

> Though need may drive Man into society, and Reason implant social principles in him, Beauty alone can confer on him a *social character.* Taste alone brings harmony into society, because it establishes harmony in the individual. All other forms of perception divide a man, because they are exclusively based either on the sensuous or on the intellectual part of his being; only the perception of the Beautiful makes something whole of him, because both his natures must accord with it [p. 138; Letter 27].

No greater claim for the aesthetic education of man has ever been staked out.

Kant, it will be remembered, left behind him a system that presented a number of challenges to his successors and in particular two challenges that were felt most keenly by the Idealists, and taken up with great enthusiasm. First, his "Copernican revolution" guaranteed the a priori validity of certain categories of thought (and consequently of certain principles), as applied to nature, by demonstrating the extent to which nature itself is what it is because the mind applies these very categories. Philosophers who were exhilarated by this powerful affirmation of spirit's dominion over brute fact naturally wondered whether Kant's revolution could be surpassed, by deriving not only the form of the external world (as he did), but even its content, from the nature of mind itself. Thus, for example, Fichte based his own system on the principle that "the Ego posits the non-Ego," that is, the self (not the individual self, but the greater self which it manifests) calls nature into existence as a foil to itself, to make possible moral effort and an actively good will. Second, Kant's system attained its precarious stability through the delicate adjustment of certain oppositions—between the matter of experience, which is given, and the form, which is contributed by understanding; and between the phenomenal world, which we can know empirically, and the noumenal world of things-in-themselves, which lies beyond knowledge but somehow is the source of the given in experience. The resulting dualisms appeared to the Idealists as a demand to be overcome, or overridden; and this seemed possible only if philosophy could secure an absolute standpoint, a perspective higher, or deeper, than Kant thought possible.

It was the philosopher Friedrich Wilhelm von Schelling (1775–1854), in his precocious youth as professor at Jena, who first claimed to have achieved such a standpoint. That later on he renounced his earlier views does not matter to our story, for it was these views that were most influential. Nor does it matter that his chief work on aesthetics, the lectures on *The Philosophy of Art*, was not published until 1859, for these lectures, given at Jena (1802–3) and elsewhere, were widely circulated in manuscript, and much discussed at the time. What does, perhaps, matter from our point of view, is that Schelling, for all his claims to system, could never discipline or control his effervescent thought, and though the general shape of his metaphysics and aesthetics can be made out (together with many eloquent though often puzzling passages on particular points), the arguments and connections—as Hegel, his early friend and philosophical debtor, complained—are far from clear or cogent. Nevertheless, Schelling (as will be evident in my next chapter) became the inspired and inspiring philosopher of the Romantic movement, especially in the central and exalted position he gave to art itself.

Not since Plotinus, in fact, and never again since Schelling, have aesthetic concerns been made the highest and dominant feature of a systematic philosophy. This point was reached first in Schelling's *System of Transcendental Idealism* (1800). In his earlier works, Schelling had developed the "Philosophy of Nature" that was so exciting to contemporary poets and critics. He attempted to do away with the antithesis of Nature and Spirit, by conceiving of Nature itself as an unconscious form of thought, with the capacity to evolve conscious thought in man. In the second phase of his thinking, the problem of relating the self and Nature is felt more deeply, and the task of transcendental philosophy is taken to be precisely that of bridging this gap, by deriving Nature from Reason. There is, he says, in the *Transcendental Idealism,* a radical "contradiction" in the post-Kantian philosophy, for our ideas must shape themselves to conform to objects, in order to be true, but objects must conform to ideas, that is, yield to our will, if there is to be moral striving. Neither theoretical nor practical (that is, ethical) philosophy can overcome this difficulty; what is required is another way of exhibiting an underlying harmony between Nature and Self. Schelling postulates that the forms (organic beings, crystals, etc.) we find in nature are produced by a creative process that is, though unconscious, the same creativity we can find in ourselves; and this is the harmony that is sought for.

> Only *aesthetic* activity is of this kind, and every work of art is intelligible only as the product of such an activity. The ideal world of art and the real world of objects are therefore products of one and the same activity. The confluence of the two (conscious and unconscious activities) *without* consciousness gives rise to the real world, and *with* consciousness to the aesthetic world [*System of Transcendental Idealism*, Introduction, § 3; *Werke*, III, 349; trans. Albert Hofstadter].[1]

The problem of transcendental philosophy, for Schelling, is to show how the inner harmony of Nature and the Self (or Ego) can be made manifest to the Self. This can only be understood through the discovery of an "intuition" in which the Self is both conscious and unconscious at once. And this intuition can only be "artistic intuition," since artistic activity combines both a conscious (deliberate) element, which he calls *"Kunst,"* and an unconscious (inspired) element, which he calls *"Poesie"* (see Section 5). With this clue, Schelling undertakes (in Section 6) nothing less than a transcendental deduction of the necessity of art, and of the basic principles of a philosophy of art. The argument is very obscure, and choked with characteristic Schellingian oppositions of abstract concepts whose relationships are by no means fully explained. Apparently he conceives of artistic production as a unique process that begins with an inner contradiction between the conscious and the unconscious, and resolves this contradiction by objectifying intelligence for itself, in a product that unifies freedom and necessity. In the satisfaction that comes from carrying through this process (and from contemplating the result) we become aware of the infinite harmony of Self and Nature.

In Schelling's lectures on the *Philosophy of Art*, his "Transcendental Idealism" becomes Absolute Idealism. The Absolute

----

[1] From Albert Hofstadter and Richard Kuhns, eds., *Philosophies of Art and Beauty* (New York, 1964), pp. 354–55.

itself is simple self-identity, but not an empty identity, because its unity is that of a whole within which, from a finite point of view, we can distinguish degrees of reality and ideality; and in whatever exists within the Absolute both of these aspects are given a special degree of emphasis. Differences of emphasis are called "potencies," of which art turns out to be one. A philosophy aims to understand the Absolute through its potencies, and ultimately to see their connection and unity; a philosophy of art approaches the Absolute through the potency of art. Though, fundamentally, Nature and Mind are identical, they are very different in their level of reality, and hence in their striving; Nature yearns toward ideality, Mind aims toward a systematic synthesis of the finite and infinite. This it reaches through art. For art is peculiarly concerned with the realization of what Schelling calls "Ideas," which he characterizes as neither subjectively Lockean nor objectively Platonic, but as "essences," an identity of subject and object. By embodying infinite Ideas in finite objects, art becomes the symbolic representation of the Absolute, and the deepest expression of Mind—hence the highest of the potencies, compared with which science and morality are only partial and incomplete.

This general idea seems to underlie Schelling's famous Munich address "On the Relation of the Plastic [or Formative] Arts to Nature" (1807), where he criticizes the imitation theory. Paintings in which there is a realistic imitation of objects are paradoxically less "real" and vital, less powerfully "true," than those which are less realistic—and this paradox can only be explained by supposing that in representation, art reaches toward a truth higher than actuality, and that "thought is the only living principle in things" (*Werke*, VII, pp. 289 ff).

The *Philosophy of Art* goes on to discuss various arts in terms of the Ideas congenial to them. In this part of the work there are some peculiar notions—among them, the famous characterization of architecture as "frozen music" (see *Werke*, V, 593; cf. 577). But the discussion of music is remarkably original: in its freedom from space, its insubstantial existence as pure process, music is said to symbolize the unity of Being itself, the interpenetration of finite and infinite.

A great deal of what is viable in Schelling found its way into

Hegel, though transformed. I will come to that in a moment; meanwhile, there are two other thinkers who deserve mention, if only to indicate briefly (as I must so often be content to do in this short history) where certain ideas might be followed up by the reader. Karl Wilhelm Ferdinand Solger wrote a difficult dialogue, *Erwin* (1815), and published his *Vorlesungen über Ästhetik* (1829; delivered in 1819). He was much concerned with the nature of the artistic imagination (*Phantasie*), which he conceived as closely analogous to the creative activity of God, as bringing universal and particular together into a "symbolic unity"—borrowing the term "symbol," which Goethe had first introduced in this context. The difference is that the work of the finite artist is permeated with the sense of illusion, contingency, and "nothingness"—which he calls "irony," and finds to be pervasive and fundamental in great literature. Friedrich Schleiermacher, whose chief historical fame is in the field of theology, lectured on aesthetics at the University of Berlin in 1819 and later (the lectures were published in 1842). He was also much concerned with the process of artistic creation, which he interpreted in a thoroughly emotionalist fashion. Art is, in his view, self-expression, which is at the same time self-awareness, an externalization of emotion (communication is not an essential aspect of art). Schleiermacher carried farther than other thinkers that notion of the artistic impulse as "free productivity," not called upon or compelled by ends beyond itself, or external demands; in this respect it is like the dream state, which is a free productivity of images. Art is thus independent of moral and cognitive conditions; it is sui generis.

A new and determinate metaphysical role was assigned to art in the system of Absolute Idealism worked out in full complexity by Georg Friedrich Wilhelm Hegel (1770–1831). Hegel's aesthetics is intimately connected with his whole system, and that system does not yield readily to intelligible paraphrase, but perhaps, after an initial explication of a few of his fundamental concepts, it will be possible to describe, without excessive oversimplification, the main features of his theory. Our fullest source is the manuscript notes for lectures at the University of Berlin (given first in 1820; revised in 1823, 1826, and 1829), edited and published (1835) after his death as the *Philosophy of Fine Art*.

Without attempting to describe the reasoning by which Hegel arrived at this conclusion, let us begin with his principle that reality is Spirit, or Mind (*Geist*)—a systematic whole, whose self-unfolding, through its activity of thought, gives rise to the structure, and the history, of all that is. Considered in itself, Spirit articulates itself necessarily in certain basic categories of thought, whose dialectical relationships (the way in which they grow out of each other through contradiction and higher synthesis) are mapped in Hegel's *Logic*. In its course of self-development, Spirit must pass through a stage of self-estrangement, alienation, or externalization, which is Nature, the object of empirical science; but it returns to itself in its self-consciousness, on a higher level, in three grades of self-realization—Subjective Mind (the individual self), Objective Mind (the State), and Absolute Mind, which is the ultimate truth, the object of philosophical knowledge.

The categories of thought—by which we strive to grasp the Absolute, and by which the Absolute at the same time comes to terms with its own infinite richness of content—are ranged in degrees of adequacy, from the category of bare Being (which is the least one can ascribe to the Absolute) to the category that Hegel calls "Idea" (*Idee*). All of the endless variety of concepts in which thought can articulate itself are divided by Hegel into two sorts. For many ordinary and specialized purposes, we, as finite individuals, conceive of objects as grouped in series or in classes in terms of commonly shared universals (like the successor-relation in number theory, or the property of being opaque). Hegel calls these "abstract universals." But thought that aims to lay hold of the Absolute, or of some partial truth within it, must (like the thoughts of the Absolute as such) be a "concrete universal": a universal that does not exclude the particular, but contains (somehow) the potentiality of the particular within it, as part of its necessary content. The concrete universal is the "Notion" (*Begriff*): it is not barren, but full of content, and capable of dialectical development, that is, of generating other concepts. (Even the thin category of Being, which like all the categories is a Notion, is shown by Hegel's method of examination to turn into its negation, Nothing, and thus to generate Becoming, as a synthesis of Being and Nothing.) The Notion involves self-identity, but a self-identity mediated through involvement in the individuals that fall under it; it is an identity-in-difference.

These difficult doctrines, so carefully but obscurely spelled out in Hegel's *Logic*, seem to call for at least so much of a review here, since they are presupposed by two other terms that are not only fundamental to the logic, but central to the philosophy of art: "Idea" and "Ideal." In the last part of the *Logic*, the Notion, exhibiting itself in its fullest significance, becomes the Idea, defined as "truth in itself and for itself—the absolute unity of the notion and objectivity."[2] To understand how there can be such a unity—how thought in its fullest concreteness can become identical with its object, yet without becoming indistinguishable from it—we must bear in mind that from the Absolute point of view the necessary distinctions that we make between our thoughts and the objects we think *about* are valid only at the lower stages of philosophical wisdom; in the final analysis, truth is the Absolute's knowledge of itself. The richer and more concrete the Notion becomes, the more it tends toward reality; in the Idea, and most especially in the Absolute Idea, the Notion and the real coalesce (see *Philosophy of Fine Art*, trans. Osmaston, I, 149–53).

All this is germane to our purpose because it is the foundation of Hegel's theory of beauty. "The function of philosophy," says Hegel, "is to examine subject-matter in the light of the principle of necessity" (I, 14). Therefore a truly philosophical theory of art must show how the existence of art is necessarily entailed by the nature of reality itself. Now, in order to unfold itself at every level of cognitive adequacy, the Idea must be exhibited with all the resources of Spirit. Moreover, to assist its recovery from that self-alienation which posits the existence of Nature, Spirit requires a phase of activity in which the Idea can show itself (and Spirit recognize itself) in sensuous form—in which the gulf that Spirit creates between itself and matter is canceled, and the Idea allowed to "shine" through matter itself. This inevitable movement of Spirit is precisely what makes art necessary, and explains how there should be such a thing (I, 15–16). Looking from the more limited point of view of man himself, as creator and enjoyer of art, a similar necessity can be observed: because man is a *"thinking* consciousness," and "renders explicit *to himself,* and

2 See Hegel's shorter *Logic*, trans. William Wallace, 2d ed. (Oxford, 1892), §213, p. 352.

from his own substance, what he is and all in fact that exists"
(I, 41), he satisfies in works of art his need to increase his self-
consciousness and self-knowledge. For on these works

he imprints the seal of his inner life, rediscovering in them thereby
the features of his own determinate nature. And man does all this, in
order that he may as a free agent divest the external world of its stub-
born alienation from himself—and in order that he may enjoy in the
configuration of objective fact an external reality simply of himself
[I, 42].

How do works of art fulfill this function in the life of Spirit
and of man? By presenting "merely a shadow-world of shapes,
tones, and imaged conceptions *(Anschauungen)"*—not for purely
sensuous or emotional satisfaction, but "for higher and more
spiritual interests." They

summon an echo and response in the human spirit evoked from all
depths of its conscious life. In this way the sensuous is *spiritualized* in
art, or, in other words, the life of *spirit* comes to dwell in it under
sensuous guise [I, 53].

The basic and essential function of art, then, to which all other
possible uses are subordinate, is "to reveal *truth* under the mode
of art's sensuous or material configuration" (I, 77; cf. 95). This
revelation is beauty (I, 125–29)—"the *Sensuous Semblance [das
sinnliche Scheinen]* of the Idea" (I, 154).

Each work of art, then, when it achieves beauty, involves a
reconciliation of matter and content, of sensuous show and the
embodied Idea. Thus the excellence of the work "will depend
upon the degree of intimacy and union with which idea and configuration appear together in elaborated fusion" (I, 98). The idea
that finds in this way its adequate sensuous realization, the artistically embodied Idea, Hegel calls the "Ideal" (I, 100; cf.
102, 147).

"An object which is beautiful," says Hegel, is a peculiarly perfect paradigm of freedom, the essence of Spirit, because it "suffers
its own notion to appear as realized in its objective presence," and
presents itself as independent of other things, as self-determined,
self-complete, and infinite (I, 157–59). Hence the perceiving self
is caught in a rapt and fulfilling contemplation, from which passion and desire drop away. "The aesthetic contemplation of the
beautiful is a liberal education" (I, 158).

Granting that Hegel has proved the necessity of beauty, has he proved the necessity of art? For Nature has a beauty, too, as he concedes, and we have seen that Kant, for example, gives natural beauty the commanding place in his theory. But Hegel—and this is one of his important contributions to the progress of aesthetics—is quite clear that "the beauty of art stands *higher* than Nature" (I, 2). Natural beauties bear an imprint of the Idea, but a dimmer and lower one than is borne by the works that directly proceed from the human spirit. "The hard rind of Nature and the everyday world offer more difficulty to the mind in breaking through to the Idea than do the products of art" (I, 11). Man's artistic creations seize upon spiritual values and capture them with "greater purity and clarity." "And for this reason the work of art is of higher rank than any product of Nature whatever" (I, 39; cf. 10–11, 208, 212–14).

In his final estimate, Hegel makes Art, along with Religion and Philosophy, one of the three modes of apprehension of the Absolute, one of the three self-revelations of the Absolute Idea. In art, he says, we grasp Spirit in its "immediacy" (I, 8–9; cf. 138–40). This is not the highest form of knowledge of Spirit, because not every grade of truth can be expressed in art (Oriental and Greek religious concepts can be completely embodied in sense, but the highest Christian concepts resist such an exhibition)—moreover, when art strives after the expression of the most profound Idea, it overreaches itself and becomes something else, namely Religion or Philosophy (I, 11–13). Hegel seems to suggest in some rather ambiguous passages that the capabilities of Art for development and larger encompassment have been exhausted; as Spirit comes closer to its cosmic and historical goal, freedom (see I, 133), and men and their institutions and their culture become more spiritualized, art becomes less and less adequate to the realized Ideas (I, 141–42). The development—which Hegel traces at some length in Vol. II—from what he calls Symbolic art through Classical art to Romantic art, may be at an end.

Though Hegel's discussion of these distinctions has many interesting features, we need not follow it here. Essentially, since in every work, according to his theory, there is always sensuous material and spiritual content, three basic relations can be distinguished between these two aspects. In Symbolic art, characteristic of early and Oriental culture, the Idea is overwhelmed by the medium, which strains in vain to express it. In Classical art, the Idea and the medium are in perfect equilibrium. In Romantic art, the Idea dominates the medium and spiritualization is complete (see I, 102 ff). Corresponding to these distinctions, there is a further, elaborately developed, analysis of a hierarchy of the arts themselves (see III and IV). Architecture is the paradigm of Symbolic art: sculpture of classical art; and the Romantic artistic impulse expresses itself most fully in three arts, marking progressive stages of freedom from the sensuous medium and approximation toward pure thought—painting, which is less material than sculpture in having only two dimensions; music, which leaves space behind; and poetry, which is nearly all Idea (see I, 112 ff). Hegel not only gives many examples to illustrate his theses (including able discussions of particular works), but in the course of his argument treats a number of interesting topics, such as the sublime (II, 97–105) and the nature of tragedy (IV, 293 ff)—which, in his view, involves the collision (best illustrated by the *Antigone*) of antithetical ethical claims, each having some validity, and their resolution or partial reconciliation. Thus tragedy, at its highest, embodies the very dialectical movement of the world's ethical order.

The later history of metaphysical idealism in aesthetics, through the nineteenth century, need not be told here; even to sort out the various thinkers, and discuss them fully enough to distinguish their views usefully and memorably, would require far more space than (on the scale of this little history) could be justified by the significance of their contributions. Hegel himself attracted a host of now forgotten followers, many of them most faithful. Among them, Christian Hermann Weisse (*Ästhetik*, 1830) is perhaps most favorably representative. A few other thinkers belonging to the idealist tradition may deserve at least mention, on account of some novelties in the way they developed aesthetic theory, or on account of the bulk and earnestness of their work. Among them was Friedrich Theodor Vischer, whose six huge volumes of elaborate distinctions and classifications (including the *Ästhetik*, 2 vols., 1846–47, and *Die Künste*, 4 vols., 1851–57) are a monument of nineteenth-century idealistic aesthetics, though in his later years, in a remarkable piece of self-criticism, he repudiated much of what they say. Karl Rosenkranz wrote an *Ästhetik der Hässlichen* (1853), that is, a treatise on the ugly. Hermann Lotze developed his aesthetic theories in his history of German aesthetics (1868) and in the little *Grundzüge der Ästhetik* (1884; trans. G. T. Ladd, 1886). And Eduard von Hartmann wrote a systematic aesthetics (in his *Philosophie des Schönen*, Part II of an *Ästhetik*, 1890).

In general, these and the many other writers were occupied with three main issues. There was some controversy between the "abstract idealists" (like Lotze), who fell back on a kind of Platonic Idea of beauty, and the "concrete idealists" (like Hartmann), who remained faithful to Hegel's view that any Idea is a beauty when it appears in sense. A good deal of attention was given to the concept of the ugly, and its relation to beauty, the sublime, and artistic perfection. And various schemes were proposed for the classification of the arts, as alternatives to Hegel's, on various possible principles.

This may also be a good place to note the important reaction against idealist aesthetics in those who took it seriously enough to combat it, but saw in the reduction of beauty to the Idea an overintellectualization or overcognitivization of the aesthetic, a surrender of its autonomy ultimately to the dominance of religion and philosophy. The pioneer of these "formalistic" aestheticians was Johann Friedrich Herbart (*Schriften zur praktischen Philosophie*, 1808; *Einleitung in die Philosophie*, 1813). For him, the essential feature of art is form, that is sets of successive or simultaneous relations. This concept was further developed by Robert Zimmermann, in his history of aesthetics (1858), and *Allgemeine Ästhetik als Formwissenschaft* (1865). Though not strictly empiricist in his method, his concept of aesthetics as investigating the conditions under which sensuous contents elicit approval or disapproval helped lead the way to the appearance of psychological aesthetics in Fechner and Stumpf.

The German Idealists after Kant (and especially Hegel, of course)—whether or not, as they believed, they taught people to think more profoundly about the nature of art—at least introduced a new breadth into the discussion. They saw Art, capitalized, in the largest context, not only metaphysical, but social and cultural—that is, "concretely," in the way Hegel understood this term. And it was in part through their approach that, as we shall see, people were led to think about art as a social fact, with important (and discoverable) social roots and fruit.

Bibliography

Kant's Critique of Judgement, trans. J. H. Bernard, 2d ed. (London, 1914).

Immanuel Kant, *Analytic of the Beautiful*, trans. Walter Cerf (New York, 1963).

H. W. Cassirer, *A Commentary on Kant's Critique of Judgment* (London, 1938).

R. A. C. Macmillan, *The Crowning Phase of the Critical Philosophy* (London, 1912).

James C. Meredith, *Kant's Critique of Aesthetic Judgement* (Oxford U., 1911), Introductory Essays.

Barrows Dunham, *A Study in Kant's Aesthetics* (Lancaster, Pa., 1934).

Israel Knox, *The Aesthetic Theories of Kant, Hegel, and Schopenhauer* (Columbia U., 1936).

Hermann Cohen, *Kants Begründung der Ästhetik* (Berlin, 1889).

O. Schlapp, *Kants Lehre vom Genie und die Entstehung der "Kritik der Urteilskraft"* (Göttingen, 1901).

P. Menzer, *Kants Ästhetik in ihrer Entwicklung* (Berlin, 1952).

Victor Basch, *Essai critique sur l'esthétique de Kant*, 2d ed. (Paris, 1927).

A. D. Lindsay, *Kant* (London, 1934), ch. 5.

Edward Caird, *The Critical Philosophy of Immanuel Kant*, 2 vols. (Glasgow, 1889), Book III.

Humayun Kabir, *Immanuel Kant on Philosophy in General* (Calcutta, 1935), Introductory Essays (on the first Introduction to the *Critique of Judgment*).

Robert L. Zimmerman, "Kant: The Aesthetic Judgment," *Jour Aesth and Art Crit* XXI (Spring 1963): 333–44.

Harold N. Lee, "Kant's Theory of Aesthetics," *Philos Rev* XL (1931): 537–48.

T. M. Greene, "A Reassessment of Kant's Aesthetic Theory"; Barrows Dunham, "Kant's Theory of Aesthetic Form"; R. W. Bretall, "Kant's Theory of the Sublime"; in G. T. Whitney and D. F. Bowers, eds., *The Heritage of Kant* (Princeton U., 1939).

Herbert M. Schueller, "Immanuel Kant and the Aesthetics of Music," *Jour Aesth and Art Crit* XIV (December 1955): 218–47.

René Wellek, "[Kant's] Aesthetics and Criticism," in C. W. Hendel, ed., *The Philosophy of Kant and Our Modern World* (New York, 1957).

Harry Blocker, "Kant's Theory of the Relation of Imagination and Understanding in Aesthetic Judgments of Taste," *Brit Jour of Aesth* V (1965): 37–45.

Frederic Will, *Intelligible Beauty in Aesthetic Thought from Winckelmann to Victor Cousin* (Tübingen, 1958).

Friedrich Schiller, [*Letters*] *On the Aesthetic Education of Man*, trans. Reginald Snell (Yale U., 1954).

Frederick Ungar, *Friedrich Schiller: An Anthology for Our Time*, Part I (New York, 1959).

Otto Harnack, *Die klassische Ästhetik der Deutschen* (Leipzig, 1892).

S. S. Kerry, "The Artist's Intuition in Schiller's Aesthetic Philosophy," *Pubs of the Eng Goethe Soc* N.S. Vol. XXVIII (Leeds, 1959).

Eva Schaper, "Friedrich Schiller: Adventures of a Kantian," *Brit Jour of Aesth* IV (1964): 348–62.

Elizabeth E. Bohning, "Goethe's and Schiller's Interpretation of Beauty," *German Quart* XXII (1949): 185–94.

Friedrich von Schelling, *Sämmtliche Werke*, 14 vols. (Stuttgart and Augsburg, 1856–61).

Friedrich von Schelling, "Concerning the Relation of the Plastic Arts to Nature (*Über das Verhältnis der bildenen Künste zu der Natur*)" (1807), trans. Michael Bullock, in Herbert Read, *The True Voice of Feeling* (New York, 1953).

Friedrich von Schelling, *The Method of University Studies*

(*Vorlesung über die Methode des akademischen Studiums*) (1803); 14th lecture, trans. Mrs. Ella S. Morgan, in Daniel S. Robinson, ed., *An Anthology of Modern Philosophy* (New York, 1931).

Friedrich von Schelling, *System of Transcendental Idealism* (1800); selection trans. Thomas Davidson, in ibid.

Jean Gibelin, *L'esthétique de Schelling d'après la philosophie de l'art* (Paris, 1934).

Emil L. Fackenheim, "Schelling's Philosophy of the Literary Arts," *Philos Quart* IV (1954): 310–26.

Herbert M. Schueller, "Schelling's Theory of the Metaphysics of Music," *Jour Aesth and Art Crit* XV (June 1957): 461–76.

G. W. F. Hegel, *Philosophy of Fine Art*, 4 vols., trans. F. P. B. Osmaston (London, 1920).

The Introduction to Hegel's Philosophy of Fine Art, trans. Bernard Bosanquet (London, 1886).

W. T. Stace, *The Philosophy of Hegel* (London, 1924), Part IV, Third Div., Ch. 1.

Israel Knox, *The Aesthetic Theories of Kant, Hegel, and Schopenhauer* (Columbia U., 1936), second part.

A. C. Bradley, "Hegel's Theory of Tragedy," in *Oxford Lectures on Poetry,* 2d ed. (London, 1909).

Günther Jacoby, *Herders und Kant's Ästhetik* (Leipzig, 1907).

Ernest K. Mundt, "Three Aspects of German Aesthetic Theory," *Jour Aesth and Art Crit* XVII (March 1959): 287–310.

There are several German histories that deal with the development of post-Kantian idealist aesthetics (but in reading them it must be borne in mind that they are written by interested parties in the disputes, and their partisanship must be allowed for). See, for example: Eduard von Hartmann, *Die deutsche Ästhetik seit Kant* (Berlin, 1886); Hermann Lotze, *Geschichte der Ästhetik in Deutschland* (Munich, 1868); G. Neudecker, *Studien zur Geschichte der deutschen Ästhetik seit Kant* (Würzburg, 1878); Max Schasler, *Kritische Geschichte der Ästhetik* (Berlin, 1872); Robert Zimmermann, *Geschichte der Ästhetik als philosophischer Wissenschaft* (Vienna, 1858).

TEN

Romanticism

The history of aesthetic thinking in the nineteenth century has a markedly different character from that in the preceding century. As we have seen, philosophic concern with aesthetic problems persisted in Germany, among the Hegelians and semi-Hegelians, and also among those "formalistic" professors whose rebellion against Hegelianism helped foster the rise of experimental psychology in aesthetics. Though considerable in quantity, German aesthetics achieved few advances of permanent note—except in the hands of two thinkers outside the academic tradition, Schopenhauer and Nietzsche, to whom we must pay due respect in the present chapter. In England, after the philosophical renaissance among the Scots philosophers, the systematic study of aesthetics, in the manner begun by Hutcheson and (as we have seen) practiced so brilliantly by many others, declined. And, there, as in France, the new ideas about art and about criticism came, for the most part, from the critical theorists and the creative artists themselves.

The nineteenth century saw the emergence, or growing prominence, of several tendencies, some of which rose and fell in a full cycle of realization and exhaustion, while others produced only a promissory note awaiting the twentieth century for redemption. An important part of the story is reserved for the following chapter, which will try to disentangle a number of threads of argument having to do with the relationships between the creative artist and his society. That general problem, however, grows in large part out of the dominant intellectual current in the first

[244]

half of the nineteenth century, that is, Romanticism. This movement, very rich in implications for a philosophy of art, is to be
considered—at least, in broad outlines—in the present chapter.

THE AESTHETICS OF FEELING

We must now go back a step, from Hegel's lectures on aesthetics, to consider some developments which, though they began
in close association with the philosophic Idealisms of Kant,
Schiller, and Schelling, ultimately led off in a different direction.
(To recite a short history of complex movements requires—and
therefore, I think, allows—some chronological license.) The Romantic Revolution was not announced by any very definite event,
a storming of the Bastille or shot heard round the world, and it
erupted at different times in different countries. The term "Romantic" itself hardly has a determinate and standard sense,
though it is somewhat more settled now than it was among the
Romantics themselves. August Wilhelm Schlegel (with some
suggestions from his brother Friedrich) developed the concept
of Romantic, as opposed to Classic, poetry and art (in his Berlin
lectures, first, but most fully in the Vienna lectures, 1809–11,
Über dramatische Kunst und Litteratur): Romantic poetry embodies a striving for the infinite; it stems from Christianity, and
is marked by inner division of spirit, a sense of a gap between
actual and ideal, hence an unsatisfied longing. Schlegel's distinction reached England (and other countries) via Madame de
Staël's *De l'Allemagne* (1813), and later through translations of
the Vienna lectures—and it became very influential. True, the
British poets whom we classify as Romantic did not apply
Schlegel's term to themselves; but most of them were conscious
of taking part in a new adventure of thought and feeling.

We had better not trouble ourselves much, then, with the history of the term itself. What is more bothersome is the difficulty
of separating, in Romanticism, the dominant aesthetic convictions from other ingredients of what is, admittedly, a rather
amorphous and formula-resistant body of ideas. The historian
who seeks to identify a Romantic aesthetics, or at least some leading principles, finds that he is drawn, willy-nilly, into a congeries
of general propositions about practically everything under the

sun, and above it. When he tries to get his bearings by defining Romanticism in general, he is again baffled, for each strand that he selects for emphasis, as peculiarly characteristic of Romanticism, turns out not to be new at all, but already noticeable in Plotinus or Bruno, "Longinus" or Shaftesbury, or another. And the discovery, a few decades ago, of "pre-Romanticism" has emphasized the continuity of the Romantic movement with eighteenth-century antecedents.

Looking for novelty, then, we must be content to find that it is not the ideas themselves so much as the particular constellation of them, the importance attached to them, and the extent of their influence, that defines Romanticism—at least in so far as we can concern ourselves with it here. For our purposes it will be enough to consider three main features of Romanticism, all of which had a significant bearing on the course of modern, and of present-day, aesthetics. First, the advent of Romanticism involved some changes in basic values, including qualities valued in works of art (especially literature). Certainly the leading spirits of the late eighteenth and early nineteenth centuries, in Western Europe, came to enjoy and to demand different qualities in works of art, and they set less store by (though many of them were not incapable of appreciating) the best literary productions of the preceding century. We can at least say that eyes were opened to new aesthetic vistas. But of course a new awareness of what is desired in poetry may lead to a new concept of what is to be accounted good poetry, or the best poetry; and this, in turn, may lead to a new (or partly new) concept of what all poetry is, in some degree, though not to the same degree—and therefore to new aesthetic theories.

Second, a very important ingredient, I think, of Romanticism, was its epistemology (again, not wholly new, but carried further and given a greater emphasis): a kind of emotional intuitionism, regarded as superseding or correcting the previously dominant rationalism and empiricism. As we shall see, this philosophical development bore within it the seeds of an aesthetic that could give to art, and to the artist, a new status among the important elements of life and culture—a glorification of art, such as had never quite been envisioned before, except in some pages of Plotinus and the Renaissance Neoplatonists.

Third, Romanticism brought into prominence, if not dominance, some categories of thought that had not previously been stressed—leading notions in terms of which reality, and art, were to be thought about. Of these, the category of organism was fundamental. This aspect of Romanticism, along with others, has been excellently analyzed by Meyer H. Abrams. Though he remarks that "In aesthetics, as in other provinces of inquiry, radical novelties frequently turn out to be migrant ideas which, in their native intellectual habitat, were commonplaces," he also argues (very effectively) that Coleridge's organismic theory of mind "was, in fact, part of a change in the habitual way of thinking, in all areas of intellectual enterprise, which is as sharp and dramatic as any the history of ideas can show."[1]

I shall now fill out my sketch of these three aspects of Romanticism.

Perhaps the most obvious feature of Romanticism is a new impulse to the enjoyment of feeling and emotion. In the creation and appreciation of art, this involves cultivating a more intense awareness of felt quality—even (if need be) at some sacrifice of form and balance, of classical order and repose. In aesthetic theory it means several things. The scope of good, or great, art, is widened to include works whose comparative loosening of form is considered to be offset by a more poignant or more individualized presentation of personal emotions; the way has been prepared by the eighteenth-century "sublime." Artistic production comes to be conceived as essentially an act of self-expression; and the critic, as the century moves on, feels a growing concern with the artist's sincerity, with the details of his biography, with his inner spiritual life. I will illustrate these, and other, generalizations by a few quotations selected from a great number that might be cited; even so, it should always be borne in mind that all these generalizations have exceptions and require qualifications that would have to be supplied in a fuller account.

In one respect, an emotionalist concept of art is by no means new; we have seen that it was held by some eighteenth-century aestheticians that the purpose of art is primarily to arouse emotions. Ironically, as René Wellek has pointed out (*History*, II,

[1] *The Mirror and the Lamp: Romantic Theory and the Critical Tradition* (Oxford U., 1953), pp. viii, 158.

242), a remark of Victor Hugo's that well expresses the Romantic view—"What indeed is a poet? A man who feels strongly and expresses his feelings in a more expressive language" (from his essay on Chénier)—is promptly supported by a quotation from Voltaire: "Poetry is almost nothing but feeling." Other eighteenth-century writers had made attempts to break away from the reiterated formula that poetry is imitation; and to introduce a new emphasis on emotion. In the 1770s, J. G. Sulzer, in his four-volume encyclopedia of aesthetics,[2] had written: "The poet is . . . put into a passion, or at least into a certain mood, by his object; he cannot resist the violent desire to utter his feelings; he is transported" (trans. Abrams, p. 89)—echoing, no doubt, the Longinian transport, but giving it a Romantic cast by the inclusion of "a certain mood." Sir William Jones, in an essay appended to a volume of translations of oriental poetry (1772),[3] had argued "that the finest parts of poetry, musick, and painting, are expressive of the *passions*"—the "inferior" parts being "descriptive of natural objects." And Hugh Blair, in his *Lectures on Rhetoric and Belles Lettres* (1783), had asserted that "the most just and comprehensive definition which, I think, can be given to poetry, is, 'that it is the language of passion, or of enlivened imagination, formed, most commonly, into regular numbers.' "[4]

In the Romantic view of poetry, this doctrine became central and primary; the imitation theory was set aside, or relegated to a subordinate position, and a form of expression theory took its place. The poet's state of mind, the spontaneity and intensity of his emotions, became the focus of attention. One of the most memorable statements of this view is, of course, Wordsworth's remark (in the 1800 Preface to *Lyrical Ballads*) that "all good poetry is the spontaneous overflow of powerful feelings"—though he hastens to add that good poems "were never produced . . . but by a man who, being possessed of more than usual organic sensibility, had also thought long and deeply" (see Hynes and Hoffman, p. 16). It is echoed frequently by the French Romantics: by Alfred de Vigny ("*La Poesie, c'est l'enthousiasme cristallisé*"[5]),

---

[2] *Allgemeine Theorie der schönen Kunst* (1771–74), in the article "Gedicht" (II, 322–23).

[3] "Essay on the Arts Called Imitative" (*Works* [1807]; VIII, 379).

[4] Lecture 38 (London, 1823), p. 511.

[5] *Journal* (1837); like Wordsworth, however, he found he worked best with emotion recollected in tranquillity; see *Oeuvres* (1946), II, 903.

by Alfred de Musset (*"l'art c'est le sentiment"*[6]). John Stuart Mill characterized poetry as "the expression or utterance of feeling," to be distinguished from "eloquence" by its making the utterance of feeling an end in itself, rather than a means of arousing it in another ("What is Poetry?" [1833]; in Hynes and Hoffman, pp. 197–98).

We have seen how Aristotle's theory of *katharsis* (as usually interpreted) was a kind of emotionalist theory, but the contrast is important to note: the Romantic view is that poetry is a *katharsis* for the poet primarily, and only secondarily for the reader. The poet, says Shelley, is an overheard nightingale, "who sits in d⌐rkness and sings to cheer its own solitude with sweet sounds" (*Defense of Poetry*, 1821; Hynes and Hoffman, p. 167). In writing his poem, the poet gets rid of the overflow of emotion. The imagination "gives an obvious relief to the indistinct and importunate cravings of the will," William Hazlitt says in his essay "On Poetry in General" (1818).[7] Hazlitt combined this view with an early form of the wish-fulfillment theory: "We shape things according to our wishes and fancies, without poetry; but poetry is the most emphatical language that can be found for those creations of the mind 'which ecstasy is very cunning in'" (V, 3). The Reverend John Keble carried this even further in his Oxford lectures on poetry (1832–41):[8] "Poetry," in his definition, "is the indirect expression in words, most appropriately in metrical words, of some overpowering emotion, or ruling taste, or feeling, the direct indulgence whereof is somehow repressed" (from his review of Lockhart's *Life of Scott*). Poetry can "act as a safety-valve, preserving men from actual madness" (*Lectures*, I, 55)—at least it protects the poet himself from his neuroses, and, Keble suggests, affords a similar therapy to the reader.

The fullest systematic development of the emotionalist aesthetic—art as the expression of feeling—came later in the century in *L'Esthétique* of Eugene Véron (1878).

It is an interesting sign of those times that the parallel of poetry and painting—the *ut pictura poesis* principle—that was so much in the aesthetician's mind from the Renaissance up to the

---

[6] "Un Mot sur l'art moderne" (1833), *Oeuvres complètes en prose*, ed. Maurice Allem (Paris, 1951), p. 898.

[7] *Complete Works*, ed. P. P. Howe (1930–34), V, 8.

[8] *De poeticae vi medica* (1844; 2 vols., trans. E. K. Francis, 1912).

late eighteenth century, now gave way (and first in Germany) to
a new parallel: music was increasingly felt to be the true sister
of poetry, because music is most fully, purely, pre-eminently the
expression of feeling—especially longing—which poetry aims to
be. In his essay on "Beethoven's Instrumental Music" (1813; see
Strunk, *Source Readings*, p. 775), E. T. A. Hoffman said of music:
"It is the most romantic of all the arts—one might almost say,
the only genuinely romantic art—for its own sole subject is the
infinite." There is a striking contrast of music with words in the
Phantasien über die Kunst (1799) of the German Romantic
Wilhelm Heinrich Wackenroder; but if we take the hint here
that the words he means are those of ordinary, discursive language, then there is also the suggestion that the language of
poetry may be closer to music.

I shall use a flowing stream as an illustration. It is beyond human art
to depict in words meant for the eye the thousands of individual waves,
smooth and rugged, bursting and foaming, in the flow of a mighty river
—words can but meagerly recount the incessant movements and cannot
visibly picture the consequent rearrangement of the drops of water. Just
so it is with the mysterious stream in the depths of the human soul;
words mention and name and describe its flux in a foreign medium. In
music, however, the stream itself seems to be released. Music coura-
geously smites upon the hidden harp strings and, in that inner world of
mystery, strikes up in due succession certain mysterious chords—our
heart-strings, and we understand the music [trans. Lussky, in Walzel,
pp. 122–23].

But it is not until later that we find the first clear-cut anticipation
of a semiotic distinction that the twentieth century was to make
much of, between descriptive and emotive language. Burke, in
the fifth book of his *Enquiry*, had suggested a distinction between
"a clear expression and a strong expression," which he assigned
to the understanding and to the passions respectively. In a remarkable essay on "The Philosophy of Poetry," in *Blackwood's
Magazine* (December 1835), a Scotsman, Alexander Smith, proposed that poetry is to be defined as "the language of emotion"—
that is, "the language in which that emotion vents itself—not the
description of the emotion, or the affirmation that it is felt." In
the end, he fell back on intention, distinguishing the two forms
of language more in terms of the user's purpose than in terms of

the language itself, but his essay showed one direction in which the Romantic theory could go.

The emotional-expression theory brought about a fundamental reorientation in the Romantic approach to art: what now became of the highest importance and interest was not so much the work itself as the man behind it. The most concise statement of the new view is that of Carlyle: Shakespeare's works "are so many windows, through which we see a glimpse of the world that was in him" ("The Hero as Poet"[9]). Not (let us notice) a window (like that of the Renaissance painter) through which we see the world, or another world behind the phenomenon, or even human nature in general—but one that looks in upon the inner life and personality of the individual creator himself. In the same spirit, Coleridge said that "In the Paradise Lost—indeed, in every one of his poems—it is Milton himself whom you see" (*Table Talk*, Aug. 18, 1833; London 1888 ed., p. 250). And Keble actually worked out a whole methodology, with canons of inference like Mill's methods, for reconstructing the character and temperament of the author from his writings (the method is applied in detail to Homer in Lectures 6 to 16).

Various critical corollaries might be drawn from the reduction of poetry to feeling. It might be taken to imply that rational criticism is impossible; thus Wackenroder argued that the only possible, or proper, response to the work is to feel along with it. "An eternal hostile gulf is fixed between the feeling heart and the investigations of research. Feeling can only be grasped and understood by feeling" (trans. Wellek, II, 90; from the *Phantasien über die Kunst*). It might lead to Friedrich Schlegel's early view (which gave way later to sounder principles) that it takes a poet to appreciate poetry, and that the critic's artistic judgment (*Kunsturteil*) should itself be a work of art (*Kunstwerk*)—a view echoed later by Walter Pater and others (see Schlegel's early prose writings, 1882 ed., II, 200). At the very least, it would suggest the importance of considering the relation between the poet's real and his professed emotions, the adequacy or sincerity of the expression. Thus Wordsworth thought it important that the poet be sincere; Keble made sincerity a basic criterion of critical

9 *On Heroes, Hero-Worship and the Heroic in History* (1841; *Works*, 1896–1901), V, 110.

evaluation; Carlyle wrote that "The excellence of Burns is . . . his *Sincerity*, his indisputable air of Truth" (essay on Burns; *Works*, XXVI, 267), and sincerity is a recurrent theme of "The Hero as Poet" ("It is a man's sincerity and depth of vision that makes him a poet," *Works*, V, 84). And Matthew Arnold regarded "the high seriousness which comes from absolute sincerity" as a necessary condition of "supreme poetical success" ("The Study of Poetry," 1880[10]).

THEORIES OF THE IMAGINATION

That poetry (and art in general) is essentially the expression of feeling can, then, be taken as the first principle of Romantic aesthetics, and this statement will serve as a first approximation to a distinction between Romantic aesthetics and neoclassical aesthetics. Wordsworth's rejection (in his 1800 Preface; see Hynes and Hoffman, 20 n) of the dichotomy of poetry vs. prose, and his substitution of "the more philosophical one of Poetry and Matter of Fact, or Science," reflected the general view. For a closer approximation to Romantic aesthetics, we must, however, add qualifications. First, though the Romantics insisted that the expression of feeling can be an end in itself, and rejected the conception of poetry as teaching abstract moral truths—nevertheless, some of them, especially Wordsworth and Shelley, believed in a moral value of poetry, and argued (again like Wordsworth's Preface; see Hynes and Hoffman, pp. 16, 22) that the refinement and enlargement of the capacity to feel, and especially the capacity for those feelings that bind human beings together, is an ultimate justification of poetry. The poet "ought, to a certain degree, to rectify men's feelings, to give them new compositions of feeling, to render their feelings more sane, pure, and permanent" (Letter to John Wilson, 1800).[1] Second, though the didactic view of poetry was rejected in favor of the emotionalist one, the concept of poetry as having a kind of cognitive status was not rejected, but transformed—at least by some of the Romantic theorists.

[10] *Essays in Criticism*, 2d Series (1888), p. 48.
[1] *Wordsworth's Literary Criticism*, ed. Nowell C. Smith (London, 1905), p. 7.

For feeling, in the Romantic theory of art, is not only the primary cause and most important effect of art; it can also be a source of knowledge. The antecedents of this emotional intuitionism, or insight-theory, can, like other Romantic ideas, be traced back into the eighteenth century: perhaps to the "inner sense" of Shaftesbury and Hutcheson, at least to the theory of sympathy, or the moral sentiment, in Hume and Adam Smith. But in the Romantic poets and novelists, these epistemological concepts blossomed into a more ambitious, if much less clear, notion of a special gift, the ability to participate feelingly, not only in the inner life of other human beings, but in the inner life of the world itself. In a letter to Fougué (1806), August Wilhelm Schlegel said that he found in the great poets (Homer, Dante, Shakespeare) "the oracular verdict [*Orakelspruch*] of the heart, those deep intuitions in which the dark riddle of our existence seems to solve itself" (trans. Wellek, II, 43).

It was the claim to this form of knowledge that gave rise to a new theory of the imagination—or, perhaps better, that was marked by a new extension of the term "imagination," to cover not only a faculty of inventing and reassembling materials, but a faculty of seizing directly upon important truth. These two ideas —of invention and discovery—were, in fact, often identified, under the influence of Kant's "Copernican Revolution," and the metaphysical theories of Fichte. Kant's theory that the form of our experience is contributed by the understanding itself, imposing its a priori categories upon the data of sense, and Fichte's theory that reality is itself a non-Ego "posited," as he said, by the Ego for self-realization, gave the mind some part in making reality what it is, so that to some extent in coming to know reality it recognizes its own work. This is what Wordsworth seems to say in *The Prelude* (II, 255–60):

> For feeling has to him imparted power
> That through the growing faculties of sense
> Doth like an agent of the one great Mind
> Create, creator and receiver both,
> Working but in alliance with the works
> Which it beholds.

The Romantic fusion of cognition and creation meant at least that both are present in every important mental act; that neither can occur in a pure form, unmixed with the other, since on the one hand nothing can be known without being to some degree molded by the knower, and on the other the imagination cannot invent anything, however wild, without seeing something new. It also meant that in every cognition the line between what is contributed by the self and what is contributed by external data cannot be sharply drawn. Coleridge's favorite symbol of mind, the wind-harp, or Aeolian lyre (see his poem "The Eolian Harp," and its echo in Shelley's *Defense of Poetry*), combines the two elements, but in a way that allows the stress to fall on either mental activity or mental passivity—depending on whether the wind is interpreted as the objective power of nature, awakening the poet, or the inspiration sweeping over the poet from within.

The attempt to combine and balance in one cognitive theory the concepts of revelation and of creation, knowing and making, is distinctive of Romantic aesthetics, and is the root of many difficulties. One method of reconciliation is to bring imagination and feeling together: what the poet especially grasps is reality as colored by his own emotions. But this is also, confusingly, combined with the view that the "secondary" and "tertiary" qualities immediately given in experience are the concrete reality to which the poet attends, from which scientific truth is only an abstraction.

William Blake was one of the earliest English poets to speak in the new, lofty, way of imagination, or "Visionary Fancy." "One Power alone makes a Poet: Imagination, the Divine Vision," he says (*Annotations to Wordsworth's Poems*).[2] "This World of Imagination is the world of Eternity; it is the divine bosom into which we shall all go after the death of the Vegetated body" (*A Vision of the Last Judgment*).[3]

Shelley's *Defense of Poetry* contains philosophical puzzles enough, and from the general extravagance of his language throughout the essay we are, no doubt, not to expect very determinate theses. But when he proposes to define poetry "in a general sense" as "the expression of the imagination" (Hynes and Hoffman, p. 161), and later argues (169) that "the great instrument of moral good is the imagination," because it gives us

[2] *Poetry and Prose,* ed. Geoffrey Keynes (London, 1927), p. 1024.
[3] Ibid., p. 830.

immediate participation in the inner life of other men, it is evident that Shelley attributed a high and special cognitive value to the imagination, and consequently to poetry. Keats was even more emphatic, though in his usual somewhat cryptic fashion, in the famous letter to Benjamin Bailey (Nov. 22, 1817), when he wrote:

I am certain of nothing but the holiness of the Heart's affections and the truth of Imagination—What the imagination seizes as Beauty must be truth—whether it existed before or not . . . I have never yet been able to perceive how anything can be known for truth by consequitive reasoning . . . [*Letters,* ed. H. E. Rollins (Harvard U. 1958), I, 184–85].

William Hazlitt's writings, when collected and compared, sum up a large part of Romantic doctrine. "This intuitive perception of the hidden analogies of things, or, as it may be called, this *instinct of the imagination,* is, perhaps, what stamps the character of genius on the productions of art more than any other circumstance: for it works unconsciously, like nature . . ." ("On the English Novelists" [1819]; *Works,* VI, 109). Imagination is contrasted with reason as synthetic rather than analytical, concrete rather than abstract, individual rather than general, intuitive rather than discursive. Poetry "describes the flowing, not the fixed" ("On Poetry in General" [1818]; V, 3), he remarks in a Bergsonian spirit (see also "On Reason and Imagination" [1826], XII, 46).

On the Continent, those Romantic theorists groping their way toward symbolist poetics also assigned the imagination a central cognitive role. Joseph Joubert, for example, wrote that "Imagination is the faculty of making sensuous what is intellectual, of making corporeal what is spirit: in a word, of bringing to light, without depriving it of its nature, that which in itself is invisible" (see *Les Carnets* [1938 ed.], II, 493). The sensuous vehicle through which the unseen is revealed to sight is the creation of imagination. To Baudelaire, "Imagination is, as it were, a divine faculty, which perceives directly, without the use of philosophical methods, the secret and intimate relationships of things, their correspondences and analogies" (Introduction to his translation of Poe, the *Nouvelles Histoires extraordinaires* [1857], *Oeuvres complètes,* VII [1933], xv). The "correspondences" are between the outer and inner worlds, the natural and the supernatural; everything is a symbol, a "hieroglyphic," for poets to decipher, by the faculty of imaginative insight, "the queen of the faculties" (see also the "Exposition Universelle de 1855," in *Curiosités esthétiques*).

Perhaps the most famous product of Romantic theorizing about the imagination is the puzzling distinction that Coleridge proposed between the imagination and the fancy—his conviction "that fancy and imagination were two distinct and widely different faculties, instead of being, according to the general belief, either two names with one meaning, or, at furthest, the lower and higher degree of one and the same power" (*Biographia Literaria* [1817], ch. 4; Shawcross, I, 60–61).

The primary IMAGINATION I hold to be the living Power and prime Agent of all human Perception, and as a repetition in the finite mind of the eternal act of creation in the infinite I AM. The secondary Imagination I consider as an echo of the former [ch. 13; I, 202].

The "primary imagination" here, following Schelling, is unconscious and involuntary, but active and creative, in both natural processes and human perception; the "secondary imagination" is the conscious poetic power.

To the fancy, Coleridge relegates those activities that had been called imagination by the eighteenth century, and that the associationists had long been trying to explain. The fancy, he says, receives its data from sense, "emancipates" them from space and time, rearranges them according to the laws of association, and produces combinations whose mechanical novelty consists only in a different order of essentially unchanged elements. It "has no other counters to play with, but fixities and definites" (I, 202). But the imagination, the "coadunating faculty," transforms the elements themselves by fusing them or blending them into new wholes, from which new qualities emerge, as food is digested and transformed in the growing body (see *Statesman's Manual* [1816], Appendix C, xxvii; included in *Biographia Literaria* [1898], ed. Bohn; see pp. 343 ff, 353). After the abandonment of his earlier enthusiastic attachment to the mechanistic psychology of David Hartley, as set forth in the *Observations on Man* (1749), and the reinforcement of his own intellectual tendencies by successive waves of metaphysical reading—in Plotinus, in the seventeenth-century British Platonists, in the German Idealists—Coleridge's attack on associationism, and his gropings toward a more adequate theory of artistic creation, became dominant themes of his work. Coleridge has often been criticized, and probably undervalued, partly because so many of his cherished ideas have been traced back to others, from whom he borrowed with general gratitude but inadequate acknowledgment, and partly because he never completed his project of working out a clear and satisfactory psychology. Nor did his view advance rapidly against the prevailing associationism, buoyed up as it was by assurance that much mental activity had already been explained by analytical and atomistic methods, and by confidence that the remainder would yield to the same methods. But among poets and literary theorists, Coleridge took hold, and in time—certainly in our time, when he has been more carefully read than ever—the importance of his challenge was recognized as helping lead to a new consideration of the problem of artistic creation.

The poet, according to this Coleridgean view, has a "synthetic and magical power" which "reveals itself in the balance or reconciliation of opposite or discordant qualities" (II, 12). The Hegelian dialectic is reflected here, and also the idea of a literary work as a living, vital whole in which internal tensions, ironic contrasts, contribute by their very opposition to the unity of the whole. Coleridge's formula for beauty is "Multëity in Unity," or "that in which the *many*, still seen as many, becomes one" (see his interesting three-part essay "On the Principles of Genial Criticism" [1814]; ed. Shawcross, II, 232; cf. 239). He here echoes an ancient formula, but with a difference: in Coleridge, the whole "is presupposed by all its parts" (see *Hints Toward . . . a . . . Theory of Life*, ed. S. B. Watson [1848], p. 42). On this principle, Coleridge, as practical critic, makes the goodness of a work consist in part in its richness, "the variety of parts which it holds in unity" ("On Poesy or Art" [1818]; ed. Shawcross, II, 255—this essay being in large part a paraphrase of Schelling's essay "On the Relation of the Plastic Arts to Nature"). Literary works are not to be tested by the older system of rules, which are mechanical measurements; the critic's job is to look for deeper unities. Coleridge tried to show that Shakespeare's plays, for example (unlike the plays of Beaumont and Fletcher, which he called "mere aggregates without unity"), have "a vitality which grows and evolves itself from within," so that such works could not have been produced by a merely associative mind, but only by one with creative power, in his sense.[4]

In this department of his thought—in bringing into English aesthetic theory the category of organic form—Coleridge made one of his greatest contributions. Aristotle and Plato, as we have seen, compared a literary work to a living animal. And, on the metaphysical level, the notion that the world of nature may itself be a great living thing, with a soul of its own, went back to Plato, Plotinus and Renaissance thinkers (such as Giordano Bruno), and reappeared in Shaftesbury's world soul. It came to its greatest flower, and connected with concern about art, among the great German Romantic thinkers. The way was paved in Germany by the dominance of Leibniz's metaphysics, with its concept of "a world of creatures, of living beings, . . . in the smallest particle of matter" (*Monadology* [1714], §§ 65–69). A little book by Karl Philip Moritz, *Über die bildende Nachahmung des Schönen* (1788), deriving an organic conception of beauty from Leibniz, was cited with approval by A. W. Schlegel, in his Berlin lectures. In the Vienna lectures on dramatic art (Lecture 22), Schlegel had explicitly contrasted the form of a work of art with "mechanical form"—the former "unfolds itself from within," but the latter "is imparted to a material merely as an accidental addition, without relation to its nature" (trans. Wellek, II, 48).[5] And Coleridge clearly had this very passage in mind when he made his own distinction between the mechanical and the organic:

> The form is mechanic when on any given material we impress a pre-determined form, not necessarily arising out of the properties of the material . . . The organic form, on the other hand, is innate; it shapes as it develops itself from within, and the fullness of its development is one and the same with the perfection of its outward form [*Shakespearean Criticism*, ed. Raysor, I, 224].

Meanwhile, the depth and significance of the organic category was being further developed by the hands of two other German thinkers, Herder and Goethe.

[4] See his *Miscellaneous Criticism*, ed. T. M. Raysor (1936), pp. 44 n, 88–89; cf. *Shakespearean Criticism*, ed. T. M. Raysor (1930), II, 170–71.

[5] See A. W. Schlegel, *A Course of Lectures on Dramatic Art and Literature*, trans. John Black (London, 1846), p. 340.

Though Johann Gottfried Herder's philosophy contains elements of all the numerous eighteenth-century thinkers whose works he absorbed, it stirs them together into a new mixture, poured out through numerous volumes in a fervid style. From these writings emerge many of the leading ideas of Romantic aesthetics, in an early form: poetry as the art of emotional expression; criticism as empathy with the author; and—an idea that I have not so far mentioned, though it was taken up by others, including Shelley—the theory that metaphor and myth are the original language of man, which gets overlaid by rational reconstructions, but in the shape of poetry can still be the medium through which we know the nature of reality and the inwardness of each other (see his *Über den Ursprung der Sprache* [1772], and the essay "Über Bild, Dichtung and Fabel" [1786]).[6] For nature herself is a living organism, of which man is an organic part, with powers that express and exemplify the whole; and it is in works of art, because of their own plantlike germination in the mind—largely in the unconscious mind—of the artist, that the nature of reality is best reflected (see also his *Vom Erkennen und Empfinden der Menschlichen Seele* [1778]).

In the ever-active thought of Goethe, these leading ideas took root and flourished, and they played an important role in all his thinking about art. At one time or another, he found occasion to reflect on most literary problems, usually with penetrating insight, yet he did not attempt a systematic formulation of his aesthetic views, and only a few of them can be mentioned here. Goethe, like Herder, had a deep sense of the organic unity of all nature, and of man as a part of nature, and of works of art, as growing out of, and expressing, man's unity with nature (see,

---

[6] In this theory, Herder was anticipated by Giambattista Vico, whose strange book, the *Scienza Nuova* (1725), has been made so much of in the twentieth century (as, for example, in Croce's *Aesthetic*). Since Vico's work seems to have made no impression on his contemporaries or other eighteenth-century aestheticians—though an indirect connection has been traced between Vico and Herder via an Italian and a German translator of the poems of "Ossian"—I have not discussed it in Chapters 7 and 8 above. Vico's theory of "poetic wisdom" as the original metaphysics of man, a product of primitive mythological imagination, is part of a general philosophy of history, and does not lend itself to any very clear statement [see, e.g., sections 367 and 375, trans. T. G. Bergin and M. H. Fisch (Ithaca, 1948); Erich Auerbach, "Vico and Aesthetic Historicism," *Jour Aesth and Art Crit* VIII (Dec. 1949): 110–24].

for example, his early essay on German architecture, "Vom Deutscher Baukunst" [1772]). "Why does a perfect work of art appear like a work of nature to me also?" asks "Spectator" in Goethe's little dialogue, "Über Wahrheit und Wahrscheinlichkeit [Truth and Probability] der Kunstwerke" (1797; trans. S. G. Ward, in Spingarn, p. 57), and "Agent" replies, "Because it harmonizes with your better nature. Because it is above natural, yet not unnatural. A perfect work of art is a work of the human soul, and in this sense, also, a work of nature." Goethe expounded a similar view in that remarkable conversation about beauty with Eckermann (April 18, 1827; trans. Oxenford, p. 248): "The artist has a twofold relation to nature; he is at once her master and her slave."

Thus every good work of art, says Goethe (speaking of the opera), "creates a little world of its own, in which all proceeds according to fixed laws, which must be judged by its own laws, felt according to its own spirit" ("Über Wahrheit und Wahrscheinlichkeit"; Spingarn, p. 54). For this reason, in one of his last recorded conversations, he objected vigorously to the French term "composition," for the act of artistic creation—"a thoroughly contemptible word."

How can one say, Mozart has *composed* [componiert] Don Juan! Composition! As if it were a piece of cake or biscuit, which had been stirred together out of eggs, flour, and sugar! It is a spiritual creation, in which the details, as well as the whole, are pervaded by *one* spirit, and by the breath of *one* life; so that the producer did not make experiments, and patch together, and follow his own caprice, but was altogether in the power of the daemonic spirit of his genius, and acted according to his orders [June 20, 1831; Oxenford, p. 556].

Another interesting application of Goethe's organicism appears in a late paper on Aristotle's *Poetics* (1827; see Spingarn, p. 105), in which he argues that Aristotle's *katharsis* should not be interpreted as a psychological effect of the tragedy, but rather as a relationship within the tragedy itself: "When the course of action is one arousing pity and fear, the tragedy must close *on the stage* with an equilibration, a reconciliation, of these emotions." Here he strikingly anticipates a recent reinterpretation of Aristotle by Gerald Else (see Chapter 3 above).

Romantic intuitionism is, then, an attempt at a new way of recovering for literature an important cognitive status, without making it didactic in the neoclassic sense, a bearer of general truths, of Aristotelian universals, of teachable abstractions. The very feeling at the center of poetic life turns out to be a kind of insight. It is interesting to note how Wordsworth and Shelley, for example, say, or almost say, how poetry is, or contains, knowledge. "Poetry," says the former (1800 Preface; Hynes and Hoffman, p. 25), "is the breath and finer spirit of all knowledge; it is the impassioned expression which is in the countenance of all science." And again (pp. 25–26), "Poetry is the first and last of all knowledge—it is as immortal as the heart of man." From his previous agreement with Aristotle about poetry that

its object is truth, not individual and local, but general and operative; not standing upon external testimony, but carried alive into the heart by passion; truth which is its own testimony, which gives competence and confidence to the tribunal to which it appeals, and receives them from the same tribunal [p. 23],

it seems that Wordsworth means that the truths of poetry are, first, about perennial characteristics of human nature and the universe, and, second, not fully propositional and inferential, but direct and heartfelt. Shelley says that "A poem is the very image of life expressed in its eternal truth" (*Defense*; Hynes and Hoffman, p. 166), and that "It is at once the center and circumference of knowledge; it is that which comprehends all science, and that to which all science must be referred" (p. 185). Here we find a tacit acknowledgment of a kind of tension between scientific and poetic truth, and the will to resolve it without rivalry, by placing poetry on a level (hardly very well defined) where it will seem at once to *make* less of a claim, and yet somehow *have* a greater claim, than publicly verifiable empirical propositions.

Along with poetry's claim to its own order of truth goes a double implication: in one way, poetic truth is the kind that all men possess, or once possessed as children, before reason and prudence impinged (the "beginning" of knowledge, the "center" of knowledge); in another way, it is rare and precious like the mystic's illumination (the "end" of knowledge, the "circumference" of knowledge). And out of this second thought grows a new version of the theory of genius, the conception of the poet as a higher order of being. "The genuine poet," said Novalis (Friedrich von Hardenberg), "is always a priest" (see *Works* [1945], II, 41; trans. Wellek, II, 83). In his essay on German architecture Goethe calls the artist "God's anointed" (Spingarn, p. 12). "The poet is a priest," says Victor Hugo. "He is God's tripod" (*William Shakespeare* [1864]; trans. Gilman, p. 216). For Shelley, the poet unites the character of legislator and prophet (Hynes and Hoffman, p. 163); "Poets are the hierophants of an unapprehended inspiration . . . the unacknowledged legislators of the world" (p. 190). Carlyle makes the poet a "hero," a "great soul" (a term from "Longinus"), a seer, a *vates*, or prophet—a term used earlier by Sir Philip Sidney, but in a rather different spirit ("The Hero as Poet," in *Heroes* and "Death of Goethe" [1832] in *Works*, XXVII). He is, says Emerson ("The Poet" [1844]) the "namer," and "the true and only doctor" (Allen and Clark, pp. 376, 382).

The transfiguration of the artist takes two divergent forms. In the early stages, under the influence of Schelling and Goethe, the artist is himself a natural force, the Aeolian wind-harp, Shelley's fading coal awakened to transitory brightness, the sensitive plant —a sacred instrument by which Nature works to surpass herself. In the words of Victor Hugo, "Nature is God's immediate creation, and art is what God creates through the mind of man" (*Philosophie*, I, 265; in *Oeuvres complètes* [1904–52]). Later the other concept becomes more prominent—though it, too, is expressed early by Goethe. Under the felt pressure of alienating forces (which I shall discuss in the following chapter), the artist may become a Promethean figure, the rival of Nature and God, cursed with a tragic but glorious doom.

The culmination of these various tendencies was the French Symbolist movement that arose and receded in the 1880s and 1890s, leaving behind not only a body of haunting poetry but some doctrines that have become part of the permanent possession of twentieth-century poetics. Out of all the strange manifestoes and overheated pronouncements of the Symbolists, and despite the illogical mixture of mysticisms and whimsies involved in their theorizing, there emerged more definitely than ever before the concept of a poem as a structure of words and meanings, constituting a complex symbol or meaningful utterance, whose peculiar value lies in its internal ironic tensions and richness of suggestiveness.

The roots of the Symbolist aesthetic—if that is not too grand a term for the general notion that a work of art is in some sense (in some one of many related senses) a "symbol"—go back into the German Romantics, and, through them, of course, to the Middle Ages and antiquity. Goethe, in his essay "Über die Gegenstände der bildenen Kunst" (1797), was one of the earliest to make a sharp distinction between allegory, which brings the universal and the particular together externally, and symbolism, in which subject and object coincide and an ideal meaning is suggested to the mind (see also his *Maximen und Reflexionen*, Nos. 279, 314, 1112, 1113; in *Works* [Zurich, 1949], Vol. IX). Friedrich Schlegel, in his *Gespräch über die Poesie* (1800), made much of the importance of myth for poetry—meaning a system of culturally significant symbols. Other contributing ideas were the "significant image [*Sinnbild*]" of August Wilhelm Schlegel, his emphasis on the central role of metaphor, myth, and symbol in poetry (see his *Vorlesungen über schöne Litteratur und Kunst*, ed. Minor, I, 92–93), and his concept of art as a way of knowing by means of signs, a *"bildlich anschauender Gedankenausdruck"* (thinking in terms of images?)—see his Vienna lectures on aesthetics (1798; the *Vorlesungen über philosophische Kunstlehre* [1911], p. 23). Composing poetry, he wrote, is "an eternal mode of symbolizing: we either seek an outer covering for something spiritual, or we draw something external over the invisibly inner" (trans. Abrams, p. 90; from the Berlin lectures, 1801–2, *Deutsche Literaturdenkmale*, XVII, 91–95). German idealism, especially in the manner of Schelling, emphasized the idea that a symbol can connect the material with the spiritual (see Coleridge's poem "Destiny of Nations" [1797]). Theodore Jouffroy in his *Cours d'esthétique* (1843; lectures given in 1826) echoed Victor Cousin's statement that "all nature is symbolic," and stated that "Poetry is but a series of symbols presented to the mind to make it conceive the invisible" (p. 132)—and in the appendix recalled, as others did, Diderot's term *hiéroglyphe*, to characterize matter as the silent speaker of a spiritual language.

In England, without any very ambitious theorizing, the new poetic symbol appears in the great nature poetry of Blake, Wordsworth, Coleridge, Shelley, Keats. The lyric poem is conceived as the discovery of correlatives of human experience in the visible landscape—not, as in so much eighteenth-century nature poetry, the bringing of the natural object and the human feeling together deliberately in a sort of loose simile, but the blending of the two into a single symbolic unity, in which the heart dances with the daffodils, the impetuous West Wind trumpets a prophecy, and the nightingale sings of magic casements opening on the foam of perilous seas.

The Symbolist movement in French letters, was a more self-conscious theory and practice. Even if we could stick with some comparatively narrow sense (as launched, say, by the manifestoes of Jean Moréas in 1885), its short, but volatile, history would require much time to trace, through the maze of articles, slogans, attacks, and counterattacks in the journals and reviews. And there are no sharp boundaries to mark it off from a variety of increasingly wild and woolly movements that developed among the avant garde in the late nineteenth century—musical theories of poetry; the appeal to dreams, the unconscious, automatism; anarchism, decadence, and proto-surrealism. The "symbol" was, at various times and sometimes ambiguously, the word itself and the object referred to by the word; but though the mystical exaltation and Romantic glorification of poetry was carried to all extremes, the burden of all these claims, in the long run, instead of weighing poetry down or dissolving the poem into several other things, somehow served to support and emphasize its autonomy. Consider Rimbaud (in his *Saison en enfer,* Délires II, "Alchimie du verbe"): "*J'expliquai mes sophismes magiques avec l'hallucination des mots.*" Baudelaire's general theory of "correspondences" has already been mentioned. In his thinking, the similarities of qualities and relations within different sensory orders, the synaesthetic comparability of sounds and colors, for example, suggests a system of universal analogy, in which all phenomenal objects are deeply related to other objects, and capable of becoming symbols of them (see his poem "Correspondances"). The poet, or the artist in general, is gifted in noting these analogies, and expressing them (see the articles on Gautier and Hugo in *L'Art romantique* [1869]). Similar ideas—the "inherent symbols" formed in the "Great Memory"—are found in Yeats' early essays (see "Magic" [1901]; "Symbolism in Painting" [1898]; "The Symbolism of Poetry" [1900]; in *Ideas of Good and Evil* [1903]). All of these poets enjoyed extravagances from which we may now feel quite remote, but in their late-century transformations of Romantic theory, they succeeded in turning it around. Instead of treating a poem as a piece of autobiography, a cry of the heart through which we look to a living soul, they turned attention to a simple notion that was to be of some revolutionary force in the twentieth century—that a poem is, first of all, a feat of language, a composition of words, with an ontological status of its own.

SCHOPENHAUER AND NIETZSCHE

Since a philosopher's significance in the history of his subject is determined not only by what he has to give, but by what is received from him, there can sometimes be a question where he should be placed by the historian. This is especially true of Arthur Schopenhauer (1788–1860) in the history of aesthetics, for he began his thinking in the post-Kantian climate, claiming Kant and Plato as his teachers, but found hardly any sympathetic listeners, while those Idealists whom he scorned were in the ascendent; yet after the middle of the century he came to fame and exerted a strong influence, not only on later Romantic thought and practice, but on the rise of twentieth-century process-philosophies. Schopenhauer's philosophy of art is expounded in the third book of his chief work, *Die Welt als Wille und Vorstellung* (*The World as Will and Idea* [1819; second edition, with a supplement of fifty chapters, 1844]).

Schopenhauer's system rests upon a contrast between two ways of looking at the "world"—that is, the whole of things. From one point of view, he says, in Book I, the world is a phenomenon, that is, a congeries of "ideas," or sense perceptions, in the minds of sentient beings. Each of us can truly say, "The world is my idea." But the phenomenal world is not a random flux; it includes material objects and orderly relations of space, time, and causality. In short, it is subject to what Schopenhauer calls "the principle of sufficient reason," which is his simplification of the Kantian categories of the understanding. Our ordinary practical consciousness necessarily takes the things of the phenomenal

world to stand in spatial and temporal relations, and to be connected by causal laws; and common-sense inquiry, as well as
empirical science, is governed by this a priori condition in seeking
to understand and to explain events.

But behind the phenomenal world lies a noumenal world, the
Kantian "thing in itself [*Ding an Sich*]"—the "kernel" or inward
side, as Schopenhauer says (trans. Haldane and Kemp, I, 39).
Kant thought he had proved that the thing in itself is unknow-
able, though we can make assured postulates about it on moral
grounds. Schopenhauer's original and striking suggestion was
that the thing in itself is really an irrational and limitless urge,
which he called "the Will to Live." When we look at the system
from this angle, the phenomenal world, with all its varied classes
and grades of objects, is recognized as "objectification" of the
primal Will. In the elemental forces of nature, microphysical or
meteorological—in the striving for survival that grips all organisms from plants to mammals, but with greater intensity as the
scale rises—and in man's drives, desires, and emotions—the Will
expresses or manifests itself. Schopenhauer presents his theory of
the Will in Book II. Being noumenal, it is free of the principle
of sufficient reason (space, time, causality); it is a sheer striving,
without direction, goal or end. Though in itself one and undivided, its objectification somehow involves appearing in multiplicity, in the form of distinct objects and organisms—this dog,
this cat, both embody and evince the force of the whole Will.
Hence arise, everywhere in nature, "strife, conflict, and alterna-
tion of victory, and . . . that variance with itself which is essential
to the Will" (I, 191). There is no rest for any individual, including human beings. We are condemned, so long as we live, to live
amid threats and perils, to suffer want and deprivation while we
strive to satisfy our desires, and to suffer boredom and satiety
during those relatively rare moments when our desires are mo-
mentarily stilled. This is the basis of Schopenhauer's classic
pessimism: his argument that life is inherently and inescapably
evil.

I recall these features of Schopenhauer's general view because
they are essential to his philosophy of art, the main point of
which is just that art exists and justifies itself as a means of escape
from the tyranny of will and the misery of existence. It is not a

complete and permanent escape—for that, we must go to Schopenhauer's moral philosophy, which recommends asceticism and a Buddhist renunciation of desire and selfhood. But apart from this higher saintliness, art alone makes life at times tolerable. We must now see how that happens.

What makes art possible, in Schopenhauer's view, is another element of his metaphysical theory—a segment of Platonism grafted onto his Kantian phenomenalism and his own theory of the Will. Somehow, in objectifying itself phenomenally, the Will not only proliferates a multiplicity of individual things, but expresses itself in various discrete degrees of fullness or of intensity. Thus the objects of the phenomenal world fall into classes or species: different minerals, different groups of animals, etc. Moreover, these species fall into hierarchies, or levels, each representing a "grade of objectification" of the Will. Such a grade of objectification of will, Schopenhauer calls a "Platonic Idea" (Book II, §§ 25 ff). The Idea is Platonic because it is itself outside space and time (cf. III, 123), a subsistent form—not like the individuals that fall under it. The Ideas are related to their particulars "as archetypes to their copies" (Book III, § 30; I, 219). Schopenhauer describes the various grades of Will, the various sorts of Idea, from the lowest to the highest—from the inorganic up to the values of human character.

The relationship between the one Will, the many Ideas, and the innumerable individual things of the phenomenal world is not wholly clear. Because the Idea stands between the Will and the particulars of the world, it is the only "direct" objectivity of the will. Because it is not subject to the principle of sufficient reason, it is the only "adequate" objectivity of the Will (§ 32). In any case, there are now two radically different kinds of "knowledge" available to man. The knowledge we have in ordinary life, or as scientists, approaching things through the principle of sufficient reason, is knowledge we acquire as individuals, "always subordinate to the service of the Will" (§ 33; I, 230). Ideas, on the other hand, can be objects of knowledge only in so far as we can break away from "interest" or the practical orientation, and indeed from our very individuality (§ 30). The connections in Schopenhauer's mind among all these concepts is perhaps best shown in this passage:

If, raised by the power of the mind, a man relinquishes the common way of looking at things, gives up tracing, under the guidance of the forms of the principle of sufficient reason, their relations to each other, the final goal of which is always a relation to his own will; if he thus ceases to consider the where, the when, the why, and the whither of things, and looks simply and solely at the *what*; if, further, he does not allow abstract thought, the concepts of the reason, to take possession of his consciousness, but, instead of all this, gives the whole power of his mind to perception, sinks himself entirely in this, and lets his whole consciousness be filled with the quiet contemplation of the natural object actually present, whether a landscape, a tree, a mountain, a building, or whatever it may be; inasmuch as he *loses* himself in this object (to use a pregnant German idiom), *i.e.*, forgets even his individuality, his will, and only continues to exist as the pure subject, the clear mirror of the object, so that it is as if the object alone were there, without any one to perceive it, and he can no longer separate the perceiver from the perception, but both have become one, because the whole consciousness is filled and occupied with the one single sensuous picture; if thus the object has to such an extent passed out of all relation to something outside it, and the subject out of all relation to the will, then that which is so known is no longer the particular thing as such; but it is the *Idea*, the eternal form, the immediate objectivity of the will at this grade; and, therefore, he who is sunk in this perception is no longer individual, for in such perception the individual has lost himself; but he is *pure, will-less, painless, timeless subject of knowledge* [§ 34; I, 231].

In this remarkable sentence, various earlier observations on aesthetic experience are gathered together, and new and important suggestions added. Schopenhauer mentions concentration on the object, attention to presented quality, the "framing" of the object, loss of self-consciousness, disinterestedness, and detachment. And he describes the experience as a pure, unclouded knowledge of the Platonic Idea, which puts to sleep the restless craving of the Will, and for a time deadens the pain of being (cf. ch. 30, Supplement).

Schopenhauer does not use the term "aesthetic" for this experience. He first characterizes it, and tries to show that it is possible in a world that is both Will and Idea—though there are a good many difficulties here, for example in explaining how, as he says, "the accident (the intellect) overcomes and annuls the substance (the will), although only for a short time" (III, 129). Then he makes the connection with art: "But what kind of knowledge is concerned with that which is outside and independent of all

relations, that which alone is really essential to the world, the
true content of its phenomena," etc.? "We answer, *Art*, the work
of genius" (§ 36; I, 238–39; cf. § 49). He in fact proposes to define
art as "the *way of viewing things independent of the principle
of sufficient reason*" (I, 239). The capacity to know "the Ideas in
themselves" probably exists in all men, but in widely varying
degrees—"unless indeed there are some men who are capable of
no aesthetic pleasure at all" (§ 37; I, 252). This pleasure "is one
and the same whether it is called forth by a work of art or directly
by the contemplation of nature and life." But

That the Idea comes to us more easily from the work of art than directly
from nature and the real world, arises from the fact that the artist, who
knew only the Idea, no longer the actual, has reproduced in his work
the pure Idea, has abstracted it from the actual, omitting all disturbing
accidents [§ 37; I, 252].

"Things as they are in truth," says Schopenhauer in his Supplement, "cannot be directly discerned by every one through the
mist of objective and subjective contingencies. Art takes away
this mist" (III, 177).

For Schopenhauer, then, it is plain, art is essentially a cognitive
enterprise, with its own special object of knowledge, the Ideas.
These are grasped and revealed. But since this knowledge is
utterly removed from the Will and its servant, the ordinary intellect, it has no practical use; its value lies in the experience
afforded by its contemplative reception, the gratification itself of
becoming a *"pure will-less subject of knowledge,"* freed from the
burden and the curse of self-assertion (§ 38; I, 253). In this state,
"we keep the Sabbath of the penal servitude of willing; the wheel
of Ixion stands still" (I, 254). This double aspect of the aesthetic
situation, the objective and subjective, or cognitive and affective, is reflected in the predication of beauty, according to
Schopenhauer:

When we say that a thing is *beautiful*, we thereby assert that it is an
object of our aesthetic contemplation, and this has a double meaning;
on the one hand it means that the sight of the thing makes us *objective*,
that is to say, that in contemplating it we are no longer conscious of
ourselves as individuals, but as pure will-less subjects of knowledge; and
on the other hand it means that we recognize in the object, not the
particular thing, but an Idea [§ 41; I, 270–71].

Schopenhauer draws another consequence:

> Since, on the one hand, every given thing may be observed in a
> purely objective manner and apart from all relations; and since, on the
> other hand, the will manifests itself in everything at some grade of its
> objectivity, so that everything is the expression of an Idea; it follows
> that everything is also *beautiful* [I, 271]. . . . But one thing is more
> beautiful than another, because it makes this pure objective contempla-
> tion easier, it lends itself to it, and, so to speak, even compels it, and
> then we call it very beautiful [I, 272].

Schopenhauer takes up, with originality and force, a number
of other aesthetic topics that were of special interest to his contemporaries and predecessors. He borrows suggestions from the
British Empiricists and from the German Idealists, but he gives
them new shapes and new settings in his own system, which they
seem to fit quite well. For example, he can allow Kant's distinction between the mathematical and the dynamical sublime, but
his basic explanation of the sense of the sublime is quite different.
When the contemplated object has a "hostile relation to the
human will in general" (§ 39; I, 260), but

> if, nevertheless, the beholder . . . forcibly detaches himself from his will
> and its relations, and . . . quietly contemplates those very objects that
> are so terrible to the will, comprehends only their Idea . . . so that he
> lingers gladly over its contemplation, and is thereby raised above him-
> self, his person, his will, and all will:—in that case he is filled with the
> sense of the *sublime* [I, 261].

Schopenhauer also devotes a considerable discussion to analysis
of artistic genius, which he defines as the capacity for knowing
Ideas as such—that is, for having aesthetic experience, as he conceives it (§§ 36–37; cf. ch. 31 of Supplement). And finally, he
tackles the problem of the classification and ordering of the arts—
in this case, armed with a general theory that provides him with
some new and interesting principles of order.

Works of art exist to present Ideas. Ideas exist in various
grades, and works of art in various media; we would not be sur-
prised to find, then, that each art is specialized with respect to
content: that is, it takes as its special province a certain range of
Ideas. Thus architecture makes use of, and thereby brings into
contemplatable embodiment, "the conflict between gravity and
rigidity," which are elemental natural forces (§ 43; I, 277; cf.

ch. 35 of Supplement). Sculpture is especially suited to the expression of human beauty and grace (§§ 44–45); painting (especially in its highest mode, historical painting), to traits of human character (§§ 46–50; cf. ch. 36 of Supplement). But character traits, and the qualities of human relationships, and especially the Ideas in the natures of highly individual people, are the special domain of literature, of lyric and epic and dramatic poetry (§ 51; cf. ch. 37 of Supplement). The "summit of poetical art, both on account of the greatness of its effect and the difficulty of its achievement" (I, 326) is tragedy. "Our pleasure in tragedy belongs, not to the sense of the beautiful, but to that of the sublime" (III, 212). For it brings us face to face with the misery of life; it shows us life in all its terror and futility, stripping away the veil of illusion. It shows "the strife of the will with itself" (I, 326), through the conflict of different individuals in whom the same Will exerts itself, reminding us that the individuals are thus phenomenal only, since in reality they are one. Thus tragedy "has a *quieting* effect on the will, produces resignation, the surrender not merely of life, but of the very will to live" (I, 327).

So far, the correspondence of the modes of art with the grades of Will is argued with ingenuity; Schopenhauer is most original, however, in discussing the role of music. Music, he says, does not belong in the preceding scheme at all. "It stands alone, quite cut off from all the other arts. In it we do not recognize the copy or repetition of any Idea of existence in the world" (§ 52; I, 330; cf. ch. 39 of Supplement). It is "the *copy of the will itself*"—"as *direct* an objectification and copy of the whole *will* as the world itself, nay, even as the Ideas, whose multiplied manifestation constitutes the world of individual things" (I, 333). We cannot pause to consider the interesting way in which Schopenhauer works out this thesis of the metaphysics of music, analyzes the expressive effects of melody, harmony, and rhythm, and accounts for the supreme power of music by its daring to confront us with, to let us hear in it—though we are still quiescent—the ceaseless urge of the Will itself.

Schopenhauer's basic philosophy of music played a major role in later nineteenth-century reflections on musical aesthetics—a subject that took on new vigor and interest in that period. The rise of purely instrumental music, and the heights it had reached in the hands of the Austrian composers, posed again, but in a new way, the old problems about the expressiveness of music, and its essential or natural or ideal relation to words, images, and concepts. The musical theorist needed a theory that would, paradoxically, explain both the enormous effect of pure symphonic and chamber music, and the remarkable capacity of music to enter into alliance, or union, with words. And the adventurous composer, seeking for ways in which the Romantic feeling could be more fully expressed by musical means, created music of a new order of emotional intensity, and experimented with genres—for example, the symphonic poem of Berlioz and Liszt—that might raise art, as the expression of feeling, to a new height. Some of the resulting problems, and ambivalences, can be seen in the essay on "Berlioz and his *Harold* Symphony" (1855) that Liszt wrote with Princess Caroline von Wittgenstein. Their first principle is that "Music embodies *feeling* without forcing it . . . to contend and combine with *thought*," and they speak of "its supreme capacity to make each inner impulse audible." "It is the embodied and intelligible essence of feeling" (see Strunk, p. 849). Yet they are soon defending the value of providing a program for the music, as though its capacity needed strengthening by being forced to combine (somehow) with thought.

These problems were a matter of great concern to Richard Wagner for several decades. His study of *The World as Will and Idea* (which he first read in the autumn of 1854) moved him deeply, and helped work a fundamental shift in his aesthetic theories as well as his compositional practice. The contrast in doctrine between *Opera and Drama* (1851) and the essay on Beethoven (1870), like the contrast in style between *Das Rheingold* (finished May 1854) and the third act of *Siegfried* (finished February 1871), reflects a fundamental change in Wagner's philosophy of music.

The early doctrine—still the one most famously associated with his name—was quite at variance with Schopenhauer's view of the uniqueness of music among the arts. In his book *The Art-Work of the Future (Das Kunstwerk der Zukunft,* 1850), Wagner called for a new and ultimate art form, an ideal drama, in which all the arts would be synthesized to produce the highest and most powerful emotional expression. His theory of this synthesis was a culmination of an old Romantic dream of the ultimate union of the arts, though Wagner did not neglect to stipulate that in contributing to the whole the special nature of each art must be respected. But Wagner was also proclaiming a social doctrine of art—his ideal drama would be an art of the people, an expression of their ideals and aspirations. In both senses it would be a *Gesamtkunstwerk*, a collective art. This theory was further developed in *Opera and Drama* (1851), which laid out (in Part III) the details of the artistic synthesis required for the ideal drama, in which, Wagner says, everything will be subordinated to feeling, and to that form of knowledge that comes only through feeling. Word, action, design, and tone would be completely fused.

It was the possibility of this fusion, with its requirement of an accommodation between the music and the other elements of the work, that Wagner found to be challenged by Schopenhauer's theory of the arts. Wagner's assimilation of Schopenhauer, and his formulation of a new concept of the music drama, occupied his later writings in aesthetics. His first tentative attempt was made in an essay ironically entitled "The Music of the Future" (1861), which he prefaced to a French prose translation of his operas. He argued that music is the greatest of all arts, in its freedom from the laws of logic and causality, which enables it to yield the deepest revelations—but words, in the music drama, can help to mediate these difficult messages and make the auditor more receptive to them by stirring his real-life emotions. The essay on Beethoven (1870) shows the pervasive influence of Schopenhauer, and uses his basic concepts. In the music drama, says Wagner, the word embodies the Platonic Idea, while the music expresses the Will itself; what both refer to, or center on, is the action of the drama, as we see it on the stage. Only through the music, with its penetrating and revelatory powers, does the action become fully intelligible; and so the laws of music, he suggests, are a kind of a priori condition of drama, considered in itself as Will, somewhat in the way the forms of sufficient reason are (for Schopenhauer) the a priori conditions of phenomena. *The Destiny of Opera (Über die Bestimmung der Oper,* 1871) proposed some further modifications of this theory.

The range of reflection in nineteenth-century musical aesthetics can best be seen by setting Wagner's serious, though somewhat mysterious, theories beside those of two other thinkers who also took Schopenhauer's doctrine as a point of departure, but moved off in a very different direction. Eduard Hanslick, the great Viennese music critic, published his little book on *The Beautiful in Music* (*Vom Musikalisch-Schönen*) in 1854, and revised it several times through its nine editions. The main thrust of his argument throughout was counter to the theory of *Gesamtkunstwerk*, the amalgamation of the arts; Hanslick defended the autonomy, the self-sufficiency, of music. Music does not need words, or thoughts, or actions, to achieve its greatest perfection, he said. The belief that it does arises from the false assumption that music has something special to do with feeling or emotion. And his fire was directed most sharply and persistently (in language marked by eloquence and sharp wit) at this most prevalent and (in his view) most dangerous confusion.

> On the one hand it is said that the aim and object of music is to excite emotions, i.e., pleasurable emotions; on the other hand, the emotions are said to be the subject matter which musical works are intended to illustrate.
> Both propositions are alike in this, that one is as false as the other [trans. Cohen, p. 9].

Hanslick shows, first (ch. 1), that, apart from conventional associations (as in parades or churches), music cannot, by itself, arouse emotions, for "there is no invariable and inevitable nexus between musical works and certain states of mind" (p. 15). And he shows (ch. 2) that, since emotions involve a concept, which music cannot provide, music cannot represent emotions, either. It can only present the "dynamical quality" of the emotion:

> The *whispering* may be expressed, true, but not the whispering of love; the *clamor* may be reproduced, undoubtedly, but not the clamor of ardent combatants [p. 21].

This is shown by the fact that when different people are asked to describe specific subjects of music, they diverge widely, and none can be proved wrong. It is also shown, Hanslick argues, by the fact that very different words can go well with the same music, and vice versa. Dynamical qualities can correctly be described by metaphors, as graceful or vigorous, but "the essence of music is sound and motion" (p. 48). And the beauty, or aesthetic value, of music, is peculiar to it, independent of anything else, perceived and enjoyed by the contemplative imagination. "A composition that looks us in the face with the bright eyes of beauty would make us glad, though its object were to picture all the woes of the age" (p. 100). Hanslick does not say very much about the nature of beauty, or of the faculty that perceives it; his chief concern is to show that the beauty of music cannot depend on its effects, either physiological or psychological, or on its supposed content, or its meaning, or any other external circumstance: "Its nature is specifically musical" (p. 47).

Another remarkable book, though by no means as influential, was *The Power of Sound* (1880), by Edmund Gurney. Gurney deals at some length, always clearly and rationally, with a number of problems about music, among them musical "expression." His discussion of expression (ch. 14) begins with an admirable analysis of various senses of the term, very much in the spirit of contemporary analytic philosophy (see pp. 312–13, esp. note 1). He holds that music *can* be expressive, "in the sense of definitely suggesting or inspiring images, ideas, qualities, or feelings belonging to the region of the *known* outside music" (p. 314). There Gurney seems to part company with Hanslick.

But the great point, which is so often strangely ignored . . . , is that *expressiveness* of the literal and tangible sort is either *absent or only slightly present* in an immense amount of *im*pressive music; that to suggest describable images, qualities, or feelings, known in connection with other experiences, however frequent a characteristic of Music, makes up no inseparable or essential part of its function [p. 314].

On this point he and Hanslick are as one.

Schopenhauer and Wagner were the two powerful influences under whom Friedrich Nietzsche (1844–1900) began his reflections on art, as well as on philosophical problems in general—the former' through his book, the latter in close personal association for several years. Though Nietzsche later repudiated something in each of them, they left their mark on his mature thought. Nietzsche's philosophy of art, in its main features, is set forth in his first book, *The Birth of Tragedy from the Spirit of Music* (1872); it is supplemented by scattered passages in later works, including the two anti-Wagner polemics written in 1888, and especially the notes collected by his sister and published posthumously as *The Will to Power* (first in 1901, as Vol. XV of the *Works*; then, much expanded, in 1910–11, as Vols. XV and XVI of the *Works*).

In one of his late notes, Nietzsche remarks that

> Our aesthetics have hitherto been women's aesthetics, inasmuch as they have only formulated the experiences of what is beautiful, from the point of view of the receivers in art. In the whole of philosophy hitherto the artist has been lacking [*Will to Power*; trans. Levy, p. 256].

The main focus of all Nietzsche's thinking about art is on this previously neglected area: he wanted to probe more deeply than had ever been done the deep sources of artistic creation, the nature of the impulse to make works of art. He began with an inquiry, highly speculative but fertile in psychological suggestions, into the origin of Greek tragedy; the important elements of his explanation became the basis of a general theory of art.

Tragedy arose, according to Nietzsche, from the conjunction of two strong impulses deep in human nature, which were allowed unusually free play of expression in Greek culture. The Apollonian spirit is cool—a love of order and measure, expressing itself in an art of formal beauty and proportion. The Dionysian spirit is wild—glorying in a state of elation or intoxication (*Rausch*) that accepts fully and joyfully the excitement and the pain of existence. Dionysian man, the worshiper of life, the taster of all its ecstasies, comes face to face with "the terror or the absurdity of existence" (*Birth of Tragedy*, § 7; trans. Fadiman, p. 209). In his orgiastic hour of worship, he annihilates himself and his terror, but he is always in danger of falling back into awareness of the real nature of life, "of longing for a Buddhistic [and Schopenhauerian] negation of the will. Art saves him, and through art life saves him—for herself" (p. 208).

> *Art* approaches, as a redeeming and healing enchantress; she alone may transform these horrible reflections on the terror and absurdity of existence into representations with which man may live. These are the representation of the *sublime* as the artistic conquest of the awful, and of the *comic* as the artistic release from the nausea of the absurd [p. 210].

In music, the paroxysms of Dionysian ecstasy are subjected to the Apollonian order and measure; they are formalized into art, and become the satiric chorus of the dithyramb, the first form of Greek tragedy.

It is music, the mating of Dionysian and Apollonian impulses, that gives rise to tragedy—and here Nietzsche makes use of Schopenhauer's theory, subtly reinterpreted by himself.

According to the doctrine of Schopenhauer . . . we may understand music as the immediate language of the will, and we feel our fancy stimulated to give form to this invisible and yet so actively stirred spirit-world which speaks to us, and we feel prompted to embody it in an analogous example [§ 16, p. 276].

That is, we seek and construct symbolic images to translate conceptually the insight of the music, just as the Will itself seeks for embodiment in a world.

If now we reflect that music at its greatest intensity must seek to attain also to its highest symbolization, we must deem it possible that it also knows how to find the symbolic expression for its unique Dionysian wisdom [p. 277].

This symbol is the tragic myth—the true image—correlate of music. "That striving of the spirit of music towards symbolic and mythical objectification" (p. 281) first gives rise to the proto-tragedy, which celebrates the sufferings and death of Dionysius, and Dionysius remains in Greek tragedy the essential and universal tragic hero, under whatever names and masks—Prometheus, Oedipus, Orestes, etc. (§ 10; p. 229).

Tragedy, then, is assigned a most important and original function in Nietzsche's aesthetics.

Art is not merely an imitation of the reality of nature, but in fact a metaphysical supplement to the reality of nature, placed beside it for purpose of conquest. Tragic myth, in so far as it really belongs to art, also fully participates in this transfiguring metaphysical purpose of art in general [§ 24, pp. 334–35; cf. § 8, p. 214].

Tragedy "presents the phenomenal world under the form of the suffering hero" (p. 335), making us look at it, and overcome it. "Only as an esthetic phenomenon may existence and the world appear justified," says Nietzsche; "and in this sense it is precisely the function of tragic myth to convince us that even the ugly and unharmonious is an artistic game in which the will plays with itself in the eternal fullness of its joy" (p. 336; cf. §22, p. 320).

The Birth of Tragedy was written in the period of Nietzsche's closest association with Wagner, and deepest admiration of him; the book was dedicated to Wagner, and its main argument leads, in the end, to a defense of Wagner's music drama. If tragedy was born out of the spirit of music, then, after many centuries, it can be reborn. Wagner's music, especially *Tristan und Isolde*, which Nietzsche so much admired (that music in which Wagner "put his ear to the heart-chamber of the world-will," § 21, p. 313), gives rise, in Wagner's verse, to new myths, in which the suffering hero appears once again in full glory, and once more the heights of the tragic transfiguration can be, are about to be, attained.

We need not follow the sad and tortuous developments of the Nietzsche-Wagner affair. The meaning of tragic, and generally artistic, "transfiguration," calls, however, for more explanation. And fortunately we have, in the later notes, important clues to Nietzsche's further thinking about art. In the meantime, he had discovered and sharpened his theory of the Will to Power as the basic human drive, and under the guidance of this concept he had reflected a good deal more on the effect of art, as well as its cause.

The Dionysian intoxication, says Nietzsche, is "equivalent to a sensation of *surplus power*" (*Will to Power*, II, 241), a super-abundance of life-force (sometimes kept up by a kind of sublimation of sexual energy) that overflows into creativity. The artist has an "inner compulsion to make things a mirror of [his] own fulness and perfection" (p. 254). The "aesthetic state" is one of those Dionysian states "in which we transfigure things and make them fuller, and rhapsodize about them, until they reflect our own fulness and love of life back upon us" (p. 243). This explains that cryptic passage in which, after rejecting the identification of the good, the true, and the beautiful, as "unworthy of a philosopher," he says: "Art is with us in order that we may not perish through truth" (p. 264). The real world, our intellect tells us, is cruel, senseless, and absurd. "We are in need of lies in order to rise superior to this reality, to this truth—that is to say, in order to live. . . . That lies should be necessary to life is part and parcel of the terrible and questionable character of existence"

(p. 289). The "lies" referred to here are not the lies of self-deception, but the lies of transfiguration: out of his own abundant vitality, the artist makes the world a mirror of himself, *gives* it sense and beauty. And thus he makes it liveable. This is why Nietzsche says, "In the main I am much more in favor of artists than any philosopher that has appeared hitherto" (p. 262).

The effect of great art, then, is to revitalize the perceiver. "All art works as a *tonic*; it increases strength, it kindles desire (*i.e.*, the feeling of strength), it excites all the more subtle recollections of intoxication" (p. 252). "Art is essentially the affirmation, the blessing, and the deification of existence" (p. 263; cf. 290). Here is where Schopenhauer, with his pessimistic aesthetics, and especially his theory of tragedy, went so badly wrong, according to Nietzsche. Art is not a "denial of life" (p. 257)—at least great, strong, healthy art is not. "Tragedy does not teach 'resignation' " (p. 264)—any more than it exists to teach morality, or purge the emotions (pp. 285, 287). Tragedy, and all art, say Yea to life (p. 288)—in every aspect, from the depths to the heights.

It may seem unfair of this little history to give Nietzsche a place he would no doubt have scorned—at the close of a chapter on Romanticism. Nietzsche hated Romanticism ("Romantic art," he said, "is only an emergency exit from defective 'reality,' " p. 269; cf. pp. 279 ff). Yet in several important respects, his philosophy of art belongs with Romantic theories, to which it is linked by Schopenhauer. The voluntarism and antirationalism, the glorification of the artist and the tragic hero, speak of their Romantic origins, despite their new shapes. Nevertheless, with Nietzsche we have come a long way, and we can also discern in him ideas that, in their fuller development, belong to a later time: our own. His Existentialism invites a deeper study of the function of art and of artistic truth. The Dionysian impulse implies a more positive and fundamental relationship of art and life, closer in some ways to twentieth-century instrumentalism and naturalism than to the vague Romantic longing for the unattainable.[7]

[7] Cf. Nietzsche's "Skirmishes in a War with the Age," in *The Twilight of the Idols* (1889), especially the rejection of *L'Art pour l'art* in §24 (*Complete Works*, ed. Oscar Levy, 18 vols. [London 1909–11]), XVI, 79–81.

Bibliography

G. W. Allen and H. H. Clark, eds., *Literary Criticism: Pope to Croce* (New York, 1941).

Samuel Hynes and Daniel G. Hoffman, eds., *English Literary Criticism: Romantic and Victorian* (New York, 1963).

René Wellek, *A History of Modern Criticism: 1750–1950* (Yale U., 1955), Vol. II.

Meyer H. Abrams, *The Mirror and the Lamp: Romantic Theory and the Critical Tradition* (Oxford U., 1953).

Walter Jackson Bate, *From Classic to Romantic* (Harvard U., 1949), chs. 5, 6.

Oskar Walzel, *German Romanticism*, trans. A. E. Lussky (New York and London, 1932), Part I.

A. E. Powell (Mrs. A. E. Dodds), *The Romantic Theory of Poetry* (London, 1926).

C. M. Bowra, *The Romantic Imagination* (Cambridge, Mass., 1949).

John Theodore Merz, *A History of European Thought in the Nineteenth Century* (Edinburgh and London, 1924), Vol. IV, ch. 7.

George Brandes, *Main Currents in Nineteenth Century Literature* (New York, 1902), Vol. VI.

Paul Reiff, *Die Ästhetik der deutschen Frühromantik* (Ann Arbor, 1946; Illinois Studies in Language and Literature, XXXI).

Margaret Gilman, *The Idea of Poetry in France from Houdar de la Motte to Baudelaire* (Harvard U., 1958).

Maurice Z. Shroder, *Icarus: The Image of the Artist in French Romanticism* (Cambridge, Mass., 1961).

A. G. Lehmann, *The Symbolist Movement in France, 1885–1895* (Oxford, 1950).

Joseph Ciari, *Symbolism from Poe to Mallarmé: The Growth of a Myth* (London, 1956).

A. O. Lovejoy, " 'Nature' as an Aesthetic Norm," *Essays in the History of Ideas* (Baltimore, 1948), 69–77.

A. O. Lovejoy, "The Meaning of Romanticism for the Historian of Ideas," *Jour Hist Ideas* II (1941): 257–78.

René Wellek, "The Concept of 'Romanticism' in Literary History," *Compar Lit* I (1949): 1–23, 147–72.

Morse Peckham, "Toward a Theory of Romanticism," *PMLA* LXVI, March 1951, 5–23.

Morse Peckham, "Toward a Theory of Romanticism: II. Reconsiderations," *Studies in Romanticism* I (1961): 1–8.

Elizabeth Schneider, *The Aesthetics of William Hazlitt* (Philadelphi⌐ 1933).

John M. Bullitt, "Hazlitt and the Romantic Conception of the Imagination," *Philol Quart* XXIV (1945): 343–61.

Samuel Taylor Coleridge, *Biographia Literaria*, 2 vols., ed. J. Shawcross (Oxford U., 1907).

J. W. Mackail, ed., *Coleridge's Literary Criticism* (London, 1908).

James V. Baker, *The Sacred River: Coleridge's Theory of the Imagination* (Louisiana State U., 1957).

I. A. Richards, *Coleridge on Imagination* (New York, 1950).

John H. Muirhead, *Coleridge as Philosopher* (New York, 1930), ch. 7.

Gordon McKenzie, *Organic Unity in Coleridge*, U. of Calif. Publications in English, VII, No. 1, 1–108 (U. of Calif., 1939).

R. H. Foyle, *The Idea of Coleridge's Criticism* (U. of California, 1962).

R. L. Brett, "Coleridge's Theory of the Imagination," in *English Studies*, New Series, 1949 (London, 1949).

Walter Jackson Bate, "Coleridge on the Functions of Art," in Harry Levin, ed., *Perspectives of Criticism* (Harvard U., 1950).

Clarence D. Thorpe, "Coleridge as Aesthetician and Critic," *Jour Hist Ideas* V (1944): 387–414.

James Benziger, "Organic Unity: Leibniz to Coleridge," *PMLA* LXVI, March 1951, 24–48.

Goethe's Literary Essays, ed. J. E. Spingarn (New York, 1921).

Conversations of Goethe with Eckermann and Soret, trans. John Oxenford (London, 1874).

Paul Frankl, *The Gothic* (Princeton, 1960), ch. 3.

Vivian C. Hopkins, *Spires of Form: A Study of Emerson's Aesthetic Theory* (Harvard U., 1951).

Charles R. Metzger, "Emerson's Religious Conception of Beauty," *Jour Aesth and Art Crit* XI (September 1952): 67–74.

André Ferran, *L'Esthétique de Baudelaire* (Paris, 1933).

Arthur Schopenhauer, *The World as Will and Idea*, trans. R. B. Haldane and J. Kemp, with Supplements, 3 vols. (6th ed., London, 1907–9); also trans. E. F. J. Payne (Indian Hill, Colorado, 1958).

Arthur Schopenhauer, *Complete Essays*, trans. T. Bailey Saunders, 4 vols. (New York, 1923).

Frederick Copleston, S. J., *Arthur Schopenhauer: Philosopher of Pessimism* (London, 1946), chs. 5, 6.

John Stokes Adams, *The Aesthetics of Pessimism* (Philadelphia, 1940).

André Fauconnet, *L'Esthétique de Schopenhauer* (Paris, 1913).

Patrick Gardiner, *Schopenhauer* (Baltimore, 1963), ch. 5.

Jack M. Stein, *Richard Wagner and the Synthesis of the Arts* (Wayne State U., 1960).

E. A. Lippman, "The Esthetic Theories of Richard Wagner," *Musical Quart* XLIV (1958): 209–20.

E. J. Dehnert, "Parsifal as Will and Idea," *Jour Aesth and Art Crit* XVIII (June 1960): 511–20.

P. L. Frank, "Wilhelm Dilthey's Contribution to the Aesthetics of Music," *Jour Aesth and Art Crit* XV (June 1957): 477–80.

Eduard Hanslick, *The Beautiful in Music,* trans. Gustav Cohen, ed. Morris Weitz (New York, 1957).

Edmund Gurney, *The Power of Sound* (London, 1880).

Friedrich Nietzsche, *The Birth of Tragedy*, trans. Clifton Fadiman (New York, 1927).

Friedrich Nietzsche, *The Will to Power*, 2 vols., trans. Oscar Levy (London, 1910), Vol. II, 239–92.

John E. Smith, "Nietzsche: The Conquest of the Tragic through Art," in *Reason and God* (Yale U., 1961).

ELEVEN

The Artist and Society

The nineteenth century brought radical changes in the political, economic, and social position of the artist, and posed unprecedented problems, both practical and theoretical, about the artist's relation to his art and to his fellow-men. The political scene was marked by a growing aspiration for individual freedom and political expression, with spasms of revolution and reform punctuating periods of dictatorialism and reaction, but with a broadening of educational opportunity and political participation. The advancement of mechanized industry and the factory system forced a revision of people's attitudes toward economic goods, toward production and utility. The emergence of social classes built primarily upon wealth, of the middle class, brought into existence a new determinant of morals and of aesthetic taste. How could the artist, in his own sphere, attain his share of the liberty promised by the age of revolution and the overthrow of eighteenth-century despotisms? How could artistic creation find its place and flourish in the age of mass-production, governed by supply and demand, the cash-payment nexus? How could works of art, with their peculiar sort of value, compete in the open market under a system that put primacy on useful objects? How was the artist to deal with a situation in which—the old system of private patronage being largely gone—he must win recognition, and obtain an income, from a middle class to whose taste he could cater, it would seem, only by being unfaithful to his own sense of beauty and vision of life?

The reflective artists, more than the technical philosophers, were the ones who wrestled with these problems and their manifold implications. No full-fledged aesthetic theories resulted, except (it might reasonably be contended) in the mind of Tolstoy, at the end of the century. But different possibilities were explored, and different tendencies of thought can be distinguished—some of them the immediate ancestors of important aesthetic positions today. And these are part of our story, though they have to be treated sketchily here, without the detailed documentation that would emphasize their pervasiveness in nineteenth-century thought.

ART FOR ART'S SAKE

The alienation of the artist from his society—the sense of incompatibility and of conflict, different in quality and in degree from anything that could have been felt before in the history of the arts—was one of the earliest themes of Romantic thought. It appeared in the German Romantics of the late eighteenth century: in Wackenroder's musician hero, Berglinger, who learns that the artist can at best be understood and appreciated by only a few; in Tieck, who felt that the life of art and the ordinary life of man are antithetical, and cannot be combined or reconciled. At first, the concept of alienation came from the Romantic artist's sense of his divine mission, and special endowments—his superiority to other men. Later there was added the sense of being rejected by society, as superfluous in a political and economic system running by its own hard and self-sufficient laws.

A mark of the Romantic artist and hero, from the beginning, was hypersensitivity—a livelier sympathy with other men, a quicker and more refined reaction to the beauty and ugliness of things. This was something to be proud of, though it makes others envious and hostile, and though it condemns the artist to feel pains that others cannot feel, and to suffer more acutely. That is the artist's burden, and his curse: e.g., Shelley's "sensitive plant," Vigny's Moïse, Baudelaire's albatross, hindered from walking the earth by his giant wings. This was the Romantic poet's interpretation of his favorite Orpheus legend. But actual poets, the martyred ones, also came to play a large iconographic role in the pantheon of the Romantic:

From the elaboration of the image of Tasso, wandering from city to city, to that of Chatterton, draining a vial of poison in a room strewn with his shredded manuscripts, one fact remained constant: the curse of genius, as it was interpreted by the French Romantics, referred most often to the persecution that the artist receives at the hands of a hostile society.[1]

Later, Baudelaire made of Poe the prime example of the poet whose fatal destiny it is to suffer and die for the sake of his art. The necessity of the poet's martyrdom was also explained in Vigny's preface to his play *Chatterton* (1835), and by Balzac, in an article on "Des Artistes" (1830)—and it was given memorable (and influential) expression in his short story "Le Chef-d'oeuvre inconnu" (1845).

From the assumption of this inevitable conflict between artist and society, a number of possible deductions can evidently be drawn—or, perhaps better, a number of possible stances or gestures may be suggested to the artist. One of these is withdrawal, the renunciation of social obligations for aesthetic monasticism. This is the ivory tower. The metaphorical meaning of this term, *"tour d'ivoire,"* was assigned by Sainte-Beuve to describe the life of Alfred de Vigny.[2] The implications of the metaphor are extremely rich, and have not been exhausted to our own day. Most of the strands in the theme of alienation are comprised in it, including the artist's need for protection, for solitude, for special care; his self-imposed or at least resignedly accepted uniqueness, carrying his curse as a pride; the transcendent importance of his calling; and something of Mallarmé's view that the artist practices a mystery, which cannot be revealed to the masses who are not initiated into its rites (see Mallarmé, "L'Art pour tous," written in the early 1860s).

It is this cluster of ideas that came to be summed up in the famous slogan of the nineteenth century, "Art for Art's Sake." The phrase *"L'art pour l'art"* was apparently used first by Benjamin Constant, in his *Journal intime* (February 10, 1804;

[1] Maurice Z. Shroder, *Icarus: The Image of the Artist in French Romanticism* (Cambridge, Mass., 1961), p. 35—to which I am much indebted for material in this section.

[2] See Sainte-Beuve's poem, "Pensées d'août" (1837); and Harry Levin, "The Ivory Gate," *Yale French Studies*, no. 13 (1954), 17–29 (references taken from Shroder, *op. cit.*, 124 n; cf. p. 236, on the Decadents' transformation of the Ivory Tower into Axel's Castle).

not published until 1895), and in a context that connected the theory with Kant. It (or something close to it) was used by Victor Cousin, in his lectures on *Le Vrai, Le Beau et le Bien* (1818; published 1836). We have seen how the Kantian aesthetics aimed to carve out a sphere of autonomy for art, which Schiller went on to enlarge and celebrate: the aesthetic object is something utterly different from all utilitarian objects, for its purposiveness is without purpose; the motive that leads to its creation is distinct, and independent of all others (that is, the free play of imagination under the understanding's general conditions of lawfulness); and the enjoyment of beauty and of the sublime brings to man a value that nothing else can provide, since it has nothing to do with cognition or with morality. The sources of what came to be called "art for art's sake" are mostly there in the Kantian system, though they no doubt had to be somewhat exaggerated and oversimplified, and they came to be so intermixed with other thoughts and feelings that they are best discussed as a cluster of ideas rather than as a special theory. Nor can a paradigm art-for-art's-sake theorist be found to represent this set of ideas. The Romantic poets and critics often shifted their view, wavered, or even left conflicting views unreconciled. Baudelaire, for example, can be placed in some respects with the art-for-art's-sake group. He wrote that the idea of utility is "the most hostile in the world to the idea of beauty" (Introduction to the *Nouvelles histoires extraordinaires, Oeuvres complètes,* VII [1933], xiv). He defended the importance of pure art, free from moral limitations, and his flowers of evil symbolize beauty's independence of, and superiority to, all other considerations. Yet he attacked "the childish utopianism of the *art for art's sake* school, in ruling out morals" (see *L'Art romantique* [1869], in *Oeuvres complètes,* II [1925], 184). But he seems to have meant here not so much that art is, in the final analysis, subject to the ordinary moral code, but that it has its own code of morality, to which it has an obligation to conform (see III, 284, 382).

In France, Théophile Gautier was probably the clearest and most outspoken representative of art for art's sake—first in his *Premières poésies* (1832), and then in the prefaces to *Albertus* (1833) and *Mademoiselle de Maupin* (1834). The third of these writings is the most famous, for its sarcastic humor and its barbs at contemporary customs and values. Gautier defends the right of art to be itself, and of the artist to go his own way; he is against moralists and against those who reject art on materialistic utilitarian grounds. His own value theory is hedonistic. Moralists complain that certain novels should be prohibited, or their wives and daughters will be ruined: the wives, says Gautier, don't read anyway, and "As for their daughters, if they have been to boarding-school, I do not see what these books could possibly teach them" (trans. Sumichrast, in Eugen Weber, p. 84). The utilitarians are always asking, "What is the good of this book? In what way can it be applied to the moral and physical improvement of our most numerous and poorest class? Why, there is not a word in it on the needs of society, nothing civilizing, nothing progressive." And to them Gautier replies, "A book cannot be turned into gelatine soup, a novel is not a pair of seamless boots" (85)—its practical value is that it earns money for author and publisher, and its "spiritual" value is that it keeps people from "reading useful, virtuous, and progressive newspapers, or other indigestible and degrading drugs" (86). Poems are no more "necessary" than flowers, but "I would rather do without potatoes than without roses" (87); and beauty is something different from, something utterly above, mere use, as those who can see it know. "I am aware that there are people who prefer mills to churches, and the bread of the body to the bread of the soul. I have nothing to say to such people. They deserve to be economists in this world and in the next likewise" (87).

In England, the best-known expressions of art for art's sake are the Conclusion of Walter Pater's *Studies in the History of the Renaissance* (1868); the "Ten O'Clock" lecture of the painter James A. McNeill Whistler (first delivered February 20, 1885; later incorporated in *The Gentle Art of Making Enemies* [1890]); and the essays of Oscar Wilde published in various periodicals and collected under the title *Intentions* (1891). Pater's concluding words, urging the reader to get "as many pulsations as possible" into the limits of his life, through a "quickened sense of life, ecstasy and sorrow," have often been taken as the most fervid statement of the doctrine:

Only be sure it is passion—that it does yield you this fruit of a quickened, multiplied consciousness. Of such wisdom, the poetic passion, the desire of beauty, the love of art for its own sake, has most. For art comes to you proposing frankly to give nothing but the highest quality to your moments as they pass, and simply for those moments' sake [in Weber, p. 200].

Apart from its roots, then, in the opposition of artist-genius to bourgeois society, the art for art's sake doctrine is essentially a brief for the intrinsic worth of aesthetic experience, quite apart from other values, and a Declaration of Aesthetic Independence for the artist who alone makes that experience, at its highest, possible. Sometimes unclearly, and with all the overtones of rebellion and scorn, these theorists were making an apology rather unlike any made before—just that beauty is a self-sufficient joy. Since they were doing this in a society that was inclined to feel little sympathy with the whole artistic enterprise (except within certain conventional and authorized limits), they had also to stake out a new and forceful claim for the artist's sovereignty in his own domain, his right to follow his own bent or his ideal, to experiment artistically as he wishes. Victor Hugo became the most inspiring defender and exemplar of artistic freedom; in his famous Preface to *Hernani* (1830), he wrote:

This loud and powerful voice of the people, likened to the voice of God, declares that henceforth poetry shall bear the same device as politics: TOLERATION AND LIBERTY [trans. Mrs. Newton Crosland; in Weber, p. 60].

On one level the demand for artistic freedom can be construed as economic: in the largely laissez-faire (though not wholly unmanaged) market of free enterprise, the artist was a producer of objects, too, but he did not have the prestige of the economic entrepreneur. He felt something of an urge to unionize, to found a brotherhood under another banner than material progress, or at least to grope toward a common sense of valid social purposiveness. And to survive at all, he had to advertise his goods on the fringes of the market, claiming wares better than the penny press and the music halls. On a higher level, the artist was making an assertion of a new human right: the freedom of self-expression for the gifted individual who must express himself or perish. Such an assertion was by no means academic under the fluctuating political conditions of France and the limitations on the press in England, for a number of the best novelists and poets had to cope constantly with censorship, with suppression of books and threats of imprisonment. On a still higher level, art for art's sake was a code of professional ethics. In the minds of writers like Flaubert, with his "religion de la beauté," his single-minded dedication to his craft and his commitment to perfection—see his letters to Louise Colet, *Oeuvres complètes, Correspondence*, I (1926), 225; cf. III (1927), 294—the demand for freedom from external pressures was a demand for the chance to live up to the artist's own highest obligation, to his art itself. That art has its own laws, which must be obeyed—not the old rules of neo-classicism, but the demands made by each particular work itself, to be developed and perfected in its own terms—might be a corollary of the concept of art as "play" in the sense of Kant and Schiller. And in the nineteenth century, the ivory tower was not a voluptuary paradise for most writers, but a sanctuary where, away from the politicians, the police, and the money-hungry people, the artist might polish away at his verse, might weigh every syllable (as Flaubert did) to create his finished work of art.

When art for art's sake is thought of on this plane, it is not as far as it might seem from its opposite view, in the nineteenth century; the ivory tower becomes, in a sense, a social institution, and the retirement of the poet to his refuge might be like the experimental scientist's retirement to his laboratory—demanding unconditional release from immediate obligations for a time, but only so that, in the long run, he can return with something of the highest value that cannot be achieved in the rush of ordinary affairs. The artist may limit himself to the search for formal beauty, but beauty is not an abstraction; it appears only in infinitely varied concrete forms, each one of which can only be realized by an artist with his unique personality and style. Gautier was fond of asserting (as for example in his program for *L'Artiste*, when he became editor, December 14, 1856), "I believe in the autonomy of Art; for me Art is not a means, but an end . . ." Yet even he wanted also to say that, in a more fundamental and roundabout way, the artist gives something to his society which he cannot give unless he goes his own way. "The verses of Homer, the statues of Phidias, the paintings of Raphael, have done more to lift up the soul than all the treatises of the moralists" (*L'Art moderne* [1856], p. 153; compare a similar view expressed by Leconte de Lisle in *Les Poètes contemporaines* [1864]). The artist's paradox is that of the mystical saint; both need their lonely wilderness retreat, if they are to bring back to society the fruits of meditation.

The nineteenth-century controversies over art-for-art were often more warming than illuminating because the important theses were so commingled with the easily ridiculed ones, the claim to a higher artistic responsibility confounded with the claim to irresponsibility. But I think we should see in them another step in the long historical process of thinking by which the uniqueness and independence of art is to be understood, its own sphere marked out. The art-for-art theorists foreshadowed the further attempts of twentieth-century "formalists," for example, Clive Bell and Roger Fry, to mark out a distinctive value in a distinctive aesthetic emotion, and to say that the poet or painter does his duty in cultivating that emotion just as surely as the doctor or lawyer does by his activities.

REALISM

If the nineteenth century was an "age of ideology," as it has been called, it was also, of course, an age of science—one may say that it was the age when natural science became professional, entered the economic system, the universities, and the popular consciousness as one of the most important segments of civilization. And this development was reflected, in art, in the movement known as Realism.

To the literary historian, Realism is a kind of literature, a practice that developed in the nineteenth century, partly out of, and partly in reaction to, Romanticism, and is still vital today, though seldom found in a pure form among the finest contemporary works of drama or prose fiction. It is a method, or a collection of methods, that can be described with some definiteness, and that was noted from the start by critics and reviewers, often with hostility. To the historian of criticism, Realism is a theory about what kind of literature is most to be admired, or is most needed—a self-conscious program, such as was frequently announced and defended by the great French Realists of the nineteenth century, in their prefaces, essays, and letters. The aesthetician's interest in this literary movement and critical school is necessarily more abstract and selective. In so far as Realism, in theory or practice, rests upon general assumptions about what literature is, or ought to be, and about its relationship to other human concerns, then it reflects, or implicitly presupposes, aesthetic theories. These are the theories we must take note of here.

The fullest and most vigorous defense of Realist aesthetics is to be found in the writings of Émile Zola, and principally in two long essays, "The Experimental Novel" and "Naturalism in the Theatre" (in *Le Roman experimental* [1880]; they had appeared previously, in Russian, in *The Messenger of Europe*). His theories owed much to the novelists who preceded him, especially Flaubert and the Goncourts; from the start, Zola was also much influenced by the sociological theories of Hippolyte Taine, and after he had formed the main features of his position, he found in Claude Bernard some principles of scientific method that enabled him to work out the position in detail.

Taine's approach to the study of literature, as explained in the Introduction to his *History of English Literature* (1864), can be considered, in one aspect, as a continuation of the historical approach to literature conceived in the late eighteenth century, and effectively used by Herder and by the Schlegels. Underlying their work was a new, or at least newly definite, concept of a literary work as a human artifact that appears in a particular society at a particular time and—they believed—needs to be understood in this context. Auguste Comte redefined this view in terms of his "Positive Philosophy," and added the theory—which Taine was determined to clarify and prove—that, like all other objects, literary works are completely determined by, and therefore in principle fully explainable in terms of, their contexts. The relevant causal, and explanatory, factors Taine sorted out into three categories, according to the now-famous formula: "the race, the surroundings, and the epoch" (*race, milieu, moment*; trans. Van Laun, in Weber, p. 153). Taine did not succeed in using these categories consistently, but he tried to explicate them in terms of mechanics: "the permanent impulse" (or initial thrust), the environment (with its friction and its settled forces), and "the acquired momentum"—which includes, for example, the literary tradition in which the poem appears (see Weber, pp. 155–56). The scientific historian's problem is to discover the general laws governing the production of various elements of human culture— religions, philosophies, poems, and plays. And, in the light of these laws, to solve particular problems of the form: Given this literary work, what conditions of race, circumstance, and epoch must have been required to produce it? "Just as in its elements astronomy is a mechanical and physiology a chemical problem, so history in its elements is a psychological problem" (Weber, p. 161).

From this general view of literature, Taine suggests, certain important critical corollaries may be derived. First, "a work of literature is not a mere play of imagination, a solitary caprice of a heated brain, but a transcript of contemporary manners" (Weber, p. 145). Even when it is about old, unhappy, far-off things, or faery lands forlorn, it is still a product of its social context, and to the instructed inquirer reveals the nature of its roots. But, second, some books show more transparently, more explicitly, and more fully, what sort of society it is that produces them, and these are the most valuable. "I would give fifty volumes of charters and a hundred volumes of state-papers for the memoirs of Cellini, the epistles of St. Paul, the Table-talk of Luther, or the comedies of Aristophanes" (Weber, p. 162). Hence Taine's principle of evaluation:

The more a book represents visible sentiments, the more it is a work of literature; for the proper office of literature is to take note of sentiments. The more a book represents important sentiments, the higher is its place in literature; for it is by representing the mode of being of a whole nation and a whole age, that a writer rallies round him the sympathies of an entire age and an entire nation [Weber, p. 162].

These criteria provide the rationale for attributing the highest value to the work of every Realistic novelist—notably the great series, *The Human Comedy* (completed in 1846) by Balzac, who had died in 1850. They are clearly also capable of becoming a vocation and an inspiration for later novelists, and especially Zola, the first volume of whose own Rougon-Macquart series appeared in 1871.

Claude Bernard's *Introduction to the Study of Experimental Medicine* (1865) is a landmark in the history of science. In this work he formulated, more clearly than had ever been done, the modern concept of scientific method as consisting in the testing of hypotheses by controlled observation and, where possible, experiment. And he laid the groundwork on which physiology could become an exact experimental science. That a living thing, however complex and delicate, can be studied by the same quantitative methods as the inorganic—that it is a dynamical equilibrium whose energy input and output can be measured, and whose chemical processes can be deterministically explained—is the central thesis. It was this powerful concept of scientific method, of its range and potentialities, that aroused the enthusiasm of Zola, whose essay on "The Experimental Novel" quotes Bernard copiously, interprets him with understanding, and makes of his theories a springboard for a literary aesthetics. It is true that before reading Bernard, Zola had already begun (no doubt in response to the developing temper of his age) to think of the novelist as a kind of scientist—in the Preface he added to the second edition (1868; but before he read Bernard) of *Thérèse Raquin* (1867), he defended himself, uncompromisingly, against the attacks on the first edition, by saying "that my aim has been a scientific aim, above all. . . . I have carried out, on these two live bodies, the analytical work that surgeons do on corpses" (trans. Philip G. Downs [1955], p. viii). (He also took as a motto for this work the famous words of Taine: "Vice and virtue are products, like vitriol and sugar"; see Weber, p. 150.) And other novelists had spoken in a somewhat similar vein; for example, the Goncourts, in their Preface to *Germinie Lacerteux* (1864): "the study that follows is the clinical analysis of Love" and "the Novel has taken up the studies and the duties of science" (trans. Weber, pp. 143–44). And Flaubert in various letters: Flaubert wrote of *Madame Bovary*, on which he was at work, as "a work of criticism above all, or rather of anatomy" (to Louise Colet, January 1854; *Correspondence* IV, 3; trans. Becker, p. 94). "Art ought, moreover, to rise above personal feelings and nervous susceptibilities! It is time to give it the precision of the physical sciences, by means of a pitiless method!" (To Mlle Leroyer de Chantpie, March 18, 1857; IV, 164–65; Becker, p. 95.) But it was Bernard's book that enabled Zola to see more clearly, and defend more cogently, the kind of novel he wanted to write.

From the time of the earlier Realistic French novelists, Stendhal, Mérimée, Balzac, critics had constantly noted, and sometimes praised, their ruthless candor—"la complète vérité," "la vraie vérité," "la vérité nue." Nothing but the truth, was the idea, and something like the whole truth, too—or at least far wider stretches of truth, in terms of social classes, occupations, psychological impulses, were steadily brought into the range of novelistic treatment, from 1830 on. Zola claimed for Realism an even more central place in literary tradition. "All criticism from Aristotle to Boileau," he said (in "Naturalism in the Theatre," trans. Becker, p. 197), "has set forth the principle that a work ought to be based on truth." If this can be agreed upon—that literature contains, always and essentially, at best and at worst, a claim to truth—then the next question is only: What is true? Or: What can we know? Combine this cognitive principle with the Romantic epistemological premise that the free intuitive imagination takes wing to penetrate reality beyond what the senses teach, and you derive, as a conclusion, one theory about literature. Combine the same principle with another premise, that all we reliably know comes by patient accumulation of, and induction from, empirical observations, and you derive a different conclusion. For then it is, in the broad sense, scientific knowledge that literature must claim to be, and to give.

The novelist, like the empirical scientist, begins by observing how people behave and trying to understand them—that is the basis of the Realistic theory. And in a fairly clear sense, Realist literature can be defined as literature that presents as objectively as possible, with as little distortion or manipulation as may be, human beings in action, so that their motives and drives are understandable to the reader. As a corollary, we could then further say that Realist literature is to be defined in terms of a set of specific devices or special traits, whose utility to the writer comes from the aid they give him in making his work Realistic. For example,[1] the writer will deal with contemporary life, which he can know at first hand; he will be wide-ranging in his interests, visiting stock exchange, madhouse, hospital, cafe, etc.; he will use ordinary language and the technical jargon of the trades

[1] These points are well summarized by Bernard Weinberg, *French Realism: The Critical Reaction, 1830–1870* (New York, 1937), p. 126.

and professions; he will omit no aspect of life, however dull or
seamy, that helps to explain why people act as they do; he will
be greatly interested in concrete details, of furnishings and of
surroundings, though he need not be unselective, since his central
interest is man, and objects concern him in so far as they are clues
to human psychology; he will allow the plot to move as the
characters seem to guide it, not sacrificing plausibility to a well-
constructed tale; he will not intervene, as narrator, to comment
or moralize, any more than the natural scientist needs to edi-
torialize on his work. Many of these principles are expressed in
Flaubert's letters.

That's what is so fine about the natural sciences: they don't wish to
prove anything. [I take it Flaubert means that they have no axe to
grind.] Therefore what breadth of fact and what an immensity for
thought! We must treat men like mastodons and crocodiles. Does anyone
fly into a passion about the horns of the former or the jaws of the latter?
[to Louise Colet, March 31, 1853; III, 154; Becker, p. 92; cf. letter of
March 19, 1854: "the personality of the author is *completely* absent,"
Becker, p. 94].

It is this collection of ideas that had best be called "Realism,"
it seems to me. Zola himself subscribed to them, and stated them
quite forcefully (in "Naturalism in the Theatre"; see Becker,
pp. 207–210): "The imagination no longer has a function," he
concluded (p. 207), thus breaking profoundly with the Romantic
view. But actually, his main point (which Bernard helped him
to define for himself) went somewhat beyond the Realistic theory
—which is why he himself preferred to call it "Naturalism," rather
than Realism. Now, the relations between these two terms are
much too complicated to deal with adequately here. It seems to
me useful to reserve the term "Naturalism" for a certain type of
metaphysical view, either a very abstract one (Naturalism vs.
Supernaturalism) or a more specific one, say, pessimistic materialistic determinism, a nineteenth-century reductionistic view, as if
one said that virtue and vice are *no more than* vitriol and sugar.
But in Zola, Naturalism is to Realism what (in Bernard) experiment is to observation. "We have experimental chemistry and
physics," says Zola ("The Experimental Novel," trans. Becker,
p. 171); "we shall have experimental physiology; later still we
shall have the experimental novel." The essential notion is that

the novelist selects his characters, places them in a situation, and lets them interact to see what will happen. Therefore he is no mere photographer, or chronicler, or amasser of facts; like the laboratory worker, he arranges, he sets up the apparatus, he observes consequences, he tests hypotheses.

When we come to this point, we may well feel that we are a long way from the main lines of aesthetic thought that we have traced more or less continuously through previous chapters. One measure of the distance is given by the question: Where does beauty enter in? On this point there is a considerable ambivalence among the Realists. Flaubert was quite frank about it: the novelist's duty, in the Realist view, is an unpleasant one; he must have a strong stomach to face up to reality, which is often ugly, and perhaps ugliest where it is most in need of being faced—as in the life of Emma Bovary or in the condition of the lowest social classes. "I execrate ordinary life" (to Laurent-Pichat, October 2, 1856; IV, 125; Becker, p. 94). And yet, sometimes, he put it a different way: everything, even the humblest object, has its poetry: "So let's become accustomed to considering the world as a work of art, the ways of which we must reproduce in our works" (to Louise Colet, March 27, 1853; III, 138; Becker, 92). It is the same in painting. The attempt to reproduce visible objects exactly, however lowly, just to report their colors and textures and the patterns they make, struck academic painters and public as a cultivation of ugliness, when Courbet held his own exhibition in 1855 (calling himself a "Realist" in his manifesto) and later when Manet and the other Impressionists made the same resolution to be true to appearance. John Constable, who, in his fourth lecture at the Royal Institution (1836) declared that painting is "a branch of natural philosophy, of which pictures are but the experiments," once remarked to a lady, "No, madam, there is nothing ugly; *I never saw an ugly thing in my life*: for let the form of an object be what it may,—light, shade, and perspective will always make it beautiful."[2] In the same spirit, Zola, writing on "The Realists of the Salon of 1866" (1866), says, "I negate no artist. I accept all works of art on the same grounds, as being manifestations of the human spirit. . . . They all have true beauty: life, life in its thousand expressions, ever changing, ever

2 See C. R. Leslie, *Memoirs of the Life of John Constable* (1843) (London, 1951), pp. 323, 280.

new" (trans. Weber, p. 182). The literary theorist who becomes convinced, like Zola, that scientific method is the only reliable source of knowledge, must resolve a new and difficult dilemma about the relationship of beauty and truth. Should the novelist aim at truth, expecting beauty to tag along with it? Or should the novelist aim at beauty, and leave truth to the scientists? This dilemma was to grow more formidable in the twentieth century.

Another indication of the seriousness of the Realistic challenge to older and well-established aesthetic assumptions is provided by an interesting essay on Maupassant by Tolstoy (originally in *Arena* [1894]; trans. Charles Johnston, in Becker). He blames Maupassant for lacking the most important of

the three qualities necessary for the production of a true work of art. *These three conditions are: a true, a moral attitude towards his subject; clear expression, or, what is the same thing, beauty of form; and, thirdly, sincerity—unfeigned love or unfeigned hatred for what he depicts* [Becker, p. 414].

If these three qualities are indispensable, it would seem to follow that Realism is incompatible with art. For the passionless scientific detachment required of the Realistic narrator, calmly absorbed in the chemical reactions of personality, excludes all moralizing, and all feelings of approval or disapproval. And above all, he must not tamper with the experiment, no matter how tempted by the thought of a more perfect structure or style.

It is evident, I think, that there is a kind of kinship, in one respect, between the Realistic view and the school of art for art's sake: each demands its own kind of discipline, even if one be to labor for the perfection of beauty and the other, more ascetic, for the perfection of empirical knowledge of human nature. The Realist, as strongly as the believer in art for art, begins by affirming his right to inquire freely—especially when the bourgeoisie begins to call his works obscene and pornographic because he observes immorality so keenly and so calmly. But when pressed, he wants to claim that his ultimate justification is a social one. The goal of physiology and of experimental medicine, says Zola, is "to master life in order to direct it," and the same is true of the experimental novel ("The Experimental Novel," Becker, pp. 176–77). The deepening of human understanding, the widening of human freedom, are the goals. This line of thought, the importance of art as a contributor to the

general welfare, is another development in the nineteenth century that deserves (and will in a moment receive) attention on
its own account.

Before coming to that, however, we must note a somewhat
parallel movement among literary theorists in Russia. It began
with V. G. Belinsky, who was at first (like Taine) under the influence of German Idealism and Romanticism, but came to emphasize the historical context of literature, and finally attached the
highest importance to verisimilitude and the reflection of social
conditions (see his last two annual surveys of Russian literature,
1846–47). This last theme was the main emphasis of N. G.
Chernyshevsky, in his famous dissertation on *The Aesthetic Relations of Art to Reality* (1855; see also the preface written for an
unpublished reissue in 1888). Here art is taken as essentially a
reproduction of reality, of "facts," in many cases inferior to the
model, but sometimes useful in that it makes certain aspects of
reality more accessible—a person who cannot get to the sea can
use a painting or a photograph as a substitute (see trans. by
S. D. Kogan, in Becker, pp. 63–64). "The first purpose of art is
to reproduce reality" (p. 64); the second is "explaining life"
(p. 72)—and here its virtue is chiefly that it helps understanding
by being attractive and arousing interest. Chernyshevsky's position was strongly endorsed by D. I. Pisarev, in his paper on "The
Destruction of Aesthetics" (1865), in which the musical and
visual arts are said to have no social use—though literature may
help convey social ideas. Pisarev was no doubt trying to arouse
concern by startling the reader; but he did raise important questions that had to be faced. Can we argue, for example, that since
the artist's creative imagination is limited, and he is necessarily
the product of his age, therefore the only way to get better art is
to improve the social conditions it necessarily reflects? Or, even
in a naturalistic theory, can we ascribe to the artist a power to
mould and guide social progress, make him an effective agent?
Pisarev seems to have been very dubious of the latter claim.

SOCIAL RESPONSIBILITY

Nineteenth-century thinkers, under the double impact of revolutionary political developments and the emergence of a truly

scientific social science, took up a theme that had not been given such serious attention between Plato and Schiller: the role of art in human society. They were concerned with the general Platonic problem, whether art as such is a boon or a menace, or can be controlled so that it will be one and not the other; but they gave it, ultimately, a new direction, by raising the question of the individual artist's responsibility to his society. The artist is a citizen or a subject, and has his obligations in this role; are these obligations to be subordinated to—or are they to take precedence over—his obligations to his art? In the twentieth century, in a time of totalitarian tyrannies and their underground resistances, this problem has sometimes been acute, and many thinkers, from the Marxists to the Existentialists, have wrestled with it (see, for example, Jean-Paul Sartre, "What is Literature?" [1947]).

This part of our story may begin (since we have already looked into Schiller) with the early French social reformers and social philosophers, who undertook to project systematic plans of what a rational society should be, and who were led to ask themselves what role, if any, the arts might (ideally) be asked to play in such a scheme. In the social order, purged of feudalism and ecclesiasticism, envisioned by the Comte de Saint-Simon and his disciples, the artist was to take his place along with the artisan and the scholar, or scientist, as a contributor to progress and general welfare, whose works would be appreciated for their genuine value by his fellow-workers (see, for example, *Du Système industriel*, 1821). This central idea, which was highly influential, took effect in many different ways. It could help, for example, to inspire Victor Hugo's sense of social mission (see "La Fonction du poète," 1839), and lay behind his remark that "Art for Art's sake may be fine, but art for the sake of progress is still more beautiful" (*Philosophie*, II, 172, in *Oeuvres complètes* [1880–92]; trans. Shroder)—though Hugo's context made it clear that he considered poetry to work best for progress precisely when it was most itself. Saint-Simon also set the scene for several other systematic thinkers—including Auguste Comte, who was for some years his secretary.

Comte outlined his philosophy of art in his *Discours sur l'ensemble du positivisme* (1848; ch. 5). To him, the cultivation of art for its own sake, and its separation from the rest of life, was a self-defeating tendency. It reflects the fact that "Reason has been divorced for a long time from Feeling and Imagination" (trans. Bridges, p. 203)—a breach which the Positivistic political system was designed to heal. In the projected Comtean society, the arts would be the basis of education; they would unite with industry to produce new human satisfactions; and they would exercise their true function in conveying that Religion of Humanity which Comte preached for modern man. Art is "an ideal representation of Fact; and its object is to cultivate our sense of perfection" (p. 208), by strengthening those sympathies with one another, those bonds of affection and mutual love, that are the true basis of social order (pp. 207, 211). The fullest flowering of art awaits the coming of a world from which, by the development of science and the increase of good will, war and oppression and economic servitude will be eliminated. This ideal of a society in which art would take a high place, and realize itself by becoming indispensable to the society, appeared to many people as one of the brightest features of Comte's utopian vision.

Somewhat earlier than Comte's fully developed Positive Philosophy, another utopian, Charles Fourier, had also thought of art, and of beauty, as essential to a healthy social and economic system. In his book *Cités Ouvrières* (1849), the description of a future city worthy of humanity, Fourier condemned the ugliness and disorder of existing cities, and imagined a city in which the buildings, by their harmonious colors, order, and good proportions, would gratify the eye, giving aesthetic satisfaction (as well as physical satisfaction) to man.

The political economist, Pierre-Joseph Proudhon, included a reference to social purpose in his Comtean definition of art as "an idealized representation of nature and of ourselves, its end being the physical and moral perfection of our species" (*Du Principe de l'art et de sa destination sociale* [published posthumously, 1865] 1939 ed., ch. 3, p. 68). "L'art pour l'art is nothing"; separated from "right and duty, cultivated and investigated as the highest thought of the soul and the supreme manifestation of humanity," he said, art becomes only "an excitation of fantasy and sensation," "the cause of the corruption of manners and the decadence of the state" (ch. 4; pp. 70–71). From these premises he derived the principle that the judgment of art belongs to the general public:

"The artist whose work . . . pleases the greatest number will be rated the greatest of all, since his ideal is the most powerful; there is no other rule" (*De la Justice dans la revolution* [1858; revised ed., 1860], III, 344). But he was emphatically opposed to the reduction of art to luxury or entertainment; and in a violent chapter (ch. 16) on "the prostitution of art," he attacked with Puritan zeal and righteous indignation the putting of art to unworthy uses.

In the line of French sociological aestheticians, one other should be credited with much vigorous thought. Jean-Marie Guyau, in his book *L'Art au point de vue sociologique* (1887), tried to break down separations of art from other aspects of culture. He emphasized, especially, the connections and continuities of beauty with utility, for example, in architecture and practical objects (see *Les Problèmes de l'esthétique contemporaine* [1884], pp. 15 ff). And he denied any essential difference between aesthetic emotions and other emotions that bring men together (ibid., p. 26). Art is essentially social. "True art, without pursuing externally a moral and social end, has in itself its profound morality and its profound sociability, which alone give it its health and its vitality" (Preface). The literary genius is one who possesses an unusually intense sympathy and social feeling, which enables him to enter into the characters he creates, and bring about new worlds of living beings (see *L'Art*, 3d ed., ch. 2; esp. p. 27).

In England, the approach to art in terms of its social context, and the argument for its social responsibility, was first fully developed by John Ruskin: these were, indeed, the lifelong themes of his thought and the main thrust of all his many works. In certain respects, he was the heir of Romanticism—in his attempt to make the imagination into a supreme cognitive faculty, and in his concept of the artist's high calling, for which he was indebted to Carlyle. But he belongs more to the Victorian age than to its predecessor—and some of the lessons he kept trying to teach it were profoundly needed. His significance can be overlooked because he is so easy to make fun of. As an art critic and connoisseur, the arbiter of taste (so he conceived himself), he does not survive well. R. H. Wilenski has pointed out, for example, the irony that he began his career as art critic by resolving to defend

Turner against the critic in the *Literary Gazette* (1842) who said that Turner's pictures were produced "as if by throwing handfuls of white and blue and red at the canvas, letting what chanced to stick, stick"—but achieved his most notorious public defeat thirty-five years later when he wrote in the same vein of Whistler's *Nocturne in Black and Gold: The Falling Rocket*: "I . . . never expected to hear a coxcomb ask two hundred guineas for flinging a pot of paint in the public's face."[1] But in his reflections on the ills of his society, and his grasp of its aesthetic as well as its economic dimension, Ruskin must be considered one of the great prophetic voices.

Ruskin's aesthetic theory, his basis of artistic judgment, was first set out in Volumes I and II (1846, 1853) of *Modern Painters* (Vol. III–V, 1856–60). Essentially it is a rather limited imitation theory. Volume I was to explain the first principle of art (or at least, of painting), namely truth. And Volume II was to explain the second, namely beauty. But they turn out to be much the same thing.

> I say that the art is greatest which conveys to the mind of the spectator, by any means whatsoever, the greatest number of the greatest ideas; and I call an idea great in proportion as it is received by a higher faculty of the mind, and as it more fully occupies, and in occupying, exercises and exalts, the faculty by which it is received [*Modern Painters*, Part I, Sec. I, ch. 2, § 9; *Works*, III, 92].

Great ideas are true to experience, though not narrowly imitative (ch. 5). Ruskin calls an object beautiful in the broad sense if it "can give us pleasure in the simple contemplation of its outward qualities without any direct and definite exertion of the intellect" (ch. 6, § 1; III, 109). In Volume II of *Modern Painters*, however (Part III, Sec. 1, ch. 2), beauty becomes somewhat narrower. Here Ruskin first describes "Aesthesis" as sensuous perception of enjoyable qualities—"But I wholly deny that the impressions of beauty are in any way sensual" (§ 1; *Works*, IV, 42).

> Now the mere animal consciousness of the pleasantness I call Aesthesis; but the exulting, reverent, and grateful perception of it I call

---

[1] See Wilenski, *John Ruskin* (New York, 1933), p. 198; and Whistler's account of the trial, reprinted in R. L. Peters, ed., *Victorians on Literature and Art* (New York, 1961).

Theoria. For this, and this only, is the full comprehension and contemplation of the Beautiful as a gift of God [§ 6; IV, 47].

The term "aesthetics," he suggests later on, should be reserved for "the inquiry into the nature of things that are in themselves pleasant to the human senses or instincts, though they represent nothing, and serve for nothing, their only service *being* their pleasantness" (*Aratra Pentelici*, Lecture 1; *Works*, XX, 207). He hastens to add (XX, 208) that, when so conceived, "Nearly the whole study of aesthetics is in like manner either gratuitous or useless." "Beauty" properly signifies two different things, says Ruskin:

First, that external quality of bodies . . . which . . . may be shown to be in some sort typical of the Divine attributes, and which therefore I shall, for distinction's sake, call Typical Beauty: and, secondarily, the appearance of felicitous fulfillment of function in living things . . . ; and this kind of beauty I shall call Vital Beauty" [*Modern Painters*, Vol. II, Part III, Sec. 1, ch. 3, § 16; *Works*, IV, 64].

In either form, the characteristic or the functional, beauty belongs to objects, and the virtue of art lies in its capacity to discover and convey such beauties.

In his two early works on architecture, *The Seven Lamps of Architecture* (1849) and *The Stones of Venice* (1851), Ruskin was deeply concerned with the relations between buildings and the men who build and use them. He argued that great works of architecture are expressions of builders with moral quality, and he argued that they have a profound effect upon the society in which they appear. The famous chapter on "The Nature of Gothic" (*Stones of Venice*, Vol. II, ch. 6) analyzed the moral and spiritual character of Gothic architecture, and pleaded for a return to social and economic conditions in which the division of labor would not be a division of men, from each other and within themselves (§ 16), in which social usefulness would be the basic principle of production (§ 17), and in which the workman would be a creative craftsman, not a mere instrument or machine (cf. *The Two Paths* [1859], Lecture III; and the Lecture on "Traffic" in *The Crown of Wild Olives* [1866], Lecture II). This became the main burden of his later lectures and writings: that art is moral in causes and effects—and art here includes not only paintings and poetry, but churches, banks, streets, gardens, pots and clothes. At times the doctrine he preached was close to Puritanical rigor, as when he said that

the entire vitality of art depends upon its being either full of truth, or full of use; and that, however pleasant, wonderful or impressive it may be in itself, it must yet be of inferior kind, and tend to deeper inferiority, unless it has clearly one of these main objects,—either *to state a true thing,* or to *adorn a serviceable one* [*Lectures on Art* (1870); *Works,* XX, 95–96].

Ruskin's form of functionalism struck a note that called forth powerful echoes in the minds of others who had been disturbed or appalled by the arid aesthetic wastes and the inhumanities that were the by-product of the Victorian economic process. Among the first to catch his spirit, and follow his lead, was that many-sided and dedicated man, William Morris. While producing epic poems and translations at a tremendous rate, learning numerous crafts of dyeing, weaving, etc., and managing (after 1860) the workshops of Morris and Co., in which he aimed to bring back good taste and good workmanship, Morris preached his doctrines in numerous addresses and pamphlets. Patiently and earnestly, in clear, strong and often moving words he stated over and over again, in various ways, his main themes.

The English aesthetic situation, so to speak, which Morris observed and diagnosed, was characterized, first, by a separation of the two main species of art: fine art, which he calls "intellectual," and "decorative" art, or craft (see "Art Under Plutocracy" [1883]; *Works,* XXIII, 165). Though they may be distinguished, these species are mutually dependent, says Morris, and their separation has led to the degeneration of both—the reduction of fine art largely to a trivial source of amusement to a few, and the almost complete disappearance of craft before the march of manufacturing. The only path to health lies in a reuniting of the two, that is, in the last analysis, a close companionship of use and beauty.

Now, Morris had very little to say about works of fine art as such; perhaps he thought that, if they do little of the good they might be made capable of, they at least do much less harm than the far more numerous and familiar objects of practical life that confront us constantly. When Morris talks about "art" in general,

he speaks of it in just about the same terms that, on other occasions, he specifically applies to the decorative arts. For example,
he says,

> To give people pleasure in the things they must perforce *use*, that is
> one great office of decoration; to give people pleasure in the things they
> must perforce *make*, that is the other use of it ["The Lesser Arts"
> (1877); *Works*, XXII, 5; cf. "The Arts and Crafts of To-day" (1889);
> *Works*, XXII, 356].

But, speaking in general terms, Morris also often says, "That
thing which I understand by real art is the expression by man of
his pleasure in labor" ("The Art of the People" [1879]; *Works*,
XXII, 42; cf. "Art Under Plutocracy," *Works*, XXIII, 173). And
he expands this formula, speaking of "the seed of real art, the
expression of man's happiness in his labor—an art made by the
people, and for the people, as a happiness to the maker and
the user" ("The Art of the People," *Works*, XXII, 46; cf. "The
Beauty of Life" [1880], and "The Aims of Art" [1887], *Works*,
XXIII, 84).

It would seem, then, that decorative art, the simultaneous, but
not merely parallel, making of the useful object, with pleasure
and for pleasure, is the highest and best artistic activity. And it is
precisely in making such activity impossible for a great many
people that the primary wrong of Victorian industrial society
consisted. There were two sides to the indictment.

First, from the side of the maker. When Morris thinks of decoration, of adding designs to the pottery or caring for the appearance of a printed book, he is thinking of something added by
the maker, freely, as an individual, out of the spontaneity of his
joy. He makes

> forms and intricacies that do not necessarily imitate nature, but in
> which the hand of the craftsman is guided to work in the way that she
> does, till the web, the cup, or the knife, look as natural, nay as lovely,
> as the green field, the river bank, or the mountain flint ["The Lesser
> Arts," *Works*, XXII, 5].

Morris is untiring, in essay after essay, in his exposure of the
present by contrast with the past; his constant historical theme
is that before industrialism, those who made useful objects, however deprived and depraved their lives were in other respects, had

in their grasp that one indispensable part of happiness, that they could express themselves in their work. Ruskin's chapter on "The Nature of Gothic" was his inspiration, and sometimes his text. Industrial civilization "turned the man into a machine" ("The Hopes of Civilization" [1888]; *Works*, XXIII, 68); the conditions of manufacture condemn the greater part of civilized men to labor in which they can take no intrinsic satisfaction, "which at the best cannot interest them, or develop their best faculties, and at the worst (and that is the commonest, too) is mere unmitigated slavish toil" ("The Beauty of Life," *Works*, XXII, 66; cf. "Art, Wealth, and Riches" [1883], *Works*, XXIII, 157).

Second, from the side of the receiver. Here there are two aesthetic tasks, in both of which industrial society has failed, says Morris. The first is to preserve the "natural beauty of the earth" ("The Prospects of Architecture" [1881]; *Works*, XXII, 125); and it is precisely this beauty which the slum, the railway, the smoking chimney, the junkyard, have recklessly destroyed (see "Art, Wealth, and Riches," *Works*, XXIII, 157).

Not only have whole counties of England, and the heavens that hang over them, disappeared beneath a crust of unutterable grime, but the disease, which, to a visitor coming from the times of art, reason, and order, would seem to be a love of dirt and ugliness for its own sake, spreads all over the country, and every little market-town seizes the opportunity to imitate, as far as it can, the majesty of the hell of London and Manchester ["Art Under Plutocracy," *Works*, XXIII, 170]—

an ironic inversion of "art for art's sake." The second is to make man's works fit substitutes for what they replace—to give his buildings, for example, beauty, just as the trees and brooks before them had beauty. The duty here is to keep in mind the welfare of all the inhabitants of earth. "Art will not grow and flourish, nay, it will not long exist, unless it be shared by all people; and for my part I don't wish that it should" ("Art and the Beauty of the Earth" [1881]; *Works*, XXII, 165).

Only fundamental changes in the system, Morris concluded, could bring back art to the everyday life of man, surrounding him with forms worthy of his manhood and allowing him to be an artist. Therefore, Morris became a Socialist, and much of the character of British socialism is due to his humanism, his breadth of spirit, and his hope for man (see "Art Under Plutocracy,"

Works, XXIII, 172; "Art and Socialism" [1884]). If an aesthetically fulfilling social order cannot be achieved, it might be better to have no art at all ("The Lesser Arts of Life," *Works*, XXII, 237). On the whole, however, it seemed to Morris that a long-range optimism must be justified: that, however skillful people are at adjusting themselves so they can live with ugliness and squalor, these evils must gradually become more and more apparent and insupportable—and finally be done away with (see "The Aims of Art," esp. *Works*, XXIII, 94–97).

Another extraordinary Victorian also deserves to be recorded, along with Morris, as a follower of Ruskin, but one who struck out on his own in many directions. The work of Patrick Geddes, biologist, city-planner, educational theorist, has still not been adequately recounted and evaluated. His book with Victor Branford, *The Coming Polity* (London, 1919), and numerous scattered articles and reports, develop the aesthetic tests of industrial society in what he called the "paleotechnic" stage of development: the degree of beauty in the environment, of quality in works produced, of creative satisfaction in the activity of production. For him, these tests were summed up in a standard of "vital value," of genuine suitability for the fullest human life; and he looked forward to a "biotechnic" era, in which this standard would prevail throughout the whole of society. Geddes' ideas have been further developed, in a vital way, by Lewis Mumford (see *The Culture of Cities* [1938]).

In the United States, a functionalist aesthetics was stated early, but tersely and decisively, by Horatio Greenough. His essay on "American Architecture" (which appeared in *The United States Magazine and Democratic Review*, August 1843, and was reprinted as ch. 9 of his book, *The Travels, Observations, and Experiences of a Yankee Stonecutter* [1852]) rejected the imitation of old styles of building, and urged the architect to "observe the skeletons and skins of animals" and note how "the law of adaptation" to use and need produces expressiveness and beauty. As he wrote to Emerson (Dec. 28, 1851; see article by T. M. Brown, in bibliography below), he found in the principle that beauty follows from function a theory that "will do for all structure from a bedstead to a cathedral," and he saw "in the ships, the carriages and the engines a partial illustration of the doctrine

and a glorious foretaste of what structure can be in this country
in ten years time . . ."

Emerson himself had been moving in the same direction. In his
"Thoughts on Art" (published in *The Dial*, January 1841), he
had propounded a Schellingesque basis for art in the processes
of nature, bringing use and beauty into alignment: "The gayest
charm of beauty has a root in the constitution of things" and
"The most perfect form to answer an end, is so far beautiful"
(see *Works*, IV, 67). In his essay on "Beauty," in *Conduct of Life*
(1860), Emerson insisted that

Beauty rests on necessities. The line of beauty is the result of perfect
economy. The cell of the bee is built at that angle which gives the most
strength with the least wax; the bone or quill of the bird gives the most
alar strength, with the least weight. "It is the purgation of superfluities,"
said Michel Angelo [*Works*, III, 193].

And he treated mere ornament and embellishment as deformity
(cf. the essay "Art," in *Essays, First Series* [1841]).

It was Leo Tolstoy (1828–1910) who carried through the concept of the social responsibility of art in the most thorough and
uncompromising way. After the peak of his work as a novelist
(the production of his two masterpieces), Tolstoy passed through
the great spiritual crisis that brought him to a new and purified
religious conviction. All the main aspects of his society, and of
his own life, came under review, and had to be re-evaluated in
the light of his new faith—among them, art, "a decoy of life"
(see *My Confession*, written 1878–79, chs. 2, 4). The results of
his long meditations on the role of the arts in European culture
and on the significance of his own literary activity were finally
formulated in his book *What is Art?* (published in a censored
and distorted version, in Russia, and in an authorized English
translation by Aylmer Maude [1898])—a work so unorthodox in
its main conclusions that its serious challenges have generally
been shrugged off. But this book is a fitting climax to nineteenth-
century thinking about social aspects of art, and some of the
questions it raises, so simply and forcefully, go to the heart of
twentieth-century concerns.

Tolstoy begins (ch. 1) in a novel way, by observing that the
arts are evidently taken to be important, by those people who

count in Western society, since they require enormous sacrifices of time and labor, the exploitation of people and of physical resources—to produce operas, fill the picture galleries, train musical virtuosi, etc. So it seems reasonable to ask: what good is art, that so high a cost should be paid? It becomes necessary "to find out whether all that professes to be art is really art," whether "all that is art is good, and whether it is important, and worth those sacrifices which it necessitates" (trans. Maude, p. 133). Hence arise Tolstoy's questions: What is Art? and What is good art?

The usual answer to the first question, says Tolstoy (ch. 2), is that art is what produces beauty. So we must ask: what is beauty? And to this a most bewildering and confusing variety of answers has geen given. Tolstoy reviews a large sample of them (ch. 3), but comes to a simplifying conclusion. They all fall into two main classes, he says: either they are metaphysical and "mystical" (beauty is transcendental, or divine—"a fantastic definition, founded on nothing," p. 162) or they reduce to "a very simple, and intelligible, subjective one, which considers beauty to be that which pleases" (p. 162—it is not necessary to add "disinterestedly" here, he says, since that is implicit in the concept of pleasing). This second definition of beauty is the only one worth considering (cf. p. 189 n). Tolstoy even includes a little "ordinary language" analysis to show that it is good Russian to use the word "beauty" (*krasota*) only for "that which pleases the sight" (p. 138)—"Such is the meaning ascribed by the Russian language, and therefore by the sense of the people" (p. 139).

To define art in terms of beauty, then, once we set aside all high-flown metaphysics, is to define it in terms of pleasure; and to judge art by its beauty is to judge it by the pleasure it affords. But this is a completely mistaken way of going about the understanding of art. In the first place, it is question-begging, says Tolstoy (ch. 4). The usual so-called "science of aesthetics" begins by selecting a class of artistic productions, on the ground that they are pleasing to the upper classes in society; "a definition of art is then devised to cover all these productions" (p. 165). In this way "No matter what insanities appear in art," they are accepted if they please (p. 165). But the correct method is to give "a definition of true art" and then determine "what is and what is not good art by judging whether a work conforms or does not conform to the definition" (p. 165). Tolstoy begins with the activity of art production.

> If we say that the aim of any activity is merely our pleasure and define it solely by that pleasure, our definition will evidently be a false one. . . . Everyone understands that the satisfaction of our taste cannot serve as a basis for our definition of the merits of food . . .
>
> In the same way, beauty, or that which pleases us, can in no sense serve as a basis for the definition of art . . . [p. 166]
>
> . . . And since discussions as to why one man likes pears and another prefers meat do not help towards finding a definition of what is essential in nourishment, so the solution of questions of taste in art (to which the discussions of art involuntarily come) not only does not help to make clear what this particular human activity which we call art really consists in, but renders such elucidation quite impossible until we rid ourselves of a conception which justifies every kind of art at the cost of confusing the whole matter [p. 167].

These statements set forth Tolstoy's basic orientation. Two points should be especially noted. Though, as will emerge more clearly later, there is a distinction in Tolstoy's mind (not consistently kept in view) between defining art and saying what makes a work of art good, these two processes are closely connected in his thinking. If artistic production is an activity, its products are to be defined in terms of the function they serve (so he evidently holds): hence to get a correct definition, we must consider, not how much people like or dislike them (any more than we would raise this question in defining "shoe" or "typewriter"), but how they connect up causally with other things, what effects they have, in what way they are "conditions of human life" (p. 170). But once this is decided, we have at hand the information we require for introducing normative considerations, for we can ask which works of art serve this purpose best. The method is basically Aristotelian.

What, then, is the real function of art? "Viewing it in this way we cannot fail to observe that art is one of the means of intercourse between man and man" (p. 170). Just as speech is a medium for communicating thoughts, so art is a medium for communicating feelings. Communication is "infection"—making the perceiver share the feelings of the creator, and making different perceivers share each other's feelings, by arousing the same feelings in each (p. 171). Hence Tolstoy's proposed definition:

Art is a human activity consisting in this, that one man consciously, by means of certain external signs, hands on to others feelings he has lived through, and that others are infected by these feelings and also experience them [p. 173].

The most astonishing parts of *What is Art?* are those chapters (10–15) in which Tolstoy launches a broad attack against most of the works of music, painting, literature, and drama, that have been regarded as the highest productions of Western artistic genius—and at the same time repudiates all of his own earlier works except a couple of short stories (see p. 292 n). It is this attack (see pp. 229, 265) that has so shocked and confounded his readers: if Shakespeare and Beethoven do not hold up on his theory of art, this in itself seems the best possible reductio ad absurdum of the theory. But Tolstoy's arguments must be met, if they can be met, on more basic grounds, and we must try to be as clear as we can about what he actually claims. This involves keeping track better than he often does of the elusive distinction between counterfeit art and bad art.

The basic distinction between art and non-art, for Tolstoy, follows immediately from the definition of art: "infection [is] a sure sign of art" (p. 275). This infection may occur in various degrees, or it may fail; and the factors that are required for it are three: "the greater or lesser individuality of the feeling transmitted"; the clarity of its transmission; the sincerity of the artist, i.e., the extent to which he is himself moved (p. 275). Of these, says Tolstoy, sincerity is fundamental, but "The absence of any one of these conditions excludes a work from the category of art and relegates it to that of art's counterfeits . . . If all these conditions are present, even in the smallest degree, then the work, even if a weak one, is yet a work of art" (p. 277).

Communication involves two parties, and can fail at either end; hence there are two fundamental ways in which pseudo-art occurs. The first is when the artist pretends to feel what he does not feel. This is insincerity (pp. 241, 231): the artist only imitates other works of art, or tries to shock and excite (ch. 11). The second is when the perceiver cannot understand the work, so the communication is not carried through (ch. 10). Tolstoy is himself somewhat uncommunicative about the exact nature of this stipulation; he seems to be saying part of the time that a work cannot be wholly private in its appeal, restricted to a tight group, without failing to be art altogether; at other times, he seems to be saying that the work is art if it can affect someone, but not *good* art unless it can affect most people, or all people. Thus, for example, he objects to the plea that some works of art "are very good but very difficult to understand." This "is the same as saying of some kind of food that it is very good but that most people can't eat it" (p. 223). "Art cannot be incomprehensible to the great masses only because it is very good,—as artists of our day are fond of telling us. Rather we are bound to conclude that this art is . . . very bad art, or even is not art at all" (pp. 226–27). (Hence, he adds, there is no need for critics and criticism, for in genuine art there is nothing to explain or explicate, p. 242.)

Communication may fail, then, if the work is obscure—or if the feelings it contains are too exclusive, too unhealthy and limited to a social class. The chief subjects of present-day art, says Tolstoy, are "honor, patriotism, and amorousness" (p. 195)—or pride, sexual desire, and weariness of life (p. 200)—and to feel these, you have to be perverted by your mode of life: the ordinary healthy peasant simply cannot share them (cf. pp. 223, 196).

It is clear that we have already, at some point, passed from the distinction between art and pseudo-art to the judgment of artistic goodness. In his explicit formulation of his criterion for judging good art, apart from its content, Tolstoy proposes one quantitative criterion: "*The stronger the infection the better is the art*, as art" (p. 275)—and he means here the intensity of the feeling. Throughout his discussion of the exclusiveness of modern music and poetry, as we have seen, he frequently presupposes a second quantitative criterion—the number or range of people who can respond to the work. Great art, he says, is universally "accessible and comprehensible" (p. 225). Hence Beethoven's D Minor Symphony (No. 9) "is not a good work of art" (p. 295).

But the purely quantitative judgments, says Tolstoy, mean little by themselves; we can't judge a work good merely because it evokes feelings any more than we can judge a fire good without knowing what is burning. The ultimate and inescapable judgment of artistic goodness has to be on the basis of a genuine standard that tells us *what* feelings are worth having, and which are harmful. And such a standard is ultimately religious. Tolstoy's own conception of religion is presupposed here. "In every age and in every human society there exists a religious sense, common to that whole society, of what is good and what is bad, and it is this religious conception that decides the value of the feelings transmitted by art" (pp. 177–78). Good art in a particular society is what transmits the highest feelings recognized by the religion of the time (p. 179). Of course, some spoiled classes of people may not share that religion, and to them art will be only a means of pleasure (pp. 182–83). But there is always an advancing edge of religious insight, or ethical perception (p. 278–79), which it is the function of art to foster. In our time, says Tolstoy, the highest religious sense is the sense of the brotherhood of man under the Fatherhood of God (ch. 16; see pp. 281–82, 285). Good art, in our time, then (qualitatively speaking), is that which communicates this feeling, in either of two ways. First, directly, by evoking Christian feelings (*Les Miserables, A Christmas Carol, Uncle Tom's Cabin*); or second, indirectly, by dealing with basic human experiences which can be shared by all men, and thereby increasing the emotional area in which men can feel together and increase their sense of human brotherhood (pp. 288–90)—*Don Quixote, David Copperfield*, the comedies of Molière.

The requirement is stringent, but Tolstoy sees no way in which the social costs of art can be justified unless it performs this service. Good art is indispensable: it is a means "of the movement of humanity forward towards perfection" (p. 278). "The task of art is enormous" (p. 331)—for only by its help can love and trust replace the vast apparatus of police, courts, war, and force that now makes up the structure of society; only thus can Tolstoy's ideal of non-violence be attained (p. 331). Meanwhile, there is no neutrality; art that does not bind all men together necessarily parts some men from others (ch. 17), and continues to stunt the lives of its servants—for example, the little ballerinas— as it helps to pervert its patrons and admirers—intensifying those destructive feelings of patriotism, class pride, sensuality, and superstition (pp. 305–6) that constantly increase the cruelty of man to man.

Bibliography

Gay Wilson Allen and Harry Hayden Clark, eds., *Literary Criticism: Pope to Croce* (New York, 1941).

Eugen Weber, ed., *Paths to the Present: Aspects of European Thought from Romanticism to Existentialism* (New York, 1962).

Robert L. Peters, ed., *Victorians on Literature and Art* (New York, 1961).

O. B. Hardison, Jr., ed., *Modern Continental Literary Criticism* (New York, 1962).

Melvin Friedman, "Passages on Aesthetics from Flaubert's Correspondence," *Quart Rev of Lit* IV (1949): 390–400.

Rose Frances Egan, "The Genesis of the Theory of 'Art for Art's Sake' in Germany and in England," in *Smith College Studies in Modern Languages*, Part I, in Vol. II, July 1921; Part II, in Vol. V, April 1924.

Albert Cassagne, *La Théorie de l'art pour l'art en France* (Paris, 1906).

John Wilcox, "The Beginnings of L'art pour l'art," *Jour Aesth and Art Crit* XI (June 1953): 360–77.

Irving Singer, "The Aesthetics of 'Art for Art's Sake,'" *Jour Aesth and Art Crit* XII (March 1954): 343–59.

George J. Becker, ed., *Documents of Modern Literary Realism* (Princeton U., 1963).

H. A. Needham, *Le Développement de l'esthétique sociologique en France et en Angleterre au XIXe siècle* (Paris, 1926).

J. H. Bornecque and Pierre Cogny, *Réalisme et naturalisme: l'histoire, la doctrine, les oeuvres* (Paris, 1958).

Bernard Weinberg, *French Realism: The Critical Reaction, 1830–1870* (New York, 1937).

T. M. Mustoxidi, *Histoire de l'esthétique française, 1700–1900* (Paris, 1920).

Horace M. Kallen, *Art and Freedom*, 2 vols. (New York, 1942), esp. Books II–IV.

Hippolyte Taine, *The Philosophy of Art*, in *Lectures on Art*, trans. John Durand (New York, 1875).

Stefan Morawski, "The Problem of Value and Criteria in Taine's Aesthetics," *Jour Aesth and Art Crit* XXI (Summer 1963): 407–22.

René Wellek, "Social and Aesthetic Values in Russian Nineteenth-Century Literary Criticism," in E. J. Simmons, ed., *Continuity and Change in Russian and Soviet Thought* (Harvard U., 1955).

Herbert E. Bowman, "Art and Reality in Russian 'Realist' Criticism," *Jour Aesth and Art Crit* XII (March 1954): 386–95.

V. V. Zenkovsky, *A History of Russian Philosophy*, trans. George L. Kline (New York and London, 1953), Vol. I, ch. 11.

N. G. Chernyshevsky, *Selected Philosophical Essays*, ed. M. Grigoryan (?) (Moscow, 1953).

Stefan Morawski, "Polish Theories of Art Between 1830 and 1850," *Jour Aesth and Art Crit* XVI (December 1957): 217–36.

Joseph C. Sloane, "The Tradition of Figure Painting and Concepts of Modern Art in France from 1845 to 1870," *Jour Aesth and Art Crit* VII (September 1948): 1–29.

Auguste Comte, *A General View of Positivism* (*Discours sur l'ensemble du positivisme*), trans. J. H. Bridges, 2d ed. (London, 1880).

P. J. Proudhon, *Du Principe de l'art et de sa destination sociale*, in *Oeuvres complètes*, ed. Bouglé & Moysset (Paris, 1939).

Jean-Marie Guyau, *L'Art au point de vue sociologique*, 3d ed. (Paris, 1895).

The Works of John Ruskin, ed. Cook and Wedderburn, 39 vols. (London, 1903–12).

Henry Ladd, *The Victorian Morality of Art: An Analysis of Ruskin's Esthetic* (New York, 1932).

Frank D. Curtin, "Aesthetics in English Social Reform: Ruskin and his Followers," in Herbert Davis *et al.*, eds., *Nineteenth-Century Studies* (Cornell U., 1940).

Albert Bush-Brown, " 'Get an honest bricklayer!': The Scientist's Answer to Ruskin," *Jour Aesth and Art Crit* XVI (March 1958): 348–56.

William Morris, *Collected Works,* ed. May Morris, 24 vols. (London, 1910–15).

Ralph Waldo Emerson, *Works,* 4 vols. in 1 (New York, 193–).

C. R. Metzger, *Emerson and Greenough: Transcendental Pioneers of an American Esthetic* (U. of California, 1954).

C. R. Metzger, *Thoreau and Whitman: A Study of Their Esthetics* (U. of Washington, 1961).

Theodore M. Brown, "Greenough, Paine, Emerson, and the Organic Aesthetic," *Jour Aesth and Art Crit* XIV (March 1956): 304–17.

Vivian C. Hopkins, *Spires of Form: A Study of Emerson's Aesthetic Theory* (Harvard U., 1951).

Leo Tolstoy, *What is Art?* trans. Aylmer Maude, in *Tolstoy on Art* (Oxford U., 1924).

Don Geiger, "Tolstoy as Defender of a 'Pure Art' That Unwraps Something," in *The Age of the Splendid Machine* (Tokyo, 1961).

TWELVE

Contemporary Developments

W hen the historian, picking his way carefully through the varied remains of human thought and activity that mark the centuries past, comes within hailing distance of his own time, his determination to keep hold of a proper perspective becomes more desperate than ever. It is difficult enough to weigh in judgment the permanent significance, or at least the apparent present significance, of past thinkers or their theories. But to decide how much attention and emphasis is deserved by a contemporary development, in comparison with classical Greece or the eighteenth century, taxes intolerably the most scrupulous writer, by demanding of him a timeless and Olympian stance that he could certainly not sustain, even if he could achieve it.

Another hazard awaits the historian who ventures across the threshold of his own time. Consider the political, military, or diplomatic historian; the qualifications for his task are not generally expected to include active participation in the events he chronicles (and, indeed, if he is in fact a retired politician, general, or diplomat, his readers judge him by a different, and perhaps more tolerant, standard, since he no doubt has errors to excuse and enemies to pay off). Even such a historian is plunged into a vast perplexity when he tries to estimate the comparative significance of contemporary events, without the prior screening provided by the disappearance of evidence and the helpful hints provided by hindsight. But the historian of ideas has an added dilemma, since his reader can fairly hope that he knows whereof he speaks, as one who has taken some part (however modest) in the intellectual movements of which he writes—yet if his thinking has earned him any opinions of his own, he must resist the temptation to turn his history into an argument to support them, as (it must be confessed) some extant histories of aesthetics have turned out to be.

On behalf of my own method of treating the material of the present chapter, I can only say that I have tried to look at what has recently been going on in aesthetics—an extraordinarily diverse and vital cluster of intellectual activities—both close-up and at a distance, to let its own gestalt appear, as far as might be, without shoving and pushing. (In the end, of course, I had to do a little tidying up, to make a reasonably clear picture, and I hope I will be forgiven by living writers who have not been placed in what would be their favorite category, and whose views have consequently been oversimplified or slighted.)

I shall divide up the great quantity of work done so far in the twentieth century into what seem to be main lines of thought or general orientations. I confess at once that there is no single *principium individuationis* of my several section headings, but I think they have some perspicuity, and they enable me to give, with economy, at least a general notion of where things have been going, and where they stand at present. In a reasonably short space, if I am to avoid a mere bibliographical clutter, I shall have to be selective; names and works that might well have equal claim will turn up missing. I cannot include all that has been done, only the sorts of thing that have been done, but I shall try to give credit to those to whom the greatest credit is clearly due. A small group of philosophers have been selected for special attention, at the start of the chapter, because (as it either seems to me or has evidently seemed to a good many others) they have most to say. Other philosophers who have left their mark are treated more succinctly, but I hope with due deference, in relation to particular movements.

CROCE AND THE METAPHYSICIANS

Twentieth century aesthetic discussion may be said to have been opened by Benedetto Croce (1866–1952), unquestionably the most influential aesthetician of our time. His persistent engagement with aesthetic and critical problems (as well as other philosophical problems) for half a century has made its impression upon everyone who has thought seriously about these problems. His success is not hard to understand. He came with a radically new concept of the aesthetic, and it had two great virtues. First, it interpreted aesthetic phenomena in the context of a respectably Idealist metaphysics that many of his readers recognized as Hegelian, yet in a manner so concrete, so down to earth, and so close to actual works of art, that many of his conclusions could readily be translated into naturalistic terms. Second, it was a refreshingly simple philosophy of art, while claiming to embrace a multitude of complexities; and Croce delighted in showing, in his sharp and ingenious way, how one traditional question after another could be dismissed as nonsensical or unnecessary if art were conceived in his fashion. Everything fell into a new, but natural, place; and the central formula, "intuition = expression," seemed to many philosophers to crystallize profound and unprecedented insights.

The main outlines of Croce's theory were presented in 1900 to the Accademia Pontaniana (the paper was called "Fundamental Theses of an Aesthetic as Science of Expression and General Linguistic"); its fullest, and best-known, statement is that in the *Aesthetic as Science of Expression and General Linguistic* (*Estetica come scienze dell' espressione e linguistica generale* [1902]). This is the first of four volumes, collectively entitled *Filosofia dello Spirito,* in which Croce's system is set forth.

Philosophy, in Croce's view, is the study of Mind, or Spirit, which is reality. Mind is essentially an activity that takes two basic forms, knowing and doing. Doing can be directed either to the useful or to the good, which are studied by the "practical sciences" of economics and ethics, respectively. Knowing (as Croce tells us at the start of the *Aesthetic*) aims at either "intuitive knowledge" or "logical knowledge." The "science" of logical knowledge, of concepts, is logic; the science of intuitive knowledge, or images, is aesthetic (Ainslie trans., p. 1).

An intuition is a particular image (not necessarily visual, of course) held in consciousness, an "objectified" impression (p. 4)—"this river, this lake, this brook, this rain, this glass of water"

(p. 22). All percepts are intuitions, but not all intuitions are percepts (if percepts are by definition veridical) for some are memories, or ostensible memories. "The distinction between reality and non-reality is extraneous, secondary, to the true nature of intuition" (p. 3)—in the realm of intuitive knowledge, this distinction has not yet arisen, for it is conceptual. Pure intuitions, without any conceptualization, can occur; Croce's examples are "The impression of a moonlight scene by a painter; the outline of a country drawn by a cartographer; a musical motive, tender or energetic" (p. 2). On the other side, Croce distinguishes intuitions from bare "sensations," which are passive and formless, and reveal no "spiritual activity" (p. 6). Pure sensation (a limiting concept) cannot really occur in consciousness, for whatever occurs is intuition, and "every true intuition or representation is also *expression*" (p. 8).

We come now to the most celebrated, and (it must be acknowledged) most often attacked, of Croce's principles. There is, he says, "a sure method" of distinguishing intuition from what is "inferior to it." "That which does not objectify itself in expression is not intuition, . . . but sensation and mere natural fact" (p. 8). Thus

> It is impossible to distinguish intuition from expression in this cognitive process. The one appears with the other at the same instant, because they are not two, but one [p. 9].

Croce treats the proposition "intuition = expression" in a curious way. At first he argues for it empirically: how can you really claim to have an accurate image (intuition) of a geometrical figure unless you can draw it on the blackboard (expression)? But this is a slip, as will become clear shortly, for what he really means by "expression" is precisely the clear mental vision of the figure—which is also the intuition—and the physical activity of drawing is quite another matter. To do justice to his meaning, we must think of the same image as both an intuition and an expression, but considered in two aspects, so to speak. However, these aspects are very difficult to distinguish in Croce's account. For he insists upon using the two terms in a way that rigorously excludes any possibility of a disparity between them. If it is suggested that an intuition (or inspiration) may not be fully expressed, Croce's reply is scathing: "as if Beethoven's Ninth Symphony were not his own intuition and his intuition the Ninth Symphony" (p. 11).

Croce's next step is simply to identify art with intuitive knowledge—or to say, what amounts to the same, that art is expression. He analyzes and rejects all attempts to distinguish artistic expressions (or intuitions) as a special class; there are only differences of degree, in depth and breadth (pp. 13–14). All men are artists in so far as they possess images. And this he regards as important, for he believes the progress of aesthetics has been hindered by failure to recognize "the true nature of art, its real roots in human nature"—by a separation of art from the rest of "spiritual life" (p. 14). The simplest and most elementary level of mind has been taken for the most complex. Fine art is just the most highly developed form of intuition-expression, as science is the most highly developed form of logical knowledge. The relation between art and science is carefully stated by Croce. First, he argues that while intuition can occur without concepts (so that elementary preconceptual art is possible), concepts (being essentially relational) cannot occur without intuitions to relate. Just as a true intuition must be an "expression," so a concept must have symbolic representation—there can be no thought without "language" in the broad sense (pp. 23–24). (Hence there can be no such thing as clear thought expressed in an obscure style, p. 24.) Now, in most works of art, of course, both intuitions and concepts are combined. But every concept has its intuitive side, so to speak; that is, we can contemplate it without employing it abstractly, and so when concepts appear in a work of art, they "are no longer concepts . . . for they have lost all independence and autonomy" (p. 2). (Philosophical theses in literature are no longer conceptual, but revelations of character, or part of the drama.) Whether a mixture, or fusion, of concepts and intuitions is, as a whole, science or art, "lies in the difference of the total effect aimed at by their respective authors" (p. 3). Actually, "Every scientific work is also a work of art" (p. 25), since it can be read, not for its logical knowledge, but for its qualities as the record of a process of thought.

Croce's theory of intuition, and consequently his theory of art, underwent important changes in his later thinking. There were two main additions, or alterations. The first was the *Breviary of Aesthetic* (lectures at Rice Institute, 1912; reprinted in the *New Essays on Aesthetics*, 1926), in which Croce discovered the "lyrical" nature of art. The argument is briefly this: An artistic expression is always a complex, whose constituent expressions correspond to individual intuitions; but it has a unity of its own, that makes it a single expression, which therefore must correspond to (or be identical to) a single intuition. This intuition, Croce proposes, is always an emotion or feeling: "what gives coherence and unity to the intuition is feeling: the intuition is really such that it represents a feeling, and can only appear from and upon that" (trans. Ainslie, p. 247). Thus all art is expression of emotion, and since the lyric poem is the quintessence of such expression, Croce borrows the term "lyrical" and generalizes it to all art:

Artistic intuition, then, is always *lyrical* intuition: this latter being a word that is not present as an adjective or definition of the first, but as a synonym, another of the synonyms that can be united to the several that I have mentioned already, and which, all of them, designate the intuition [p. 249].

The second major change appeared in an essay on "The Character of Totality of Artistic Expression" (1918, also in the *New Essays*), in which Croce proposed that while every intuition (and expression) is—as the *Aesthetic* insisted—individual and individualizing, in virtue of its form it is universalized. Artistic intuition is not only "lyrical" but "cosmic." We need not consider these later views further. For the earlier doctrines remain the more influential, challenging, and consistently developed.

And from this basic position, secure in his fundamental principle of identity, Croce launches an impressive array of attacks against existing assumptions about art and criticism. Some of them strike hard at first, and then turn out, after concessions, to be meant in a less startling sense than it first seemed. Others are subtle and telling, the kind of thing that, once it is pointed out, seems almost truistic. I will not attempt to survey all of the interesting points, by any means—most of them are of special concern to the literary theorist. But I shall mention a few, as examples of Croce at his most stimulating and penetrating. He argues that it is misleading to say (as some say) that every work of art is a "symbol." If "symbol" is just a synonym for intuition-expression, well and good; if it implies a distinction between the work as vehicle and some "meaning," it separates intuition from expression, and exemplifies the "intellectualist error," of imposing concepts on literature (*Aesthetic*, p. 34). The same error is even more evident in the theory of literary and artistic kinds (or genres), which Croce attacks most vigorously (pp. 35 ff). There is no doubt that works of art resemble each other in many ways, and can, with arbitrariness, be sorted into groups; but these groups are not true species, with genera and subspecies: their resemblances "consist wholly of what is called a *family likeness*" (p. 73). In a sense there are such things as tragedies, epics, eclogues, etc.; "Error begins when we try to deduce the expression from the concept," that is, to judge the unique works in these categories and to set up "laws" for them (pp. 36–37).

The separation of the theoretical from the practical in Croce's philosophy has another important consequence, which has been much disputed.

The aesthetic fact is altogether completed in the expressive elaboration of impressions. When we have achieved the word within us, conceived definitely and vividly a figure or a statue, or found a musical motive, expression is born and is complete; there is no need for anything else [p. 50].

To sing or play the melody, to paint the picture, to write the word—that requires an act of will, and so belongs to the practical, with which the aesthetic has nothing to do. The real work of art, then, lies in the artist's mind; the external artifact serves only to facilitate its being shared or recalled (pp. 96–97). Aesthetic expression is utterly different from showing anger, and other physical activities; "there is nothing in common between the science of spiritual expression and a *Semiotic*, whether it be medical, meteorological, political, physiognomic, or chiromantic" (p. 95). The separation of the physical from the aesthetic by this sharp blow of the axe renders senseless many familiar questions. For example, Lessing and Schopenhauer asked: What are the limits of expression in each medium, sound, color, or word? And Schopenhauer and Hegel asked: Which is the highest or lowest, most powerful or expressive, art, or combination of arts? Such questions, Croce argues (pp. 114–16), involve a confusion of the work, as internal, with its physical externalization, and once we see this distinction, we can no longer be bothered by them.

Finally, there is a new theory of beauty, in terms of the new system. Beauty is simply *"successful expression"* or, rather *"expression* and nothing more, because expression when it is not successful is not expression" (p. 79). There are no degrees of beauty, but there are degrees of ugliness, through inadequate or incomplete expression. Aesthetic fault is always a failure of expression. Croce cannot of course consistently mean that there was something in the intuition that was not expressed, for what was not expressed was not really intuited. Somehow, raw sensations—or inarticulate "impressions"—struggle to become intuition (= expression), but may fall short. This is a most puzzling part of his theory, and one that his commentators have labored to clarify and amplify.

Croce's most widely studied and highly regarded follower in English-speaking countries was R. G. Collingwood. The extent of his actual indebtedness is not clear, but it must be considerable (despite the fact that Collingwood hardly refers to Croce in his works), even if we allow—as we must for such a strong and go-it-alone mind as Collingwood's—that he could have worked out a great many of the ideas himself, given only a few basic suggestions. Collingwood is not to be dismissed as a mere follower, in any case; his own originality shows in his determined search for the differentia of art, as opposed to all manner of things confused with it, and in his detailed analysis of "imaginative expression" as a process in which inchoate emotion becomes articulate and self-aware (see *The Principles of Art* [1938]; and cf. *Speculum Mentis* [1924], ch. 3).

The influence of Croce is strongly evident in several other works on aesthetics, though not without important and deliberate divergences. Among the more notable of these are Bernard Bosanquet, *Three Lectures on Aesthetic* (1915), E. F. Carritt, *Theory of Beauty* (1914), T. M. Greene, *The Arts and the Art of Criticism* (1940), and C. J. Ducasse, *The Philosophy of Art* (1929)—the last a book highly critical of Croce, and itself distinguished by a vigorous empiricist and analytical style of argument.

A very different notion of intuition is presented in the philosophic system of Henri Bergson (1859–1941). But it, too, has been welcomed by some aestheticians for the special cognitive role it offers to the arts—just as it has been welcomed by some philosophers of religion for its support of mysticism. Bergson's suggestions toward an aesthetics developed largely in the context of his primary concerns with other problems; I believe the best way to review them will be to note their progress through his works.

The *Essai sur les Données Immédiates de la Conscience* (1889; trans. as *Time and Free Will*) aimed to show how pseudo-problems about the will and its freedom have arisen from a false phenomenology of mental states—essentially, a tendency to conceive and describe them in spatial terms. What Bergson calls the "aesthetic feelings" (particularly the "feeling of grace") turn up as examples in a subtle discussion of the question whether psychical states can strictly speaking be said to differ in magnitude.

The object of art is to put to sleep the active or rather resistant powers of our personality, and thus to bring us into a state of perfect responsiveness, in which we realize the idea that is suggested to us and sympathize with the feeling that is expressed [trans. F. L. Pogson, p. 14] . . . The feeling of the beautiful is no specific feeling, but . . . every feeling experienced by us will assume an aesthetic character, provided that it has been *suggested*, and not *caused* [pp. 16–17].

These provocative but undeveloped observations were expanded in *Le Rire* (*Laughter* [1900]). This "Essay on the Meaning of the Comic" confines itself largely to its initial question, what makes us laugh? And the argument (that the comic consists essentially of "something mechanical encrusted on the living") is worked out with great ingenuity. In the first part of the last chapter, however, there is a section in which Bergson broadens out for a moment to speak about art in general. Here he describes our normal way of experiencing: it is responding to things as members of classes (not as individuals), noting only the "labels" affixed to them rather than the things themselves (trans. C. Brereton and F. Rothwell [1911], p. 153). And he contrasts this experience with a kind of experience in which we might "enter into immediate communion with things and with ourselves" (p. 150). If all our experience were of the latter sort, "probably art would be useless, or rather we should all be artists" (p. 150). But in fact it is only rarely and "in a fit of absentmindedness" that "nature raises up souls that are more detached from life" (p. 154) who can "vibrate in perfect accord with nature" (p. 150)—at least occasionally—and create works of art to reveal nature to us.

So art, whether it be painting or sculpture, poetry or music, has no other object than to brush aside the utilitarian symbols, the conventional and socially accepted generalities, in short, everything that veils reality from us, in order to bring us face to face with reality itself [p. 157].

The nature of this penetrating artistic cognition was further explored by Bergson (though not in connection with art) in his "Introduction à la métaphysique" (1903). Here he introduces his theory of intuition as "the kind of *intellectual sympathy* by which one places oneself within an object in order to coincide with what is unique in it and consequently inexpressible" (trans. T. E. Hulme [1949], p. 23). The method of intuition is contrasted with that of conceptual analysis; the former dispenses with symbols, which are required by the latter (pp. 24, 33). Both the character of intuition as a faculty, and its role in philosophy, were enlarged and deepened in Bergson's next, and greatest, work, *L'Évolution Créatrice* (*Creative Evolution* [1907]). In this work, in terms that owe much to Schopenhauer, reality is described as essentially a process of change, which Bergson calls "duration" (*durée*) and "vital impulse" (*élan vital*). Man's intellect has developed in the course of evolution as an instrument of survival, and has evolved language and symbols for manipulating reality. It comes to think inevitably in geometrical or "spatializing" terms that are inadequate to lay hold of the ultimate living process. Hence arise the basic insoluble metaphysical puzzles about permanence and change, the one and the many. But intuition—which is now defined as "instinct that has become disinterested, self-conscious, capable of reflecting upon its object and of enlarging it indefinitely" (trans. Arthur Mitchell, p. 176)—goes to the heart of reality, and enables us to find philosophic truth. It is the "aesthetic faculty" in man that "proves" the possibility of this knowledge: the artist who draws a curve to picture the tense or flowing character of a living being, for example, intuits movement as such, "in placing himself back within the object by a kind of sympathy, in breaking down, by an effort of intuition, the barrier that space puts up between him and his model"

(p. 177). It is the function of art then, to find ways to bring us close to reality, where intellect with its discursive categories and its analytical bent cannot go. (This theme is also developed in Bergson's first Oxford lecture on *La Perception du Changement* [1911].)

Though Croce professed himself (but in his own special sense) "antimetaphysical" (*Aesthetic*, pp. 64–65), his "philosophy of mind" is a metaphysics, a form of Idealism, and his aesthetics is a remarkably essential and inherent part of it. Since Bergson's aesthetics also relies upon a worked-out ontological and epistemological context, this seems a suitable place to accord due mention to some other twentieth-century ventures distinguished by a similar metaphysical character. One of the most recent is that by Paul Weiss, in two companion volumes (*The World of Art* [1961], and *Nine Basic Arts* [1961]). He assigns to the arts the function of revealing the "texture of existence" and "the import" of existence for man—the category of existence being one of the four basic categories (along with actuality, ideality, and God) of Weiss's metaphysics. In a wide-ranging and thoughtful book on *Art and the Human Enterprise* (1958), Iredell Jenkins has distinguished three dimensions of man's world—the "import," the "connectedness," and the "particularity" of things—and has argued that the third aspect is what is taken hold of, expressed, and illuminated by art. One of the most influential essays in metaphysical aesthetics is *Art et Scholastique* (1920), by Jacques Maritain, in which this neo-Thomist philosopher reanimates St. Thomas's theories of art and beauty, and proposes to expand the Thomistic system by making beauty one of the transcendentals. The case of Alfred North Whitehead is also interesting. Whitehead's argument, in *Science and the Modern World* (1925, ch. 5), that poets have an eye for fundamental qualitative features of the world and a vital sense of the unity of experience, his dense analysis of beauty in *Adventures of Ideas* (1933; chs. 17, 18), and, most of all, the quasi-aesthetic categories of eternal objects, ingression, prehension and creativity that play such a fundamental role in his metaphysics—all suggest that his system would readily support an aesthetics which he did not get around to writing. One way of working this out has been sketched by Donald W. Sherburne in *A Whiteheadian Aesthetic* (1961).

SANTAYANA AND DEWEY

In grouping together, somewhat adventitiously perhaps, certain twentieth-century aestheticians as taking a metaphysical approach to their problems, I have left out one species of philosophy that could also be said (and would, by some) to be a metaphysics. This is the philosophy that might be designated "American Naturalism," a title broad enough, I think, to embrace a number of philosophers who have called themselves Naturalists, Materialists, Pragmatists, Instrumentalists, or Contextualists. It is true that the distinction between Naturalism and other forms of metaphysics has been questioned, and I do not propose to defend its usefulness here. Perhaps some of the philosophers whom I mentioned in the previous section would prefer to be placed in this, and could, if pressed, justify a transfer. To them I offer apologies for not reading them aright.

Several of the most noteworthy American Naturalists—William James, for example—have not paid very close or persistent attention to aesthetic problems. But two have been outstanding among twentieth-century aestheticians, and several others have made significant contributions.

I begin with George Santayana (1863–1952), whose thought, in my judgment, belongs to our century, though his first book on aesthetics anticipated its arrival by four years. Santayana taught a metaphysics (though he was reluctant to call it such) which he called "naturalism" or "materialism" (a term he preferred, and considered more exact). True, he distinguished four "realms of being," and dwelt upon them in his longest work, with all the richness of his imagination; yet they do not turn out ontologically distinct, for in the end they are all aspects of the same basic underlying reality, the "profound fertility and darkness" of matter. The "realm of essence" consists not of existents, but of the qualities and forms of matter; and the "realm of spirit" is epiphenomenal—a kind of emergent from, but ultimately bound to, the material substratum. At least, this is the general idea that Santayana gives, for unfortunately he does not quite explain in a clear and definite way what matter really is, or how it gives rise to the other realms.

In any case, metaphysics is not his goal. As with the ancient materialists—for example, Epicurus—the metaphysics is chiefly a way of setting man free from oppressive ontological commitments, clearing the air for the central things of life. In this sense, Santayana is primarily the moralist: not the moralist who lays down rules, but he who teaches man how to live. Born with many interests in a world that may favor or refuse them, a man must learn to harmonize them at all levels, framing for himself a wholeness of life that gives it quality and character, and realizes some dominant or central good—like the life of the Franciscan or Buddhist monk, the dedicated civil rights leader, the painter or poet. This "rational pursuit of happiness" is the "Life of Reason" (see *Reason in Art* [1903], Vol. IV of *The Life of Reason*, p. 151). And the main drive of Santayana's philosophy of art is to settle the role of the aesthetic in this whole design.

He did not see it quite so broadly at first. *The Sense of Beauty* (1896) was primarily a psychological study—partly introspective, partly speculative—of the experience of beauty and its conditions. In one way, the book was a kind of throwback, for the sort of inquiry Santayana undertook was very much like the work of the eighteenth century aesthetic empiricists. In another way, considered in its immediate context—the dominance of Hegelianism in the academic world and the rudimentary stage of experimental aesthetics—the book was indeed very fresh and surprising. The book's main novelty lay in the attempted psychological explanations of two aesthetic phenomena, beauty and expression. From a present-day vantage-point, the psychology cannot be called very sophisticated, but these two discussions had both charm and persuasiveness, and they carried to many readers the invigorating sense that here, at last, we are getting back to experience, down to earth. Both explanations have been respectfully discussed by many aestheticians, and have left their mark.

The experience of art, Santayana begins, is a pleasure, a positive and intrinsic value (p. 35). This pleasure, like other sensations, can be transformed by the mind into "the quality of a thing" (p. 44).

If we say that other men should see the beauties we see, it is because we think those beauties *are in the object*, like its color, proportion, or size. Our judgment appears to us merely the perception and discovery of an external existence, of the real excellence that is without [pp. 44–45].

This projective transference, says Santayana, "is radically absurd and contradictory," since beauty is a "value," which can exist only in perception. "A beauty not perceived is a pleasure not felt, and a contradiction" (p. 45). Hence his formula: "Beauty is pleasure regarded as the quality of a thing" (p. 49), or "pleasure objectified" (p. 52). There is really not much here by way of psychological backing; Santayana simply appeals to what he considers a general tendency, or capacity, of the mind—"a tendency originally universal to make every effect of a thing upon us a constituent of its conceived nature" (p. 48). Many years later, in a footnote to his paper on "The Mutability of Aesthetic Categories" (1925), he said he would "not now use the phrase 'objectified pleasure,' because I see that a term does not become subjective merely because an intuition of it occurs"; pleasures, like colors, are neither objective nor subjective, but neutral (*Philosophical Review* XXXIV, p. 284 n).

After presenting his account of beauty, Santayana devotes the remainder of his book to an extended discussion of the kinds, or conditions, of beauty, which he divides into three classes. There is beauty of "material" (e.g., the pleasure of colors and sounds), of "form" (e.g., pleasure in symmetry and proportion), and of "expression." Expression occurs, he says, when the "hushed reverberations" of some feelings associated with a certain percept linger on in memory, but dimly, and "by modifying our present reaction, color the image upon which our attention is fixed" (p. 193). If the associated element is fully conscious, so that we take the present content only as a clue to it, and turn our thought wholly to it, expression does not occur. But "Let the images of the past fade, let them remain simply as a halo and suggestion of happiness hanging about a scene" (p. 194); then the present content becomes expressive.

In all expression we may thus distinguish two terms: the first is the object actually presented, the word, the image, the expressive thing; the second is the object suggested, the further thought, emotion, or image evoked, the thing expressed [p. 195].

The remainder of the book is largely an extended, and interesting, argument that only positive values, even when involved with evils originally, survive to become expressed contents of art, so that "Nothing but the good of life enters into the texture of the beautiful" (p. 260).

Reason in Art begins with a general account of the rise of "art" (where this term is taken broadly: "Any operation which thus humanizes and rationalizes objects is called art," p. 4). What we would ordinarily call practical skills and activities are then set aside. "Productions in which an aesthetic value is or is supposed to be prominent take the name of fine art" (pp. 15–16). But Santayana, from the start, is unwilling to withhold the terms "practical" and "useful" from the fine arts, and he is uneasy about divorcing "the aesthetic function of things" from the "practical and moral." "The rose's grace could more easily be plucked from its petals than the beauty of art from its subject, occasion, and use" (p. 16). One of his dominant feelings throughout this work is a mistrust of all "aestheticism," and a conviction that the estrangement of the "aesthetic good" from other goods that were, he says, "hatched in the same nest," will lead to a devitalization and trivialization of fine art (cf. pp. 183–94, 208–15, and the article "What is Aesthetics?" [1904], in *Obiter Scripta* [1936]).

This double view, that there are distinguishable aesthetic goods and yet that they depend for their existence on a close relationship with other goods, is one that Santayana has some difficulty keeping in balance. In his discussion of music, for example (one of the best of the discussions of various arts), he gives a beautiful description of musical process just as it is in itself, and of its inherent delight (pp. 44–47, 52–56); but then he adds that music is rescued from this "pathological plight" of meaning nothing because its emotional expressiveness lends itself to infinite uses to the ends of prayer, mourning, and dancing (pp. 56–57). Its rational justification, in his view, seems to be incomplete until it is related to something more substantial.

In the course of his book, Santayana says many interesting and impressive things about the arts, severally and collectively; and he concludes with a general case for them. The "justification of art" (ch. 9) begins somewhat apologetically with the point that they cannot do much harm—Santayana seems to feel that Plato requires to be answered again—and whatever ill they may produce is probably slight and transitory. But innocence is not their only virtue. For in so far as they are intrinsically delightful,

they become exempla of life itself. As an instance of fully harmonized and rationally controlled pleasure, "art in general is a
rehearsal of rational living" (p. 172), a model, as well as a constituent, of the Life of Reason. When the artist is called to
account,

> Appearances, he may justly urge, are alone actual. All forces, substances,
> realities, and principles are inferred and potential only and in the moral
> scale mere instruments to bring perfect appearances about. To have
> grasped such an appearance, to have embodied a form in matter, is to
> have justified for the first time whatever may underlie appearance and
> to have put reality to some use. It is to have begun to live [pp. 218–19].

It would be easy enough, if space could be spared, to point out
numerous ways in which the spirit of Santayana's philosophy is
alien to that of John Dewey (1859–1952), but in the fundamental
decision, as Dewey saw it, they were on the same side. In his
Carus lectures, *Experience and Nature* (1925; rev. ed. 1929),
Dewey stated this choice as follows:

> There are substantially but two alternatives. Either art is a continua-
> tion, by means of intelligent selection and arrangement, of natural tend-
> encies of natural events; or art is a peculiar addition to nature springing
> from something dwelling exclusively within the breast of man, whatever
> name be given the latter. In the former case, delightfully enhanced per-
> ception or esthetic appreciation is of the same nature as enjoyment of
> any object that is consummatory. It is the outcome of a skilled and
> intelligent art of dealing with natural things for the sake of intensify-
> ing, purifying, prolonging and deepening the satisfactions which they
> spontaneously afford. That, in this process, new meanings develop, and
> that these afford uniquely new traits and modes of enjoyment is but
> what happens everywhere in emergent growths [p. 389].

This passage gives a very exact and yet packed statement of the
perspective upon art obtained from Dewey's "empirical naturalism or naturalistic empiricism" (p. 1a).

Dewey was over seventy years old when he got around to the
task of working out this view fully and articulately, but his book
Art as Experience (1934) has an air of spontaneity and new discovery, freshness of vision, enormous richness of suggestion, and
a special Deweyan eloquence, with his characteristically oblique
but steady and inexorable advance of argument. It is, by widespread agreement, the most valuable work on aesthetics written
in English (and perhaps in any language) so far in our century.

It is the kind of book that may lose its reader the first time around but, once it begins to open up, yields surprising new insights every time it is read; and numerous passages return to memory and ask to be quoted, for the vigor or pungency with which they seem to seize upon a most important truth.

Though much in *Art as Experience* felt new (at least as coming from Dewey), its way had actually been prepared for in his earlier publications, and indeed its main underlying principles had nearly all been made explicit in *Experience and Nature*. There was his basic category of "experience," as the interaction between organism and environment—not the subjective pole only, but the whole transaction (pp. 421–23)—man's "doing and undergoing," as he says in *Art as Experience* (p. 48). Experience divides up, not sharply or ultimately, into strands—beginnings and endings, dependencies and independencies of causal line—which he calls "histories" (*Experience and Nature*, pp. 100, 163). These are the prototypes of "*an* experience" in the later book. No more than any other sort, is aesthetic experience "something private and psychical" (1st ed., p. 24). But the notion of a "sort" of experience may be misleading. Any experience, to some degree, involves attention to presented quality as such, involves "objects which are final" (2d ed. p. 80), that is, afford "consummations" (p. 81)— and this is always an aesthetic aspect, or phase, of the experience. Nor are the qualities that we take this interest in to be thought of as "projections" or "objectifications":

Empirically, things are poignant, tragic, beautiful, humorous, settled, disturbed, comfortable, annoying, barren, harsh, consoling, splendid, fearful; are such immediately and in their own right and behalf. If we take advantage of the word esthetic in a wider sense than that of application to the beautiful and ugly, esthetic quality, immediate, final or self-enclosed, indubitably characterizes natural situations as they empirically occur. These traits stand in themselves on precisely the same level as colors, sounds, qualities of contact, taste and smell [p. 96; cf. p. 108].

Though when we look back over Dewey's long and enormously active philosophical life we do not see many sharp corners, perhaps *Experience and Nature* was something of a turning point. Up to this time, Dewey had been largely concerned with developing the central doctrines of his "instrumentalism," especially his doctrines of logic (as the theory of inquiry), of knowledge (as operational, or instrumental to action), of value and ethical good (as a form of empirical knowledge, to be gained and tested, in the long run, like all other forms of knowledge). The stress was on means, on methods, on process—and had to be, to make good his long struggle against intrinsic values, final ends, the "spectator-theory" of knowledge, supernaturalism, and all dualisms: the separation of mind from body, of theory from practice, of knowing from doing, etc. Now Dewey spoke more fully than before of what he called the "consummatory" aspect of experience and nature. And the adjustment between this and the instrumental features of experience was reached in these terms:

When this perception dawns, it will be a commonplace that art—the mode of activity that is charged with meanings capable of immediately enjoyed possession—is the complete culmination of nature, and that "science" is properly a handmaiden that conducts natural events to this happy issue [p. 358; see the whole of ch. 9].

Compare with this passage the last one quoted from Santayana above—changing "appearances" to "immediately enjoyed qualities."

Let us turn now to *Art as Experience* and see how much of its wealth of ideas can be picked out and exhibited fairly in a few pages. Dewey begins (as he often does) by searching out trouble-making dualisms. The practical separation of art from life, symbolized by museum and concert hall (making art, he says, "the beauty parlor of civilization," p. 344), is paralleled by a philosophical tendency to try to understand art apart from its sources in ordinary experience.

The task is to restore continuity between the refined and intensified forms of experience that are works of art and the everyday events, doings, and sufferings that are universally recognized to constitute experience [p. 3].[1]

The clue to a sounder view of art is provided by what we know of primitive civilizations, and of earlier stages of Western Civilization, where we find the arts existing in close association with

---

[1] It is an interesting sidelight on Dewey's development as a philosopher that even in 1893, in his review of Bosanquet's *History of Aesthetic*, he was saying, "The entire conception . . . of a fixed distinction between the realm of art and that of commonplace reality seems to me to need a good deal of explanation" (*Philosophical Review* II, 68).

other cultural activities, as celebrations and commemorations of the qualities of experience encountered in worship, in hunting, in sowing and reaping (pp. 6–7, 11). To understand the aesthetic, "one must begin with it in the raw" (p. 4), says Dewey. And though some may find his references to fire engines and baseball players (p. 5) and dogs howling and crouching over their food (p. 13) rather too raw, Dewey's basic method, to start with an account of the "live creature" interacting with nature, has given to many philosophers in our time a persuasive and inspiring vision of art.

Dewey's description of experience in its generic traits is now classic. For example:

> Direct experience comes from nature and man interacting with each other. In this interaction, human energy gathers, is released, dammed up, frustrated and victorious. There are rhythmic beats of want and fulfillment, pulses of doing and being withheld from doing [p. 16; cf. pp. 14, 22, 24].

In experience, there are periods when the organism loses its integration with the environment. Emotion is the sign of a break, actual or impending (p. 15); and, in man, conscious exercise of intelligence is called upon to repair the situation and restore equilibrium and order. Consciousness notes causes and effects, antecedents and consequents, and converts them into "relations of means and consequence" by deliberately manipulating the one to obtain the other (p. 25). Objects become instruments. "With the realization, material of reflection is incorporated into objects as their meaning" (p. 15).

This sentence is somewhat cryptic, and it is also crucial, for Dewey's concept of meaning plays a central role in his aesthetics. Nor are some of his other statements about meaning less mysterious: that there are "intrinsic meanings" (p. 21) and that "There is no limit to the capacity of immediate sensuous experience to absorb into itself meanings and values that in and of themselves— that is in the abstract—would be designated 'ideal' and 'spiritual' " (p. 29). I think Dewey's basic idea can be put this way. In a moment of danger, a man may seize a rock and use it as a weapon. He may label it and place it on the mantel as a conversation piece, so it will remind him of his fortunate escape—this is what Dewey calls "association." But suppose the rock has certain qualities, of shape, texture, and weight, that commend themselves directly to vision, so it *looks* like something handleable, throwable, destructive. Then its meaning—its weaponness—is "embodied" in it (p. 22; cf. pp. 44–45). Or the primitive hunter may carve a picture of his victim on the handle of his knife (cf. p. 259). When we use tools that have such "incorporated" meanings— when the recognition of its function and the enjoyment of its immediate qualities fuse together—then experience is more unified, and more like art. "Art is the living and concrete proof that man is capable of restoring consciously, and thus on the plane of meaning, the union of sense, need, impulse and action characteristic of the live creature" (p. 25).

Embodied meanings bring together in experience means and ends that have been analytically separated for purposes of intelligent control. By this creation of unities, they promote that distinction of one experience from another which is already encouraged by the pulses and discontinuities of life—sleep, satisfaction of hunger, the carrying through of a task or project. We have not only experience; sometimes we have *"an* experience," an experiential whole carved out from the loose flow of experience in general. This concept is fundamental to Dewey's aesthetics, and he takes great care to point out those features of experience that make *an* experience. (1) There is completeness. "We have *an* experience when the material experienced runs its course to fulfillment" (p. 35). We are puzzled; we solve the puzzle; and that strand of life is finished; there are no loose ends. (2) There is internal impetus. The experience "moves by its own urge to fulfillment" (p. 39), rather than being impelled by external forces. (3) There is continuity. "Every successive part flows freely, without seam and without unfilled blanks, into what ensues" (p. 36). It is the joining of ends and means in perception that gives this continuity. (4) There is articulation, however—not a mere shapeless flow. "There is no sacrifice of the self-identity of the parts" (p. 36). (5) There is cumulativeness, the buildup of intensity and significance—"a sense of growing meaning conserved and accumulating toward an end that is felt as accomplishment of a process" (p. 39). (6) There is a dominant quality; for the unity of *an* experience "is constituted by a single

quality that pervades the entire experience in spite of the variation of its constituent parts" (p. 37). This quality Dewey sometimes calls "emotion," as when he says "Emotion is the moving
and cementing force" (p. 42); however, he also insists that
"Experience is emotional but there are no separate things called
emotions in it" (p. 42), and adds that "significant" emotions
are "qualities . . . of a complex experience" (p. 41; cf. "Qualitative thought" in *Philosophy and Civilization* [1931]).

Under favorable conditions, ordinary life affords many occasions for enjoying *an* experience, according to Dewey. Practical
and intellectual tasks when motivated from within and carried
through satisfactorily are patterns of this sort, and have inherent
as well as instrumental worth. They differ from aesthetic experience only in that in the latter there is a dominant attention to
presented quality (rather than, say, mathematical symbols or
tools).

An object is peculiarly and dominantly esthetic, yielding the enjoyment
characteristic of esthetic perception, when the factors that determine
anything which can be called *an* experience are lifted high above the
threshold of perception and are made manifest for their own sake [p. 57;
cf. p. 38].

Dewey next turns to the exposition of another difficult part of
his aesthetics, his theory of expression. Before coming to that,
though, we must try to clarify in our own minds two confusing
features of Dewey's terminology. Like so many of the trouble-
some features of Dewey's philosophy, they proceed from his
determined opposition to all dualisms. Haunted by the spectre
of separations and oppositions, he often deplores distinctions—
even distinctions that have been carefully won by long thought,
and have proved helpful to many. For example, there is Dewey's
use of the term "work of art." When he says that practical and
intellectual processes aim at a result with value "on its own
account," such as a housing project or a verified theory, but
"In a work of art there is no such single self-sufficient deposit"
(p. 55), the term "work of art" means the experience itself; and
that the experience is the "real" work of art he reminds us on
several occasions (see p. 64). Yet he also seems to allow a distinction—though not a separation (pp. 146–47)—between the work

of art and the experience of it (see p. 139), or at least between the "art product" as mere "potentiality" and the "work of art" as it actually figures in experience (p. 162). To remain in the spirit of Dewey, we must be on guard against dichotomies, but it does not seem to me to misrepresent him if we speak both of the object (the sculpture) and of the experience of it (which includes more than the perception of the qualities of the sculpture, by Dewey's own description).

Second, there is the problem of the relation between two experiences, that of the creative artist and that of the perceiver. Dewey's description of *an* experience is certainly an excellent account of the experience of reading a poem or listening to a whole musical composition; yet in certain features, especially when the emphasis is on its continuity with other experience, it purports to be a description of the poet's or composer's experience as well. Again, Dewey is very uneasy about separating the two (see pp. 46 ff), and especially because he (properly) wants to insist that aesthetic perception is not a passive state, but an active participation (p. 52). But of course this could be maintained without insisting that the perceiver "must *create* his own experience. And his creation must include relations comparable to those which the original producer underwent" (p. 54). Perhaps "comparable" is loose enough here to be safe. But Dewey, it seems to me, never does satisfactorily clear up the similarities and differences between the two kinds of experience—aesthetic and artistic—even though further light is thrown on the problem by his discussion of the two aspects of expression.

Dewey deals, in successive chapters, with "the act of expression" and "the expressive object." His views on these two matters turn out to be somewhat more disjunct than Dewey hoped they were. Dewey's account of the act of expression—to consider that first—is, as usual, his own. To express is not merely to vent emotions; it differs from plain discharge in two ways. First, it is undertaken with a sense of the consequences, a conscious grasp of meaning (see pp. 62–63); second, it has a medium, so that the emotion is released indirectly. "Only where material is employed as media is there expression and art" (p. 63). Two rather subtle ideas are involved here. One is Dewey's concept of the medium—he says that a material element becomes a medium when employed with other materials in some order, so that it becomes part of an inclusive whole (p. 64). The other is his theory of the role of emotion in expression. In all expression there is emotion, which is temporarily blocked and thereby subjected to control (p. 66), so that it can work itself out through the act of chipping marble, etc. As the medium is worked, and matter transformed, the emotion is transformed, too (pp. 74–75). Thus the emotion at the end is not what it was at the start, and so the emotion at the start, though it is necessary to initiate the process, and functions as a "magnet" to draw material together (p. 69), is not what is expressed at all—it is not the "significant content" of the artistic product (p. 69). For example, a person is irritated and works it off by putting his room to rights: "if his original emotion of impatient irritation has been ordered and tranquillized by what he has done, the orderly room reflects back to him the change that has taken place in himself . . . His emotion as thus 'objectified' is esthetic" (p. 78).

Since it is the object that tells us what is really expressed in it, Dewey's interest is really in the product rather than the process— though (of course) he insists that you can't separate them (p. 82). Dewey begins his analysis of expression in the objective sense (in the sense in which we say the *work* expresses rather than that the *artist* expresses) by asking what "representation" means— "since it must be representative in some sense if it is expressive" (p. 83). In all art, he argues, there is some reference to the world— even if, quoting A. C. Barnes (p. 94), it is only that by having a color the painting represents the quality of color that all objects share. When meanings "present themselves directly as possessions of objects which are experienced," they are "intrinsic," like the "meaning" of a flower-garden (p. 83). In aesthetic expressiveness, we have "meanings and values extracted from prior experiences and funded in such a way" that they fuse with the qualities directly presented in a work of art" (p. 98). In his ensuing discussion of regional qualities of lines, Dewey rejects both the associationist view that these qualities are mere associations and the alternative view that "*esthetic* expressiveness belongs to the direct sensuous qualities" (p. 99). Instead he says that lines (wavering, majestic, crooked, aspiring) "carry with them the properties of objects," as "transferred value" (p. 119) but so deeply embedded in them that they are wholly "fused" (pp. 100–3).

Dewey's extended and interesting discussions of various common features of the arts, and of the individual arts, cannot be reviewed here. Nor, once we have seen his initial premises and the direction in which his thought must move, will it be necessary to recount all of the general theses (however important) that he advances toward the close of his book. There are, for example (ch. 11), extremely penetrating criticisms of alternative characterizations of aesthetic experience—as "contemplation," "equilibrium," "disinterestedness," "detachment." Throughout this discussion, I have the impression that Dewey is overemphasizing his difference from the others; that he is overanxious to avoid associating with any of those terms, because in each case there is a misleading implication. His main concern is expressed in an often quoted passage:

Not absence of desire and thought but their thorough incorporation into perceptual experience characterizes esthetic experience, in its distinction from experiences that are especially "intellectual" and "practical" [p. 254].

Other aestheticians had seen something of this truth; perhaps Dewey has stated it most effectively. Yet he does not really mean, of course, to deny distinctions—only to substitute his own. Aesthetic experience can assimilate any intellectual and emotional elements, provided quality is in control; yet there is a fundamental difference between the way aesthetic experience restores unity by squeezing meanings and qualities together, and the experience of cognitive inquiry, in which qualities and their meanings are set apart for study. In another famous statement (p. 85), Dewey says:

The poetic as distinct from the prosaic, esthetic art as distinct from scientific, expression as distinct from statement, does something different from leading to an experience. It constitutes one.

Then, in ch. 12, Dewey launches his criticisms of various "theories of art," such as the view of art as make-believe, as play, as imitation, as revelation. He sees some truth in them, but they are too one-sided—each in its own way fails to keep its eye firmly on the central organism-environment situation which is at once the cradle of all art and the source of all its glory. With respect to the revelation theory, Dewey's own position is perhaps not fully clear. In part, yes: he is clearly against making art a mode of knowledge rivalling science (pp. 288–89); yet he agrees that the "sense of disclosure and of heightened intelligibility of the world" which he experiences in art "remains to be accounted for" (p. 289). In the understatement of the century, Dewey says "I have from time to time set forth a conception of knowledge as being 'instrumental' " (p. 290)—and if anything is to be contrasted, in this respect, with knowledge it is art. Yet in the last analysis (ch. 14), the question of art's relation to the rest of life and culture remains to be faced—and here Dewey expresses some of his deepest and most profound convictions. From the point of view of the society or the culture, there is this to say:

Esthetic experience is a manifestation, a record and celebration of the life of a civilization, a means of promoting its development, and is also the ultimate judgment upon the quality of a civilization [p. 326; cf. 81, 270–71].

In its capacity to further communication between man and man, even across barriers of language and culture, art is one of the important humanizing forces (see pp. 244, 332, 335).

From the point of view of the individual, Dewey also has much to say. He finds the value of art in its "refreshment" (p. 139), its quickening of the sense of "ideal" possibilities in natural experience (p. 185)—quoting Santayana (p. 139). Not by being moralistic, but by its power "to remove prejudice, do away with the scales that keep the eye from seeing, tear away the veils due to wont and custom, perfect the power to perceive" (p. 325), it has the highest moral value (cf. *Human Nature and Conduct* [1922], pp. 160–64). And in an even deeper capacity—as it "elicits and accentuates this quality of being a whole and of belonging to the larger, all-inclusive, whole which is the universe in which we live" (p. 195)—it has a religious quality, in the naturalistic sense of "religious" taught by Dewey in *A Common Faith*, which appeared in the same year as *Art as Experience* (and cf. *The Quest for Certainty* [1929], p. 235).

The influence of Dewey's thought, in aesthetics as elsewhere, is incalculable. Hardly any student of the subject, even if confirmed in a radically different position, has been left untouched by him. One group of philosophers, however, may be singled out as belonging especially closely to Dewey's general tradition. Some of them were working along related lines even before *Art as Experience*, but consciously aware of their debt to his general philosophy. Albert C. Barnes, whose earlier study with Dewey at Columbia led to a long and remarkable association, dedicated his book *The Art in Painting* (1925; revised in 1928, 1937) to Dewey, who returned the compliment in *Art as Experience*. For many years Dewey was in close and fruitful touch with the Barnes Foundation (Merion, Pa.), which has been fundamentally concerned with the problem of art education. Its teaching owes a great deal to Dewey's educational philosophy; and Barnes contributed very much to *Art as Experience*.

Teaching at California and at Harvard, David W. Prall worked out a naturalistic aesthetics, with emphasis on "aesthetic surface," which he presented in two widely read and much-respected books, *Aesthetic Judgment* (1929) and *Aesthetic Analysis* (1936). C. I. Lewis's "Conceptualistic pragmatism" (*Mind and the World Order*, 1929, p. xi) made a place for the aesthetic experience as "the nearest approach to pure givenness" (p. 402); in his later work, *An Analysis of Knowledge and Valuation* (1946), he has dealt with problems about the ontological status of aesthetic objects and the nature of aesthetic value in an impressive way (chs. 14, 15). Stephen C. Pepper's aesthetics was first set forth in *Aesthetic Quality: A Contextualistic Theory of Beauty* (1937), though even in that book (p. 4) he described aesthetic "contextualism" as but one among several possible "hypotheses" that can be used to "illuminate the field." The three alternatives were formulated more fully in *The Basis of Criticism in the Arts* (1945). Pepper has also written *Principles of Art Appreciation* (1949) and *The Work of Art* (1955).

SEMIOTIC APPROACHES

Future historians of ideas, I believe, will record with some astonishment—but also, I hope, with sympathetic understanding —the remarkable preoccupation of the twentieth century, through many of its best minds, with the meaning of meaning. In so many varied concerns and achievements—symbolic logic, linguistics, the interpretation of dreams and neurotic behavior, the explication of poetry, cultural mythology, religious symbolism, communication, philosophical analysis—our attention has concentrated on the problems of *semiosis*, the process in which one thing functions as a sign of something else. "Semiotic" is now the philosophically accepted term for the study of semiosis, and I shall use it here—rather than the more common, but inaccurate, term "semantics."

If it is not too extravagant to say, it is as though Western Civilization in our day has broken through to a new level of consciousness, or self-consciousness—has learned to think easily in terms of the distinction of sign from significatum (or referent), and characteristically approaches problems in awareness of their semiotic dimension. No previous age has quite achieved this. I do not mean to deny, of course, that most of our ideas have antecedents in former times, and I do not mean to claim that the semiotic facility and concern is by any means universal today; but it can be argued, I think, that this combination of fascination with meanings and at-homeness with the manipulation of signs, is a pervasive characteristic of the most advanced intellectual activity of our age, and marks an important advance in human thought.

There is no opportunity here to explore the general cultural situation. Within the field of aesthetics, one of the significant contemporary developments, in my opinion, is the emergence of a number of ways in which semiotic ideas and principles have been drawn upon for solutions of long-standing problems about the arts.

In the main line of modern attempts to give an account of what it is for something to mean something else, *The Meaning of Meaning*, by C. K. Ogden and I. A. Richards (1923), was the pioneering work. Their subtitle, "A Study of the Influence of Language upon Thought and of the Science of Symbolism," gives some notion of the ambition (but not of the zest) with which they set forth. It was a remarkable try, especially considering that it was one of those books with almost nothing in the way of a precedent. Their contextual analysis of "reference" stimulated a host of successors, of increasing degrees of sophistication and precision down to our own day, to improve upon it. The authors finally emerged with a distinction between different "language functions" and especially between the "referential function," in which a word (for example) becomes fully symbolic, and the "emotive function," in which it serves as a sign of the speaker's feelings (see 5th ed., pp. 149, 223). This distinction between referential and emotive functions—or between two kinds of language, in which one function or the other exclusively or predominantly appears—has had its own notorious and complicated history over the past decades. We must note here at least two effects on aesthetic theory.

The first aesthetic application was suggested by Ogden and Richards immediately: here was, it seemed, the long-sought essential difference between poetry and scientific discourse (or "prose"). "Instead therefore of an antithesis of prose and poetry we may substitute that of symbolic and emotive uses of language" (p. 235). The fundamental importance of this distinction, in all fields, was heavily underlined in *The Meaning of Meaning* (see esp. ch. 7), and its influence was forceful. Richards himself, when later on (see *Practical Criticism* [1929]) he studied the problem of explicating poetry, treated poetry far more as cognitive ("referential") than as emotive discourse; nevertheless, the view that poetry is somehow essentially emotive language underlay his influential little book on *Science and Poetry* (1926), and has often been repeated—mainly by those who have not reflected very hard about the nature of poetry (for example, the early Logical Positivists). Second, the theory of "emotive meaning," refined and strengthened by such later thinkers as Charles L. Stevenson (in his *Ethics and Language* [1944]), suggested the possibility that critical judgments themselves might be neither true nor false, but simply expressions of approval or disapproval. Ogden and Richards argued that conflicts over the real nature of beauty reflect the confusion of linguistic functions. Generally, they said, "terms such as Beauty are used in discussion for the sake of their emotive value" (p. 147). And this emotive theory of value, including aesthetic value, has also figured prominently in the philosophic debates of the twentieth century.

The Meaning of Meaning was a semiotic call to arms. It was also a healthful irritant, which did much to start up thinking about meaning in general, and about the sense or senses in which (precisely) poems may be said to mean differently, or something different, from scientific treatises, and in which paintings and musical compositions may be said to have any meaning at all. The problems in what might be called the General Theory of Interpretation (including under this heading, for the moment, the explication of literature) were formulated more explicitly and more broadly than hitherto. What happens when we understand a meaning—whether verbal or visual or auditory—and what are the criteria of correct understanding? In several of Richards' later works, this is the dominant interest: for example, *The Philosophy of Rhetoric* (1936), and *Interpretation in Teaching* (1939). The "New Critics" have carried the craft of explication to a new level of precision (see pp. 365–66 below). And in the fine arts, under the leadership of such scholars as Erwin Panofsky (see *Studies in Iconology*, 1939), the analysis of symbolism and iconological reference in painting has been highly developed. Meanwhile, some of the most important work in the philosophy of art has been carried on by philosophers strongly interested in just these questions. See, for example: John Hospers, *Meaning and Truth in the Arts* (1946); Charles L. Stevenson, "Interpretation and Evaluation in Aesthetics" (1950); Morris Weitz, *Philosophy of the Arts* (1950); Isabel C. Hungerland, *Poetic Discourse* (1958); Joseph Margolis, *The Language of Art and Art Criticism* (Wayne State U., 1965); and many interesting papers by Henry Aiken, Arnold Isenberg, Kingsley Price, Vincent Tomas, and others (which may be found via the general works listed in the Bibliography below).

Meanwhile, both the theory and the practice of the arts (especially literature) have felt a powerful influence from a quite different direction: the field of anthropology, especially studies of the phenomenon of myth. The designation of the term "myth" seems not to be very securely fixed, and the anthropologists, amateur and professional, who have dealt with the subject, either in first-hand field-studies or in a more theoretical way, employ a considerable variety of definitions. They are no doubt saved from ultimate confusion by the fact that a great many things—for example, the Homeric stories of the Gods and the legends of the Algonquins—would universally be included in the denotation of the term. But then it appears there is almost as great a variety of explanations of myth—that is hypotheses about its origin and its relations to such other cultural phenomena as ritual, religion, magic, science, art, and social cohesion. Fascinating as are the many questions that have been discussed over the past century, since the study of myth began to be carried on with the persistence, scope, and orderliness that mark the scientific spirit, we shall have to set most of them aside here, and consider (but sketchily) the implications of these investigations for our general view of art.

The work of the nineteenth-century mythologists—that is, the wealth of the material they collected and connected, more than their actual theories about the nature and origin of primitive myth—has had its own career in the twentieth century as material for literature. It has provided symbolically charged objects and events for the poet (most notably, of course, the T. S. Eliot of *The Waste Land*) to play with for his own purposes. Sir James G. Frazer, whose twelve volumes of *The Golden Bough: A Study in Magic and Religion* appeared between 1890 and 1915, has had the greatest impact. The influence of mythology upon literary theory came about more indirectly, when a group of British classical scholars, inspired by Frazer, began to inquire into the origins of Greek myth and Greek tragedy. The turning point was the publication of Jane Ellen Harrison's *Themis: A Study of the Social Origins of Greek Religion* (1912), containing sections contributed by Gilbert Murray and F. M. Cornford. With great insight and considerable evidence, Harrison argued the revolutionary proposition that the tragic myth "arose out of or rather together with the ritual, not the ritual out of the myth" (p. 13); the myth was "the spoken correlative of the acted rite" (p. 328). In *Ancient Art and Ritual* (1913), she investigated, along the same lines, the ritual origin of ancient plastic art.

During the following decades, the origins of Greek tragedy were explored further by a number of writers, who pointed out the apparent traces of that origin which that tragedy seems to have preserved. (For a critical assessment of the available evidence for various speculative theories, see A. W. Pickard-Cambridge, *Dithyramb, Tragedy and Comedy* [1927; rev. ed. 1962]).

Not surprisingly, once a connection between literature and myth was made, it was found to have a wide extension. In what ways, one might ask, do Shakespeare's tragedies, say, contain ritual echoes, and to what extent are the ancient myths, in some disguised or partly disguised form, still at work in them? The field of investigation thus opened out has been very actively cultivated during recent decades. The assumption that mythical and ritualistic elements are present in all great literature, and await the imaginative critic to tease them out, underlies a large body of criticism, and may perhaps now be said to be accepted and applied to some extent by most critics in western countries.

This form of criticism would not, however, have become so live had it not been reinforced from another quarter. In 1922, Carl G. Jung read a paper "On the Relation of Analytical Psychology to Poetic Art," in which he applied his theory of the "collective unconscious" to literature. In a truly "symbolical art-work," the source of the images are not to be found in the personal unconscious of the author, he argued (that would make the work "a symptomatic rather than a symbolical product"), but "in that sphere òf unconscious mythology, the primordial contents of which are the common heritage of mankind" (*Contributions to Analytical Psychology*, trans. Baynes and Baynes, p. 245). In the mythologies of all cultures, and in their dreams and literary creations, there appear these "primordial images" or "archetypes" (p. 246), which belong not to individual or cultural minds, but to the vast unconscious mind underlying them all. And it is the appearance of these archetypal patterns in great literature that gives it its powerful emotional impact—"we feel suddenly aware of an extraordinary release, as though transported, or caught up as by an overwhelming power" (p. 247), for we find up opened up to us, as it were, the "deepest springs of life" (p. 248).

Jung has pursued this theme, and developed it a little further, in several of his works. In an essay on "Psychology and Literature" (in *Modern Man in Search of a Soul*, 1933) he criticizes Freud—who is discussed on pp. 383-84 below—for his approach to art in terms of the individual unconscious. (But Jung's collective unconscious turns out to be rather nationalistic in this essay.) In his book with C. Kerenyi, *Essays on a Science of Mythology* (1949), he says that the "archetypal content" expresses a *"figure of speech"* (an identification of sun with king, or child with God), and is part of a myth. Myths have "an *unconscious core of meaning*" that cannot really be brought into consciousness, though it can be loosely approximated in description (trans. Hull, pp. 104–5). Greater optimism has animated a number of critics who have applied Jung's theory in searching out the archetypal patterns of literature and trying to interpret them. Archetypes have been found at various levels of abstraction, by those who uncover a welter of thematic structures (such as Death-and-return or the Quest) and by those who reduce all archetypes to a single myth. Of these critics, two outstanding ones are Maud Bodkin (*Archetypal Patterns in Poetry* [1934]), the first to apply the method systematically, and Northrop Frye (*Anatomy of Criticism* [1957]; see also "The Archetypes of Literature," in *Kenyon Review* [1951]).

Probably the most ambitious attempt to construct a systematic philosophy of language—indeed, a general philosophy of human culture, or "philosophical anthropology"—was made by Ernst Cassirer (1874–1945). Drawing, with immense learning, on anthropological studies of primitive myth, on depth psychology and brain physiology, on a thorough acquaintance with physical science and mathematics, and on a broad humanistic experience with the arts, Cassirer has proposed a new way of seeing the arts in relation to the other aspects of human culture. This theory is set forth at length in his *Philosophie der Symbolischen Formen* (3 vols., 1923, 1925, 1929). *Sprache und Mythos* (*Language and Myth* [1925]) summarizes the leading ideas of this work; and Cassirer's final thoughts on these problems are presented in his last book, written in English after he came to the United States, *An Essay on Man* (1944). (Cassirer planned to write an *Aesthetics*, but did not live to finish it.)

The key to Cassirer's enterprise is his discovery (as he believed) that Kant's "transcendental method" can be given a much broader application than Kant realized (see *Philosophy of Symbolic Forms*, trans. Manheim, II, 29). Kant held that our experience of a common world of events and objects presupposes the forms of intuition (space and time) and the categories of the understanding (substance, causality, etc.) which we impose upon the raw data to give them form. And we can never get behind the phenomenon thus produced to the "thing-in-itself." Cassirer surveyed the evidence from psychology and anthropology, and concluded that the very language, or symbol-system, we use to talk about, and think about, the world around us (for Cassirer agreed with Croce that symbol and thought, expression and intuition, are inseparable), determines in important ways what that world will be. These great symbol systems or "symbolic forms"— mythology, language, art, science, religion—are not modeled on reality, he argued, but model it; nor can we think of getting to some untainted reality behind them. They are expressions of the creativity of spirit, or mind, itself, and so when we study art, or religion, or science, as a symbolic form, we discover not ultimate reality, but our own human power. To use Cassirer's metaphor (*Symbolic Forms*, III, 1), the various symbolic functions are "refractions" of something beyond, inescapable if there is to be vision at all; the philosopher of symbolic forms can only discover the "indexes of refraction," their laws and necessities (cf. *Language and Myth*, trans. Langer, p. 8).

Cassirer's theory of myth is defended in Vol. II (*Das mythische Denken*) of the *Symbolic Forms*, and sketched in *Language and Myth*. Language and myth, he tells us, began as one. They originally "stand in an indissoluble correlation with one another, from which they both emerge but gradually as independent elements"; they spring from the "same impulse of symbolic formulation . . . a concentration and heightening of simple sensory experience" (*Language and Myth*, p. 88). Primitive man at this stage grasps his world through *"metaphorical thinking"* (p. 84), "a type of apprehension that is contrary to theoretical, discursive thinking" (p. 56)—and his world, as structured by this symbolic form, is very different from ours. "What myth primarily perceives are not objective but *physiognomic* characters" (*An Essay on Man*, p. 102). But language "bears within itself, from its very beginning, another power, the power of logic" (*Language and Myth*, p. 97), and develops in one direction toward science, while myth develops into art (p. 98), a very different kind of symbol. Though now "emancipated" from its cradle of myth, however, "there is one intellectual realm in which the word not only preserves its original creative power, but is ever renewing it"—this is the "aesthetically liberated life" of poetry (p. 98), especially lyric poetry. "The greatest lyric poets, for instance Hölderlin or Keats, are men in whom the mythic power of insight breaks forth again in its full intensity and objectifying power" (p. 99).

So bald a summary of so elaborate an argument may obscure connections, but some of the gaps left here are present in the original. The "insight" that breaks forth in the last sentence above, for example, seems to be important to Cassirer, yet it is not quite prepared for by the preceding steps. The general view of art as a primary forming power is vivid, and some have found it inspiring. It is art, Cassirer says in his *Essay on Man*—along with science, myth, and religion—that places man not merely in a universe but in a "symbolic universe" (p. 43). "Like all the other symbolic forms art is not the mere reproduction of a ready-made, given reality. It is one of the ways leading to an objective view of things and of human life. It is not an imitation but a discovery of reality" (p. 183). At the same time, "Language and science are abbreviations of reality; art is an intensification of reality" (p. 184)—and again there seems to be an unresolved ambivalence. For (once more) art is "an interpretation of reality—not by concepts but by intuitions" (p. 188)—and still "the forms of art . . . perform a definite task in the construction and organization of human experience" (p. 212). Constructing something new and interpreting what is already there, could be rather different functions. Cassirer's argument seems to be that since reality is only what it is (for us) as made by the symbolic forms, in art (as in the other forms) discovery and creation merge into one.

Cassirer's philosophy of language first became widely known in the United States through two writers who were deeply influenced by him, though in quite different ways because of the very different philosophical apperceptive masses with which they came to him. The first was Wilbur Marshall Urban (*Language and Reality* [1939]), who brought a strongly Hegelian metaphysics to the study of language. Urban distinguishes symbols from signs as "expressive or significant" (p. 407), and he distinguishes "insight symbols" from the others (pp. 415–16), as a class to which "aesthetic symbols" belong, among other types (p. 466). The aesthetic symbol embodies an ideal content, holding it forth for enjoyment; like all insight symbols, it contains implicitly a revelatory truth (pp. 481–85). Thus Urban puts his emphasis on one side of Cassirer's double view. "Poetry is covert metaphysics" (p. 501).

The second philosopher who has been strongly influenced by

Cassirer is Susanne K. Langer, whose concern with problems of semiotic began with an interest in symbolic logic, but drew also upon much experience of poetry and music. The title of her book, *Philosophy in a New Key* (1942), called attention to a dominant theme of twentieth-century philosophy, which she described as a realization of the role played by "symbolic transformations" in man's relations to his world. Like Cassirer she takes man as essentially a symbol-using animal, but her own development of Cassirer's philosophy is original and imaginative. And her book, with its impressive style, its wide range of topics, and its illuminating suggestions, has been very widely read and discussed.

In *Philosophy in a New Key*, Langer proposed a distinction between two kinds of symbol, "presentational" and "discursive" (ch. 4), and with the help of this distinction presented a theory of musical meaning (ch. 8). In her next book, *Feeling and Form* (1953), which she asked to have considered as "Volume II of the study in symbolism that began with *Philosophy in a New Key*" (vii), she extended the theory to the other basic arts, modifying it somewhat in the course of development. Her aesthetics is one of the most fully worked out in recent years, and further light is thrown on it in her many essays (see *Problems of Art* [1957] and "Abstraction in Science and Abstraction in Art," in Paul Henle, ed., *Structure, Method, and Meaning* [1951]).

Langer's theory of music begins with the recognition of the point made earlier by Hanslick, Gurney, Carroll C. Pratt (in *The Meaning of Music* [1931]), and others: that "The tonal structures we call 'music' bear a close logical similarity to the forms of human feeling"—to use words from her summary of the earlier book, in Ch. 3 of *Feeling and Form* (p. 27). Because it is capable of exhibiting the same patterns as sentience in general, "Music is a tonal analogue of emotive life" (p. 27). In virtue of this similarity, music is a "presentational symbol" of psychic process—that is, it symbolizes the (morphological) features of that process by exhibiting these features itself: "forms of growth and of attenuation, flowing and stowing, conflict and resolution, speed, arrest, terrific excitement, calm, or subtle activation and dreamy lapses" (p. 27). Whereas the "discursive" symbolism of language, with its fixed denotations, syntactical rules of combinability, and analytical character, cannot reflect directly the nature of psychic process, the "nondiscursive" symbolism of music can (*New Key*, pp. 66, 78). But music is an "unconsummated symbol" (p. 195), because it lacks fixed dictionary denotations. "We are always free to fill its subtle articulate forms with any meaning that fits them; that is, it may convey an idea of anything conceivable in its logical image" (*Feeling and Form*, p. 31). So music does not have "meaning" in familiar senses (p. 29), but has "vital import," and can be called a "significant form." "Feeling, life, motion and emotion constitute its import" (p. 32). It can be said to be "expressive," but, again, what it expresses is not anyone's emotion, but the "idea" of emotion (pp. 26, 59).

Feeling and Form shows how this general concept of art as symbol, in this sense, can be applied to other major arts—and the development of the idea is carried through with great sensitivity and concreteness. Every work of art, in whatever medium, is, says Langer (p. 49), an "appearance," or "semblance" (but not necessarily a semblance *of* anything real—this term is her equivalent of Schiller's *Schein*). It creates "a realm of illusion" (p. 59). But again the sense must be carefully guarded. It is, like a rainbow, "a merely virtual object" (p. 49). The essential nature of each art is analyzed in terms of its own special semblance-nature: painting is "virtual space," music "virtual time," and so on. Merely to name these formulas here may be invidious, for they are far from suggesting the richness of interesting ideas with which they are filled out, especially in relation to drama and the dance. But the general outline of her aesthetics may be reasonably clear. The basic view of art as presentationally symbolic remains in *Feeling and Form*. But the stress (it seems to me) is on what is presented rather than on its symbolic use.

A few years before *Philosophy in a New Key* (that is, in 1939), another philosopher of language, Charles W. Morris, published a pair of articles setting forth a general semiotic view of art that has close affinities with Langer's. The articles were "Esthetics and the Theory of Signs" (*Journal of Unified Science* [*Erkenntnis*] [1939–40], VIII) and "Science, Art and Technology" (*The Kenyon Review* I [1939]). (See also his later systematic work, *Signs, Language and Behavior* [1946], pp. 136–38, 190–96.) Morris was working in a thoroughly empirical frame of reference, where he felt that both American pragmatism and Vienna Circle Logical Positivism (or Logical Empiricism) could find a home. He claimed that his own theory of art "agrees in all essentials with the formulation given by John Dewey in *Art as Experience*," but also that

esthetics, conceived in pragmatic terms . . . can be given a much more precise formulation (though not such a pleasing one), and its relation to the whole of the scientific edifice be much more clearly seen, when it is approached specifically in terms of a theory of signs [*Journal of Unified Science*, VIII, 131 n].

When Morris came to examine aesthetics, he had already laid down the basic categories of semiotic in his monograph, *Foundations of the Theory of Signs* (1938). He had proposed the definition of semiosis as "mediated taking account of"—a sign is anything by means of which we take account in any way of something else. He was interested in working out a system in which all the basic aspects of human culture, considered as various types and functions of signs could be related, and he was looking for the specific differentia of the "aesthetic sign," i.e., the work of art. Later on, he changed his mind somewhat: "the attempt to isolate the fine arts by isolating a special class of esthetic signs seems now an error" (*Signs, Language and Behavior*, p. 195; cf. 274 n). But he still maintained that the theory so confidently, clearly, and persuasively set forth in the two earlier articles was an essential part of the truth about art, and it is this theory that has played such an important role in contemporary thinking.

In any sign process, there is always the sign-vehicle (i.e., the physical work of art), the interpreter who takes it as a sign (i.e., the enjoyer of art), and the "designatum" of the sign, that is, what it leads the interpreter to take account of (say, a cloud). There is always a designatum; but there need not be a "denotatum," for what is designated may not exist—the cloud depicted in the painting may not ever have occurred (see *Journal of Unified Science*, VIII, 132–34). Now, the "aesthetic sign" is distinguished from all other signs by a combination of two features. First, it is an "iconic sign"—a term that Morris borrowed from the philosopher Charles Peirce. Morris distinguishes "two main classes of sign vehicles: those which are like (i.e., have properties in common with) what they denote, and those which are not like what they denote." An iconic sign is one that "denotes any object which has the properties (in practice, a selection from the properties) which it itself has" (VIII, 136). A picture signifies by similarity, according to Morris; here is one of the plainest examples of an iconic sign. But a poem or a dance or a musical composition does the same. Stravinsky's *Rite of Spring* has as its (approximate) designatum "primitive forces in elemental conflict" (*Signs, Language and Behavior*, p. 193). And even the most abstract visual design is simply an "extreme case" of generality of reference (VIII, 140). Second, however, not all iconic signs are aesthetic signs (maps, for example, are not), but only those whose designatum is what Morris calls a "value property"—that is a property that is related to an interest (VIII, 134). Morris's interest theory of value is involved here, but it does not seem essential. What he has in mind are such qualities as these: "an object can be insipid, sublime, menacing, oppressive, or gay in some contexts just as it may have a certain mass or length or velocity in other contexts" (*Kenyon*, I, 415). It is iconic signification of such human regional qualities that distinguishes aesthetic signs from other iconic signs.

Morris claims both novelty and ancestry for his view. It is, in a broad sense, he says, the ancient imitation theory (I, 414), but given a more technical formulation and more scientific grounding. It clearly shows the paradoxical character of art: that in one and the same experience "there is both a mediated and an immediate taking account of certain properties" (*Journal of Unified Science*, VIII, 137); what the object means, or intends, it also presents for our inspection; we seem to be led beyond it in some way as we feel its significance, and yet at the same time everything is there, for what it means is already within our grasp.

The Iconic Sign Theory of Morris and the Presentational Symbolism Theory of Langer have become part of the thinking of a number of aestheticians. And they have stimulated a great deal of valuable debate. The suggestion that works of art are best understood as being, or as featuring, some form of symbol has been followed up by several writers, in different ways. Thus, Milton C. Nahm (*Aesthetic Experience and its Presuppositions*,

1946) has elaborated an account of the work of art as a symbol of the artist's feelings; Edward G. Ballard (*Art and Analysis,* 1957) has proposed a view of the work of art as a "self-significant natural symbol"; Martin Foss's position (*Symbol and Metaphor in Human Experience,* 1949) belongs to the same general class, though he reserves the term "symbol" for the bearer of conceptual meaning, and places art in the "metaphorical sphere." Morris's concepts play an important role in the theories of Max Bense (*Aesthetica: Metaphysicische Beobachtungen am Schönen* [1954]; *Aesthetica II: Aesthetische Information* [1956]).

MARXISM-LENINISM

Despite their common love of literature and philosophical concern, neither Karl Marx nor Friedrich Engels worked out an aesthetic theory. But the system of philosophy which they jointly evolved—the system later named Dialectical Materialism—contained partial foundations for an aesthetics, with suggestions as to how to build. And when the system was filled out by V. I. Lenin and other Marxist theoreticians, it was found to accommodate a significant and still developing philosophy of art. This philosophy owes much to the nineteenth-century discussions of the social milieu and social functions of art which I have discussed in Chapter 11, but it has followed its own path to interesting conclusions. The world-view of Dialectical Materialism, and its categories and methods of inquiry, give its aesthetics a special character, which is further intensified by the circumstance that it has partly grown within a political framework imposing external standards of ideological orthodoxy. Yet the aesthetics has shown itself capable of reaching out to new ideas, and of engaging in fundamental debate within its ranks over a number of issues.

The fundamental principle of Dialectical Materialist aesthetics was formulated by Marx: that art, like all higher activities, belongs to the cultural "superstructure," or dominant class ideologies. This superstructure—a generalization of Ludwig Feuerbach's theory of religion—is determined by socio-historical conditions, especially by basic economic conditions, i.e., the methods of producing and distributing the means of subsistence in a given society at a given stage of history. When artistic activity is seen in the context of production in general, certain aspects are thrown into prominence, while others, featured in alternative philosophies, are played down. Thus Marxist aesthetics takes a general interest in the social matrix in which the artist works, and out of which his work emerges—the limits of his freedom from social forces, under capitalism and socialism. Marx, for example, in his early *Economic and Philosophical Manuscripts* (written in 1844, but not published until 1932), made a profound phenomenological analysis of the "alienation" of labor that, in his view, must characterize production within a system of private property, and his analysis contains many important implications for artistic production, as well.

A more specific corollary was also derived from the general thesis of a causal dependence of art upon social conditions: that a connection can always be traced between the particular work and its peculiar conditions. It was taken to follow that until that connection is grasped, the work itself can neither be fully understood nor correctly judged. One of the hardest recurrent tasks of Marxist aestheticians has been to determine the nature of the relation between the work of art and social forces, and to define its closeness and directness. Marx himself did not regard it as a simple one-to-one correspondence; in a famous passage in his *Contribution to the Critique of Political Economy* (1859), he said:

It is well known that certain periods of highest development of art stand in no direct connection with the general development of society, nor with the material basis and the skeleton structure of its organization. Witness the example of the Greeks as compared with the modern nations or even Shakespeare [see the Marx-Engels selections on *Literature and Art*, p. 18].

But later the orthodox Marxist view came to be that art is, in some sense, always a "reflection of reality"—a conclusion derived from Lenin's epistemological position by considering art as a mode of cognition. In his sustained attack on the nineteenth-century positivists as "crypto-idealists" (see, e.g., *Materialism and Empiriocriticism* [1908]), Lenin held that all thought necessarily mirrors social reality; and the view that art is also "a special form of reflection, of the cognition of the world" is emphasized in the latest Soviet textbook of aesthetics, *Essays of Marxist-Leninist Aesthetics* (2d ed. [1960]; from Max Rieser, in *Jour Aesth and Art Crit* XXII, 49).

In the period before the October Revolution of 1917, the thinker who contributed most to the working out of a Marxist aesthetics was G. V. Plekhanov. His *Art and Social Life* (1912) was a spirited attack on the separation of art from life, the "art for art's sake" view as he interpreted it. This view arises "when discord exists between the artist and his social environment" (trans. Leitner et al., p. 43). It is self-defeating, since "there is no such thing as a work of art completely devoid of ideological content" (p. 65). Its supporters are conscious or unconscious defenders of a social order in which exploitation of one class by another continues. This inevitably leads to a decadence of art, for *"When a work of art is based upon a fallacious idea, inherent contradictions inevitably cause a degeneration of its aesthetic quality"* (p. 66). Plekhanov also argues the inverse claim that *"any artist of proven talent will increase considerably the forcefulness of his work by steeping himself in the great emancipatory ideas of our time"* (p. 93).

Another important Marxist view is brought out well by Plekhanov. The whole concept of art as inherently and essentially propagandistic seems to him to follow from its necessary role as a product of social forces, and remains even when the social forces are beneficent. The Marxist aesthetician, like the champion of art for art's sake, was rebelling against the reduction of art to a mere commodity, and of its value to market value—exactly what, in his view, must happen under capitalism (see p. 92). But the art-for-art movement asks too little of art, in making it an instrument of sensuous gratification. If a nobler vision of art is to be realized, it must become the servant, through its sensuous appeal, of a higher social purpose. The Hegelian theory of the Idea shining through sense, and the Tolstoyan rejection of mere pleasure as the test of art, come together here, with the influence of the nineteenth-century Russian Realists, Belinsky and Chernyshevsky (cf. pp. 33–35).

It was Lenin who stamped firmly and decisively upon Marxism its rigid political pragmatism: a tendency to make the furtherance of revolutionary goals the criterion of doctrinal acceptability. This had its long-range effect on aesthetics, as well. In his paper on "Party Organization and Party Literature" (1905), Lenin argued the need for political control over educational, scientific, economic publications, etc. At least, this was the main thrust of his argument, though the key term *"literatura"* could cover (and in some contexts, for Lenin, did cover) imaginative literature as well. This ambiguity made it possible for this essay to become, in the 1930s, the textual justification for submitting all works of literature, music, and other arts, to complete Party, and therefore government, control.

Lenin himself, when he came to power, was not concerned to impose restrictions on the arts, though other Bolsheviks did discourage the remarkable flowering of creative work in painting and in poetry that had marked the prerevolutionary period in Russia. After the revolution, and throughout most of the twenties, there was again much brilliantly creative experiment in various forms of art—notably, motion pictures, drama, poetry. And this was paralleled by free and vigorous aesthetic debate. At the extremes, in point of both the posture and intensity of their theories, were the Formalists (to be discussed below), who began about 1915 to emphasize and demonstrate the autonomy and independence of literary works, and the rigid Marxists (the "proletarians"), such as G. Lelevich and the periodical *On Guard*. Another Marxist anti-Formalist, A. V. Lunacharsky, transcended the narrower Marxists in breadth of view, and his periodical, *Press and Revolution*, was perhaps the freest organ of theoretical discussion.

. . . The crucial question or questions which confronted the Marxian literary theorists in the twenties could be stated thus: is literature a mere by-product of social strife, just another weapon in the class struggle, however potent and strategic, or does it have exigencies of its own which cannot be derived either from its "class roots" or from its social import?[1]

But the scene was dominated by thinkers who, without accepting Formalism, maintained a flexible theory of class-determinism, which allowed for aesthetic value in nonsocialist writers and for a legitimate concern with artistic form. Leon Trotsky, before his

[1] Victor Erlich, "Social and Aesthetic Criteria in Soviet Russian Criticism," in E. J. Simmons, *Continuity and Change in Russian and Soviet Thought* (Harvard U., 1955), p. 406.

fall and exile, held that art is "a deflection, a changing and a transformation of reality, in accordance with the peculiar laws of art" (*Literature and Revolution* [1924]; trans. Strunsky, p. 175). These peculiar laws, presumably not reducible to those of social change, would be the domain of the art student, who must judge art in terms of them (p. 178). Nikolai Bukharin (in various papers of 1925–27, translated as *Problems of Soviet Literature* [n.d.]) criticized Formalism as a wrenching of art from its social context, but found formal analysis a necessary part of the spadework required for full understanding of a work of art. A. Voronsky (in his *Proletariat and Literature*, 1927) argued that there are "supraclass" aspects of every genuine work of art—which explains how a noncommunist writer may produce a work both aesthetically and ideologically better than a writer in the Party.

The disputes of the twenties also dealt persistently and sharply with a related internal problem of Marxist-Leninist aesthetics. The principle of socio-historical determinism posed a difficult paradox of practical application. Marxism from the start was conceived as a pragmatic philosophy: not merely to understand the world, but to change it. But unless the "superstructure" (to which philosophies belong) is more than epiphenomenon, philosophy itself would seem fairly helpless. Now if the correspondence of art works to their social matrix is very close (even if not perfect), all forms of political control over art would seem to be both futile and unnecessary. Futile, because until the matrix is changed, art cannot be changed either (though it can be suppressed); and unnecessary, because once a society moves from capitalism into socialism, its art will be bound to change, too—a healthy society will express itself inevitably in a truly humane art. On the other hand, if this consequence is not automatic, some degree of political adjustment may be required to bring the painter's and the poet's activity into acceptable alignment with social needs; art may be more than a mirror of change; it may be a means of indoctrinating the people for their new role in a coming socialist society.

Discussion of these problems came to a climax toward the end of the decade, when forces were set in motion by Soviet authorities to end the debate, fruitful though it had been—to discourage disagreement about aesthetic matters. The Party, under the leadership of Stalin, felt that the time had come to bring the various groups together, insist on a united front, and clarify the basic principles of Marxist-Leninist aesthetics. This task was completed at the First All-Union Congress of Soviet Writers, in 1934, at which "Socialist Realism" was proclaimed the aesthetics of Marxism-Leninism. This concept was defined by Andrei Zhdanov in the Statute of the Union of Soviet Writers:

> Socialist Realism is the fundamental method of Soviet Literature and criticism: it demands of the artist a true, historically concrete representation of reality in its revolutionary development. Further, it ought to contribute to the ideological transformation and education of the workers in the spirit of socialism [see Hankin, "Soviet Literary Controls," p. 448; and Eugen Weber, *Paths to the Present*, pp. 395–96].

The two principles enunciated here are evidently in peril of contradiction: it is easy to think of occasions on which either the demand for truth or the demand for effective propaganda must yield to the other. In Marxism-Leninism, however, the propositions are reconciled in the phrase "reality in its revolutionary development." The basis for this reconciliation had actually been laid by Marx and Engels. Marx admired Balzac because, despite his misguided royalism, he was able to discern the moving social forces in the decadent society he depicted so fully and accurately. Thus he could portray, prophetically, characters that were only coming into existence under Louis Philippe, and would flower under Napoleon III (see Paul Lafargue, "Marx and Literature," in Marx-Engels selections, p. 139). Looked at "dynamically," a social condition reveals its vectors and promises, the future within it. The two tasks of revealing this implicit goal and of helping its realization will, then, coincide. Similarly, Engels wrote to Margaret Harkness (April 1888), about her novel *City Girl*, that even though the working class may appear as a "passive mass," her novel would be more "typical" if it showed the masses as having in them the seeds of revolutionary activity. The sense in which the term "typical" is to be taken has been clarified by a later Marxist aesthetician: "A character is typical, in this technical sense, when his innermost being is determined by objective forces at work in society."[2]

---

[2] Georg Lukács, *The Meaning of Contemporary Realism*, trans. John and Necke Mander (London, 1962), p. 122; English translation of *Wider den missverstandenen Realismus* (Hamburg, 1958).

During the thirties, some work was done by Marxist critics in Western European countries and in the United States. For the most part, this criticism merely illustrated (sometimes brilliantly, sometimes in a drudgelike manner) the methods and principles of Marxism-Leninism, without extending or sharpening them. Two of the theorists whose work illustrates some of the better thinking of that time are Ralph Fox, *The Novel and the People* (1937), and Christopher Caudwell (pseud. for Sprigg), *Illusion and Reality* (1937), *Studies in a Dying Culture* (1938), and especially *Further Studies in a Dying Culture* (1949).

Socialist Realism was proposed as a critical theory—a method for interpreting and judging art—and as a guide to artistic practice. In the former respect, it was a rigidifying and standardizing of principles that had been developing for several decades. In the latter respect, it was an act of state—an attempt to determine the course of artistic production, as well as distribution, by political will. It reached degrees of restrictiveness that we need not detail here—for example, in the climactic cracking down on composers in 1948, when Soviet Russian officialdom insisted on more program music, on singable melodies and easy harmonies. Andrei Zhdanov, with the support of the aging Maxim Gorky, became the official interpreter and executor of Socialist Realism; his statement at the 1934 Congress laid down the rule for artistic creation and government censorship. At its best, Socialist Realism expressed a spirit of determination to encourage and inspire the highest type of socially responsive art. As A. V. Lunacharsky said in an article in 1933 (trans. Hankin, p. 449):

To indicate where to direct artistic forces, artistic attention, artistic talent—that is the natural conclusion from all our understanding of socialist construction. We know very well that we have the right to intervene in the course of culture, starting with mechanization in our country, with electrification as part of it, and ending with the direction of the most delicate forms of art.

The electrification program leads to the aesthetic one; if one can be planned and directed for the best, why not the other? So, if laws and administration could do the job, the arts were to become affirmative and optimistic (not like the "critical realism" of the nineteenth century), inspiring and uplifting—in every way worthy of the high ideals of the society that produced it. That was the hope.

Like other aspects of that period under Stalin, the repression of art has now been agonizingly reappraised. Since this is not a book on the politics of art, I shall not attempt to trace the apparent variations of freedom and control that have marked recent years. Individual writers, painters, and composers are officially censured from time to time, and the standing question is raised again whether Dialectical Materialist aesthetics entails government prohibition of all art but Socialist Realism. Nevertheless, signs of vigorous and independent thinking are evident within the Marxist movement.

For example, the Austrian writer Ernst Fischer has published a forceful and yet thoughtful book on *The Necessity of Art: A Marxist Approach* (*Von der Notwendigkeit der Kunst* [Dresden, 1959]; trans. Anna Bostok [Baltimore, 1963]). He argues in detail for the dependence of form upon content in the several arts (ch. 4), alleges various artistic tendencies (alienation, escapism, dehumanization, etc.) to be inevitable under capitalism (ch. 3), and concludes with a vivid, and frequently eloquent, description of the values and functions of art in a completely socialistic society (ch. 5).

The greatest living Marxist aesthetician is the Hungarian Georg Lukács. Though at present out of official favor in the Soviet bloc for having been Minister of Culture in the short-lived Imre Nagy regime (1956), he has, over two decades, made his own independent and subtle contributions to Marxism-Leninism.[3] Lukács, in his detailed studies of individual writers and styles, has done much to clarify the differences between Socialist Realism and other forms of Realism, and the ways in which (in Marxist theory) literature "reflects" reality. "In no other aesthetic does the truthful depiction of reality have so central a place as in Marxism" (*The Meaning of Contemporary Realism*, p. 101). But "truth" does not mean either what the writer sees on the surface, or what he wants to see.

In the writing of the Stalinist period, however, the real problems were overlooked and—as with economic subjectivism—the correctness of par-

[3] His main essays were reprinted in *Essays über Realismus* (1947), revised under the title *Probleme des Realismus* (1955); the remarkable later essay on "Socialist Realism and Critical Realism" (1955) is in *The Meaning of Contemporary Realism*, referred to above. He is now working on a systematic *Aesthetics*, of which Vols. I and II were published in 1963.

ticular solutions became a matter for dogmatism. Literature ceased to reflect the dynamic contradictions of social life; it became the illustration of an abstract "truth." The aesthetic consequences of such an approach are all too evident. Even where this "truth" was in fact true and not, as so often, a lie or a half-truth, the notion of literature-as-illustration was extremely detrimental to good writing [p. 119].

In Poland, Stefan Morawski, of Warsaw University, has published a significant article, "Vicissitudes in the Theory of Socialist Realism" (1961), in which he aims "to decorticate the theory of socialist realism from the Zhdanovian envelope which ended by choking it" (p. 136). Morawski emphasizes the elements of Socialist Realism in the great Russian works produced during the twenties, and argues for the artist's freedom of experimentation in form as a necessary condition of his being able to carry out his social and ethical purpose in the best way. "The theory of socialist realism must be an *open theory*; I mean by that, it must be ready to enter into polemics with other contemporary theories with regard to problems which have been put forward; and it must stand comparison with new artistic phenomena" (p. 136).

Actually, as Morawski has pointed out, Marxist-Leninist aesthetics developed at every crucial stage in close dialogue with other and opposing strains of thought, first in opposition to the Hegelians, later to the Croceans and the Formalists. Marx's method of "assimilation by polemics" is illustrated in this development as in others. On a number of crucial questions of serious concern to all aestheticians—such as the origin and function of art, the interpretation and evaluation of works of art, the objectivity or subjectivity of beauty, the possible future directions of artistic creation, the artist's involvement with and alienation from his society—much thinking is being done by Marxist-Leninist philosophers, as by non-Marxists. Moreover, insights already achieved on each side have yet to be adequately taken advantage of by the other.

PHENOMENOLOGY AND EXISTENTIALISM

Several contemporary strains of thought have combined to carry a good deal farther than ever before a tendency that we have noted from time to time in earlier chapters, and especially in the "art for art's sake" movement: the recognition of a work of art as an object in its own right, intelligible and valuable as such, with intrinsic properties independent of its relation to other things and to its creator and perceiver. Among leading critics and critical theorists in various arts there has been a marked revolt against efforts to dissolve the aesthetic object into its causal conditions or emotional effects, and to reduce criticism either to biography or to autobiography.

Perhaps the first clear and firm voice in this company was that of Eduard Hanslick, whose highly significant little book on *The Beautiful in Music* (1854) was discussed in Chapter 10. Hanslick insisted that to listen to music is to respond to objective qualities of the sound pattern itself, and that the secret of musical beauty is to be found here, rather than by searching the mind of the composer ("The thrilling effect of a theme is owing, not to the supposed extreme grief of the composer, but to the extreme intervals; not to the beating of his heart, but to the beating of the drums," p. 54) or by introspecting one's own emotions ("We might as well study the properties of wine by getting drunk," p. 13). Sir Donald Tovey's masterly essays in music analysis exhibit the same conviction.

A parallel plea for the autonomy of the plastic arts was made by Konrad Fiedler (*Über den Ursprung der künstlerischen Tätigkeit* [1887]), who held that the forms the painter sees and presents do not depend on concepts and references for their aesthetic value. Much of the extraordinarily valuable educational work of Clive Bell (see *Art* [1914]) and Roger Fry (see *Vision and Design* [1920]) consisted in helping people to look at paintings without predispositions and preconceptions, and without being distracted by irrelevant associations with the representational subject-matter. They made famous the term "significant form," introduced by Bell as a name for the quality common to all good visual art—roughly, unified organization with vitality of regional quality—and used it to focus attention on the work itself.[1] In Germany, art historians such as Heinrich Wölfflin (see

---

[1] Clive Bell's Objectivism (i.e., his conception of the work as an object in its own right) owed much to the influence of G. E. Moore, especially the latter's theory of goodness as a simple, unanalyzable property, and his definition of "the beautiful . . . as that of which the admiring contemplation is good in itself" (*Principia Ethica* [Cambridge U., 1903], p. 201; cf. Teddy Brunius, *G. E. Moore's Analyses of Beauty* [Uppsala, 1964], and George Dickie, "Clive Bell and the Method of *Principia Ethica*," *Brit Jour of Aesth* V (1965): 139–43.

especially his *Kunstgeschichtliche Grundbegriffe* [1917]) and Wilhelm Worringer (see *Formprobleme der Gotik* [1911]) were treating the history of art as the history of styles that develop out of each other in some independence of other social factors— "a history of art without names," as Wölfflin suggested. This general attitude is also reflected in André Malraux's concept of the "museum without walls" (*Les Voix du Silence* [1951]).

In literature, one of the first to speak up strongly for the autonomy of the work was A. C. Bradley, in his famous essay, "Poetry for Poetry's Sake" (*Oxford Lectures on Poetry* [1909]). During the following decades, two independent movements, one in Russia (spreading to Poland and Czechoslovakia), the other in the United States and England, vigorously championed the same view. Russian "Formalism" (a name given it by its enemies) was launched in 1915–16, both in Petersburg and in Moscow. Essays by various members of the Petersburg group appeared in *Studies in the Theory of Poetic Language* (1916) and *Poetics* (1919), which contained detailed studies, especially of the sound-texture of poetry. Roman Jakobson, Victor Shklovsky, Boris Eichenbaum, and Boris Tomashevsky (*Theory of Literature* [1925]) were among the leaders during the next decade. The Formalists produced many analytical essays, and developed important critical principles—without crystallizing their views into a full-fledged aesthetics—while carrying on a running battle with the Marxists, who finally (by about 1930) outlawed their theories in Soviet Russia. They took seriously the basic principle that a literary work is a piece of language, which can be studied independently of its author. They found it useful to make a sharp distinction between verbal and nonverbal art. They investigated the distinguishing feature of literary, as opposed to nonliterary, discourse, and marked it by the term *Differenzqualität*, borrowed from the German writer Broder Christiansen (*Philosophie der Kunst* [1909]). This "quality of divergence" consists in literature's "creative deformation" of reality, in the use of deviant discourse (linguistic devices departing from normal speech), in alterations of existing formal literary conventions (that is, the novelty and originality of the work, considered in relation to the history of literature).

The central thesis of the so-called "New Critics" has also been that a literary work should be read as an organic whole, self-existing and self-sufficient, in all its complexity and unity. The first great teacher of this lesson was I. A. Richards, in his *Practical Criticism* (1929). His *Principles of Literary Criticism* (1924) had called for a new psychology of literature, and made interesting suggestions toward it, but *Practical Criticism* was a revelation, in its thorough and subtle investigation of the processes involved in understanding poetry and in misunderstanding it. *Seven Types of Ambiguity* (1930), by his pupil William Empson, brought the methods of explication to the highest degree of refinement, and set a model for all successors. The Objectivist approach to poetry is evident in the essays of many of the "New Critics"—a term that now means just the serious analytical critics who attempt with some success to help readers find in poetry what is there. See, for example, Cleanth Brooks, *The Well Wrought Urn* (1947), William K. Wimsatt, Jr., *The Verbal Icon* (1954), René Wellek and Austin Warren, *Theory of Literature* (1949). The autonomy of the work has also been the theme of two well-known papers by Wimsatt and Monroe C. Beardsley, "The Intentional Fallacy" (1946) and "The Affective Fallacy" (1949), which argued for keeping clear the distinction between a work and both its author's intention and its readers' responses. This pair of essays (to be found in *The Verbal Icon*) formulated and named assumptions that were already widely operative among critics, though not without vigorous opposition. Beardsley has since stressed—if not overstressed—the independent existence of aesthetic objects in his *Aesthetics: Problems in the Philosophy of Criticism* (1958).

These Objectivist tendencies have been given strong support by Gestalt psychology (see following section). And they have been reinforced by the philosophical movement called "Phenomenology," which pledges absolute and total respect for the "given" (as distinct from the inferred and conjectured) in human experience. This complex and subtle method of philosophical inquiry was first worked out by Edmund Husserl in various books and essays, but notably in his *Logische Untersuchungen* (2 vols., 1900–1) and his *Ideen zu reiner Phänomenologie und phänomenologischen Philosophie* (Vol. I [1913]; Vols. II and III published posthumously [1952]). With various modifications, it has been adopted and practiced by a number of contemporary philosophers, especially in Germany and France. And out of this movement have come important aesthetic studies, bringing to the phenomena of art the same willingness to grasp and explore in detail what is presented and what is felt in aesthetic experience. Husserl's slogan "To the things themselves" (*Zu den Sachen*) has proved fruitful here, as elsewhere.

The basic concept of Phenomenology was formulated by Franz Brentano in his *Psychologie vom empirischen Standpunkt* (1874). Seeking for a criterion to distinguish mental from physical states, he found it in the phenomenon of "reference to a content, the directedness toward an object [which in this context is not to be understood as something real] or the immanent-object-quality" (trans. Herbert Spiegelberg, *The Phenomenological Movement*, I, 39). When we see, it is always something that we see (even if we are having a hallucination); love and hatred are *of*, or *toward*, someone; a thought is *about* a concept or a proposition. To mark this general character of consciousness, Brentano borrowed the scholastic term "intention," and gave it a new sense. Thus, in his terminology, when Ponce de Leon sought for the Fountain of Youth, the Fountain of Youth was the "intentional object" of his thought and desire; in that role it had "intentional inexistence."

Because of this peculiar feature of "psychical phenomena," that something is contained in them by way of intentionality, or reference, it becomes theoretically possible to investigate the intentional objects, or referential contents, of consciousness wholly apart from any theoretical assumptions about them—as to whether, for example, the Fountain of Youth actually exists or not. Different people can think of the same intentional object, and compare notes about their thoughts of it, to discover in what ways these concepts overlap or differ. Therefore this Phenomenological investigation can yield intersubjectively valid results. It was Husserl who worked out the method. Fortunately, only a part of his difficult doctrine need be considered here; without attempting to do adequate justice to his immense work, I will touch briefly on two features of the Phenomenological method that have a bearing upon aesthetics.

First, the Phenomenologist, selecting a certain area for study (such as beauty, or the sense of personal responsibility toward others, or the meaning of freedom), aims to grasp, as fully as he can, what is actually experienced, and to describe it faithfully. To do this, he must set aside all his culturally-determined preconceptions about the phenomenon, all the theoretical constructs that he may have been relying on in ordinary practical life. This may be extremely difficult; part of the task is precisely to become keenly aware of what is in fact given, and to recognize what is imported, and therefore needs to be compared freshly with the actual presented content. The inquirer sets aside, too, any concern about whether the object actually exists—a Phenomenological analysis of the Fountain of Youth would simply consider it, without acceptance or rejection. This is the operation of "bracketing" existence (*Einklammerung*). But it is not simply an ignoring of belief—the fact that the inquirer finds himself believing, or hoping, or hoping against hope, may also be part of his experience, and should be noted. He merely refuses commitment to the belief, at the time; he does not allow any assumptions about actual existence or nonexistence to influence his conclusions about the nature of the phenomenon itself. The phenomenon is freed from all "transphenomenal" elements. This process is the so-called "Phenomenological reduction"—which is not really a reduction, since it proposes only to face, without management or manipulation, experience in all its richness, and is thus regarded by the Phenomenologist as opposed to all reductionistic philosophies, such as earlier and more primitive forms of the "sense-datum" theory.

A second feature of the Phenomenological method—enabling it to go beyond pure receptivity, and thus to derive a kind of knowledge that can (as is claimed) resolve the long-standing problems of philosophy—is the intuition of general essences (*Wesensschau*), "eidetic intuition." The inquirer can recognize the particulars presented to him *as* particulars, and in so doing he can also grasp them as instances of universals. The Fountain of Youth is an instance of fountains in general; and so the universal *fountain* is also given in experience, or, better, can be taken from it by the Phenomenological inquirer. And once he possesses, clearly and distinctly, sets of general essences, he can also investigate the essential relations between them—to discover which ones are necessarily connected. That all colors are necessarily extended, for example, would be known in this way.

Apart from its fruitfulness as a general philosophical method—a question I cannot discuss here—there are two evident ways in which Phenomenology has affinities for aesthetics. First, "The spirit of free acknowledgment of the qualitative richness of true experience on the one side and the insistence on the qualitative irreducibility of its essential characters on the other proved to be congenial to art."[2] The human regional qualities in which works of art may shine—their warmth, energy, elegance, grandeur—have sometimes found themselves unwelcome in narrower empirical descriptions of experience, insisting on a more atomistic and more limited vocabulary. If the areas in a painting must be described as red or blue, triangular or curved, the energy and elegance of the painting are relegated to the subjective or contingent in some odd sense. But Phenomenology (like the phenomenological objectivity of Gestalt psychology) restores them, without prejudice, to the full account of the given.

Second, in return for this kindness, art might promise to help the Phenomenologist. For the Phenomenologist's presupposition-less openness to what is presented, suspending practical and theoretical concerns, comes close to being a description of all aesthetic experience (cf. *Ideen*, § 111). In some part, to have an aesthetic experience is to perform a Phenomenological reduction—or so it might be argued. Thus, seeking for ways to perfect his own method, the Phenomenologist could be urged to turn to artistic works, which might be described as objects specially designed to facilitate the "bracketing" of irrelevancies, and to reward utter absorption in the given.

Husserl's ideas had an influence on the Russian (and Polish and Czech) Formalists. The most brilliant use in aesthetics of the Phenomenological method (those parts of it which I have described above) has been made by one of his early students who remained in close touch with him throughout his life. The Polish philosopher Roman Ingarden applied the method to literature, in a very remarkable study, *Das Literarische Kunstwerk* (1930), and later to painting and music (see especially his essay on the structure of the picture, published in French and Polish [1946]:

[2] Fritz Kaufmann, "Art and Phenomenology," in Marvin Faber, ed., *Philosophical Essays in Memory of Edmund Husserl* (Harvard U., 1940), p. 193.

"De la structure du tableau," "O Budowie Obrazu").[3] His Phenomenological contributions, still continuing, to other branches of philosophy have been considerable; here, however, I shall discuss only his aesthetics, and that sketchily.

Das Literarische Kunstwerk set itself to answer, fully and carefully, two main questions about literary works of art—and, in so doing, to provide a set of categories in terms of which the traditional problems of aesthetics could be tackled in relation to all the arts. First: What is the mode of existence (*Seinsweise*) of the literary work? And second: What are the essential and crucial features of literary works in general?

The answer to the first question uses the basic concept of Phenomenology. A poem (to take that species for convenience) is something quite distinct from its "concretions" (*Konkretisationen*)—that is, particular occasions of reading it—yet at the same time it is somehow related to, and dependent upon, those concretions, even though none of them exhausts its properties and some of them may be more in the nature of *misreadings* (§ 63). The poem, says Ingarden, is best understood as an intentional object which the concretions more or less adequately intend; it is neither an "ideal entity," an abstraction like a number or a function, nor an "actual entity," like the inkmarks on paper in the printed book (§ 3).

The answer to the second question is that a literary work is a "many-layered," or "multiply stratified," creation (*ein mehrschichtiges Gebilde*, p. 24). In every literary work, Phenomenological analysis discloses four distinct strata, in an order of dependence and emergence; and it also shows how the strata cooperate together to produce the wholeness of the work. Ingarden deals with each of the strata illuminatingly. The first stratum is the sound (*sprachlichen Lautgebilde*)—not sound-tokens or utterances, but sound-structures (*Gestalten*) and their qualities. The second stratum is meaning (*Bedeutungseinheiten*), including its emergent qualities, such as lightness, simplicity, complexity of

---

[3] There are also *Studies in Aesthetics* (*Studia z estetyki*, 2 vols. [1958]) , and *Untersuchungen zur Ontologie der Kunst* (Tübingen, 1962). Parts of the former are translated as "The General Question of the Essence of Form and Content," trans. Max Rieser, *Jour Phil* LVII (1960): 222–23; and "Aesthetic Experience and Aesthetic Object," trans. Janina Makota, *Phil and Phenomenological Res* XXI (March, 1961): 289–313.

style. The third stratum is that of the objects exhibited (*darge-stellten Gegenständlichkeiten*), the "world of the work" in space and time. These objects are purely intentional, and differ (phenomenologically) from "real" objects in several ways, which Ingarden analyzes with subtlety—a fictional character, for example, does not have all his properties determinate like a real person. The fourth stratum is that of the "schematized aspects" (*schematisierten Ansichten*). Out of the relations among persons, places, and things in the third stratum arise certain "perspectives" of the work; these are schematic, in the sense that each reader must fill them in, but his interpretation of the work is guided, and its correctness is limited, by the structure of the work itself.

Each of the strata has its own "aesthetic value-qualities." The highest are those that suffuse the work as a whole, qualities such as the sublime, the ugly, the tragic, the holy, which Ingarden calls "metaphysical qualities." The work of art is an "aesthetic object" because of the "polyphonic harmony" of all its aesthetic values. "The polyphonic harmony is precisely that feature of the literary work of art which, together with the metaphysical qualities that are revealed in it, makes it a *work of art*" (p. 384).

In his later *Studies in Aesthetics* (see footnote above), Ingarden applies his concept of strata to other forms of art; thus music turns out, on his analysis, to have but one stratum, while representational painting has three.

Another important study in Phenomenological aesthetics is Mikel Dufrenne's *Phénoménologie de l'Expérience Esthétique* (2 vols., 1953). Taking as his starting point not so much Husserl's Phenomenology as the version worked out (with some differences) by Maurice Merleau-Ponty and Jean-Paul Sartre (see I, 4 n), Dufrenne undertakes a detailed examination of the aesthetic object (the "work of art" as it enters into experience), and of aesthetic experience. And he carries it through with considerable clarity, insight, and originality. Part I considers the aesthetic object as phenomenally given, and examines its general features, which are sharpened by contrast with other objects in our phenomenal field—natural objects, useful objects, etc. An aesthetic object appears *in* the ordinary world of space and time, and yet is not wholly *of* it (I, 199). It is "privileged" (I, 201) over the other objects about it in space, as the painting lords it over the gallery wall, and refuses to sink into its background (I, 202). And despite its historical character as an object created and destroyed, it preserves an air of timelessness, or time resistance (I, 217, 220).

Dufrenne finds that the aesthetic object is distinguished in a deeper way still: it is not only in a world, but it *has* a world—indeed, a double one. There is its "represented world" of persons, places, and things—Ingarden's third stratum (I, 224 ff). And there is its "expressed world," more difficult to describe (I, 232 ff). A novel or painting or musical composition has its own special quality or spirit or *Weltanschauung*, which gives it "the coherence of a character" (I, 234), that is, makes it hang together in the way a person does. It is a quasi subject, with a double mode of being, for it combines (in Sartre's terms) the "being in itself" (*en-soi*) of all presented objects, which exist as objects of consciousness (I, 286), with the "being for itself" (*pour-soi*) of consciousness. Its hidden depths and inexhaustible richness give it a special "truth" that makes demands on us in somewhat the way another human being does. Aesthetic perception is unlike all other kinds; when I lose myself in the object, "it is then that I recognize in the object an interiority and an affinity with myself" (I, 296). This final view is reached by Dufrenne after a criticism of alternative ontologies of the aesthetic object, such as the "ideal existence" attributed to them by Sartre.

The analysis of aesthetic experience that Dufrenne gives in Part III makes it co-ordinate with the preceding analysis. Aesthetic perception requires the co-operation of imagination and "understanding" (*entendement*). This response, which Dufrenne calls "sentiment," is not emotion, but a kind of "knowledge," since it "reveals a world," while emotion is a reaction to "a world already given" (II, 472). Sentiment is detached to some degree:

> At a comedy, it is not necessary that the spectator be gay as if he were situated in the world represented; it is enough for him to have comic sentiment, and if he laughs, it is a calm laughter that proceeds from knowledge, not from surprise [II, 472].

But in the end the aesthetic sentiment is a response of the whole self and its accumulated experience to the object; the depth (*profondeur*) of the aesthetic object speaks to the depth of the self (Part III, ch. 4).

Contributions to Phenomenological aesthetics have also been made by others who should be noted. Moritz Geiger, in his *Zugänge zur Ästhetik* (1928), made a careful Phenomenological study of aesthetic enjoyment, distinguishing it from other pleasurable experience, as directed to objects or states of affairs that have an "intuitive abundance" (*anschauliche Fülle*), so that "outer-concentration" (*Aussenkonzentration*) can be complete (see pp. 12 ff). Some degree of distance from the self is a condition of aesthetic enjoyability; but with an effort to avoid ego-involvement, a person can come to enjoy aesthetically even tastes and smells and the qualities of his own moods. Nicolai Hartmann, though not strictly a member of the Phenomenological movement, practiced a kind of Phenomenological method. His unfinished and posthumously published *Ästhetik* (1953) applies Max Scheler's concept of "strata," or modes of being, to works of art, which he interprets as complexes consisting of a "real foreground" and a "background of appearance." This was his way of acknowledging a tension or duality within aesthetic objects, without the dualistic temptation of the form-content distinction. In Italy, Guido Morpurgo-Tagliabue has contributed a Phenomenological analysis of style: *Il Concetto dello Stile* (1951).

In his later thinking, Husserl evolved a concept which he called the "life-world" (*Lebenswelt*), the totality of each man's lived experience; this is found, not in his published works, but in his unpublished manuscripts, and it was partly through studies of those manuscripts, and reflection on this concept, that Phenomenology came to link up with another contemporary movement, Existentialism. It is not easy to select the core of this philosophy, as it has gathered itself together from strains of thought in Pascal, Nietzsche, and Kierkegaard, to become the highly developed system of today—most notably in Martin Heidegger, *Sein und Zeit* (1927) and Jean-Paul Sartre, *L'Être et le Néant* (1943). The Existentialist (at least, of the nontheistic variety) teaches that each man is alone in a world without meaning, except such meaning as he himself can create in it out of his absolute freedom, as a being who is not made, but always in the making. It is from the recognition of this human condition, in which the certainty of death and the perilousness of life are inherent, that the Existentialist draws both the deepest anxiety and the highest sense of absolute personal responsibility.

In the thinking of Heidegger, the method of Phenomenology came to the support of Existentialism, to produce a combined philosophic view that is called "Existential Phenomenology." The insights of the Existentialist, and his vision of the human predicament, have found their fullest expression in literature—in the images of the man about to be executed, or the hell without an exit, or the prisoner tried for a crime whose name he is not told. But only in very recent years have there been systematic attempts to draw out the implications of Existential Phenomenology for aesthetic theory.

To see how such an aesthetics might be derived, we must look a little more closely at the whole philosophy. Man's essential condition Heidegger describes as "being-in-the-world" (*in-der-Welt-leben*), and he sets himself to discover, by Phenomenological analysis, the structure and the modes of this being-in-the-world. Only man "exists," in his terminology; that is to say, only man is a person rather than a thing or object. His existence (*Dasein*) is simply possibility or potentiality; he has no antecedent "nature," or essence, but is only what he becomes through his complete personal spontaneity of action. When he becomes a creature of routine habit, or lives under the control of externals, allows himself to be made into a machine or an economic good or an abstraction, he lives an "inauthentic" life. But when he exerts his freedom in creation and self-assertion, recognizing at the same time that he has been cast into the world, and that all values depend on him for their being—when he is resolved to face and overcome his existential dread—he lives "authentically." One aesthetic question that arises, then, is this: in what way does art, considered in its deepest terms, contribute to man's realization of authenticity in his existence?

An interesting and thoughtful answer to this question has been given by Arturo B. Fallico, in *Art and Existentialism* (1962). What is primary in a work of art, says Fallico, is that it is a "*free essence* . . . born out of spontaneity itself*" (p. 23); it is the paradigm case, so to speak, of a free act (or the product of one). As such, the work is always implicitly related, in our grasp of it, to its creator—even a piece of driftwood exhibited on the mantel has "the stamp of personality," because it was chosen by a person (p. 30). Art does not exist for truth, but for "truthfulness"; its raison d'être is what it shows "about how the existent feels and imagines existence itself, apart from any and all projects initiated to carry out a life" (p. 26; cf. pp. 87–88). Thus every work of art, so far as it is itself "authentic" (i.e., sincere, in this sense), has existential import—if I may abuse a logical term—in that it offers "a clear vision of the joy, the despair, the mystery, and the possibility of meaning or of meaninglessness of our existence" (p. 27). Hence arises its "pathos"—its implicit reminder of disillusionment with life (p. 71)—because it represents "a deep endeavor to 'complete' the primordial act of purposing which underlies existence" (p. 66); it is an attempt to carry through free, self-sustaining and self-justifying action in a way that life seldom if ever permits. But at the same time, "Art places on exhibit a way of validating existence, however meaningless or meaningful it may be" and thus "makes life itself meaningful and tolerable" (p. 81), saving us from ultimate cynicism and "nihilism" (p. 83) by revealing the root-spontaneity present in all men, and by showing how the power to create value, to impose meaning on life, remains intact. There is thus in art a "renewal of spontaneity," "the renewal of the very springs of feeling and imagination" (p. 120), which, in the final analysis, is its greatest gift to man and its contribution to authentic existence (see p. 125).

Heidegger's own philosophy of art, so far as he has worked it out, is contained in a long essay on "The Origin of the Work of Art" ("Der Ursprung des Kunstwerkes," in *Holzwege* [1950]). The art work is distinguished from the "mere thing" and from the useful object ("equipment") by being that which "in setting up a world, sets forth the earth" (trans. Hofstadter,[4] p. 673). These two concepts, *world* and *earth*, are deeply embedded in Heidegger's philosophy, and have rich technical senses, which can only be sketched here. A Greek temple, he says, houses a god, focuses the outlook and the concerns of the Greek people at one stage of their historical development. It discloses, opens up into the light, the meanings they attached to things, the challenge

[4] In Albert Hofstadter and Richard Kuhns, eds., *Philosophies of Art and Beauty* (New York, 1964).

and response of their culture. This is what Heidegger means by "setting up a world." At the same time, the temple glorifies the luster of its stone in the sunlight, shows the power of the rocky soil that supports it, points up by contrast the shapes of leaf and bird nearby. In this sense, it "sets forth the earth." Because the art work is always in a physical medium, in it matter (stone, paint, spoken word) is manifested, brought a little way out of its natural shyness and "closedness."

Though "the setting up of a world and the setting forth of earth are two essential features in the work-being of the work," and compose a unity within it, they are in tension with each other (p. 674), for they pull in opposite directions—the world to bring earth into the light of meaningfulness, earth to draw world down into itself. "The repose of the work that rests in itself thus has its essence in the intimacy of strife" (p. 675).

It is in this strife that truth "happens," or comes to be—truth, that is, in Heidegger's sense of revelation or "unconcealment" of what *is*. Art's function is to unwrap the "hiddenness" of being. When (to cite his other main example) Van Gogh depicts a worn pair of peasant shoes, so that we see in them the marks of the worker's "toilsome tread," of his contact with damp spring loam and hard wintry paths, then we can say that "The art-work has told us what shoes are in truth" (p. 664). There is a "setting-itself-into-work (*sich-ins-Werk-setzen*) of the truth of what *is*" (p. 665; cf. p. 680). Then, too, there is beauty, which is "one way in which truth occurs as unconcealment" (p. 681). "The beautiful belongs to the self-advent of truth" (p. 700).

EMPIRICISM

One distinguishing feature of contemporary philosophical Empiricism is its contention that the traditional problems of philosophy will yield to solution when (and only when) they, or their components, are sorted into two distinct classes. The first class consists of empirical problems, which are to be tackled by the methods of empirical science; the second, of logical problems, problems about concepts, terms, and methods, which are to be tackled by the techniques of philosophical analysis. It is usually not obvious in a philosophical problem, as formulated and discussed by earlier philosophers, which elements in it are empirical and which logical, so that there is a great deal to be done by the Empiricist, as he understands his task. But his hope is that when the separation is made, the way will be clear for the psychologist, anthropologist, or other qualified investigator, to set about finding answers to the first set of questions; and the remaining ones, seen in their true light as having to do with the clarification of terminology and the examination of logical inferences, can be approached by the philosopher with confidence of success.

As in other fields of philosophy, the problems of aesthetics have begun to be sorted out according to this program, and one of the important achievements of twentieth-century thinking about the arts has been to sharpen and emphasize the distinction between the two types of problem. It is not surprising, though it may be regrettable, that the recognition of this difference has sometimes led to a dispute over the possession of a name—whether it is the scientific study of artistic phenomena and their relations to other phenomena, or the philosophical analysis of our talk about art, that is most properly called "aesthetics." To save time and toil here, we may as well give them different names—"scientific aesthetics" and "analytical aesthetics." The important thing is to say something about each of them. For some of the scientific discoveries, especially by psychologists, have deeply affected our way of thinking about the arts, and others will certainly do so in the future. And the extension of the methods of philosophical analysis to aesthetics has also changed the manner in which a great many aestheticians go about their business.

The concept of aesthetics as an empirical science—at least, a hybrid one, on which various sciences might converge—has roots that go some way back into the past. The eighteenth-century British Empiricists, the French sociologists of the nineteenth century, the Marxists, and such philosophers as John Dewey in our own time, have certainly considered aesthetics as a broadly empirical study. In the twentieth century aestheticians have formulated the program of making aesthetics a rigorous and broad-gauged discipline—recommending

a scientific, descriptive, naturalistic approach to aesthetics; one which should be broadly experimental and empirical, but not limited to quantitative measurement; utilizing the insights of art criticism and philosophy as hypotheses, but deriving objective data from two main sources—the analysis and history of form in the arts, and psychological studies of the production, appreciation, and teaching of the arts.[1]

In these words, in 1951, Thomas Munro summed up the program which he had set forth in 1928, in his *Scientific Method in Aesthetics* (reprinted in *Toward Science in Aesthetics* [1956]).

As Munro has pointed out, this enterprise was envisioned early in the century. Max Dessoir led the way in his *Ästhetik und allgemeine Kunstwissenschaft* (1906, 1823). Charles Lalo followed, in several volumes, beginning with *L'Esthétique expérimentale contemporaine* (1908), and Étienne Souriau in *L'Avenir de l'esthétique: Essai sur l'objet d'une science naissante* (1929). In the United States, Thomas Munro himself has undoubtedly been the most forceful proponent of this approach to aesthetics, over many years. In a series of studies, notable individually for their care and thoroughness and collectively for the wide range of artistic phenomena that have engaged his interest, he has exemplified the kind of work that, in his view, aesthetics needs at the present time more than any other.

As the above quotation indicates, one source of "objective data" for the scientific aesthetician was to be the systematic work done by art historians and art critics. There have been many outstanding examples of such work in the twentieth-century, too many to attempt an adequate sample list here.[2]

The other source was to be the work of psychologists, and certain aspects of this work are so germane to the problems I have been tracing throughout this whole history that they require some attention.

This part of the story begins most naturally in the middle of the nineteenth century, with some problems raised by Darwin's evolutionary theory, as set forth in his *Origin of Species* (1859) and *Descent of Man* (1871). A propensity to delight in artistic work, or at least in ornament and decoration, is almost universally observable among men (however variable the admired objects may be). But how can this widespread trait be accounted

---

[1] Thomas Munro, "Aesthetics as Science: Its Development in America," *Jour Aesth and Art Crit* IV (March, 1951): 164.

[2] They can be tracked down through books listed in the Bibliography, below.

for in evolutionary terms? The "sense of beauty," as Darwin called it, can be assigned a transcendental origin by a transcendentalist theory. To the evolutionary biologist, however, it must be susceptible of naturalistic explanation. Darwin himself tried to trace the sense of beauty in man back to a subhuman preference:

When we behold a male bird elaborately displaying his graceful plumage or splendid colors before the female, whilst other birds, not thus decorated, make no such display, it is impossible to doubt that she admires the beauty of her male partner. As women everywhere deck themselves with these plumes, the beauty of such ornaments cannot be disputed [*Descent of Man*, ch. 3; Modern Library, p. 467].

Darwin did not offer to show why certain colors or patterns are found pleasing; he merely argued that if such aesthetic preferences arise, they can play a role in natural selection, and thus perpetuate the qualities.

The males which were the handsomest or the most attractive in any manner to the females would pair oftenest, and would leave rather more offspring than other males ["Supplemental Note," p. 923].

Darwin's conjecture was not found convincing, but the question he posed was challenging: what is, biologically speaking, the source of the artistic impulse and the aesthetic pleasure? Herbert Spencer tried another tack in his *Principles of Psychology* (1855; enlarged 1872) and in a number of essays on aesthetic questions collected under the title: *Essays: Scientific, Political, and Speculative* (3 vols., 1858–74). His theory was that human beings develop a surplus of energy in their struggle to survive, and this energy can be expended (indeed, must be expended, to preserve equilibrium) in the form of play. Artistic activity is simply play, though of a specially valuable sort, for in beauty we enjoy the greatest quantity and intensity of stimuli with the least effort, because of their integration into orderly patterns. Beauty follows the principle of economy. The advance of industrialism consists in transforming human life so that useful labor, work, makes room more and more for play; and the arts are destined to take a larger and larger place in the inherent satisfactions of life.

The "play theory" of art (which, it can be seen, is of an entirely different order from Schiller's theory, though often classed with it) was also adopted, and further developed, by Grant Allen (*Physiological Aesthetics*, 1877) and Karl Groos (*The Play of Man*, 1901). Another biological view was proposed by Jean-Marie Guyau, in *L'Esthétique contemporaine* (1884), who identified the joy of beauty with the organism's recovery of equilibrium and integration.

The idea of submitting aesthetic questions to laboratory experiment may have occurred to others earlier, but it was first realized in a thorough way by Gustav Fechner. His *Vorschule der Ästhetik* (1876) opened with a distinction between "aesthetics from above" and "aesthetics from below," and a resolution to take the second—the plain, empirical—road. Fechner laid the foundations of experimental aesthetics. Since that time, a great many experimental studies have been made of various aesthetic phenomena —some of them productive of concepts and principles that the philosophic aesthetician can make good use of, others of little aesthetic importance. Psychologists have investigated, for example, preferences in shapes, colors, and pictures, criteria of musical aptitude, the validity of metaphorical descriptions of music, poetic meter, the properties of color, the structure of jokes, and many other phenomena. Outstanding among systematic works on psychological aesthetics are those of Richard Müller-Freienfels (*Psychologie der Kunst*, 3 vols. [1923]), Paul Plaut (*Prinzipien und Methoden der Kunstpsychologie* [1935]), and O. H. Sterzinger (*Grundlinien der Kunstpsychologie* [1938]).

Meanwhile, out of the work of other investigators, using more introspective methods, have come three psychological terms that have become part of the standard vocabulary of aesthetics. The first is the term "empathy" (*Einfühlung*), introduced by Robert Vischer (*Das Optische Formgefühl* [1873]) but made famous by Theodor Lipps (see his *Ästhetik*, 2 vols. [1903–6])[3] and his followers, H. S. Langfeld and Vernon Lee (Violet Paget). The term was introduced to explain our perception of phenomenally objective regional qualities by saying that human feelings are projected onto inanimate objects. This theory, once widely held, has yielded to the attacks of the Gestalt psychologists. The second is the term

---

[3] His essay on "Empathy and Aesthetic Pleasure," trans. Karl Aschenbrenner, from *Die Zukunft*, LIV (1905), is in Aschenbrenner and Arnold Isenberg, eds. *Aesthetic Theories* (New York, 1964).

"psychical distance," proposed by Edward Bullough in his famous paper, "'Psychical Distance' as a Factor in Art and an Aesthetic Principle" (1912). "Aesthetic consciousness" he described as "distanced," in the degree to which the object is purged of concern with practical needs and ends. Because of the illumination of Bullough's examples and analysis, this term is felt to be almost indispensable by many contemporary aestheticians. The third term is "synaesthesis," used by Ogden, Richards, and Wood, in their *Foundations of Aesthetics* (1922) and by Richards in his *Principles of Literary Criticism* (1924), to refer to a state in which opposed impulses are harmonized in a tense equilibrium that still allows both "free play." Their view was that in aesthetic experience, at its best, the organism has this kind of integration.

The search for a mathematical formulation of aesthetic value has also attracted some interest in the twentieth century. If, as St. Augustine thought, beauty can be analyzed in terms of order, or, as Francis Hutcheson suggested, in terms of a ratio of unity to complexity, then degrees of beauty might actually be measurable. Until recent years, the most thorough attempt to work out this line of thought was George Birkhoff's *Aesthetic Measure* (1933). At present the most active, and promising, line of inquiry uses the concepts and principles of information theory to explain aesthetic value (especially in music) as a function of an optimum mixture of order and disorder, or redundancy and information. (See, for example, the *Journal of Aesthetics and Art Criticism* XVII [June 1959], for a symposium on "Information Theory and the Arts," and a related article by Leonard B. Meyer.)

Though it is impossible here to discuss twentieth-century psychological aesthetics in detail, some note must be taken of two groups of psychologists whose ideas have exerted a pervasive and no doubt permanent influence on the philosophy of art. These are the Gestalt psychologists and the depth psychologists.

The key term of Gestalt psychology was contributed by the Austrian philosopher, Christian von Ehrenfels, in his famous paper "On Gestalt Qualities" (1890), although the movement itself is usually dated from the pioneering paper of Max Wertheimer, "Experimental Studies on the Perception of Apparent Movement" (1912). It is interesting that the problems which Gestalt psychologists have set themselves to solve were first broached, by von Ehrenfels, in connection with a study of melody, as an example of a whole that is not the mere sum or sequence of the notes that compose it, and that retains its individual gestalt-qualities invariant through changes in key, timbre and tempo. Wertheimer was the first to work out the characteristic method and explanatory schema of Gestalt psychology, which was later developed by two other remarkable thinkers, Wolfgang Köhler and Kurt Koffka. They, and their followers over the past half century, have applied the concepts of Gestalt psychology to all types of psychological phenomena, but their greatest work has been done on perception. They have analyzed the nature of gestalts and gestalt-qualities, discovered the perceptual conditions under which they arise and disappear, formulated general "laws" of perception-phenomena, and elaborated neuro-physiological hypotheses to account for them. The resulting concepts (for example, that of the "good gestalt"), distinctions (for example, that between phenomenal and functional objectivity), and principles (for example, the law of "Pragnänz"—that the perceptual field tends to organize itself as fully as the perceptual conditions allow), have illuminated many aesthetic phenomena.

There have been several important aesthetic applications. Wolfgang Köhler, in *The Place of Value in a World of Facts* (1938), attempted to work out a theory of value, including aesthetic value, on the basis of the phenomenally objective gestalt-quality which he called "requiredness," the demand which one part of the field may have for another (as when a dominant seventh chord seeks the tonic in a cadence). Kurt Koffka developed several aesthetic implications of Gestalt psychology in his important paper on "Problems in the Psychology of Art" (in *Art: a Bryn Mawr Symposium* [1940]). The most extensive and illuminating treatment of the fine arts on Gestalt principles is Rudolf Arnheim's *Art and Visual Perception* (1954); Arnheim has used the same methods with great success in numerous papers and books. Leonard B. Meyer's significant book, *Emotion and Meaning in Music* (1956), uses Gestalt concepts and Gestalt principles very illuminatingly, though he is careful to point out (p. 84) that he does not subscribe to the basic theoretical explanations of Gestalt psychology.

The influence of Gestalt psychology on philosophical aesthetics can be seen in Andrew Ushenko's theory of the aesthetic "vector field" (*Dynamics of Art* [1953]) and in Harold Osborne's "con-figurational" theory of beauty (*Theory of Beauty* [1952]; *Aesthetics and Criticism* [1955]).

Freud's discovery of the unconscious (setting aside literary anticipations of it) opened up a new world of possibilities for investigation of the arts—which he himself, in his great interest in literature, was the first to follow up. A great many psycho-analytic studies have been made of writers and painters, and much material has been gathered. (Detailed references can be found through the Bibliography, below; here I shall only sum-marize the main lines of work.) First, there are the investigations of the process of art creation. Some of these are particularized: the psychoanalyst is interested (as was Freud, for example, in *Leonardo da Vinci* [1910] and in "Dostoyevsky and Parricide" [1928]) in explaining some particular feature of the work, its primary themes or images or details of the plot, by hypotheses about the neuroses of the artist—and, conversely, he is using the artistic products to throw further light on the creator. Some of the studies are generalized: the psychoanalyst is proposing an hypothesis to explain in general the unconscious sources of the creative impulse. Plato's old question, repeated through history, about the relation between inspiration and madness has found a new setting here. Psychoanalysts have investigated the relation of creativity to neurosis, the similarity of art and dream, the role of infantile sexuality in art creation. Freud himself made some tentative suggestions. A more recent writer, Harry B. Lee,[4] ex-plains art creation as a defense against repressed impulses to destruction—and explains the various ways of appreciating art (of which he distinguishes five) in the same terms. Second, there are the psychoanalytic investigations of the sources of aesthetic enjoyment—such as Lee's theory, or the interesting work by Simon O. Lesser, *Fiction and the Unconscious* (1957), which offers an explanation of our fascination with fiction, and its service to us, in terms of its effects on the unconscious.

Two other applications of psychoanalytic data to literature take us closer to the work itself. The problem of *elucidating* a

[4] See, for example, "On the Esthetic States of the Mind," *Psychiatry* X (1947): 281–306.

literary work gives rise to questions about the motivation of certain characters, where this has to be inferred from their actions and speeches: why, for example, does Hamlet not kill Claudius when he has the chance? In his *Interpretation of Dreams* (1900; *Complete Works*, V [1953], 264–67) followed by Ernest Jones, (*Hamlet and Oedipus* [1949]), Freud used psychoanalytic methods to answer this question. That is, he gave an answer in terms of Hamlet's unconscious processes. He used the same method in a number of papers on other literary characters, and most extensively in *Delusion and Dream in Jensen's Gradiva* (1907). On the other hand, the problem of *interpreting* a literary work involves describing its themes and the meanings of its symbols. The use for this purpose of the Jungian theory of the "collective unconscious" has been described earlier in this chapter.

Depth psychology has had an enormous effect on literary criticism, but in aesthetics less. It can be seen in DeWitt H. Parker's theory of art as wish-fulfillment (*The Analysis of Art* [1926]).

A related field of empirical inquiry, as yet perhaps still in its infancy, is the art of primitive cultures—embracing

such varied objects as Bushmen rock paintings, Eskimo drawings on ivory, Fijian prints on bark-cloth, and decorated ancestral skulls from New Guinea; and that is without arguing whether *primitive* is a proper adjective to apply to such relatively sophisticated products as the stone carving of ancient Mexico, the pottery of prehistoric Peru, or the cast metal work of West Africa.[5]

Ethnologists have investigated (for example) the reasons given by Pueblo Indian potters for judgments of design, ideas about beauty (in wooden milk pots) expressed by the Pakot of Kenya, responses of Melanesians to Müller-Lyer illusions, and cross-cultural responses to music and visual design. Melville J. Herskovits has gently suggested to philosophers that "their studies of the aesthetic have lacked a cross-cultural dimension" and that there is a "need to widen the base of aesthetic theory, to break through its culture-bound limits. If the aesthetic response is a universal in human experience, it must be studied as such, everywhere it is found."[6] There is no question that the widespread Western

5 E. R. Leach, "Aesthetics," in E. E. Evans-Pritchard *et al.*, *The Institutions of Primitive Society,* a series of broadcast talks (Oxford, 1961), p. 25.

6 "Art and Value," in *Aspects of Primitive Art*, by Robert Redfield, Melville J. Herskovits, and Gordon F. Ekholm (New York, 1959), p. 44.

acquaintance with primitive art has already affected our thinking about art quite deeply—almost as much, perhaps, as it has affected the development of visual art itself. But there is still much to be learned (and reflected upon) about the intercultural constancy or variability of aesthetic responses, the potentialities of form and medium (even to ancestral skulls), and the roles and functions of artistic activity in the full context of human cultures.[7]

While some aestheticians have been working to advance their subject as an empirical science, trying to ask its questions in such a way that the results of psychological and art-historical investigation can be brought to bear on them, others (often out of embarrassment at the state of aesthetics, which has frequently been deplored) have sought for help in a re-examination of the very foundation and methodology of aesthetics itself. In doing so, they have aligned aesthetics with a dominant movement in Western Empiricist philosophy of the twentieth century: the movement known widely as Philosophical Analysis. Philosophical analysts differ among themselves in many ways, but they share the conviction that philosophy has its own special task, quite distinct from science. This is the critical examination of basic concepts and basic assumptions involved in all our beliefs. The aim is to increase the rationality of those beliefs by clarifying the concepts and testing the reasoning.

In aesthetics this means that the philosopher begins with statements about works of art—any remark, from that of the casual observer to that of the professional critic, but especially remarks that provoke disagreement. He is not in a position, qua philosopher, to supply information that is needed for the dispute to be resolved; nevertheless, he can be of enormous help, if he can show that this resolution is hindered by the vagueness or ambiguity of key terms, or that some of the inferences are logically faulty, or that the question itself is posed in a misleading, even perhaps self-defeating, manner. In other branches of philosophy such philosophical analysis has been needed, and has shown itself extremely effective. Even those who cannot be persuaded that

[7] See also Robert Redfield, "Art and Icon," op. cit., esp. pp. 31–32; cf. Paul S. Wingert, *Primitive Art: Its Traditions and Styles* (Oxford U., 1963) . –

philosophical analysis is the whole task of the philosopher will generally acknowledge that the refinement of analytical techniques, both logical and semantical, to a high degree of precision and power, has been valuable.

It is only in recent decades that these methods have begun to be very extensively used in aesthetics—nearly every other branch of philosophy was well-advanced in this respect before philosophical analysis turned to the philosophy of art. But now a number of American, and some British, philosophers of the analytical school are working in aesthetics; some indication of their achievements, though by no means a complete picture, can be gained from two collections of reprinted papers: *Aesthetics and Language* (1954), ed. by William Elton, and *Philosophy Looks at the Arts* (1962), ed. by Joseph Margolis. The concept of aesthetics as metacriticism has been explicitly formulated and adopted in such systematic works as Monroe C. Beardsley, *Aesthetics: Problems in the Philosophy of Criticism* (1958), and Jerome Stolnitz, *Aesthetics and Philosophy of Art Criticism* (1960).

The rapid growth of the analytical movement in this century, and its rise to a dominant position in English-speaking countries, has been accompanied by divergences of aim and method—though fortunately the formation of subgroups has not been marked by sectarian bigotry so excessive as to prevent philosophers from teaching each other. It can be said in general that the method of analytical philosophy begins with the study of "actual usage" (what is sometimes called "ordinary language," but includes special languages, such as those of art critics). In aesthetics, analysts have examined such terms as "form," "style," "expression," "representation," and the logic of disputes about such matters as the objectivity of beauty, the relativity of critical evaluations, the relevance of truth to value in poetry. (See for example one of the earliest books of this genre, Bernard C. Heyl's *New Bearings in Esthetics and Art Criticism*, 1943). Where analysts part company is the point at which some go beyond pure usage-analysis into the formulation and recommendation of new critical language.

The aesthetic usage-analysts (or "ordinary-language philosophers") derive their methods from the posthumously published *Philosophical Investigations* (1953) of Ludwig Wittgenstein, and from others who have learned from him. They see philosophical puzzles as arising from insensitivity to the full flexibility and many-valued uses of the language in which we talk about art. We try to force words to behave in ways they were not designed for (as when we expect "form" to have one and only one meaning, or assume that all the objects denoted by "tragedy" have some set of common properties). We misconceive the "grammar" (or natural role) of a word, or misunderstand the sort of "language game" that is going on (is the critic, for example, in judging a work of art, doing something like grading apples, or awarding a prize, or handing down a verdict?). The cure for all such puzzles is to dissolve them by becoming aware of our language—seeing how it works, what can be expected of it, and what cannot. The underlying assumption of this approach has been made explicit by John Austin in his famous presidential address to the Aristotelian society ("A Plea for Excuses" [1956]):

Thirdly, and more hopefully, our common stock of words embodies all the distinctions men have found worth drawing, and the connections they have found worth making, in the lifetimes of many generations: these surely are likely to be more numerous, more sound, since they have stood up to the long test of the survival of the fittest, and more subtle, at least in all ordinary and reasonably practical matters, than any that you or I are likely to think up in our armchairs of an afternoon—the most favored alternative method.

Though the Wittgensteinian methods have not yet been very extensively used in aesthetics, some indication of their possibilities and limitations can be seen in Virgil Aldrich's *Philosophy of Art* (1963), and in a number of papers by Paul Ziff and Frank Sibley.

The other group of aesthetic analysts—patterning their work more closely after philosophers like C. D. Broad—are guided by a further goal. They aim not only to analyze and to understand the critic's terminology or argument, but to improve upon it. Their fear is that many key terms of critical discourse have come to be so loosely, vaguely, and variably used that some kind of overhauling is required: either to select and standardize certain senses or (in some cases) to invent a new technical vocabulary. This procedure, sometimes called "rational reconstruction," perhaps reflects more faith in the armchair than Austin expressed. However, the Reconstructionists do not assume that all the useful, or potentially useful, distinctions have already been made. Nor do they assume that all the useful distinctions that men *have* made in the past are still preserved in common speech. They point out that their work has already, in some quarters, noticeably reduced the tendency, for example, to apply words like "true" to art in odd and confusing senses, and has produced a greater self-consciousness and a higher standard of reasoning in aesthetics. And they look forward to the possibility of establishing a set of useful basic terms and categories that can be used by critics in various fields for more reliable communication and more fruitful discussion.

A history has to stop somewhere, and if the historian is modest he will try to avoid any suggestion that he can read the future, as well as any admission of his hopes for it. Because my story ends with the above remarks about philosophical analysis, I do not wish to imply that I think this approach is the last word, or the greatest promise. I am myself most at home with some of the analytical philosophers, and I have high expectations for them. But I do not want this confession to be part of my story—or to come through surreptitiously by way of subliminal suggestion. In this present (and final) chapter, as I see it, we have come to several different thresholds. That is, we have encountered several vital and living movements of aesthetic thought, all of which show promise of future work and future contributions. And we have noted other tendencies, some of them dormant or more limited in activity at present, any one of which may be about to burst into new life. Nor, of course, does even the fullest account of the past spell out all possibilities of the future. To me the encouraging fact is that various lines of thought are being explored with vigor and persistence. Truth has never taken kindly to monopolization. It is for each philosopher to work in the row he can cultivate most effectively; but it is also for all of us to keep open the lines of communication. If this platitude ever deserves utterance, it can surely find no more suitable occasion than at the end of a history of aesthetics.

Bibliography

For extensive bibliographies of contemporary thinkers and subjects, see the following:

M. C. Beardsley, *Aesthetics: Problems in the Philosophy of Criticism* (New York, 1958).

F. E. Sparshott, *The Structure of Aesthetics* (Toronto and London, 1963).

René Wellek and Austin Warren, *Theory of Literature* (New York, 1949).

Guido Morpurgo-Tagliabue, *L'Esthétique contemporaine* (Milan, 1960).

Stanley Edgar Hyman, *The Armed Vision: A Study in the Methods of Modern Literary Criticism* (New York, 1948).

Joseph Margolis, "Recent Work in Aesthetics," *Am Philos Quart* II (1965): 182–92.

Morris Weitz, "Aesthetics in English-speaking Countries," in Raymond Klibansky, ed., *Philosophy in Mid-Century: A Survey*, Vol. III (Florence, 1958); cf. review by Milton C. Nahm, *Jour Phil* LVII (1960): 281–86.

For collections of contemporary writings on aesthetics, see the following:

Melvin Rader, ed., *A Modern Book of Esthetics* (3d ed., New York, 1960).

Eliseo Vivas and Murray Krieger, eds., *The Problems of Aesthetics* (New York, 1953).

Morris Weitz, ed., *Problems in Aesthetics* (New York, 1959).

Morris Philipson, ed., *Aesthetics Today* (New York, 1961).

Marvin Levich, ed., *Aesthetics and the Philosophy of Criticism* (New York, 1963).

W. E. Kennick, ed., *Art and Philosophy: Readings in Aesthetics* (New York, 1964).

Joseph Margolis, ed., *Philosophy Looks at the Arts* (New York, 1962).

William Elton, ed., *Aesthetics and Language* (Oxford, 1954).

Benedetto Croce, *Aesthetic as Science of Expression and General Linguistic,* trans. Douglas Ainslie, 2d ed. (London, 1922).

Benedetto Croce, *The Breviary of Aesthetic,* trans. Douglas Ainslie (Rice Institute Pamphlet, II, No. 4, 1915), translation revised and called *The Essence of Aesthetic* (London, 1921).

Gian N. G. Orsini, *Benedetto Croce: Philosopher of Art and Literary Critic* (S. Illinois U., 1961).

Calvin G. Seerveld, *Benedetto Croce's Earlier Aesthetic Theories and Literary Criticism* (Kampen, Netherlands, 1958).

H. Wildon Carr, *The Philosophy of Benedetto Croce: the Problem of Art and History* (London, 1917).

John Hospers, "The Croce-Collingwood Theory of Art," *Philosophy* XXXI (1956): 291–308.

Alan Donagan, "The Croce-Collingwood Theory of Art," *Philosophy* XXXIII (1958): 162–67.

Merle E. Brown, "Croce's Early Aesthetics: 1894–1912," *Jour Aesth and Art Crit* XXII (Fall 1963): 29–41.

Bernard Mayo, "Art, Language and Philosophy in Croce," *Philos Quart* V (1955): 245–60.

E. F. Carritt, "Croce and his Aesthetic," *Mind* N.S. LXII (1953): 452–64.

Angelo A. De Gennaro, "The Drama of the Aesthetics of Benedetto Croce," *Jour Aesth and Art Crit* XV (September 1956): 117–21.

Katherine Gilbert, "The One and the Many in Croce's Aesthetic," in *Studies in Recent Aesthetic* (North Carolina U., 1927).

Alan Donagan, *The Later Philosophy of R. G. Collingwood* (Oxford U., 1962), ch. 5.

R. G. Collingwood, *Essays in the Philosophy of Art,* ed. Alan Donagan (Indiana U., 1964).

T. E. Hulme, "Bergson's Theory of Art," in *Speculations* (New York and London, 1924).

Arthur Szathmary, *The Aesthetic Theory of Bergson* (Harvard U., 1937).

Raymond Bayer, *Essais sur la Méthode en Esthétique* (Paris, 1953).

Arthur Berndtson, "Mexican Philosophy: the Aesthetics of Antonio Caso," *Jour Aesth and Art Crit* IX (June 1951): 323–29.

Donald W. Sherburne, *A Whiteheadian Aesthetic: Some Implications of Whitehead's Metaphysical Speculation* (Yale U., 1961).

Bertram Morris, "The Art-Process and the Aesthetic Fact in Whitehead's Philosophy," in Paul Schilpp, ed., *The Philosophy of Alfred North Whitehead* (Northwestern U., 1941).

George Santayana, *The Sense of Beauty; being the Outlines of Aesthetic Theory* (New York, 1907).

George Santayana, *Reason in Art* (New York, 1903).

George Santayana, *Obiter Scripta,* ed. J. Buchler and B. Schwartz (New York and London, 1956).

Willard E. Arnett, *Santayana and the Sense of Beauty* (Indiana U., 1955).

George Boas, "Santayana and the Arts," in Paul A. Schilpp, ed., *The Philosophy of George Santayana* (Northwestern U., 1940).

John Dewey, *Art as Experience* (New York, 1934). (The paperback reprint, Capricorn Books, 1958, is a reduced facsimile, with the same pagination).

John Dewey, *Experience and Nature* (2d ed., Chicago, 1929), esp. chs. 3, 4, 9, 10.

John Dewey, "Aesthetic Experience as a Primary Phase and as an Artistic Development," *Jour Aesth and Art Crit* IX (September 1950): 56–58.

John Dewey, exchange with Croce in *Jour Aesth and Art Crit* VI (March 1948): 203–9.

Jack Kaminsky, "Dewey's Concept of *An* Experience," *Philos and Phenom Res* XVII (March 1957): 316–30.

E. A. Shearer, "Dewey's Aesthetic Theory," *Jour of Phil* XXXII (1935): 617–27, 650–64.

Stephen C. Pepper, "Some Questions on Dewey's Esthetics," in Paul A. Schilpp, ed., *The Philosophy of John Dewey* (Northwestern U., 1939).

Sidney Hook, *John Dewey, An Intellectual Portrait* (New York, 1939), ch. 10.

Horace M. Kallen, *Art and Freedom* (New York, 1942), Vol. II, ch. 32.

Van Meter Ames, "John Dewey as Aesthetician," *Jour Aesth and Art Crit* XII (December 1953): 145–68.

Stephen C. Pepper, "The Concept of Fusion in Dewey's Aesthetic

Theory," *Jour Aesth and Art Crit* XII (December 1953): 169–76.

Sidney Zink, "The Concept of Continuity in Dewey's Theory of Esthetics," *Philos Rev* LII (1943): 392–400.

Charles E. Gauss, "Some Reflections on John Dewey's Aesthetics," *Jour Aesth and Art Crit* XIX (Winter 1960): 127–32.

D. W. Gotshalk, "On Dewey's Aesthetics," *Jour Aesth and Art Crit* XXIII (Fall 1964): 131–38.

Irwin Edman, "Dewey and Art," in Sidney Hook, ed., *John Dewey: Philosopher of Science and Freedom* (New York, 1950).

Art and Education (selections from Dewey, Barnes, etc.) (3d ed. Barnes Foundation, Merion, Pa., 1954).

C. K. Ogden and I. A. Richards, *The Meaning of Meaning*, International Library of Psychology, Philosophy, and Scientific Method (5th ed., New York and London, 1938).

David Bidney, *Theoretical Anthropology* (Columbia U., 1953).

Papers by David Bidney, Lord Raglan, Stanley E. Hyman, Philip Wheelwright, in T. A. Sebeok, ed., *Myth: A Symposium* (Philadelphia, 1955), American Folklore Soc. Bibliographical and Special Series, Vol. 5.

Henry A. Murray, ed., *Myth and Mythmaking* (New York, 1960).

Haskell M. Block, "Cultural Anthropology and Contemporary Literary Criticism," *Jour Aesth and Art Crit* XI (September 1952): 46–54.

Jane E. Harrison, *Themis: A Study of the Social Origins of Greek Religion* (Cambridge U., 1912).

Richard Chase, *Quest for Myth* (Louisiana State U., 1949).

Stanley Edgar Hyman, "Myth, Ritual, and Nonsense," *Kenyon Rev* XI (1949): 455–75.

C. G. Jung, *Contributions to Analytical Psychology*, trans. H. G. and C. F. Baynes, International Library of Psychology, Philosophy, and Scientific Method (New York, 1928).

C. G. Jung, *Modern Man in Search of a Soul*, trans. W. S. Dell and C. F. Baynes (1933).

C. G. Jung and C. Kerenyi, *Essays on a Science of Mythology*, trans. R. F. C. Hull (New York, 1949).

Morris Philipson, *Outline of a Jungian Aesthetics* (Northwestern U., 1963).

Ernst Cassirer, *Philosophy of Symbolic Forms*, trans. Ralph Manheim, 3 vols. (Yale U., 1953, 1955, 1957).

Ernst Cassirer, *Language and Myth*, trans. Susanne K. Langer (New York and London, 1946).

Ernst Cassirer, *An Essay on Man* (2d ed., New York, 1953).

Katharine Gilbert, "Cassirer's Placement of Art," in Paul A. Schilpp, ed., *The Philosophy of Ernst Cassirer* (Vol. VI; Evanston, Ill., 1949).

Herbert Read, *Icon and Idea* (Harvard U., 1955).

Wilbur Marshall Urban, *Language and Reality: The Philosophy of Language and the Principles of Symbolism* (New York, 1939).

Susanne K. Langer, *Philosophy in a New Key: A Study in the Symbolism of Reason, Rite, and Art* (2d ed., New York, 1948).

Susanne K. Langer, *Feeling and Form* (New York, 1953).

Richard Rudner, "On Semiotic Aesthetics," *Jour Aesth and Art Crit* X (September 1951): 67–77.

E. G. Ballard, "In Defense of Semiotic Aesthetics," *Jour Aesth and Art Crit* XII (September 1953): 38–43.

Max Rieser, "The Semantic Theory of Art in America," *Jour Aesth and Art Crit* XV (September 1956): 12–26.

Max O. Hocutt, "The Logical Foundations of Peirce's Aesthetics," *Jour Aesth and Art Crit* XXI (Winter 1962): 157–66.

Karl Marx and Friedrich Engels, *Literature and Art: Selections from Their Writings* (New York, 1947).

George V. Plekhanov, *Art and Social Life*, trans. as *Art and Society* by P. S. Leitner et al. (New York, 1937).

Stefan Morawski, "Lenin as a Literary Theorist," *Science and Society* XXIX (Winter 1965): 1–25.

Leon Trotsky, *Literature and Revolution*, trans. Rose Strunsky (New York, 1925).

Nikolai Bukharin, *Problems of Soviet Literature*, ed. H. G. Scott (New York, n.d.).

Andrei Zhdanov, *Essays on Literature, Philosophy, and Music* (New York, 1950).

Nicolas Slonimsky, *Music Since 1900* (New York, 1949), Part III, pp. 684–712.

Georg Lukács, *Beitrage zur Geschichte der Ästhetik* (Berlin, 1954).

Stefan Morawski, "Vicissitudes in the Theory of Socialist Realism," *Diogenes* No. 36 (1961), pp. 110–36.

Stefan Morawski, "Über Vieldeutigkeit und Mehrfunktion des Kunstwerkes," in *Acts of the Third International Congress of Aesthetics* (Venice, 1956).

Stefan Morawski, "On Realism as Artistic Category," in *Proceedings of the Fourth International Congress of Aesthetics* (Athens, 1960).

A. G. Kharchev, "On the Problem of the Essence and Specifics of the Beautiful," *Soviet Stud in Philos* Vol. I. No. 3, pp. 50–55 (trans. from *Filosofskie Nauki* [Philos. Sciences], 1962).

Victor Erlich, "Social and Aesthetic Criteria in Soviet Russian Criticism"; Robert M. Hankin, "Main Premises of the Communist Party in the Theory of Soviet Literary Controls"; and Ernest J. Simmons, "Review"; in Simmons, ed., *Continuity and Change in Russian and Soviet Thought* (Harvard U., 1955).

Abram Tertz, *On Socialist Realism*, trans. George Dennis (New York, 1960).

Max Rieser, "The Aesthetic Theory of Socialist Realism," *Jour Aesth and Art Crit* XVI (December 1957): 237–48.

Max Rieser, "Russian Aesthetics Today and Their Historical Background," *Jour Aesth and Art Crit* XXII (Fall 1963): 47–53.

Rufus W. Mathewson, Jr., *The Positive Hero in Russian Literature* (Columbia U., 1958), chs. 8–10.

Mikhail Lifshitz, *The Philosophy of Art of Karl Marx*, trans. R. B. Winn (New York, 1938).

Thomas Munro, "The Marxist Theory of Art History: Socioeconomic Determinism and the Dialectical Process," *Jour Aesth and Art Crit* XVIII (June 1960): 430–45.

John Fizer, "The Problem of the Unconscious in the Creative Process as Treated by Soviet Aesthetics," *Jour Aesth and Art Crit* XXI (Summer 1963): 399–406. Cf. Vera Maslow, "Georg Lukács and the Unconscious," ibid., XXII (Summer 1964): 465–70.

Olga Bradac, "Aesthetic Trends in Russia and Czechoslovakia," *Jour Aesth and Art Crit* IX (December 1950): 97–105.

N. Goncharenko, "Notes on Soviet Aesthetics," *Brit Jour of Aesth* V (1965): 191–96.

Dusan Sindelár, "Contemporary Czech Aesthetics," *Jour Aesth and Art Crit* XVIII (September 1959): 116–26.

Paul Frankl, *The Gothic* (Princeton, 1960), ch. 5.

Victor Erlich, *Russian Formalism: History, Doctrine* ('S-Gravenhage, 1955).

John Crowe Ransom, *The New Criticism* (New York, 1949).

R. W. Stallman, ed., *Critiques and Essays in Criticism* (New York, 1949).

Berel Lang, "Significance or Form: The Dilemma of Roger Fry's Aesthetics," *Jour Aesth and Art Crit* XXI (Winter 1962): 167–76.

On Clive Bell, see the special issue of the *Brit Jour of Aesth* V (April 1965).

Elio Gianturco, "Massimo Mila and Present Italian Aesthetics," *Jour Aesth and Art Crit* XI (September 1952): 15–20.

Herbert Spiegelberg, *The Phenomenological Movement: A Historical Introduction*, 2 vols. (The Hague, 1960).

Marvin Farber, *The Foundation of Phenomenology: Edmund Husserl and the Quest for a Rigorous Science of Philosophy* (Harvard U., 1943).

Fritz Kaufmann, "Art and Phenomenology," in Marvin Farber, ed., *Philosophical Essays in Memory of Edmund Husserl* (Harvard U., 1940).

Roman Ingarden, *Das Literarische Kunstwerk* (Halle, 1931).

Roman Ingarden, "Artistic and Aesthetic Values," *Brit Jour of Aesth* IV (1964): 198–213.

Anna-Teresa Tymieniecka, *Phenomenology and Science in Contemporary European Thought* (New York, 1961), esp. pp. 17–38.

Anna-Teresa Tymieniecka, review of Ingarden's *Studia z Estetyki*, in *Jour Aesth and Art Crit* XVII (March 1959): 391–92.

Philip Leon, review of Ingarden, *Das Literarische Kunstwerk*, *Mind* XLI (1932): 97–106.

Mikel Dufrenne, *Phénoménologie de l'Expérience Esthétique*, 2 vols. (Paris, 1953).

Mikel Dufrenne, "The Aesthetic Object and the Technical Object," *Jour Aesth and Art Crit* XXIII (Fall 1964): 113–22.

J.-Claude Piguet, "Esthétique et Phenomenologie" (discussion-review of Dufrenne), *Kant-Studien* XLVII (1955–56): 192–208.

Maurice Natanson, *Literature, Philosophy and the Social Sciences* (The Hague, 1962), Part II.

Eva Schaper, "The Aesthetics of Hartmann and Bense" (review), *Review of Metaphysics* X (December 1956): 289–307.

Gillo Dorfles, "New Currents in Italian Aesthetics," *Jour Aesth and Art Crit* XII (December 1953): 184–96.

Piero Raffa, "Some Contemporary Italian Aestheticians," *Jour Aesth and Art Crit* XX (Spring 1962): 287–94.

Hans Jaeger, "Heidegger and the Work of Art," *Jour Aesth and Art Crit*, XVII (September 1958): 58–71 (reprinted, with some changes, in Philipson).

Vincent Vycinas, *Earth and Gods: an Introduction to the Philosophy of Martin Heidegger* (The Hague, 1961), esp. chs. 3, § IV; 4, § IV; 7, § II; 8, § III.

Arturo B. Fallico, *Art and Existentialism* (Englewood Cliffs, N.J., 1962).

Eugene F. Kaelin, *An Existentialist Aesthetic: The Theories of Sartre and Merleau-Ponty* (Wisconsin U., 1962).

Van Meter Ames, "Existentialism and the Arts," *Jour Aesth and Art Crit*, IX (March 1951): 252–56.

Douglas Morgan, "Psychology and Art Today: a Summary and Critique," *Jour Aesth and Art Crit* IX (December 1950): 81–96 (reprinted in Philipson).

Douglas Morgan, "Creativity Today," *Jour Aesth and Art Crit* XII (September 1963): 1–24.

Albert R. Chandler, *Beauty and Human Nature* (New York, 1934).

C. W. Valentine, *The Experimental Psychology of Beauty* (London, 1962).

D. E. Berlyne, *Conflict, Arousal, and Curiosity* (New York, 1960), ch. 9.

C. C. Pratt, "Aesthetics," *Annual Rev of Psych* XII (1961): 71–92.

R. M. Ogden, *The Psychology of Art* (New York, 1938).

N. C. Meier, *Art in Human Affairs: an Introduction to the Psychology of Art* (New York and London, 1942).

Thomas Munro, "The Psychology of Art: Past, Present, Future," *Jour Aesth and Art Crit* XXI (Spring 1963): 263–82.

Thomas Munro, *Toward Science in Aesthetics: Selected Essays* (New York, 1956).

Thomas Munro, *The Arts and Their Interrelations* (New York, 1949).

Thomas Munro, "Methods in the Psychology of Art," *Jour Aesth and Art Crit* VI (March 1948): 225–234.

Thomas Munro, "Aesthetics as Science: Its Development in America," *Jour Aesth and Art Crit* IX (March 1951): 161–207.

Rudolf Arnheim, "Gestalt Psychology and Artistic Form," in L. L. Whyte, ed., *Aspects of Form* (London, 1951).

Edward Bullough, *Aesthetics: Lectures and Essays*, ed. Elizabeth Wilkinson (Stanford and London, 1957).

Harry B. Lee, "The Cultural Lag in Aesthetics," *Jour Aesth and Art Crit* VI (Dec. 1947): 120–38.

H. J. Eysenck, *Sense and Nonsense in Psychology* (Penguin Books, rev. ed., 1958), ch. 8.

George Dickie, "Is Psychology Relevant to Aesthetics?" *Philos Rev* LXXI (1962): 285–302.

See also the special issue on psychology of the *Jour Aesth and Art Crit* X (June 1952).

Ernest K. Mundt, "Three Aspects of German Aesthetic Theory," *Jour Aesth and Art Crit* XVII (March 1959): 287–310.

William Phillips, ed., *Art and Psychoanalysis* (New York, 1957); see esp. Ernst Kris, "The Contribution and Limitations of Psychoanalysis" (reprinted from his *Psychoanalytic Explorations in Art*, New York, 1952).

Frederich J. Hacker, "On Artistic Production," in Robert Lindner, ed., *Explorations in Psychoanalysis* (New York, 1953).

Daniel E. Schneider, *The Psychoanalyst and the Artist* (New York, 1950).

Herbert Read, "Psycho-analysis and Criticism," in *Reason and Romanticism* (London, 1926); expanded as "The Nature of Criticism," in *Collected Essays in Literary Criticism* (London, 1938).

Campbell Crockett, "Psychoanalysis in Art Criticism," *Jour Aesth and Art Crit* XVII (September 1958): 34–44.

Jacques Schnier, "The Function and Origin of Form," *Jour Aesth and Art Crit* XVI (September 1957): 66–75.

Carroll C. Pratt, *The Meaning of Music* (New York, 1931).

D. J. Crowley, "Aesthetic Judgment and Cultural Relativism," *Jour Aesth and Art Crit* XVII (December 1958): 187–93.

On French aesthetics, see Raymond Bayer, "Recent Aesthetic Thought in France," in Marvin Farber, ed., *Philosophic Thought in France and the United States* (U. of Buffalo, 1950), and the *Jour Aesth and Art Crit* (June 1949).

Rolf Ekman, "Modern Aesthetics in Sweden," *Jour Aesth and Art Crit* XVII (December 1958): 181–86.

Masao Yamamoto, "Aesthetics in Japan," *Jour Aesth and Art Crit* XI (December 1952): 171–72.

INDEX

Index